Blood, Sweat, and Fears

Jean Marie Stanberry

Jean Marie Stanberry

Published By Kingsmuir Press

Boston, Dundee, Auckland

http://www.jeanstanberry.com

Laying Low In Hollywood

One World United

The Illusion Of Order

DEDICATION

This book is dedicated to all the skaters in my life that have inspired me in my lifetime, and continue to inspire me artistically.

First and foremost, to Jack Adams, my inspiration for Adam. You have been my best friend, and many times in my life, my only friend. You are truly the greatest partner in the world.

To my awesome coach Heinz Grimaldi, the man that literally scared the hell out of me the first time I met him. You have been there with me for for some of the greatest times of my life, you have also been my greatest support at some of the lowest times in my life. You have shown me unwavering support and I am proud to say that you have been the one of the greatest inspirations in my life.

To Tai Babilonia and Randy Gardner, the pairs team that inspired me the most. Tai and Randy were the real pairs team that was forced to withdraw from the 1980 Olympics due to injury. Like many others, on that day I cried as well, for I felt your heartbreak.

Sending out a couple big I love you's to these other skaters I love and respect so much, they have all rose to the top and overcome tremendous obstacles on their way there. Robin Cousins, Scott Hamilton, Rudy Maricelle, Debi Thomas, Anita Curtis, Katia Gordeeva, Denise Beilman and many more, too many to count actually.

I also want to send an extra big I love you to my husband Gary, who has been putting up with me and all my crazy projects for more than twenty four years now. I love you's to my two awesome kids Ryan and Lauren who have both made me so proud, they have grown into wonderful adults

ACKNOWLEDGMENTS

Sending out a big thank you to everyone at Kingsmuir Press, especially my agent Vaughn Thompson who has been my support every step of the way.

Cover photo is a composite of images courtesy of:

imagerymajestic/freedigitalphoto.net and marin/freedigitalphoto.net

CHAPTER 1-MOSCOW MARCH 1980

Alexander pulled his hat down over his ears and his scarf up around his face to shield him from the bracing cold as he stepped out into the snowy, windswept streets of Moscow.

His brain was so consumed with a dizzying array of thoughts, he barely even noticed the scores of other Muscovites scurrying through the streets as the late afternoon light faded and darkness seemed to seep into every nook and cranny of the city.

When he finally arrived at his destination the icy cold no longer seemed as daunting. He was in no hurry to go inside. It couldn't hurt to just linger out here on the sidewalk and give himself a few minutes to process everything that had just been laid out on the table in front of him.

He stood outside the high rise flat he shared with his fiancee Marika. He tapped a cigarette from it's pack and lit it as he leaned casually against the streetlamp. He wasn't quite ready to have to deal with Marika yet, he had a lot to think about.

Alexander had lived here, in the busy city of Moscow for most of his life. He came from humble beginnings in the country, his family was very poor. In fact, the farm his family worked could barely sustain their houseful of children through the long winter months but fortunately, Alexander had a talent.

When he was just a young boy, talent scouts discovered that this strong young boy could skate across the icy ponds near his family's farm as fast as a lightening bolt. When the scouts approached his family, his father was thrilled. His son would be a hockey star, that would be good.

But there was another reason the scouts wanted Alexander for his skating ability. They planned to take him to Moscow and train him as a figure skater. His father was not quite as thrilled about this prospect, but what was a poor man to do? A full ride scholarship with room and board. As far as his father was concerned, it was a done deal. Young Alexander went off to Moscow, never to return to the little family farm outside of Ruza.

Now years later, all his hard work and determination had paid off. Alexander and his fiancee Marika were the World Champions in pairs figure skating and they had most recently won the gold medal in the winter Olympics.

Finally, things were looking up for him. Or for them, it seemed. Alexander's life was now bound to Marika's by their skating career. They had been partners for nearly eight years now, they had earned the respect of their peers. They would probably be moving into a larger flat soon, perhaps in a better neighborhood.

Marika's rich and influential family was pushing for them to marry in the fall. As far as they were concerned, Marika and Alexander were a perfect match. They would have beautiful, athletic babies.

Alexander still had his doubts about marrying Marika at all. Of course they were magic on the ice together. Too bad the same couldn't be said about their relationship in the bedroom.

They'd moved into this flat in Moscow together, since it was closer to their training rink. Alexander had reluctantly agreed to this betrothal a year ago, at the insistence of Marika's family. They didn't want their precious daughter living in sin, unless she was at least, betrothed.

Alexander had known that Marika was prone to mood swings and had a nasty temper, but since they'd moved in together he'd gotten a taste of what married life with Marika would be like and he didn't like it at all. But what could he do? His fate was essentially sealed. Marika's family was rich and powerful, it would be impossible to defy them, especially now that he and Marika were living together. If he broke up with her now, he would most likely be visited by the Russian mafia and fall victim to some sort of unfortunate "accident"

Now there was one small light at the end of the tunnel. After they won the gold medal in Lake Placid, Alexander had been contacted by a Francois Dumontier. He was the producer of a European based ice show and he was very anxious to add the world's newest Olympic gold medalists to his program.

Alexander had met with Francois today. He had an idea to match Alexander and Marika with another couple of equal speed and talent and choreograph a combined pairs number as part of his new show.

Mr. Dumontier had invited Alexander to a hotel meeting room to show him film clips of three couples he thought might mesh well with the newest Olympic medalists.

The first couple, from East Germany skated well but Alexander couldn't help but grimace as he watched the couple take their final bows.

The female partner was tiny with a forced smile and funny looking, squished nose. In fact, he was almost afraid he might laugh out loud if he saw her in person...next please.

The second couple was from Canada. They seemed promising enough. Their speed, their flow and their elements seemed to match well with Alexander and Marika's style. The female partner was tiny and attractive, that's really all Alexander cared about really.

"I hesitate to show you this next couple," said Mr. Dumontier, frowning with reticence.

"Why is that?" asked Alexander.

"Well, you are a World Champion and an Olympic gold medalist. I do not wish to offend you. This next couple is American, they are what I consider, raw talent. They are a bit unpolished and inexperienced, this was their first year skating at the senior level and they have not yet won an international competition."

Alexander frowned, he had no desire to be paired up with a couple of amateurs, he *did* have standards.

"All I'm asking is that you consider them. I believe they have great potential. I saw them perform in the US nationals and I was completely blown away by their powerful jumps. You may have seen them in Lake Placid..."

Alexander gave Mr. Dumontier a thoughtful look. "Where did they place?"

"They didn't. I am afraid there was a bit of a scandal regarding their performance there. An illegal move or something. At any rate, they were ultimately disqualified,"said Mr. Dumontier, with a bit of a frown.

Alexander thought hard, but he couldn't really remember anything about *that* particular scandal. He'd been riding high on his own success, why would he remember some unfortunate American couple that had been disqualified from the Olympics?

"Show me the clip," said Alexander shrugging half heartedly. What could it hurt?

Mr. Dumontier started the projector and Alexander couldn't help but be mesmerized by the images on the screen.

There was definitely something about this couple that made them stand out from all the others. They were young, that much was obvious. Both partners were tall, the female was just 3 or 4 inches shorter than her partner, who Alexander was guessing, was probably six feet tall.

They skated fast, with big, stunning jumps. Their spins were a bit weak, but that could be corrected easily, with the right training.

What Alexander found the most mesmerizing about this pair was the female half of the team. She looked like an adolescent after a growth spurt, she was all arms and legs, but she had a beautiful smile that seemed to light up the entire ice arena.

She was completely fearless in all the throw jumps and as she stood there on the ice taking her final bows, waving elatedly to the crowd, Alexander felt as if he'd fallen completely in love with her. He was sitting there grinning like an idiot till Mr.

Dumontier's voice cut like a knife, through his self imposed stupor.

"She is completely adorable, is she not?"

"Yes," said Alexander, he felt as if he could barely speak. As he watched her standing there, struggling to catch her breath as she blew kisses to the crowd, he felt as if he could barely catch his own breath. She seemed so happy, *passionate*.

That was exactly what his relationship with Marika was missing...passion. It was essentially an arranged marriage. They had teamed up when he was just thirteen. They had essentially grown up together and she was the only women he had ever been close to.

Over the past several years Alexander had a few one night stands. With their recent success, he had become somewhat of a Rockstar in the USSR. Women wanted him, so who was he to tell them no? It was fun, but what he really wanted was a partner in life, he had serious reservations now that Marika was the perfect partner for him.

"This couple has a unique presence on the ice, I think with a bit more work, they could be perfect," said Mr. Dumontier, giving Alexander a sly smile.

"How is it, that I have not noticed this couple before?" asked Alexander. It was a known fact, Alexander and Marika always studied other skaters, comparing moves, assessing their talents prior to competition.

"As I said, the Olympics was their first international competition. As a couple, I believe they have been partners only about three years. This year was their first year competing at the senior level. Jenna the woman, is a bit of a natural, she did not start skating till quite late in her childhood. Her mother, who is a classic stage mom and a ballerina herself, was determined to make her into a prima ballerina. It seems she wanted to skate instead. Her classical ballet training only helped her to master all the moves when she finally set foot on the ice for the first time."

"Hmmm," said Alexander, scratching his chin thoughtfully.

Maybe hooking up with an American wouldn't be a bad thing. This girl was young, she didn't even look of legal age to be traveling with their show, but she must be. Why else would Dumontier even be considering them? She was beautiful, talented, and had only been skating with her current partner for a short time. Alexander suddenly had a brilliant idea...could she be his ticket out of the Soviet Union?

Alexander tried to conceal a look of pure evil as he considered it. If he were to hook up with American, perhaps they could marry and he could defect to America...it was a perfect idea!

What a wonderful thought, to be free! Free from Marika, free from the Soviet Union and his dreary life there.

"So what do you say Mr. Peterov? Do you like the Americans?" asked Mr. Dumontier.

"Yes," said Alexander, shaking his head enthusiastically.

Jean Marie Stanberry

CHAPTER 2-ST. LOUIS MARCH 1980

Jenna looked up into the stands in the nearly deserted ice arena. There was only 15 more minutes left of practice and she was almost certain her mother would be there to take her home to Chicago today.

Jenna spotted her, she was there in the third row near the announcer's box, draped in an expensive fur coat and plaid scarf, she was filing her nails impatiently.

Jenna let an impotent sigh escape her lips, she had hoped that her parents had forgotten about her, that she'd be able to just stay the weekend here in St. Louis with her coach Hans and his wife Carolina.

Until the Olympics last month, her parents had never brought her home much in the past. They had dropped her off one morning nearly three years ago and left her there in St. Louis, to languish in her loneliness for many months.

Jenna had been left in the care of a coach whom she barely knew, in a city where she had no friends, no relatives and no history.

Now that she was finally happy, they had decided they wanted her home every weekend. She guessed it was mostly so her mother could berate her about her unfortunate disqualification from the Olympics. She had to hear about it week after week, she tried to explain to her parents it wasn't her fault. Jenna was just fifteen years old, she barely knew anything about pairs skating it was so new to her. She just did what Hans told her.

Jenna had been devastated when they'd been disqualified, but since she'd never expected to earn a place on the Olympic team in the first place, it was hard to be too upset about the whole fiasco.

Besides, she'd heard so many versions of the story from so many different sides, she still wasn't quite sure she understood *any* of it.

"Ugh, I see nurse Ratchet is here," said Hans, gesturing toward Jenna's mother in the stands, his face a mask of disgust. Jenna gave him a weak smile, Hans detested her mother, he thought she was a psychopath, hence the nickname "nurse Ratchet".

"Ugh, you should tell her we need to skate all weekend," said Adam, rolling his eyes miserably.

Jenna frowned, she had no desire to go home for the weekend, but her mother had already drove all the way here...

"She's here, there will be no changing her mind now," said Hans, shaking his head miserably.

Jenna let out a deflated sigh, more than 5 hours in the car with her mother sounded like a sentence worse than the death penalty.

When practice was over, Jenna skated to the edge of the ice and snapped her skate guards on. She was not looking forward to spending the rest of the day with her mother and the rest of the weekend with her entire dysfunctional family.

"Hello darling," said her mother, coming over and pressing a quick peck on her cheek.

"Hi mom," said Jenna, already resigned to go along with this whole senseless charade.

"You looked great out there today. Too bad it's too little, too late," said her mother.

Jenna nodded numbly, the digs were starting early. That one wasn't too bad, but her mother was just getting started.

"I've got to change," snapped Jenna, turning and heading to the locker room. Adam gave her a wry smile, he knew her weekend was going to totally suck.

When Jenna emerged from the locker room her mother was waiting for her.

"Let's go to lunch before we head out of town, I have something I've been wanting to talk to you about," said her mother.

"Sure," sighed Jenna, her insides seemed to be constricting in fear. What kind of demented plan had her mother cooked up now?

Her mother was talking mindlessly as they crossed the parking lot. Jenna was trailing along behind her. She was explaining to Jenna why she had brought her dad's car, the Lincoln town car. She was chattering nonstop about how her dad thought it was safer for highway driving, though *she* would have preferred to drive her own sports car. Her diamonds looked better in the sports car. Besides, she hated the town car, it was so "suburban". Blah, blah, blah. Jenna could barely stand the thought of spending the entire day listening to her mother's shallow rambling.

Jenna gave her a fake smile and listened patiently as they wound their way through the streets of St. Louis. They drove to her mother's favorite Italian restaurant in a part of St. Louis called "The Hill".

Jenna ordered her favorite lasagna and her mother ordered linguini with clam sauce. They remained silent for a while, Jenna really didn't know what to say.

She wasn't sure why she was here, but she knew her mother was about to drop something big on her. Her mother was a busy woman, she owned her own dance studio and kept busy doing choreography for the local theater company. Why would she drive all the way to St. Louis to bring her home for the weekend, when she had barely even spoke to her on the phone over the past three years?

"So, I wanted to talk to you a bit about the direction your skating career is heading in. I fear it may be heading in the wrong direction," said her mother, eyeing her carefully.

"Why do you say that?" snapped Jenna, she had made it all the way to the Olympics for Pete's sake. How could that possibly be the wrong direction?

"Well, perhaps your father and I were acting a bit too hasty when we allowed you to move to St. Louis to train with Hans.

"What?"

"Do I believe moving you into pairs skating was the right move? Of course I do, I really believe you have found a venue in which you can shine. Unfortunately, Hans is quite obviously inexperienced with pairs skating. Adam is a nice enough young man, but his constant attempts to sabotage your partnership have left you weak as a team. I can't help but wonder if there wasn't a better partner and coach for you out there."

Jenna stared at her in shock, she had never asked for any of this. Less than three years ago she'd been training at her neighborhood rink with her own coach Donovan. She'd been happy, she had never really considered pairs skating before Hans approached her. Hans had discovered her at the Midwest regionals in Milwaukee and he had made all the arrangements for her to move to St. Louis to skate with him. In their first year at the senior level, they had already made their way onto the Olympic team, it seemed like a fairytale, how could that possibly be bad?

"I love Hans, I don't want anyone else to be my coach. Adam and I are perfect together, he wasn't totally sold on this pairs skating thing when I first came to St. Louis, but that was three years ago. Now that we're finally skating at the senior level he's been happy. We are perfect together," cried

Jenna, she was completely stunned that her mother had brought up such a thing.

"It's just that *you* were brilliant this season, your ballet training has made you so much more graceful and concise on the ice than most of your competitors. Adam was fine too, it's just that he's a bit rough around the edges, his style is not quite as refined as yours.

You may be young, but you have a maturity and elegance on the ice that makes you a winner. I'm just afraid you're wasting your talents with these two losers," said her mother.

"Mother!" cried Jenna.

"Look Jenna, the Olympics will be coming up in another 4 years and I want you there, on the podium. If you start working with another coach and partner now, you'll be ready..."

"I don't want another coach and partner, I'm happy mother, with a little work I know that Adam and I can be on that podium too."

"Ha, I seriously doubt that, if Hans knew what he was doing you would have never ended up in the middle of this scandalous disqualification in the first place."

Jenna shook her head miserably. She could never win in an argument against her mother.

"So, I know you thought I was taking you home for the weekend, but I've arranged for you to do an audition with legendary pairs coach Cami Peters, we're going to fly out to Colorado Springs for the weekend. She has a great skater she'd like to pair you up with."

"I already told you, I don't want a different partner," cried Jenna.

"Jenna please, I'm only doing what's best for you, Cami is one of the greatest pairs coaches in the country, perhaps even the world. I have no doubt that whomever she chooses for you will be a perfect partner."

"I realize that mother, but it took me so long to feel comfortable with Adam, I just don't think I could skate with another guy."

"When you were paired up with Adam you were just a child, you have matured so much over the past several years. You were facing an uphill battle, you not only had to feel comfortable with Adam, but with your own body. You are becoming a woman Jenna, and your new programs will have to reflect that. I know you now realize that most of this is just acting. The passion, the emotion, you can fake this with any guy."

Jenna shook her head miserably, maybe that would be easy enough for her mother, to just move on to another partner, but her and Adam were best friends. She had no desire to form new bonds with someone else.

"Just let me take care of everything," said her mother.

Jenna knew better than to argue with her, it would be of no use. It was going to be a long weekend...

CHAPTER THREE

Alexander crushed his cigarette out with his foot and took the elevator up to the 12th floor. He unlocked the door to his bleak, sparsely furnished apartment. Music was blasting from the kitchen

"Alexander, is that you?" yelled Marika from the kitchen.

"Yes my darling," said Alexander, hanging up his coat and sitting on the bench near the front door to take off his boots.

"Why were you so long? I thought you would have been home an hour ago," she whined, as she appeared in the doorway, eyeing him carefully.

"To work a deal takes time. Congratulations Miss Gringkov, you are officially the headline act of the European Theater Company's ice show," said Alexander, smiling at her.

Marika jumped into his arms and hugged him excitedly. Alexander couldn't help but be surprised, it was the most affection she'd showed him in months.

"We are the stars?" she cried, completely excited.

"Of course we are, we are Olympic gold medalists, are we not?"

Marika kissed him excitedly, Alexander smiled to himself, Marika was so excited, maybe he would get lucky tonight.

He wrapped his arms around her and kissed her passionately. It had been months since she'd showed any interest at all in him. If they were going to be married he needed affection, he needed to feel loved.

"All right that's enough," she said, pulling herself from his arms.

"No it's not, kiss me some more my love," he said wrapping his arms around her and kissing her. Marika kissed him back and soon the kiss had deepened. Marika giggled as they fell onto the couch.

"You are so frisky tonight," she giggled, pressing her body against his seductively.

Alexander was getting excited as their bodies writhed frantically on the couch, it wasn't often that Marika was in a good enough mood to let him make love to her, he was ready to take advantage of the moment.

He was trailing kisses down her neck. He had already decided he was just going to take her, right there on the couch when suddenly Marika pushed him off of her, with seemingly superhuman strength.

"Oh no, do you smell that! My pirozhok are burning!" she cried, jumping up and running into the kitchen.

"Screw your pirozhok," bellowed Alexander, he was suddenly so horny, he could barely stand it.

"Oh they're ruined,"cried Marika, fanning the smoke out of the kitchen.

"Who cares? Turn them off and come back," called Alexander, even though he knew his desires were about to go unquenched, it was always *something.*

"Oh grow up, we can do that later silly," called Marika.

Alexander frowned. He knew for a fact, they would not do it later. In fact, they had only done it three times in the year since they'd become engaged. Marika told him she was just worried about becoming pregnant, and she didn't want to jeopardize their skating careers, but it was obvious to him that she just didn't like sex.

He'd tried everything he could to make it more pleasurable for her, but she had pretty much forbid him to touch her with his hands, his mouth, or any other body part, so any sort of foreplay was pretty much out of the question.

He wanted her to enjoy it, have an orgasm, but she told him sex was for men, she only did it because she had to. As result, he had resorted to having sex with any of the scores of women who threw themselves at him at various celebrations. It was shallow and meaningless, but sex with Marika was so creepy he could barely stand it. She would tell him to just do it and get it over with, she never made a sound, he found it very unnerving. When it was over she would roll to her side of the bed and fall asleep, no cuddling allowed!

Alexander was disappointed that his plans for release had been thwarted. He'd been so busy since the Olympics, he hadn't been with a woman in weeks, he could barely stand it any longer. He had decided it would almost be preferable to just spend some time in the bathroom alone with his thoughts of the American skater, Jenna. He couldn't stop thinking about her anyway.

Jenna had beautiful, long legs. He could imagine her laying there beneath him, with that exuberant smile on her face as he came inside her. Yes, she would definitely enjoy his lovemaking skills. Marika would prefer it, if she never had to make love to him again.

The more he thought about it, the more he liked the idea of seducing the American and making her his lover. It would have to be secret at first, or Marika would freak out.

They'd be working closely together, if they showed promise as partners they could be married, then they could both return to the states and he would become a US citizen.

Alexander smiled, he would have a beautiful American wife, they would live in a real house with a dog, and eventually four children. Of course, they wouldn't start making babies till their careers had peaked, maybe after the Sarajevo Olympics in four years. That would be perfect.

That would be the end of long winter nights in a dreary Moscow flat, jerking himself off because his fiancee was a frigid bitch.

CHAPTER FOUR

Jenna skated out onto the ice nervously as her mother watched excitedly from her place in the stands. They had flown to Colorado Springs so that Jenna could audition for Cami Peters. Cami was one of the most famous pairs skating coaches in the world and Jenna's mother was excited that she had agreed to have Jenna audition.

"Jenna," cried Cami, as she saw Jenna skating toward her.

"Hello."

"Wow, how tall are you?" said Cami, looking her over closely.

"I'm five foot seven," said Jenna, her face was scrunched up in confusion. What difference did it make?

"And you are how old?"

"I'm fifteen."

"Hmmm, so you're probably not done, growing yet," said Cami, her face was troubled.

Jenna shrugged in confusion. She wasn't sure why Cami seemed so upset.

"I hope I haven't just wasted your time, but I guess I didn't realize you were so tall."

Jenna looked over at her mother, who was just starting to catch on that something was not quite right.

"So are you saying I can't audition?" asked Jenna cautiously. She didn't want to get excited, but this just might be the lucky break she needed. She did not want to switch partners and she knew for sure she did not want to leave Hans and Carolina to move to Colorado Springs.

"I'll still have you skate with Richard, but he's barely taller than you, if you were to go through a major growth spurt and he didn't, there is a chance that the two of you would no longer be a good match."

Jenna tried to hide her growing smile, but it was almost impossible. Her mother was going to be *so* disappointed.

The audition went on as planned, but Richard was not only barely taller than Jenna, but he wasn't strong enough. During the star lift, he was barely able to lift Jenna above his head. Jenna's mother was disappointed, but Jenna was ecstatic when they returned to St. Louis on Sunday evening. Richard and Jenna were not a good fit on the ice, and Cami didn't have a spot for Jenna as a pairs skater.

Jean Marie Stanberry

CHAPTER FIVE

"Good morning Mr. Peterov, thank you for meeting with me on such short notice," said Mr. Dumontier, standing to shake Alexander's hand.

"You said there was a problem?"

"Yes, with the American couple we chose to be partners with you and Marika on the ice," said Mr. Dumontier, his face was grim.

"What kind of problem?" asked Alexander, his heart was suddenly pounding anxiously. This *had* to work out, it was a perfect plan.

"I guess I should have realized this, but I imagine I only saw the beauty of her skating. The woman, Jenna, is not really a woman at all, she is a mere child, just fifteen years old."

Alexander gasped, he had guessed she was young, he had been hoping that she was at least old enough that they might be able to fudge on her Visa a bit. No European country would allow a fifteen year old to travel without a chaperone, it seemed as if they would have to pick another pairs couple.

"How disappointing," said Alexander, it was quite an effort to keep his voice flat and calm, he was completely crushed, he had thought of no woman but Jenna Bruce since he had seen her skate.

"I must admit, I am quite disappointed as well. It would have been quite exciting to have all that talent on the ice at once."

Alexander gave him a sly smile, that wasn't really the part that got him excited.

"Is there no way that you can work around her age? Are her parents willing to come along and chaperone?"

"I wish, her father was most anxious to ship her away for the summer. It seems he has his hands quite full with her mother who is by all accounts, borderline certifiable. They only want her out of their house, they have no desire to travel with her and be her chaperone."

"What about her coach?"

"No, he's much too busy as well. Besides, he wasn't a fan of the idea in the first place. He had no desire to see his prized pairs team flying off to Paris to be in an ice show."

"I realize she's a minor, but what if she were married? Wouldn't that make her an adult in the eyes of the law?" asked Alexander.

"Well she is adorable, will you be proposing?"

"That would be a bit premature, seeing the two of us have never met, but in my country everything is about the paperwork. If you have the correct paperwork you can accomplish just about anything.

Mr. Dumontier gave him a puzzled look.

What I'm saying is, fake her marriage to her skating partner. They don't even have to *like* each other, they just have to have the right paperwork. Chances are, no one will question it or do any further research, I mean, why would they?" said Alexander, flashing Mr. Dumontier a sly smile.

"That's positively brilliant!" cried Dumontier.

"Do you think her parents would go for it?" asked Alexander.

"It's certainly worth a try," said Mr. Dumontier as he picked up the phone to call Jenna Bruce's father.

CHAPTER SIX-APRIL 1980

Jenna startled awake as the plane hit yet another patch of turbulence, causing it to drop like a rock momentarily, then resume it's tumultuous flight. She glanced around nervously, her clammy palms gripping her armrests tightly. Jenna had expected to hear screaming and gasps of distress, but there were none. Pretty much everyone else was fast asleep, the cabin was dark and the sounds of assorted snores seemed to engulf the entire cabin.

Jenna looked over at Adam who was sleeping in the seat next to her. He hadn't even stirred. It wasn't fair. Adam could sleep through anything, and it seemed as if, he could sleep anywhere. Jenna was finding it hard to sleep on this long flight to Paris, she feared she would be totally worthless when she finally got there.

Jenna sighed and tried to will herself to fall back to sleep before her overwhelmed brain could start, once again, nervously dissecting the series of events that had unfolded over the past several weeks. If she allowed herself to ponder all the hows and whys, she might never fall asleep.

Jenna was on her way to Paris to spend the next five months performing in the European Theater Company's ice shows. She'd been excited for weeks about this trip, it hadn't been till she boarded the plane from St. Louis, that she finally began to have second thoughts.

Jenna sighed, shaking her head miserably. What had possessed her to mindlessly agree to come on this ill conceived journey? Now that she'd had time to ponder everything in detail, it seems she'd been amazingly naive.

Her own parents had arranged everything, so at the time, Jenna had not questioned anyone's motives. Her parents wouldn't set their own daughter up for failure, would they? Jenna was now worried that might possibly be the case. Unfortunately, she had overheard the cruel whispers of some of the other skaters around the ice rink over the past several days. Were people just being catty, or was her trip to Paris truly destined to be a disaster of epic proportions?

There had been no time to ponder it really, everything had happened so fast. Jenna couldn't help but be a little rattled about this trip, her skating partner Adam, was her only travel companion. For the first time in her life, she would be on her own in a foreign country. There would be no coach, no parents, no chaperone at all. Jenna felt overwhelmed and frightened, she had never traveled anywhere without her coach, Hans. Jenna took a deep breath and shook her head numbly, as if that, could shake away the feelings of apprehension, that seemed to be completely overwhelming her.

Jenna and Adam had originally been told there was no way they would be able to go to Paris and skate, Jenna was just too young. Hans told her it would be impossible for a minor to travel to Paris without a guardian. Of course they were disappointed, they'd been so excited, but it made sense. Hans couldn't possibly go with them, not for five whole months, he was much too busy with his other skaters.

Unbelievably, several days later, Jenna's parents informed her that everything had been worked out, her and Adam would be traveling to Paris to tour with the European Theater Company's ice show for the next five months!

Jenna had been elated when she found out she was going to Paris after all, but how had her parents dealt with the chaperone issue that had seemed so daunting? No one seemed willing to explain to her, making her initial excitement, quite short lived.

Her coach Hans was angry and suspicious that everything had suddenly worked out. He had called and argued with her parents quite adamantly. Jenna wasn't sure why Hans was so upset, he was usually quite reasonable, but that day, he had thrown things and ranted to his wife Carolina, till his face was a bright crimson red. Jenna was not sure what Hans was so angry about, he refused to share any of his misgivings with her, he told her she was just too young to understand.

It made Jenna angry, why did everyone always assume that she was so stupid, just because she was young? She had been so excited when she boarded that plane, but now it all seemed so hollow to her. Her parents standing there in the terminal, waving to her with those fake smiles plastered on their faces. Smiles that Jenna had foolishly believed were truly happy for her.

Jenna had to admit, that had been a silly thought. When had her parents ever cared if she was happy or not? Jenna was beginning to think they were truly smiles of relief. Relief, that she would finally be out of their hair for the entire summer. She was just now beginning to realize, the family that she had grown up in, was not really what most people would consider a normal family.

Jenna had been skating since she was seven years old. Her father, who had been a college hockey star, had taken her ice skating one winter afternoon and had quickly discovered that she was a bit of a natural.

At the urging of Donovan, the local rink's figure skating coach, she began taking lessons compliments of her grandfather. Up to this point in her life, she had spent countless hours toiling away in her mother's ballet studio. Her mother had been determined to make her into the Prima ballerina she herself, had never become. Jenna had been quite happy to immerse herself in figure skating. In fact, she had been anxious to be involved in just about any activity that was not ballet. Jenna truly had no desire whatsoever to become a Prima ballerina, so from that point on figure skating became her life.

It had been pure fate that Hans had discovered her and somehow persuaded her parents to allow her to move to St. Louis to train with him and his most talented skater, Adam. Jenna had already known and admired Adam's skating, he was a bit older and well on his way to being a world champion at some point. As Adam entered high school though, he began to realize that the world saw him in a much different way than he saw himself. Guys at the high school teased him and told him that all male figure skaters were "queers".

Upset that many people were perceiving him in a light that wasn't true at all, Adam wanted to quit, but Hans had a plan. He rationalized that male pairs skaters were never unfairly judged that way, so he began the nearly year long search for the woman that would become Adam's partner.

At the time, Adam had just gone through a major growth spurt, so he was very tall, and still nowhere near done growing, so Hans was certain a tiny partner would never work out. Adam also had a very fast and athletic style. Hans wanted to make sure Adam's partner had a similar style.

After more than a year of searching, Hans had nearly given up hope, no one even came close to meeting his exacting specifications. Then he saw Jenna...

He had already been alerted to her talents, but he had essentially already written Jenna Bruce off. She was a relative newcomer, this was her first major competition. She was just twelve years old, which in Hans' eyes made her too young and too inexperienced to place with his most gifted skater.

Then Hans saw her skate, he was on his feet heading towards the ice before her program had even ended. He couldn't believe his eyes, he was certain she was the one.

Within weeks, Jenna's life had changed completely. Jenna had moved to St. Louis, and into the cozy guest house over Hans' garage. It had all been much easier than Hans had anticipated. He had expected a big fight from her parents, since she was just twelve years old. What he didn't realize was that her parents had never really wanted her anyway. They were quite happy to have him take her off of their hands!

Over the next three years Adam and Jenna shined. Their talents were a perfect paring and they excelled almost immediately. Adam and Jenna were perfect together, not only on the ice, but they had also quickly become best friends. Everyone who saw them skate together knew that this was meant to be, they were a perfectly suited pair.

Most recently, they had placed fourth in the National Championships, which was quite disappointing. They had not been one of the top ranked teams in the nation, but it was an Olympic year and a coveted spot on the podium at Nationals, might have ensured them a spot in the upcoming Olympics.

Their misfortune had been the result of a cruel twist of fate. They had just given the performance of a lifetime with their short program. Jenna and Adam had been virtually unknown up till that point, suddenly they were in second place, their chances of earning a spot on the podium were excellent.

Unfortunately, the next morning Jenna awoke with a fever. She was eventually diagnosed with Strep throat. The following day was the long program and Jenna was determined to perform. She'd been battling a fever all day, despite the fact that Hans was pumping her body full of antibiotics and Tylenol.

Despite her fierce determination, Jenna was weak from her illness and their performance had suffered, causing them to fall just short of their goal. Fourth place meant there was no chance that they would

go to the Olympics or the World
Championships.

They were disappointed, but of course,
that was life. They assumed the season was
over for them till Hans received a call from
Olympic officials asking them to fly to Lake
Placid and stand by.

It turns out that Gabe Gamble, the male
partner of the number one ranked US team
had been injured. The team doctors were
treating his injury the best they could, but
they were not sure he would be able to
compete. Jenna and Adam were brought in
as first alternates, in case Gabe and his
partner Lena were unable to compete.

Jenna was nervous, Gabe and his partner
Lena were fabulous, the favorites to win the
competition. They were a bit older and had
much more experience in major
competitions. Jenna and Adam were
relative newcomers in comparison. Jenna
was almost hoping that Gabe would be able
to skate, the US was almost certain to take
home the gold if Lena and Gabe skated, she
was afraid her and Adam might crumble

under the pressure, they'd never competed in a competition of this caliber before.

It turned out that Gabe's injuries were too serious to allow him to continue in the competition. It was soon announced to the media that the he would be unable to skate and the team was withdrawing from the competition.

As Jenna watched the official press conference she was shocked to realize that Lena had no idea, before that very moment, that Gabe's injuries were so bad. Lena struggled to maintain her composure, but it was obvious she was quite shaken up and emotional. Jenna had to look away, she felt so bad for Lena. That had to be the worst feeling in the world, knowing everything you've worked so hard for, is now only a dream.

Of course, it wasn't Gabe's fault, Jenna felt bad for him too. They had both worked so hard, it was just one of those things, there was nothing anyone could do.

So Jenna and Adam were brought in as the last minute replacements. Unfortunately, this effort was also destined to fail. An outdated rule, and Hans' poor understanding of the rule, ended ultimately with their disqualification. A lift they used in their long program was considered dangerous. They had used it in all their US competitions, but Hans didn't realize the move was ruled illegal in international competition.

So as scandalous as it was, Adam and Jenna were disqualified from the Olympics. They spent the rest of their time in Lake Placid dodging the press and trying to overcome their acute embarrassment.

They returned to St. Louis to resume their training and decide where their careers were heading next, that was when Hans got the phone call from Mr. Dumontier.

He had seen their performance in the short program, and though they had ultimately been disqualified from the Olympics, he thought that they would be perfect for a new act he was putting together which was going to feature Jenna and Adam, paired with the new Olympic Gold medalists, the World Champion Soviet pairs skaters

Hans had his reservations about Adam and Jenna flying off to Europe to skate in an ice show, but Jenna was completely bursting with excitement! She had never really been anywhere outside the states and her and Adam were very eager to redeem themselves in the skating world, they had accepted without a second thought. Besides, it was only for five months, what could possibly go wrong?

So now they were flying thousands of miles across the Atlantic ocean in what seemed like, a lame attempt to redeem their skating careers. Hans was not able to accompany them as he couldn't get free, he had other skaters he was training at their club in St. Louis. Besides, he was as much in the dark about the terms of their contract as Adam and Jenna were. Mr. Dumontier had made all the arrangements with Jenna's father.

Of course, Jenna and Adam were both young and naive, they had no reason to question anyone's motives, to demand answers as to why it was suddenly appropriate for a fifteen year old girl to travel to Europe without a chaperone.

Jenna was simply thrilled to be going, how was she to know her excitement was destined to be short lived?

CHAPTER SEVEN

Alexander was nervous, he'd never been this nervous in his entire life. He was on a plane, on his way to Paris and his entire life was about to change. This summer was going to be the best summer of his life and things were working out better than he had ever imagined.

He could definitely skate with Jenna Bruce, he knew that much. But would she be attracted to him? Alexander admonished himself and shook that idea from his mind, women were always hitting on him, of course she would be attracted to him.

Since he'd watched the video clips of her performance he had thought of little else but Jenna Bruce and his plans to seduce her. Now that he knew she was only fifteen years old, he worried that she might not be receptive when he told her all the things he wanted to do to her. Perhaps her age was a unexpected gift, with any luck she would be naive and easily to manipulate. That would definitely make his life easier.

Alexander wasn't sure why he suddenly couldn't get this young girl out of his head. He'd traveled the world and met hundreds of beautiful women, most of them were more than willing to do whatever he suggested to them, but all that seemed so flat and one dimensional now. Those had all been emotionless one night stands, but now he wanted something more.

Sure, Jenna Bruce wasn't the most gorgeous woman he had ever met, but there was something very endearing about her smile. Someday, when her body developed more, she might even be considered beautiful. For the moment she was still a bit like an adolescent. Her body was all arms and legs, she was skinny and shapeless.

The part that excited Alexander the most was the idea that she was most likely untouched. The idea of guiding this young woman into adulthood was very appealing to Alexander, it had been a recurrent subject of his recent dreams.

Marika had fallen asleep and her head was resting lightly on his shoulder. Alexander looked at her wistfully and wished his fiancee would be up for a quickie in the lavatory, but that would never happen...ever!

He knew he might as well rest now so he would be rested when he finally arrived in Paris. He closed his eyes and fell asleep within moments. Before long he was dreaming about Jenna Bruce again. She was laying on the bed, all that blonde hair splayed across the pillow, smiling into his eyes as he came inside her...

"Excuse me?" he jumped when the woman tapped him on the arm.

"Hello?" said Alexander. It was a beautiful blonde woman in a blue dress, she was smiling at him coyly.

"I'm sorry to wake you. Are you Alexander Peterov?" she asked. Her accent was distinctly German, her voice was deep and sexy. Alexander looked over at Marika, she was curled up by the window, still fast asleep.

"Yes," he said, still slightly disturbed. Why had this woman woke him up? It just seemed rude.

"I'm a huge fan. May I bother you for an autograph?"

"Um...sure."

"Follow me," said the woman, taking him by the hand. He followed her mindlessly, thinking she had an album or something. They arrived outside the lavatory.

The woman opened the door and looked around briefly, then she pulled Alexander inside. She locked the door and slid her hand down to his crotch, cupping him boldly in her hands.

"I couldn't help but notice that while you were sleeping, you were having a very good dream," she crooned.

Alexander smiled. Women were always coming on to him. He found it amazing that wherever he went there seemed to be no shortage of woman who just wanted to screw his brains out.

"I *was* having a good dream," said Alexander, smiling as she slowly unzipped his fly.

"I want you to finish your dream with me," said the woman as she took Alexander into her hands. Alexander gasped as she wrapped her fingers around him, it seemed like forever since a woman had touched him. How could he possibly say no?

"Wunderbar! Your cock is the biggest I have ever seen," exclaimed the woman, her eyes bulging in wonder. She didn't seem intimidated though, she continued to massage him, watching in awe as he grew even larger.

"Just you wait gorgeous," breathed Alexander as the women slid down onto her knees.

"I bet you a dollar I can take the whole thing in my mouth," said the woman, flashing him a seductive smile.

"Go ahead, amaze me," said Alexander.

In a matter of moments Alexander realized he had just lost a bet and in just moments he was on the verge of blowing his load, this woman was definitely quite talented.

The lavatory was so small, the two of them could barely fit in there together. Alexander pulled the woman to her feet and lifted her skirt, pushed her panties aside and shoved his fingers into her, causing the woman moan and convulse against him.

"Do you want it?" breathed Alexander, she felt ready to him.

"Give it to me now," she cried.

Alexander didn't want her to have to wait a single second more. He bent the woman over the sink, lifted her skirt and slid into her. She let out a shriek of delight as he slammed into her again and again. In fact, she was not quiet at all. Alexander was pretty sure in a matter of moments everyone in the entire plane knew exactly what was going on in that lavatory.

After they finished, the woman gave him a sly smile, kissed him and stuffed her panties into his pants pocket. They emerged from the lavatory to various stares and whispers from the other passengers. A stewardess gave them a dirty look and the woman whispered in her ear as she slipped past her to return to her seat.

"I just made the mile high club with an Olympic gold medalist."

The stewardess gave Alexander a blank look, then recognition flashed across her face causing her to blush, she turned and walked away quickly in acute embarrassment.

Alexander returned to his seat, unfortunately, all the commotion had woke Marika, who was glaring at him angrily as he sheepishly returned to his seat. Apparently, she hadn't missed a single moan of his little indiscretion.

"That was discreet," she told him, in a voice laced with sarcasm.

"How was I to know she was going be a screamer?"

"You have a fiancee," snapped Marika.

"You would have told me no," said Alexander.

"I have a bit more class than that, an airplane lavatory? My God, you are so sick."

"If the moment is right, why does it matter where it is?"

"The moment is always right for you. You have a perpetual boner," snapped Marika.

"Most women do not seem to mind, in fact most women are begging for me to fuck them," said Alexander, flashing her a sly smile.

Marika flashed him a look of distaste.

"Lucky for you we are not married yet. I will not tolerate my husband cheating."

"I cannot help myself. I guess I just have a thing for blondes. I promise to be faithful once we are married," said Alexander.

"No, you must be faithful now Alexander. These bimbos...what if they have diseases?"

"They don't have diseases," snapped Alexander.

"How would you know? I doubt you even caught her name. You need to grow up and think with your head, not your penis."

"Sorry, my penis just has an overactive imagination. It would be much happier if you enjoyed having sex with me."

"Enjoy sex? I fail to see how any woman could enjoy that, it is disgusting! Sex should be saved for marriage, when it is our duty. Besides, we have done it enough. I do not wish to be pregnant yet, perhaps it is best you fulfill your needs with these bimbos," said Marika, shaking her head disgustedly.

Alexander shook his head too. He wasn't a monk, he hadn't taken any vows of celibacy. He was in the prime of his life, of course his penis ruled his thoughts, wouldn't that be normal for any testosterone loaded male?

Marika was content to have sex only two or three times a year, he wanted sex two or three times a day. He didn't really want bimbos, he wanted someone who loved him, someone who would enjoy having sex with him whether they got pregnant or not, let the heavens decide when the time was right.

Alexander was done talking to Marika, there was no reasoning with her small mind. Alexander willed himself to fall back to sleep so that he could dream uninterrupted about his true love, Jenna Bruce.

Jenna would love him, he knew she would. Alexander finally fell asleep, knowing that later tonight he would finally be in Paris.

CHAPTER EIGHT

Adam and Jenna arrived safely in Paris.
Adam, of course, was well rested, but Jenna
had not rested at all en route. Jenna was one
of those people who was never able to sleep
on planes, trains, etc. When they arrived in
Paris Jenna was completely exhausted, but
living on pure adrenaline at that point.

Jenna was excited when she realized the
company had sent a limo to the airport to
pick them up, she had never ridden in a limo
before and she was excited that the company
was treating her and Adam like VIPs.

Their limo driver's name was Jean Paul,
unfortunately for Adam and Jenna, he did
not speak much English. Jean Paul was very
polite and he pointed out all the sights to
them on the way to the hotel in French, of
course. Jenna had a very limited education
in French, up to at that point, but she did
manage to recognize a few points of interest.

As they drove through the crowded streets
of Paris, Jenna was beginning to get very

nervous. She was silently wondering what would happen if no one in the company spoke English. It was a dilemma she had not considered before.

Since Jenna had come to St. Louis to skate for him, Hans had always been there for her, but he would not be there for her now. Adam and Jenna would be working under the direction of a coach and choreographer employed by the company, someone unfamiliar. Jenna was suddenly panicking! This was a nightmare!

She looked over at Adam, who looked quite amazed by all the sights, but he didn't seem worried at all. She wondered if he was exuding false confidence for her well being, or if he was just too naive to realize that the two of them might be in well over their heads.

"Adam?" asked Jenna, she couldn't conceal the shakiness in her voice, she was suddenly so scared.

"What?" he asked, looking at her quickly, his forehead wrinkled in worry, by her sudden distress.

"I'm worried. What if no one in the company speaks English?" she managed to squeak out.

"Actually, I was just thinking about that, surely at least Mr. Dumontier does, right? I mean, otherwise how could he have worked things out with Hans and your Dad? Your Dad doesn't speak French, does he?" asked Adam, giving her a sly grin.

"I wouldn't put it past him, he's full of surprises!" she told him, shaking her head absently. Truly, she couldn't be sure what her father knew, or didn't know. Jenna's dad may not have been father of the year material, but he had a genius IQ and he also had his PhD. in Education. He knew all kinds of things that Jenna didn't even realize that he knew! It's not like the two of them ever spent that much time together.

The limo pulled up in front of the massive white stone hotel. Jenna gazed up in awe, at the line of international flags whipping in the wind overhead. Her frazzled brain was suddenly racing, what on earth was she doing here?

Jenna startled when the doorman stepped over and opened the limo door. She stepped out and gazed up at the regal building in awe. Jenna sighed in distress, she was so tired at this point, she wasn't sure if she was over thinking this entire situation, or if she was just completely brain dead.

Adam took her hand and led her into the huge, bustling, hotel. They crossed the shining, elegant, lobby to the front desk, Jenna was dazzled by the shining marble and brass that touched nearly every surface, the thick rugs and shining wood furniture that filled the expansive space. The lobby was adorned with comfortable couches and massive potted plants and was bustling with neatly uniformed employees and elegantly dressed patrons.

Although Adam and Jenna were dressed nicely, it was immediately obvious that this hotel's clientele were all quite well to do. Jenna looked around in awe, trying not to gawk at the gorgeous women who were all draped in silks and designer labels and the elegantly dressed men who were standing around chatting idly.

They approached the front desk and the immaculately coiffed woman behind the desk gave them a friendly smile. She looked as elegant and well bred as the hotel's clientele and Jenna was wondering silently, if she would ever fit in here.

She worried that everyone would discover immediately, that she was not the polished, world class skater they expected, but a naive, teenager from the suburbs of Chicago. She also worried that their tarnished reputation from the Olympics had followed them here to Paris. Why would anyone want to watch these disgraced Americans who had been disqualified from the Olympics? Adam stepped up to the desk and gave the clerk a dazzling smile.

"Hello, I'm Adam Smyth, this is my partner, Jennalise Bruce. We are here with the European Theater Company, we would like to check in," Adam told the woman confidently.

"Oui Monsieur, your party is expecting you. You and your wife will be in room 4216. You may join the others in your company for drinks, right over there. The bellman will deliver your things to your room," said the woman, pointing to a large group of people who were all standing in the far corner of the lobby, drinking and socializing animatedly.

Jenna and Adam were both staring blankly at the woman. Jenna wasn't sure if she had heard the woman right, but she could have sworn that she been referred to as Adam's wife, and that they would be staying in the same room. She narrowed her eyes at the woman suspiciously...this was all wrong.

"Wait a minute, what do you mean my wife and I will be in room 4216? We're not married!" cried Adam, suddenly quite agitated.

Jenna cringed uncomfortably, as the haughty crowd in the lobby all turned in unison, to see what all the commotion was about. She sighed miserably, she really didn't want to be the center of attention, all over something that was, most likely, some sort of misunderstanding.

"Mr. Smyth, forgive me, I can only do what I have been instructed to do. If you have a problem with your accommodation arrangements, I suggest that you take it up with Francois Dumontier," said the woman, haughtily. She raised her eyebrows at Adam as she pointed again, to the group congregated in the far corner of the lobby.

Adam was just standing there, staring at her in shock, it was as if, he couldn't comprehend exactly what was going on. The desk clerk was impatiently trying to hand him the keys, Adam did not seem inclined to take them from her.

Jenna stepped over to the desk quickly. She really didn't want to cause a scene here in the lobby their first day in Paris. She thought it would be easiest if they just discussed the arrangements with Mr. Dumontier, she had no doubt that he would iron everything out immediately. Jenna smiled at the woman and held out her hand for the keys.

"It is fine, merci," said Jenna, giving the woman a fake smile, as the woman dropped the keys unceremoniously into her hand, glaring at her distastefully. Jenna took Adam by the hand and led him across the lobby to where the rest of their group was currently enjoying cocktails. The desk clerk eyed them disdainfully, as they walked away.

Jenna took a deep breath and approached the group with her best fake smile. She didn't want anyone to know how completely intimidated she felt at this very moment. Adam seemed to be completely lost at this point, and he was trailing along behind her like a lost puppy. She headed straight toward the man she was almost certain must be Francois Dumontier. He saw them approaching and broke from the crowd to introduce himself to them.

"Welcome to Paris, I am so happy you have finally arrived," he cried, extending his hand to Adam, who took it, and shook it numbly. Then the man turned and bowed formally to Jenna.

"Mademoiselle Bruce, I am Francois Dumontier, it is a pleasure to finally meet you," he said, taking her hand and kissing it, as if she were a Grand Duchess or something. Jenna bit her lower lip in an effort to conceal a giggle that randomly wanted to escape her lips. She couldn't help it, it was a nervous tic. Everyone was treating her as if she were an adult, she was not really used to all this attention.

"It is so nice of you to have us Mr. Dumontier," she said, flashing him a dazzling smile that exuded much more confidence, than she was truly feeling.

Mr. Dumontier was very excited that they had finally arrived and he proceeded to introduce them to everyone in the group. Jenna smiled confidently and shook everyone's hand, though her mind was still spinning numbly.

They met their new coach, Gail Tremone. Gail was tall and thin, with wild, curly blonde hair. She had cool blue eyes, and a spattering of freckles across her nose. Jenna wasn't sure what to make of her at this point, as Gail appeared to be assessing her quite curiously. Jenna frowned, wondering if Mr. Dumontier had failed to mention to the others in the company that she was just fifteen years old.

Next, they met their choreographer who's name was Simone Aubiere. She was small and beautiful, with perfect skin and delicate features. Her dark brown hair fell in in a silky curtain to her chin and her eyes were a piercing mahogany brown. She was obviously quiet and creative. Jenna thought she was wonderful, right away.

The rest of the people in the group were all skaters. They were all older of course, and they seemed to be enjoying the free flowing cocktails that were being provided by the company.

It didn't take Adam and Jenna long to realize that they were the only Americans. It seemed that most of the skaters were French, though the comedian of the group was Colin Anders, who was British. Jenna loved him immediately! He had a dry sense of humor and told the most hilarious stories, he was obviously born to entertain.

Jenna spoke to him at length and learned that he was a men's competitive skater, a four time British National Champion and twice a World Champion. She had watched him on television many times. She thought he was amazingly talented and she loved to watch him skate.

While Jenna was talking to Colin she could hear Adam, who was standing nearby discussing their accommodations with Mr. Dumontier. Adam was obviously distressed by the entire situation. Mr. Dumontier was listening to Adam politely as he swirled his brandy impatiently in his glass.

Mr. Dumontier looked exactly as Jenna pictured he would. He was tall and noble looking. He had dark brown hair that was peppered with silver, and a small, silver goatee. He was wearing an expensive looking charcoal wool suit and a burgundy silk tie. He was the picture of elegance as he leaned on the table, swirling his brandy wearily. His voice was velvety, with a thick, French accent, he reminded Jenna of a 1950's movie star.

He leaned closer to Adam and lowered his voice a bit, "Mr. Smyth, I admire your concern for the situation, but I am afraid I had no choice. There are laws concerning minors being abroad without a legal guardian. I doubt you want to be sent home, am I right?"

Adam gave him a blank stare. Mr. Dumontier lowered his voice a bit more and continued, Jenna made herself perfectly still, she had to concentrate hard to hear, the room seemed to be echoing with the multiple conversations that were going on around them.

"I had already decided that you and your partner would be a perfect addition to our show. What I did not realize at the time, was that Jenna was still a minor. I am sure that you are aware that hotels here in Europe will not allow a minor to stay in a room by herself, nor will they allow unmarried couples, one of which is a minor, to stay in the same room.

Jenna's father, Mr. Bruce, was well aware of the regulations we needed to contend with. He assured me that on your arrival here in Paris, the two of you would be married or at least, you would have the paperwork proving as much," said Mr. Dumontier, a look of doubt, was washing over his face.

"Married!" cried Adam, seriously close to hyperventilating now.

"Please Mr. Smyth, keep your voice down," said Mr. Dumontier anxiously. Jenna was pretending to listen to an amusing story Colin was telling her, but suddenly she was close to hyperventilating as well, this was a nightmare!

"Jenna's father did this?" cried Adam. Jenna bit her lower lip anxiously and had to look away. Adam's face was so shocked, she almost succumbed to the irrational urge to burst into hysterical laughter. This entire charade was completely ridiculous!

"I am sorry Mr. Smyth, I was not aware that you had not been informed of our little arrangement," said Mr. Dumontier, giving Adam an odd look.

Adam was standing there staring at him numbly. He opened his mouth to speak, then changed his mind. It seemed he couldn't find the words. Jenna's heart was pounding nervously, she had all but tuned poor Colin out and he was now smiling at her, waiting for her to laugh at his amusing story. She gave him a fake smile and laughed on cue, but she truly had no idea what she was laughing at.

"Jenna and I were not married, and as far as I know, there is no paperwork," said Adam, shaking his head, numbly.

Jenna was still straining to hear their conversation, the room was loud and echoing and she was suddenly feeling faint. Her father had handed her an envelope of "travel documents" before she left. She'd barely even glanced at them since no one had ever asked for anything but her passport. She assumed the envelope was still in her bag. She was now anxiously wondering if she should go get it and see what was in there, though it really wasn't that much of a surprise to learn that her father had concocted some sort of ridiculous scam.

"Jennalise?" Colin was looking at her quizzically. She gave him a guilty smile. She was sure he finally realized that she had not been paying attention to him at all.

"Yes?"

"Is everything okay? You look like you might be feeling ill," said Colin, he was staring at her with concern.

Jenna sighed. Ill didn't even begin to describe how she was feeling right now. She wanted to run away and hide. She was fifteen years old, did everyone here truly believe that she was married to Adam?

"I'm fine, thank you," she managed to mumble.

She looked over at Adam and Mr. Dumontier. Mr. Dumontier was now whispering in Adam's ear, his face was a mask of displeasure. Jenna sighed brokenly, she was getting the feeling they were going to be heading back to the States. More likely sooner, than later.

Colin watched as her gaze drifted over to Adam and Mr. Dumontier. Luckily, he assumed that she was anxious just being away from Adam, her supposed "new husband".

"I am quite sorry, Jennalise. I fear I have been monopolizing your time most of the evening and I have completely forgotten that you are a newlywed," said Colin.

Jenna tried not to visibly cringe. Apparently, everyone here thought that the two of them were newlyweds. She wondered what kind of preposterous scam her father had cooked up. She was sure that the allure of being rid of her for next five months, and being paid handsomely for it, was more than he could resist!

Jenna gave Colin another forced smile and resisted the urge to break out in maniacal laughter, she felt like her sanity was slowly slipping away. Adam was walking away from Mr. Dumontier, shaking his head miserably. She watched as he walked up to the bar and ordered a drink, something he never did.

"I'm very sorry Colin, I guess the long flight has me a bit scattered. Adam is lucky, he's able to fall right to sleep. I am not nearly as fortunate, I barely slept at all," she told him.

"Do you mind if I ask you a personal question?" asked Colin, eyeing her very seriously.

"No, I don't mind," she told him, though she was silently wondering what he had in mind.

"How old are you?" he asked, his face was completely serious.

Jenna hesitated, she was relatively sure that letting everyone in the company in on the fact that she was a minor, was probably a bad idea. They obviously thought that she and Adam were married, maybe they also thought that they were the same age.

"I'm eighteen," she told him confidently.

"Really?" he said, giving her an amused smile. It was obvious he didn't believe her.

"Yes, though I realize today I must look much older than that, considering the bags under my eyes and all," she told him, with a coy smile. It was a lame attempt to cover up her distress, she was a terrible liar.

"Actually, I was thinking you look younger than your stated age, much younger I might add. Don't get me wrong, you are obviously well read and quite intelligent. Though I must confess, your body is a dead give away, Yes, you are tall, but you are skinny and shapeless, like an adolescent. Either that, or I fear you have some sort of an eating disorder," he said, eyeing her seriously.

Jenna frowned. It was true, she had only just recently begun to develop, though she was still mainly skinny and shapeless. It had never really bothered her, in fact, she wasn't sure if she would ever develop voluptuous breasts. Her mother was a professional ballerina and she was essentially skinny and shapeless as well, though Jenna had to admit, if anyone could claim to have an eating disorder, it would be her mother. Jenna had no proof, but she suspected her mother suffered from bulimia, and she obsessed over her weight constantly.

"I've been skinny and shapeless my entire life, just like my mother, she's a professional dancer, a vegetarian, and a terrible cook," she told him.

Colin was eyeing her suspiciously when Adam appeared at her side. He was holding two drinks in his hands.

"Would you like a screwdriver?" he asked, holding one out to her.

"No," she told him, distastefully.

"Fine, I'll drink it myself," he said, sucking down the remainder of his drink and setting it on a nearby table.

"Adam Smyth," he said, extending his hand to Colin.

"Colin Anders," said Colin, shaking his hand firmly.

The two men were standing there, silently staring each other down. Jenna repressed the odd urge to giggle, that would be completely inappropriate, she was supposed to be eighteen.

"It is a pleasure to meet you Mr. Anders. Could you please excuse us, I need to speak to Jenna for a moment, if you don't mind," said Adam, taking her by the hand and leading her away.

"By all means," said Colin, bowing to them formally as Adam hauled her away. He pulled her away from the others and whispered in her ear. Jenna frowned, Adam was not himself, he was obviously very agitated.

"Do you realize what is going on here?" he whispered.

"I'm not one hundred percent sure," she told him blandly, though she was suddenly sure that she knew more than she really wanted to.

"They all think we are married! It was your father who somehow arranged this...scam, I guess you could call it. I don't know any of the details, but our staying here is contingent on our marriage, or at least, the appearance of one," Adam whispered harshly.

Jenna was staring at him in shock. "What are you saying? In order to stay here, we have to pretend that we are married?" she asked.

"We either pretend, or we go home. Mr. Dumontier was quite adamant."

"But..." Jenna wasn't sure what she wanted to say, she wanted to ask how and why her father had done this to them, but of course, Adam wouldn't know the answers to those questions.

Adam was sweating profusely and he quickly sucked down the rest of the second screwdriver he was holding. He squeezed his eyes shut as if he were thinking.

"What this means is, you and I will have to present ourselves to everyone as a married couple, we will have to stay in the same room everywhere we go. Are you okay with all of this, or should I ask Mr. DuMontier to make arrangements for us to go back to the states?" asked Adam.

Jenna gave him a stunned look. If she went home to Chicago, her parents would make her life miserable. They would be angry that she had ruined this opportunity. They were already completely freaked out because her and Adam had been disqualified from the Olympics. Jenna frowned, she

would endure just about any scam to keep
the Atlantic Ocean and half of the United
States as a buffer between herself and her
dysfunctional family.

"I want to stay, I'll go along with the little
scam, but only if you are okay with this,"
she told him.

"What choice do I have?" asked Adam, his
tone was sarcastic.

"Adam, I'm sorry that my father did this.
I didn't know..."

"I know, I'm not angry with you. I just
don't know how we can do it," said Adam,
he looked defeated.

"It will be okay," said Jenna, shrugging
slightly. She didn't mean it, and it sounded
lame. Adam just frowned.

"I seriously doubt it," said Adam, shaking
his head miserably.

"We're together all the time anyway," said
Jenna, smiling, trying to lighten his mood.

He rolled his eyes and shook his head miserably as if she didn't know what on earth, she was even talking about.

"Do you think it's a bad idea?" she asked. Adam looked uncertain, she had no idea what kind of misgivings he was having about their odd arrangement.

"Well, it's not a good idea, I know that much," said Adam. With that, he turned and headed to the bar and ordered another drink.

Jenna sighed miserably. Obviously, Adam had serious misgivings about the situation. Probably about the two of them having to stay in the same room together all summer. Whenever they had traveled in the past, they always had separate rooms. In fact, Jenna was sure that Hans would have a fit, if he knew that the two of them would be staying in the same room.

Jenna wasn't worried at all. Adam was like a big brother or a favorite cousin to her, there was no attraction between the two of them. She trusted him completely. She had no reason to believe he would loose his sense of mind and actually try something.

She figured there would be two beds in the room anyway, not really a big deal. They had a professional relationship to maintain, there couldn't be any more between the two of them...at least not at this point.

CHAPTER NINE

Jenna and Adam spent the rest of the evening meeting and socializing with the rest of the cast. Everyone was there except for the Soviets, the couple they were slated to team up with. Unfortunately, their flight had been delayed. Mr. Dumontier assured them that the couple would be at the ice arena in the morning for their first practice.

Jenna was worried about Adam, he never drank alcohol, but tonight it seemed, he had a newfound fascination for alcoholic beverages. Jenna was worried that he might overdo it, and not be functional for their first official practice with the company in the morning. The other cast members were older and she assumed, more accustomed to drinking alcohol on a regular basis. They were all still socializing much the same as they had been hours ago, while Adam seemed to be growing stupider with each passing moment.

Jenna was standing there watching Adam with a horrified look on her face. She wasn't exactly sure what to do. It was late and she had been traveling for more than twenty four hours straight, she hadn't slept much on either of their flights and the exhaustion was suddenly overtaking the elation she had felt on her arrival in Paris. The crowd in the lobby was thinning, and she was ready to retire for the night. Still, she wasn't sure how she could convince Adam to leave, he seemed to be having such a great time.

"I assume your husband doesn't drink much," said Colin, who had suddenly appeared at her side.

"He *never* drinks," Jenna told him with a sigh. She was still silently wondering why she had come here at all. She felt as if she were facing a disaster of colossal proportions. She was not eighteen, and she was not married. To pretend that she was either of those things seemed perfectly ridiculous, though she had no desire to go back to the states and spend the entire summer having her parents berate her over their Olympic failure.

"Would you like me to help you get him up to your room?" asked Colin, his kind smile radiated sincerity.

"Thank you, that would be great," she told him, breathing a silent sigh of relief.

Colin was a great gentleman. He approached Adam and whispered in his ear, in a few minutes he was helping Jenna to haul Adam into the elevator. She tried to keep a straight face as the bellman looked the three of them over curiously. Adam could barely stand up, and Colin and Jenna were both struggling to keep him upright.

The bellman took them to their room and Jenna was happy to learn that Colin was going to be in the room directly across the hall. She had to struggle to hide her surprise as the bellman led them into the elegant room. It was large and magnificently appointed with heavy cherry furnishings and soft wool rugs.

Jenna had never been in a hotel room so grand in her entire life! The one aspect of the room that had left her completely speechless though, was the huge, king sized, four poster bed that seemed to dominate the entire room. Jenna was staring at it in shock, barely able to comprehend that the two of them would be sharing this room, for the next seven weeks.

"The honeymoon suite," said the bellman, as he gave them a sweeping bow.

Jenna cringed. She had not been worried about sharing a room with Adam. He was like a big brother to her, the two of them had no romantic feelings toward each other. Unfortunately, she was worried now. She had foolishly assumed that there would be two beds in the room and she had never counted on Adam becoming completely inebriated. Coming to Paris had obviously been a bad decision.

"This room is incredible," cried Adam, suddenly pulling free from Colin and Jenna and staggering around the room, inspecting everything with interest.

"If you need anything, I am right across the hall," said Colin, squeezing Jenna's hand as he left the room. She gave him a weak smile. He was very sweet, but there was absolutely nothing Colin could do to rescue her from this mind numbing fiasco.

Jenna tipped the bellman and he went on his way also. She stood there numbly as Adam staggered all around the room, opening doors and commenting on everything.

The room was splendid, but Jenna was much too nervous about everything else to really appreciate it. Adam was not himself at all and she was silently wondering what on earth she was going to do with him, he seemed to be wound so tightly.

Jenna had very little patience for men who had overindulged in alcohol. In recent months she had found herself the unwilling object of attention at parties and she didn't care for it at all. Over the past year, her coach Hans had been very nervous. Jenna's body was slowly making the transition from that of a child to one approaching a more womanly shape, he had noticed that she was suddenly attracting the attention of men wherever they went and he had begun to lecture her constantly. He told her that all teenage guys were loaded with testosterone and only wanted one thing.

Jenna was also relatively certain that Hans had noticed the budding romance between her and Adam's best friend Matthew. Matthew had been a best friend of Jenna's too. In fact, the three of them had been close since Adam had introduced them on Christmas day nearly three years ago. The three of them did everything together and just two months ago, the relationship between Matthew and Jenna had developed into something more than just friendship.

They had all been away on vacation with Adam's family. Adam's mother had planned a huge vacation to Hawaii. Adam's family was pretty well to do, so when they went on vacation, they almost always took Matthew and Jenna along. They thought Adam would have a better time if his friends were with him.

It was on the beach, near their town home, that Matthew and Jenna had one of their first kisses, and they both realized that their friendship was growing into something more. Adam had noticed what was going on too, he seemed happy enough for them so Jenna figured that he had no feelings for her, at least not like that.

Jenna was suddenly snapped back to the present. Adam was still staggering around the room, talking non stop, as if he were in some sort of strange, manic state.

"Look champagne," he cried, holding up a bottle from a cooler on the entry table.

Jenna rolled her eyes at him, it was just what he needed...more alcohol!

He was busy opening a card that had been laying on the table next to the wine cooler.

"Newlyweds, welcome to Paris, enjoy, the management," said Adam, reading the card to her.

Jenna walked over to him and took the card from his hands.

"Maybe this was a mistake...us coming here," she said, looking at him seriously.

"Why would you say that? This is going to be great! We're getting the star treatment, why would you possibly want to go home?" asked Adam, staring at her, as if she were crazy.

"Look at this place Adam. The honeymoon suite? Everyone thinks we are newlyweds, we have to go along with it if we want to stay. I guess I'm just having second thoughts," she sighed.

"Like you said earlier, we're together all the time anyway," said Adam, with a shrug.

Jenna looked around the room again. It was quite large but the one, king sized bed, was the thing that was intimidating her. There was a small sofa as well, but Adam and Jenna were both so tall, there was no way either of them could sleep comfortably on it.

"Should we ask for another room? One with two beds?"

"That would be ridiculous, we're supposed to be married...newlyweds for God's sake. Newlyweds do not sleep in separate beds," cried Adam, rolling his eyes miserably.

"It's just that I don't think I'm comfortable sleeping in the same bed with you. I mean I know you don't like me like that but...

Adam burst out in hysterical laughter.

"Of course I don't like you like that! We'll sleep in our clothes, it's no big deal, unless you think Matt will totally freak out," said Adam, giving her a sly smile.

"Matt doesn't have to know!" she cried, suddenly more emotional than really seemed rational.

"Whoa, whoa," said Adam, holding his hands up in surrender. "I didn't mean to get you all worked up."

Jenna narrowed her eyes at him, she was nearing hysteria with the situation, and her so called best friend, didn't seem to be helping matters at all.

Unfortunately, the situation with Matt was a bit of a sore subject. Matt had been upset when he found out that Adam and Jenna were going away together for the entire summer. The fact that they were going to be spending a great deal of their time in Paris, the city of love only made matters worse. Jenna wasn't sure why Matt had been so worried, despite her assurances that she had no feelings for Adam. It had bothered her that he'd been so upset.

"I'm sorry, it's just that Matt was already worried about the two of us being together all summer," she told him with a sigh. Jenna had felt bad when she realized how serious Matt was. He had wanted to spend time with her over the summer, though Jenna wasn't sure how that would have went over with Hans or her parents. He would be away at college in Boston by the time they returned. They wouldn't get to spend any time together at all till Thanksgiving.

Actually, Jenna was happy with that prospect. At this point, no one except Adam really knew that her and Matt were a couple. She suspected it would be best if it stayed that way for a while longer. She was only fifteen, Hans wasn't keen on the idea of her having a boyfriend and she was certain her parents wouldn't be fans of the idea either.

"What's his problem? Did he think you wouldn't be able to keep your hands off of me?" asked Adam, flashing her a sly smile.

Jenna folded her arms over her chest and glared at him, he thought all of this was funny.

"Geez Jen, would you just relax! He's got absolutely nothing to worry about. It's not like I'm going to hit on you or something. I mean, you really don't do anything for me. Don't take this personally or anything, but if I were to ask a girl out, I imagine it would be some hot babe who actually had breasts. I mean, you're a nice girl and everything but..."

"Okay, I get the picture!" cried Jenna, looking away, her face red with embarrassment.

Adam dissolved into laughter and gave her a smile.

"Don't get defensive! I'm sure there are plenty of guys out there that are turned on by the skinny, shapeless girls with the wee little boobies," said Adam, dissolving into gasps of laughter again.

Jenna rolled her eyes and suddenly spied their suitcases piled by the door. She strode over to them, determined to find the paperwork her dad had faked, and inspect it for herself.

She walked over and began to rummage through her small suitcase, while Adam began to unwrap the champagne. She pulled out the envelope of documents and looked them over carefully.

Jenna's heart sank painfully as she removed the documents from the envelope and finally took a close look at them. Jenna sighed miserably as the gravity of her own deception became glaringly evident. Her own parents had indeed, fabricated this huge scam. There was a marriage license declaring that she had been married to Adam on April second, in Lake county, Illinois. Jenna shook her head disgustedly and stuffed the papers back into the envelope. Why had her parents done this?

Of course, Jenna realized she was a thorn in her mother's side. She had made that clear to Jenna, almost from the moment of her birth. In fact, both her parents were career orientated, neither of them had really wanted kids. Jenna had known her entire life that her birth had apparently been an unfortunate accident.

Her mother had been well on her way to being a prima ballerina when she found out that she was pregnant. Her mother had considered other options, but having a high profile career assured that any option other than having the baby, would be scandalous. So when Jenna was born, her mother had given domestic life, the old college try. She had been determined, for appearances sake anyway, to convince everyone that her and Jenna's father had the perfect little family. She even went so far as to have a second child three years later, Jenna's little brother Jamie.

Unfortunately, it didn't last. After just five years of being married with children, Jenna's mother had grown bored with the whole idea of domestic life and started her own ballet school, just blocks from their house in Chicago. It was at that point, that she was officially done being a mother.

Luckily for Jenna and her little brother Jamie, their grandma and grandpa Gray lived just a block away. They had assumed the care of the Bruce children, who had been essentially abandoned by their parents. At least, that was how life was until Jenna's grandfather passed away unexpectedly, just over five years ago.

It was a tragic time for the family, After Jenna's grandfather's untimely death, her mother was hospitalized with a nervous breakdown and her poor grandma Gray seemed to age twenty years, almost overnight. Since that point, Jenna and Jamie had essentially been on their own.

Jenna's mother returned from her hospitalization, but she was never the same. She was lost, she had deteriorated into nothing but an empty shell. Jenna's mother was not even capable of taking care of herself, let alone her two children.

Jenna's father had been in the midst of writing his dissertation for his Ph.D, so of course, he was much too busy to take care of his wife, who seemed incapable of caring for herself or their children. He seemed to deal with the hopeless situation, simply by ignoring it.

Grandma and Grandpa Bruce did their best to intervene, they brought the children to live with them. Unfortunately, Jenna's father felt guilty, he would always bring them back to the house, saying that is where they belonged, even though he was rarely ever there. The Bruce children were essentially on their own.

At the tender age of ten years old, Jenna had basically become the caretaker of the entire household. Neither of her parents seemed capable of taking on the responsibility for the day to day care of their children, so the chore fell to Jenna, by default.

She cooked, did laundry and made sure that Jamie was ready for school and at the bus stop on time. It had been very overwhelming for Jamie and Jenna to have to take care of each other. When Jenna left for Paris, she felt incredibly guilty for leaving her baby brother behind in the states, as he was only twelve years old now. Not really old enough to be completely on his own like that.

"Champagne?" asked Adam, holding a glass out to her.

Jenna glared at him, snapped from her unpleasant memories by her current situation, which was clearly no better. Jenna sighed miserably unable to believe that Adam had gotten so wasted, he was supposed to be the adult. He had essentially emotionally abandoned her in her time of need. She was completely irritated with him.

"No!" she snapped.

"Come on, we're in Paris. Loosen up a little bit. Did you ever think you'd be living the high life in Paris?" said Adam, giving her a sly smile.

"Adam..." whined Jenna, but she couldn't think of any argument why she shouldn't at least, try the champagne. They *were* in Paris...

"A little bit is not going to kill you," he told her with a smile.

"Oh...sure, what the hell?" she said, shaking her head absently and taking the glass from him.

"To the newlyweds," said Adam, raising his glass to her and flashing her a sly smile.

"To the newlyweds," she said, raising her eyebrows at him and returning his toast.

Jenna took a cautious sip of the champagne as the bubbles tickled her nose. Her first sip was almost overpoweringly tart, the second sip was not quite as bad, though she had already decided that champagne must be one of those things that one must acquire a taste for.

"What do you think?" asked Adam.

It's okay," she said, shrugging halfheartedly. The warmth was now spreading through her body and she decided she was done. Jenna had a sneaky feeling it would be best if one of them stayed sober tonight. She ambled slowly over to the balcony door and opened it.

She stepped out on the balcony and let the cool breeze blow across her now slightly flushed, face. Lights were blazing all over Paris and their fourth floor room afforded them a rather nice view. Jenna smiled to herself, she still couldn't believe she was actually here in Paris, it was like a dream!

Adam appeared on the balcony behind her. He seemed to be doing a little bit better, he wasn't staggering around as much. He had both glasses of champagne in his hands.

"You left your champagne behind," said Adam, handing her glass to her.

Jenna gave him a fake smile. He was trying to make her relax, though there was no relaxing her at this point. She was much too nervous.

"Adam...I.."

"Jenna just relax, we're in Paris, on our honeymoon. Have a little bubbly, take a deep breath and enjoy the view. You're so uptight, you don't always have to be the perfect one. Do something crazy for once in your life," he said, raising his eyebrows at her.

"We're not on our honeymoon!" she exclaimed, turning abruptly and heading back into the room.

"Everyone here believes that we are," said Adam, he was right behind her as she stalked back into the room, she was suddenly feeling very agitated.

"I just think it would be a good idea if one us remained sober. You are completely wasted!"

"Do you want this little scam to work or not?" asked Adam, following her. His face was completely serious.

"Of course, I want it to work. Do you actually think I want to be sent home to Chicago, so I can spend the entire summer being berated by my parents about what a failure I am!" she cried. She was aware that she was suddenly ranting at him loudly.

"First of all, your parents are idiots. You are the furthest thing from a failure, there is. Secondly, I have no desire to be sent home either, so I think we should make a concentrated effort to make this little scam work," said Adam, his voice was suddenly silky and unfamiliar sounding.

"What, exactly, do you have in mind?" asked Jenna, folding her arms across her chest and eyeing him suspiciously.

"Well, we are supposed to be a married couple, if we're going to be convincing, we're going to have to consummate our marriage," he said, flashing her a sly smile.

"Are you completely insane!" cried Jenna. She was hoping he was just messing with her, but she was getting the sinking feeling, he was not.

"No, I'm trying to be realistic."

"The answer is no Adam, absolutely not! You are being completely ridiculous, it's a bad idea," cried Jenna, already panicking at the very thought.

"You want to be convincing, don't you? It will be perfectly obvious to everyone, if we don't do it. We have to project a certain intimacy to the others, otherwise they'll never buy it."

"I vote that we just tell them you are impotent," said Jenna, stifling a little giggle. She was being catty, but he was infuriating her. He was being a drunken ass.

"I can prove to you, that I am not," said Adam, raising his eyebrows at her.

"I would rather you just sleep it off. I cannot stand another moment of this conversation. If you so much as lay one hand on me, I will call security," snapped Jenna. She almost cringed when she said the words. Really...who calls security on their own husband, on their honeymoon?

"Now you are the one who is being ridiculous. Listen Jenna, it's not a big deal and it's not something horrible. It's completely natural for two people who love each other! I love you and I know that you love me, it would be silly to be sent home over something so trivial," said Adam.

Jenna sighed, he was definitely very drunk and she doubted if he even knew what he was saying.

"Adam please...you're drunk," she was pleading with him.

"Admit it, you love me," said Adam.

"Of course, I love you Adam. But it's a different kind of love. We have to work together...if we did it...it would change everything, it would be a bad idea," she told him firmly.

"It's not wrong, we have a marriage license. I don't know what you're so upset about. It was *your* father that did this to us," snapped Adam, suddenly defensive.

"Adam, don't you realize...the license is probably a fake! This whole thing is just some sort of scam my father cooked up. Listen, I'm sorry that my dad did this to us but I have no intention of..."

"Jenna would you just grow up? You're acting like a child. Do you really want to be sent home to your mother?" snapped Adam, grabbing both of her shoulders and looking into her eyes.

Jenna was suddenly panicking, Adam knew exactly how to manipulate her to his liking. He knew she would do whatever it took to avoid being sent home to her mother. Adam knew the emotional abuse her mother would pile on her, if she were to be sent home prematurely. Jenna bit her lower lip miserably, this whole trip had been a bad idea. Now she was stuck in this hotel room with Adam, and Adam was not himself.

"Stop it Adam, you're drunk," she told him, glaring into his eyes, very seriously.

"Don't be mad at me. I didn't engineer this stupid scam. I'm just trying to make the best of it, trying to ensure that we can actually pull it off. Like it or not, you're here with me. I'm the adult, I'm the one that has to be responsible for you," said Adam, his deep blue eyes were intense and unwavering, despite the fact that he was completely wasted.

Jenna pulled away from him and walked a few steps away, trying to shake off the intensity of the situation. She did not want to be in a confrontation with her best friend, but she was positive she was not ready to do, what Adam seemed to want her to do, tonight.

"We will not be consummating our marriage tonight! If you insist that this is necessary for us to stay here, I will need to think about it before I commit. If you cannot wait for my decision, I will talk to Mr. Dumontier in the morning so that he can make arrangements for us to go back to the states," she told him, barely able to control the emotion in her voice. She suddenly felt like crying, she had been thrown into a situation she was not comfortable with at all. If she did what Adam wanted, their relationship would be forever changed. Jenna was certain, it was a bad idea.

"You're scared," said Adam, his voice was almost taunting.

"I'm just fifteen years old!" cried Jenna, her voice raising, in distress.

"We're married, what difference does it make? My grandma got married when she was fifteen, so what?" said Adam.

"You know damn well that we're not really married!" she cried angrily. Jenna was beginning to get aggravated by this entire situation. She didn't want to go back to the states, but she was sure that she couldn't do what Adam seemed to expect of her tonight.

Adam sat down on the bed and smiled at her. "Are you saving yourself for Matt? I can pretty much guarantee he's not saving himself for you," sneered Adam.

"Shut up!" snapped Jenna, her patience growing tediously thin with this entire situation.

"Yep, I knew it, you're scared," he said, flashing her an amused smile.

Jenna was pacing the room nervously. She glared at Adam, as drunk as he was, he was pushing her buttons as skillfully as ever. He always knew exactly how to get her to do something she was hesitant to do.

They were together every single day. Jenna was angry with Adam, and she was angry with herself for not seeing this coming. She felt incredibly stupid for putting herself in this compromising position.

"Adam, this is completely ridiculous! We are not married and we will not be consummating our marriage tonight. You are very drunk!" She spun around angrily to see that Adam had not heard a word she had said. He was slumped over in the bed, passed out cold.

Jenna couldn't help but laugh to herself when she saw him laying there. She pulled off his shoes and pulled the comforter up over him so he could sleep it off. She was getting the feeling he was not going to be feeling very well in the morning.

Jenna sat down on the couch to consider what she should do, but in moments she was anxiously pacing the room again, this was a nightmare! She didn't want to go home to Chicago, but coming here without Hans had been a huge mistake. She was young and naive and before tonight, Adam had treated her as if she were nothing more than an annoying little sister. If there had been any hint of attraction between them, maybe she could have seen this coming...

Jenna shook her head miserably as she continued her restless pacing of the room, she was certain that she couldn't spend the rest of the summer putting Adam off, and she was also sure that she couldn't give in to his demands. They were best friends, if she did, their friendship would be forever altered.

Jenna looked over at Adam snoring in their bed and she was suddenly worried that Adam would wake back up with "love" on the brain, so she decided she would go down and sit in the lobby for a while.

Jenna grabbed her room key and took the elevators down to the lobby. She found a sofa in a secluded corner and made herself comfortable. The lobby was nearly deserted now, most of the people who had been lingering in the lobby had moved on to nearby clubs or gone on to bed by now. Jenna didn't want any of the other skaters to see her sitting there as they returned from the clubs, but she was partially shielded by a large potted palm, so she wasn't too worried.

She had been sitting there maybe fifteen minutes when a familiar British voice spoke from behind her.

"Is sleep eluding you? I was certain that you were exhausted, you had been traveling so long," said Colin, as he approached her and sat down on the sofa beside her.

"I am exhausted, but I can't sleep," she whined.

"I am not surprised. Darling, I want you to level with me," said Colin, looking into her eyes very seriously.

Jenna nodded her head numbly.

"How old are you...truly? I am quite certain that you are not eighteen," said Colin.

Jenna was biting her lower lip, fighting the urge to burst into tears, the stress of the entire evening was finally getting to her. "I'm fifteen."

"Bloody ell!" cried Colin, staring at her in shock. "You're serious?"

Jenna just nodded her head numbly, she couldn't even speak. She felt like such a fake, she had never tried to deceive anyone, ever!

"It's worse than I had imagined, I had guessed that you were just sixteen. I cannot believe it, has the company gone completely mad?"

Jenna looked around nervously, she was sure that her tender age was not meant to be common knowledge. The elaborate lobby was not busy, but she was dangerously close to breaking down in tears, and an attractive young man at the front desk was staring at her and she really didn't want to attract attention to herself and Colin.

"I know I shouldn't be here Colin, but I can't go back home."

"But you must, you're a minor!" cried Colin.

"Shhhhh," Jenna was shussing him anxiously. "Colin, nobody can know. I can't go home to Chicago, my parents don't want me there, and they will make my life miserable. Since the Olympics I've heard nothing but what a failure I am. Adam and I came here to redeem ourselves,"

"Redeem yourself? Most people would kill to even make it so far as the Olympics! cried Colin, his voice was incredulous.

"Colin, my family is so screwed up, they really want nothing to do with me. I thought that this trip was completely legitimate, but tonight I realized I was sent here with what I can only guess, is a fake marriage license. My staying here is contingent on the illusion that Adam and I are married..." Jenna paused, Colin looked so shocked, she wasn't sure she could go on.

"Wait, you and Adam are not really married?" cried Colin, he was so shocked, his eyes threatened to bulge from their sockets

"Shhhhh," she shushed him nervously again, "No, the marriage is nothing but a ruse, the paperwork is fake," said Jenna, shaking her head miserably.

"This fiasco just gets worse and worse. I do not understand, who would do such a thing, to a fifteen year old girl? I truly cannot believe that your own parents would set you up like this, the very idea is ridiculous," snapped Colin, angrily.

"Colin please, keep your voice down," said Jenna, looking around nervously. The handsome gentleman at the front desk was staring at them curiously, Jenna tried to smooth her face into an expression that would seem less devastated, but it was nearly impossible.

"I'm sorry, it's just that I am stunned, the very idea is just ludicrous," snapped Colin.

"Unfortunately, what's done is done. I can't go back to Chicago," Jenna told him adamantly.

"Yes but..."

"No! Going back to Chicago would be worse than anything I would have to face here. I've made up my mind, I should just do whatever it takes to go along with the scam," she told him dejectedly.

"Truly, I am not sure that is such a good idea. I mean, what if the authorities were to find out? I imagine they would send you back to the states immediately, then your efforts would be in vain," said Colin.

"But how would they find out? Someone would have to tell them right? I mean, so far no one has even suspected..."

"But you've only just arrived, and of course, not many people have seen the two of you interact. I mean, I noticed right away that your relationship with Adam seemed a little, I don't know...distant..."

"Oh God, that's exactly what Adam said," cried Jenna, shaking her head miserably. "Please don't tell anyone," she begged. Jenna looked around nervously, the young man at the desk was still staring at her, making her very uncomfortable. It was as if he knew, *something* was up.

"I am not going to tell anyone, but you tell me, why are you here in the lobby at this late hour, and why is it you cannot sleep?" asked Colin.

Jenna gave Colin a nervous glance and lowered her voice. "Adam is so drunk, he doesn't know what he's saying. He suggested that we consummate our marriage," she whispered, almost cringing with embarrassment.

"Maybe you are wrong...maybe he knows *exactly* what he's saying," said Colin, raising his eyebrows at her.

Jenna frowned. "Colin, Adam and I are best friends. We've been best friends since I was just twelve years old, it's never been like that for us. He is well aware that my feelings are for his best friend, Matthew...I really don't believe..."

"I would not be so sure, people change, feelings change," said Colin, shrugging slightly.

"Adam has known me since I was a child, he treats me like a baby sister. It's not possible..." Jenna was chewing on her lower lip nervously. How could she possibly know what Adam was feeling, when she didn't even know what she, herself, was feeling right now?

"So where is he now?" asked Colin.

"He passed out, but I was worried that he might wake back up again, I needed some time to think," she mumbled.

"What is there to think about? This is completely ridiculous, you should go home to your parents," said Colin.

"That is easy for you to say, you don't know them. If you did, you wouldn't be saying that. It was my father who arranged all this," she told him, shaking her head miserably.

"Everyone is entitled to a stupid mistake," said Colin, shrugging casually.

Jenna stood up abruptly, her mind was made up. "What they did, was in no way, a mistake. I've made up my mind, I'll do whatever it takes to stay here."

"Including consummating your sham marriage?" asked Colin, eyeing her seriously.

Jenna shrugged nonchalantly. "I imagine there are worse things."

"Seriously, you believe going home to your parents would be worse?" asked Colin, looking completely exasperated.

"Like I said before, you don't know them. There are many things I would do to avoid being sent home to my parents...jump off the Eiffel tower, throw my body in front of a bus...really, the list is rather long..."

"Jenna wait, don't do anything rash. Stay with me tonight. Tomorrow everything will look different, you are tired, you need to rest," said Colin.

Jenna folded her arms over her chest and eyed him seriously. She had to agree, it probably would be a good idea, for her to just separate herself from Adam for the night. Though, she wasn't sure if spending the night with Colin was a good idea.

"It's okay...you have nothing to fear from me," said Colin, giving her a reassuring smile.

Jenna just nodded at him numbly and followed him back upstairs to his room.

CHAPTER TEN

Alexander was pacing nervously. They were stuck in Berlin, the flight that would take them on to Paris was cancelled until morning. He was angry at everyone in the terminal, didn't they realize? He *needed* to get to Paris.

He had waited for this day for weeks, the day he would meet the woman that would become his American wife. The woman that would be the reason he would finally dump his cold, unaffectionate fiancee.

He had ranted at every employee he could possibly rant at, there was no way around it, they were stuck in Berlin till morning.

"I wish you would calm down. We will be there in the morning. What difference does it make?" said Marika, rolling her eyes miserably.

"There was a reception tonight, so that we could meet the other skaters, now we've missed it." snapped Alexander angrily.

"Who cares? If they follow skating at all they already know who we are. I could care less about meeting the rest of the cast, we will be the stars."

"Did you not want to meet the other couple we will be skating with? Are you not curious?" asked Alexander.

"I have seen the clips of their skating. It will work. He is nearly as tall as you and seems quite strong. The female is nothing but a child, so young, they had to fake her marriage to her partner so that she could stay in Europe without a chaperone. I just hope she does nothing to embarrass us."

"She seems quite mature for her age...I mean her skating does."

Nyet, nyet, nyet! Do not even think about it Alexander!" cried Marika, suddenly very upset.

"What?" Alexander was trying to feign innocence. Marika knew him too well.

"I know what you have up your sleeve Alexander, do not even think it! You cannot have sex with this girl!"

"What makes you think I want to have sex with her?"

"You'd stick your dick into a rathole if you thought it would get you off. Besides, you've told me again and again you have a thing for da girls with de blonde hair. She is off limits, do you understand?"

"Marika, you know I love you," said Alexander, lamely trying to soothe her.

"I mean it! She is young and stupid, if she were to become pregnant, you know what would happen. You and I could not marry, a man should marry the woman who is carrying his baby!" cried Marika.

"We've got time now...maybe *you* could get pregnant," said Alexander, flashing her a seductive smile.

"Don't be ridiculous! We will be on tour for five months, do us both a favor and keep your dick in your pants."

Alexander sighed. That would be the story of his life if he married Marika, something he was now sure he could never do. He settled into his chair, closed his eyes and willed himself to sleep until it was time for their flight to leave. Hopefully all his dreams would be of Jenna.

CHAPTER ELEVEN

The sun was streaming through the east windows in long amber rays as it crept across the pale ivory, silk coverlet on Jenna's bed. She was still very tired, but her brain was telling her she needed to get up. Reluctantly, she forced her eyes open, stretched and looked around curiously as she realized that she was not in her little room above Hans' garage, she was in Paris.

Jenna sighed as the memories from the night before came tumbling back into her finally rested, brain. She had spent the night in Colin's room, which amazingly enough, did have two beds. She could hear him in the shower, singing loudly. She smiled, he was such a character! She frowned as she wondered how Adam was doing and if he even realized that she was gone.

Jenna still wasn't sure what she should do. She was certain she didn't want to go back to Chicago, but still, staying here in Paris didn't sound like a good option either. She had finally decided that she was going to have a heart to heart talk with Adam...sober. She scribbled a note for Colin, thanking him for taking her in for the night.

Jenna slipped silently out of Colin's room and back to her own room across the hall. As she opened the door she was greeted by the smell of a full breakfast sitting on a service cart right inside the door. Adam was sitting on the sofa wrapped in a bathrobe, he was holding a cup of coffee in his hands. He looked completely miserable sitting there, his hair was uncombed and he hadn't shaved. He jumped up, as soon as he saw Jenna walk in through the door.

"Oh my God! Where have you been? Are you okay?" he cried, excitedly.

Jenna rolled her eyes, thinking he was acting a bit dramatic. "I'm fine," she told him, with a bored shrug.

"Where were you? I was worried about you!" he cried.

Jenna was staring at him with a shocked look on her face, suddenly fighting tears.

He was treating her as if she were a child who had misbehaved.

"I spent the night with Colin. I had to get out of this room, you were being a drunken ass," it was all she could get out, before her voice seemed to fade away to nothing.

"You spent the night with Colin!" he cried, suddenly horrified.

"He doesn't drink, so he was a bit more reasonable than you were. Besides, I knew I could trust him. I guess you realize, he's gay," she told him blandly.

"I'm sorry Jenna, I..." Adam was staring at her oddly. "Oh God, what did I do?"

Jenna narrowed her eyes at him, determined not to break down in tears. He obviously remembered nothing.

"You don't remember?" she asked, folding her arms across her chest, eyeing him arrogantly, she was dangerously close to tears.

"No, I can't remember anything. I've never really drank alcohol before," he said, shaking his head miserably.

"You were being a complete ass, you suggested that we should consummate our marriage," she told him, glaring at him angrily.

"Oh shit!" he exclaimed, looking quite embarrassed. "Did we?"

"No! Because of the alcohol you were being a bit unreasonable. Luckily, you passed out. I left, because I was confused, I didn't know what else to do. Colin found me in the lobby and invited me to stay the night with him."

"Holy crap, I'm really sorry Jenna. I've never been drunk like that before," said Adam, he looked incredibly embarrassed.

"Which brings me to my next question for you. What are we going to do?" she asked.

"What exactly, are you asking?"

"I need to know...what do you expect of me, if I stay?"

"You're considering not staying?" asked Adam, his face was suddenly defeated.

"I've considered my options, to me, going home to my parents is not an option," she told him, her voice was emotionless.

"So what are you asking me then?" asked Adam, he suddenly looked baffled.

"It's this sham marriage thing...you're my best friend. I don't think I can do what you want," she managed to mumble.

"Jenna, that was a mistake, I was drunk last night. I don't even like you in that way," said Adam, his eyes were wide.

"That's not what you said last night," she told him.

"I'm sorry, it won't happen again. To everyone here in Europe, you and I will be married. In reality, we'll just be best friends. Just like we always have been. I promise, I will be a complete gentleman," he told her with a little smile.

Jenna gave him a dubious look, but he appeared to be completely sincere. She could only believe him, and hope that it truly was the alcohol that had made him into such an ass last night.

"I ordered you breakfast," he said, pointing to the service cart, which seemed to be loaded with an assortment of breakfast items.

"I'm not really hungry," she told him, she was nervous, it was always best not to eat when she was nervous like this. She glanced at the clock and realized that it was getting late, she needed to shower and dress for their first practice with the company.

In just over half an hour, they were in a car on their way to the ice arena. The arena was only five blocks away, but the company was driving them there today, until they were more familiar with the area, then they would be able to walk or ride bikes to the arena every day.

Jenna smiled as she watched the streets of Paris slip past her as they drove along. She was excited, she couldn't believe they were really there. Though when they arrived at the arena she was fighting a new wave of terror. Jenna clung to Adam's hand desperately as they walked into the large, echoing arena.

There were dozens of workers in the arena, all working busily to convert the arena from a hockey venue, to one more appropriate to hosting an all star ice show. There were construction crews, lighting crews, and sound crews, all shouting to each other in French. Jenna was completely overwhelmed by all the pandemonium as she walked with Adam through the bustling arena.

They finally reached the woman's dressing room and Jenna had to leave Adam at the door. She reluctantly let go of his hand and walked into the dressing room. She was immediately overwhelmed by all of the chaos in the cramped room. There had to be at least twenty five women in there, all chatting noisily in French. There was clothing and makeup strewn everywhere.

Jenna was shrinking back against the door, watching everyone anxiously. She was afraid to barge into this room where everyone else seemed to be completely at ease. She felt like a lost child, completely out of place.

Jenna began to wonder again, why she had even come here. All these women were older and obviously belonged here. She was suddenly worried that she was going to make a complete fool of herself.

Jenna hauled her bag over to a bench and began putting on her skates, determined to at least, give this a try. She had nearly finished lacing her skates, when a Russian tinged voice spoke from behind her, startling her.

"I am guessing you are the American, Jenna Bruce," said the woman, who was standing there behind her. The woman was looking her over carefully, her demeanor seemed quite distant.

Jenna turned around and looked at her quizzically. The woman was tiny, probably just five feet tall and maybe ninety pounds, if she was that. She had dark brown hair that was twisted into a severe knot on top of her head. Her body was rigid, with her hands on her hips, and she was glaring at Jenna with angry brown eyes.

Jenna was immediately taken aback by the hostility she could feel emanating from every pore of this woman's body. Her eyes seemed to be so bitter, they threatened to burn right through her! She shivered and wondered how someone she had never met before, could look at her with such unbridled animosity.

"Yes, that's right...and you are?" she asked. She had extended her hand to the woman, in a gesture of friendship, but she pulled it away uncomfortably when the woman showed no interest in shaking it. In fact, she was suddenly afraid this tiny woman might actually spit on it, she looked so provoked. Jenna was immediately on the defensive. Why was this woman glaring at her as if she were the enemy?

"I am Marika Gringkov...I must say, I was not expecting you to be so beautiful. You are much prettier in person, than on television. I guess you realize, you were brought here to skate with Alexander and I," the woman snapped, as her eyes continued to rake over Jenna, haughtily.

Jenna bit her lip and swallowed nervously as this all finally sunk in. Marika and her partner Alexander were the reigning World Champions from the Soviet Union. They had not only won the World Championships, but the gold medal in the Olympics. The very same Olympics, Jenna and Adam had been disqualified from.

"Oh, I didn't recognize you. I saw you in Lake Placid, I thought your long program was fabulous!" she cried, suddenly realizing who this woman was. Mr. Dumontier had mentioned that he had picked her and Adam specifically, to skate with this couple. Jenna felt very honored that Mr. Dumontier even thought that her and Adam were in the same class as Marika and Alexander, Jenna thought they were completely incredible!

"I have also admired your skating. I must admit, your style of skating does seem to be quite similar to ours, but do not get any ideas about Alexander, he is mine," snapped Marika, rather harshly. Jenna stiffened, Marika was still appraising her cooly.

Jenna gave her an odd look and resisted the urge to burst out in hysterical laughter.

Marika was insinuating that she might want to steal her boyfriend from her. Jenna stifled a giggle, she had enough problems right now, without trying to seduce Alexander away from Marika.

"Don't worry, I'm, uh...married," she managed to stutter, trying not to giggle at the very thought of her and Adam's ridiculous, fake, marriage.

"Please...spare me," snapped Marika, holding her hand up at her, and eyeing her with disgust. Jenna could only stand there and stare at her blankly.

"I am already aware that you are a minor and this whole marriage thing is...what is it you Americans say...a scam?" said Marika, she was still glaring at Jenna, her eyes narrowed with malice. Jenna shivered and wrapped her arms around herself nervously, when she caught her hostile gaze.

"Yes," sighed Jenna, nodding her head slightly. She was completely bewildered by Marika's hostile demeanor. She felt as if she'd done nothing to provoke this harsh treatment. "It is true, I am not married to

Adam, but you shouldn't worry, I have a boyfriend, he's away at college in Boston," she managed to choke out.

"You have a boyfriend, in Boston? In the United States?" Marika laughed and shook her head, suddenly completely amused. "You poor naive little child. This boyfriend you have in Boston? Are you betrothed to him?"

"What?" asked Jenna. She had no idea what Marika was talking about.

"This boyfriend, did he give you a ring? Are you to be married?" asked Marika. Her expression had changed from one of complete loathing, to one of a person who was on the verge of hysterical laughter.

"No, Matt and I...we just recently...I mean...we were friends first and then..." Jenna was so flustered, she wasn't sure what she wanted to say, she felt a bit put on the spot. Matthew was her boyfriend, but there really wasn't any commitment between them, no ring, no promises. Just those few stolen kisses, and a secret relationship she had been forced to hide from her coach Hans, who would never allow it.

Marika laughed a strange evil laugh. "I am sorry to tell you, it will be over when you return. Your boyfriend will meet many women at college. Women who will be more than happy to meet his every need, while you are here...far away in Europe."

"But.."

"You will see, Boston is much too far. The relationship will fall apart. When it does, you will want Alexander but you cannot have him, he is mine. We are betrothed," snapped Marika, glaring at her with barely restrained disdain.

"I just..." Jenna stammered, she had no idea what to say to this woman, she was completely mystified. Marika was still glaring at her, her face was a mask of barely concealed contempt. Jenna felt as if she had done nothing to provoke her. She just wanted to tell her she loved Matt, she was not interested in Alexander. Finally, Marika started laughing hysterically.

"I am worrying myself for nothing, Alexander could not possibly find you attractive, you are really nothing more than a child. Look at you, you are not yet a woman, you have no curves, you are skinny and shapeless," laughed Marika, shaking her head dismissively.

Jenna let an impotent sigh escape her lips. She was tired of being constantly reminded of her sticklike body. She was now fifteen, obviously her development had been seriously delayed, she hadn't even had her first period yet, unlike all her friends, who had got theirs at least two years ago.

"Still...I am warning you, Alexander is engaged to me! I realize, he has a thing for de girls with de blonde hair. Shapeless or not, he will be completely enchanted by you, with de blue eyes and dis pretty smile. What am I to do? You will remember, Alexander belongs to me!" she cried, staring bitterly into Jenna's eyes. Her voice seemed to raise an entire octave in distress.

"Ummm, sure," Jenna mumbled, sighing uneasily. She was chewing on her bottom lip nervously, Marika had her completely on edge. Working with this pair was going to be a challenge she had not anticipated. Marika at least, was a total nut case, she could only hope that Alexander was a bit more reasonable. She feared that Marika and her would constantly be at odds. Obviously, Marika had some serious issues...trust was one of them.

Jenna decided it would be safest if she tried to avoid being alone with her. She was getting the distinct feeling that Marika wanted to scratch her eyeballs right out of their sockets!

"So Marika, how old are you?" she asked, trying to divert her attention from the idea that she had come here specifically to steal Alexander away from her. Jenna was suddenly curious. She knew that Marika was older than her, but she seemed like a child, she was so small and delicate looking.

"I am nineteen, Alexander is twenty two. We will marry when we return to our country in the fall," said Marika, still staring at her warily. "When will you marry?"

Jenna stifled a giggle and fought the urge to roll her eyes. "I've not really considered it at all. Matthew and I, we've been friends for a while..." she didn't know what to say. She wasn't really even sure if she could consider Matt her boyfriend, they weren't engaged...there was really nothing but few stolen kisses, and a relationship she was forced to keep secret.

Hans especially, would completely freak out if he knew that Matt was more than just a friend. In fact, Jenna was sure that Hans had his suspicions about Matt recently. Before she left St. Louis, poor Matt had been pretty much been barred from their practices for weeks! Hans had been so convinced that he was ruining her concentration. Unfortunately, it was probably true, it was hard for her to concentrate on anything whenever Matt was around.

Jenna snapped to attention and suddenly realized that the room had completely emptied out except for her and Marika.

"We are late! Simone will be very unhappy with us," exclaimed Marika, jumping up and suddenly running out the dressing room door. Jenna followed her and when they arrived on the ice, Gail and Simone were already going over their plans for the show.

Simone gave them both an irritated glare as they skated breathlessly up to the group. Adam took Jenna by the hand and pulled her over by him possessively, flashing her a bug eyed glare. Jenna just shrugged at him half heartedly. Yes, she was late, but he had no idea what she'd just endured.

As Jenna listened to Simone speak, she was surprised to find out how much ice time her and Adam would have in the show, especially since it was their first season and they weren't really considered a headline act.

Jenna thought it all sounded very ambitious, they were to be in the opening number, then they would do an abbreviated version of their regular long program for their feature number. Their other number would be a combined pairs number with Alexander and Marika. Then of course, they would be in the grand finale.

Jenna was feeling nervous. She hoped that she would be able to learn everything in the next two weeks as expected. She usually learned programs pretty quickly, though at this point, she was feeling a bit overwhelmed.

Jenna's arrival in Paris had been a sobering wake up call for her. For the next five months, she would be essentially on her own. Being on her own didn't bother her, but staying in the same room with Adam seemed daunting.

Jenna was suddenly missing Hans. For the last, nearly three years, he had ruled every aspect of her life with an iron fist. He told her when to get up, when to go to practice, and he monitored her diet relentlessly. Jenna was thin, but Hans did want her and Adam to eat, what he considered, "crap". He wanted them to eat healthy foods. He didn't want Jenna to fall victim to anorexia, like so many skaters eventually did.

Hans had become more than her coach, he had become a pseudo parent to her. Jenna depended on him for everything, and besides her grandparents, he was the only person who had ever showed her any love in her entire life.

Jenna hadn't officially met Alexander yet, but she knew exactly who he was when they arrived on the ice. He was standing near the boards, assessing her carefully. In fact, he hadn't taken his eyes off of her, since she had arrived on the ice with Marika.

Alexander was attractive enough, he was tall and muscular with thick, dark hair and piercing brown eyes. Everyone else was wearing jackets, as the arena was quite cool, but Alexander was wearing black warm up pants and a tight, black t-shirt that hugged his muscular torso like a second skin.

Not that he needed a jacket, every inch of his body it seemed, was covered with a thick mass of dark, curly hair. Jenna couldn't help but be unnerved as she caught him staring at her. She shivered, as his eyes drifted up and down her body, a cool smile crossing his lips. He was standing there assessing her carefully, with his massive arms folded across his chest, he had veins the size of garden hoses bulging out from his sinewy muscles.

Jenna wrapped her arms around herself self consciously, under his intense scrutiny. She couldn't read his expression, but she imagined he was wondering why on earth they had brought in this skinny young girl to share the ice with him and Marika, the reigning World Champions.

She was nervous enough, just being here in Paris, presented to the world as an adult, when she was really nothing more than a child. Alexander caught her looking at him and flashed her a cool smile. Jenna looked away nervously, his arrogant stare gave her a little chill. She sighed anxiously, hoping that Alexander didn't hate her automatically, the way his partner seemed to.

Jenna looked up at Adam and was surprised to see that he had narrowed his eyes at Alexander and was staring him down bitterly. She was baffled when she saw the expression on Adam's face, he looked like a mad dog guarding a bone. Jenna chewed on her lower lip nervously, things didn't seem to be getting off to a very good start. Thankfully, Marika seemed focused on Simone's speech and she didn't seem to notice the sizing up that was going on between the three of them. It was a good thing, Jenna didn't want to endure anymore threats from Marika, who seemed to think her sole purpose here, was to steal Alexander away from her.

After warm ups, everyone broke up into small groups. Simone took Alexander, Marika, Adam and Jenna to the far end of the rink. She explained her new and innovative choreography for the show. She felt that pairs skating was the most beautiful discipline in figure skating. She wanted to make it even more beautiful. Her plan was to have a combined pairs number which would feature both pairs skating the same program at opposite ends of the rink, when the music changed, they would all skate to the center of the ice and change partners. For the finale, they would all skate to the center again and end as one big team.

Jenna could not help but notice how beautiful Simone was. She was petite, not much bigger in stature than Marika. She had straight, dark brown, hair that hung in a silky curtain to her chin. She had flawless skin and piercing brown eyes. Jenna was completely blown away by her talent.

Jenna was already quite familiar with
Alexander and Marika's style of skating.
She had watched the Soviets skate many
times on television, she felt very honored
that it was her and Adam that had been
selected to skate with them. She was a little
worried about Marika's odd fixation with
Alexander, but she decided to put that out of
her mind for now. Marika was obviously
more than a little screwed up!

The first order of business was to split the
pairs up, so that they could each begin to
match their skating to their new part-time,
partners. Jenna was finally introduced to
Alexander, who had been watching her
carefully as he leaned against the rink
barrier. In fact, he had barely taken his eyes
off of her since she had skated onto the ice.

Jenna had assumed that it would be the
biggest challenge for Alexander to learn to
skate with her. He was used to skating with
Marika, who was barely five feet tall and
weighed somewhere around ninety pounds.
Jenna, on the other hand, had recently gone
through a growth spurt, so she was now
5'7". Alexander was used to throwing
Marika around like a little doll. Jenna was

worried he would be in for a bit of a surprise when he needed to lift or throw her! Of course, it shouldn't be too much of an issue, he seemed to be a big, strong guy.

Simone paired Jenna off with Alexander and Marika with Adam and sent both couples to opposite sides of the arena to work on some basic pairs moves so that they could get the feel of working together.

That first week went by quickly and Jenna was very pleased. Alexander had worked hard with her, matching their strides and working on all their various lifts and throws. Jenna was amazed at how quickly her and Alexander had been able to skate as one. Their talent was closely matched, in fact, it seemed as if, they were made to skate together. Alexander seemed to have no problem whatsoever with the size difference between Marika and his new, part-time partner, Jenna. Simone and Gail were both quite excited to see that Alexander seemed to be perfectly suited to skate with Jenna.

Jenna couldn't help but be a bit relieved, after meeting Marika, she had been worried that they might both be a couple of nut cases, but her and Alexander had truly hit it off. Alexander was a true gentleman and had been nothing but polite and understanding with her. It seemed as if, he was going out of his way to be nice to her and he was always helpful and smiling. Jenna was happy that despite her initial misgivings, things seemed to be going great!

Unfortunately, Marika and Adam weren't doing nearly as well, but their skating was improving every day. Marika had proved to be difficult to work with from the start, always wanting her own way, so her personality seemed to grate on Adam's nerves.

Their biggest issue by far, was with their pairs spin. Adam thought the height difference was what was killing him. He was so tall, and Marika was so short, he said he felt like he was skating with an eight year old little girl.

Jenna was happy that despite her initial misgivings, things seemed to be going great with her and Alexander! Unfortunately, her happiness with the situation was destined to be short lived.

CHAPTER TWELVE

Alexander was happy when he finally arrived on the ice. There were about ten or eleven other skaters on the ice, all warming up, but as he scanned the faces of the skaters on the ice, he didn't see Jenna Bruce anywhere.

What had happened? Did her parents refuse to go along with the scam? Had her flight been delayed? Alexander's mind was spinning with all the possibilities. What if the Americans were unable to get fake documents? Then his trip to Paris would be for nothing. He would perform in this show all season and return the the USSR still betrothed to Marika.

His eyes frantically scanned the ice and finally he saw Adrian, or Adam or whatever the hell the guy's name was, skating around aimlessly. That was her partner, where was Jenna?

A small brunette woman skated onto the ice clapping her hands to get everyone's attention, Alexander looked around again. Where was Marika?

The woman began speaking to them, but Alexander couldn't absorb a single word she was saying. He was still looking around anxiously, hoping to catch his first glance of Jenna.

Aaron, or Adam, or whatever his name was, seemed to be looking around nervously as well. Alexander suddenly had a thought....

Marika! She wouldn't, would she? He knew she was very jealous and she had a bit of a mean streak. Alexander was suddenly worried. He wondered if he should get off the ice and into the women's locker room, just in case Marika had went off the deep end and was now murdering his would be wife.

In seconds Marika and Jenna both skated onto the ice, looking harried and embarrassed that they were late. Jenna's partner gave her a bug eyed glare, silently reprimanding her for being late. Jenna just gave him a helpless shrug. Obviously, she'd had some sort of confrontation with Marika. Jenna looked embarrassed and bewildered. Alexander narrowed his eyes at Marika, but she hardly even noticed his presence on the ice.

Alexander was pleased that Marika was ignoring him, it gave him a chance to check out his new part time skating partner.

She was taller than he'd imagined, at least five foot six, perhaps a bit taller, but she was skinny and shapeless with only the merest hint of breasts, but her legs were long and beautiful, probably the best legs he had ever seen.

He looked up and noticed that Jenna was looking his direction as well, but she looked away quickly as he caught her glance. Her face was suddenly pink with embarrassment. He chuckled to himself, she'd totally been checking him out.

He looked over at her partner...what was his name? It wasn't really important, he was now glaring at Alexander with narrowed eyes. He'd caught Alexander checking out his partner and he wasn't happy about it at all.

Alexander almost laughed out loud. Obviously, he wanted her to himself. Alexander raised his eyebrows at him as a bit of a challenge. If this man thought he had an advantage of some sort, he was wrong. Alexander would work his magic, he would have the woman.

In a matter of moments, this tiny woman, who's name was Simone, had paired Alexander up with Jenna and sent Marika and Adam to the other end of the rink. Alexander was now alone with Jenna, it was time to work his magic.

"I am Alexander, I am so happy to finally be meeting you," he said, hugging her and kissing her on both cheeks.

He would not normally greet someone so familiarly, but they were in Paris, it was how friends greeted each other, and it would quench his dire need to just touch her. He could barely stand it. He wanted to take her into his arms and kiss her passionately, but she was young and shy, this was going to take some time. Time he wasn't sure he could tolerate.

The hug had been brief, but he was already fighting arousal, just from the light touch of their bodies drifting together. Luckily, Jenna didn't seem to notice, she could barely look him in the eye she was so shy.

Alexander had worried that maybe there was something between her and her partner, but it was glaringly obvious, Jenna Bruce was a virgin.

They began to skate and work on their stroking and matching their strides on the ice. Skating with Jenna was infinitely easier than skating with Marika. Of course, she was taller, that helped, but it was obvious she was driven to make this work, she made adjustments to her style as much as he did. When he began skating with Marika, he had to conform to her style, her stride.

When their practice finally ended, he didn't want to let her go. Not only had they skated well together, but once Jenna had gotten over her initial shyness, they had fallen into an easy conversation. Alexander couldn't believe how smart and easy to talk to she was. She was perfect for him.

"Would you like to go to lunch? I would like to get to know you better," said Alexander, not wanting his time with Jenna to end.

"Ummm," she was hesitating, her partner was waiting for her at the gate, she looked over at him, she seemed torn.

"I know a perfect cafe," said Alexander, willing her to say yes, though he had not thought about what he would do with Marika. Marika would be furious.

"Maybe another time, Adam is waiting for me," she told him, though Alexander could tell she wanted to go with him. She was as intrigued as he was.

"I understand," said Alexander, giving her a nod of encouragement. Perhaps it was good she had told him no. He didn't want Marika to get all worked up quite yet. This relationship was going to take a bit more planning.

"I'll see you tomorrow," said Jenna, smiling at him.

"I cannot wait," said Alexander, he meant that, and the emotion in his voice could barely conceal it.

As Jenna skated away to her partner, Marika skated up to him.

"Well at least you managed to keep your pants on," she snapped, her face was contorted in anger.

"What do you mean? he asked innocently.

"Lucky for you she's as stupid as a box of rocks, she didn't even notice that every time you touched her, you would get a raging hard on."

"She's not stupid, she's just a bit naive," said Alexander, shrugging casually.

"I don't care what she is, you keep your horny dick in your pants. It would be easy for you to take advantage of a young girl who is so naive. If you get her pregnant, you will be stuck with her forever," snapped Marika.

"Would that be a bad thing?"

"You are betrothed to me Alexander Peterov, and don't you forget that! If I see you with her off the ice, I might just slit her throat when she's not expecting it."

"Marika, you are being ridiculous!"

"I mean it Alexander, do not mess with me. I swear I will kill that bitch," snapped Marika.

"Do not worry my darling. You are the one I want to marry. There is no need to murder a poor innocent child. Besides, I like my woman a bit more experienced."

"Well you certainly have your pick of sluts around here," said Marika shaking her head miserably.

CHAPTER THIRTEEN

Jenna's elation over her successful pairing with Alexander, had evaporated by the following week. Unfortunately, as they entered their second week of practices, Jenna began to realize that she had been completely deceived by Alexander.

The friendly and polite gentleman she had skated with last week was now beginning to test her patience. By the end of the second week Alexander had become the most obnoxious, disgusting pervert, she had ever met. He couldn't keep his filthy hands off of her. Jenna was slowly beginning to understand Marika's unexplained hatred of her.

When they arrived on the ice each morning, Alexander would abandon Marika and make a beeline straight toward Jenna. Each morning when he greeted her, he would hug her and kiss her on both cheeks.

Jenna hadn't been alarmed at first, it was just how friends greeted each other in France. Though, with each passing day, Jenna was realizing something was very wrong. The hugs were rapidly becoming more lingering and soon it seemed, her morning greeting was no longer friendly...it was almost creepy! Alexander's fondness for her was growing into a demented obsession of sorts, and it was really starting to alarm her!

****

Alexander couldn't help it, he wanted to go slow, he was trying to go slow, but when he greeted her in the morning he wanted to kiss her lips, he wanted to feel her body pressed against his. He was being tortured by her proximity and the fleeting touch of her body against his.

When he flirted with her, she would smile at him and tell him to stop being silly. How could he let her know? He wasn't being silly...he loved her!

He wasn't sure why she was being so resistant to him. The first week they'd been together had been completely perfect. They'd laughed and talked together for that hour they were together on the ice. She was amazingly smart and witty for someone so young.

Alexander was sure that her marriage to her partner Adam was nothing but a scam, why was she holding back like this?

****

It wasn't long before their practices began to suffer. Jenna wasn't completely naive, she realized that a certain amount of touching was necessary, due to the lifts and throws in the program. But soon, the accidental touches didn't seem accidental anymore. His hand sliding lightly down the length of her body, the feel of his body pressed much too tightly against hers, Alexander had been becoming bolder with each passing day.

He flirted with her all the time, but he was engaged to Marika. Jenna had already been warned, she had no intention of getting on Marika's bad side.

On this afternoon the "accidental" touching, had become almost unbearable. During the run through with music, Jenna was in a paired spiral with Alexander. At some point, Simone yelled "Stop," in a voice fraught with frustration.

Simone had been shouting at Marika and Adam, they just couldn't seem to get in sync and Simone was reaching her breaking point with the situation.

Jenna and Alexander glided to a stop as well. As they did, Alexander pulled Jenna tightly against his body and nuzzled her neck familiarly.

"Mmmmm, you even smell delicious," breathed Alexander.

"Cut it out Alexander," snapped Jenna, jerking herself out of his arms. He flashed her a seductive smile.

Jenna shook her head miserably and pretended to be interested in what Simone was saying to Adam and Marika, but she was suddenly on edge. It was finally occurring to her, after all these days, that none of this was an accident. Jenna glared at him with her arms folded across her chest. He was engaged to Marika, what was wrong with him!

When Simone had finished with the other pair, she cued the music so they could begin again. The practice was going well till the pairs spin. Alexander was supposed to have his hands at her waist during the spin, instead, he boldly slid one hand, slowly up her thigh and between her legs. Jenna was furious! She was sure that it was not an accident! She stopped skating, spun around and gave him a disgusted glare, her hands planted defiantly on her hips.

"Alexander!" cried Jenna. "That was not an accident! You keep touching me!"

"I fear I cannot stop touching you, you are very beautiful. I think you are finding me quite pleasing as well," Alexander told her, in his thick Russian accent. He raised one eyebrow at her and flashed her a sly smile. Jenna rolled her eyes disgustedly.

"I am not attracted to you Alexander. I want you to stop touching me and focus on our skating. You must keep your hands where they belong!" she cried, still completely infuriated with him.

"I will tell you exactly where my hands belong if you wish. But I think you already know. My darling, I can see it in your eyes. You want me as much as I want you," crooned Alexander, his throaty voice seemed to caress the words as he took a bold step toward her, never taking his eyes off of her for a second. Jenna swallowed anxiously, she could feel her heart rate raising in alarm. His seductive smile made her cringe in disgust.

"No Alexander, what I want, is for you to keep your hands off of me," Jenna cried angrily, her face was contorted with disgust. He was suddenly giving her the creeps!

"Do you have any idea what you have been doing to me? Do you know how hard it is for me to hold back when you are in my arms? When I want you right now?" breathed Alexander, taking a bold step toward her, smiling at her seductively.

Jenna felt a cold shiver run down her spine. In recent months, she'd had drunk men come on to her, but Alexander wasn't drunk. Her face was burning with embarrassment as she glanced around the arena to see who could save her from this awkward encounter.

"Do not be shy my darling. I realize you are young and inexperienced...I can teach you. It would be my honor to guide you into womanhood."

"Alexander, stop this right now. We have to work together, you are engaged!" snapped Jenna, taking a nervous step backwards. She kept her eyes cast down at the ice, she couldn't force herself to meet Alexander's bold, sensual gaze. She really had no idea how to deal with men like Alexander, he was completely intimidating her.

"This engagement is not my wish," snapped Alexander.

"What?"

"My betrothal to Marika, it is not my wish. I do love her, we are not compatible," said Alexander, shaking his head miserably.

"Alexander, I'm sorry, but..."

"Marika has been very jealous since you came here. I cannot hide it, she can sense how much I want you. Of course, she knows what I like, long legs, blonde hair. Like an American model. The first time I saw you, I wanted you. I know you felt it, I saw you blush and look away," he said, licking his lips and sauntering toward her seductively.

"Alexander, I am married to Adam. I told you I am not attracted to you!" Jenna snapped angrily. She was struggling to catch her breath, and her heart was pounding uneasily.

"Please Jenna, you and I both know that your marriage to Adam is nothing but a scam. A mere illusion to ensure that you can stay here in Europe without a guardian. Besides, I saw you...how do you say it? Checking me out. I believe you like what you see. You may be married to Adam on paper, but there is no chemistry...no fire. Can you feel the fire between you and I?" Alexander's Russian tinged voice was seductive and velvety, he was eyeing her suggestively.

Jenna shook her head miserably. "No Alexander, there is no fire."

"Now it is you, who is being silly. We are perfect together on the ice, we have so much in common, so much passion. I have no doubt we would be equally compatible in the bedroom.

"Alexander!" cried Jenna, looking away in embarrassment. Her face was red and she was obviously distressed that he had brought up the topic.

He grinned when he saw her embarrassment, she was such an innocent. At least, he was hoping that she was. He wanted to press her to tell him. He had to know if she had been intimate with her partner Adam.

"Tell me, how is your relationship with Adam? When he makes love to you, do you feel yourself thinking about me, wanting me?" he asked, flashing her that seductive smile again. Jenna was suddenly feeling nauseated. She took a nervous step backwards.

"Alexander please stop this, we have work to do. You are engaged to Marika, I do not want you!" cried Jenna, shuddering in distaste.

"Am I frightening you with my suggestiveness? You are not sleeping with Smyth? You are a virgin then?" he asked softly, taking another bold step toward her. He was now only inches away from her, he leaned toward her and reached out to touch her cheek.

Jenna stepped back out of his reach, she put her hands on her hips angrily. "That is absolutely none of your business!" she spat, trying to conceal her nervous shaking.

Alexander laughed a deep sensuous laugh and reached out to touch her once again. Jenna swatted his hand away nervously. He raised one eyebrow at her and gave her a seductive smile. She was so feisty!

"Don't touch me Alexander! I mean it. We cannot be lovers. I want you to keep your distance. You are to touch me only when necessary. Do you understand?" Jenna was backing away from him nervously. Alexander seemed barely daunted, he was still smiling at her, staring into her eyes.

"I knew it! There is nothing between you and your partner Adam. This so-called marriage with Smyth was never consummated, you are a virgin, are you not?" cried Alexander.

"Shhh," snapped Jenna, she didn't want this insanity broadcasted throughout the entire cast. Alexander was suddenly laughing gleefully.

"This makes me very happy, for I could not bare the thought of you in his bed every night, when it is I, who wants you so badly. Do you not understand? When you are near me, it is always necessary for me to touch you. When I touch you, I get hard. You like to feel?" he asked, sauntering closer to her again. He was smiling seductively into her eyes. Jenna rolled her eyes at him and turned away angrily. She had no intention of standing there and listening to his annoying sexual innuendo!

At the other end of the rink where Simone was busy working with Marika and Adam, they were just realizing that something was amiss between Alexander and Jenna. They were too far away, and the music was too loud, to hear the specifics of their conversation, so they were all staring dumbfoundedly across the ice, wondering suddenly, what had gone wrong. Adam could tell by Jenna's stance that she was furious about something. Though he had no idea what Alexander could have said, or done, to piss her off so badly.

Alexander's back was to them so they couldn't tell that he was inching closer to her, massaging his crotch suggestively, flaunting his obvious arousal to her. Jenna shivered, she had been sweating moments ago, though now the chill of the rink had settled over her.

She was shaking her head miserably at Alexander, he obviously hadn't heard a word she had said, and she was beginning to believe this strange obsession of his, was bordering on dangerous. She narrowed her eyes at him and gave him a disgusted glare, she had finally reached her limit with Alexander!

"I mean it, stay away from me you arrogant ass!" snapped Jenna.

At the other end of the rink Adam, Marika and Simone all watched helplessly as she spun around angrily and headed for the gate. She'd had enough of Alexander's repulsive behavior for one day. She stomped angrily off the ice!

Simone dropped what she was doing and skated quickly over to her. Jenna was standing at the gate, struggling in vain to snap her blade guards on, she was suddenly shaking so violently.

"Where are you going? Practice isn't over yet," cried Simone, visibly annoyed that Jenna would just storm out of practice like that, without any explanation to anyone.

"It is for me, until you do something with that disgusting, repulsive, obnoxious, deplorable, intolerable, horny, Russian Billy goat! I can't work with him anymore, I've had enough!" snapped Jenna, and since she couldn't think of anymore adjectives to make her point about Alexander, she turned and stormed angrily off the ice, not caring if Simone was going to follow her, or not!

Simone spun around quickly and glared at Alexander, who was now sheepishly trying to hide the lump in his crotch from her. She narrowed her eyes at him, and shook her head miserably.

"Oh my God Alexander, you horny Russian Bastard! She's just a kid!" cried Simone. "I do not know what you said to her, but she is off limits to you, do you understand? She is too young Alexander, a mere child!" snarled Simone, as she skated off the ice to catch up with Jenna.

When Simone had finally caught up to her, Jenna was in the dressing room, angrily unlacing her skates. Her face was red with anger and she was obviously not in the mood to negotiate! It was clear that Jenna had her fill of Alexander. She was done for the day!

Jenna was struggling to breathe, she was so upset, she knew she probably couldn't have skated if she tried. She was struggling just to unlace her skates, her hands were shaking so badly! Jenna's mind was racing with hundreds of thoughts, but she had already decided, she could not do the combined pairs number. She didn't want Alexander anywhere near her, he had totally creeped her out!

"Jenna, what has he done? What did Alexander do to make you so angry?" asked Simone, sitting down next to her on the bench and giving her a wry smile. Jenna sighed miserably, she was still shaking so badly, she couldn't concentrate on anything at the moment. Without thinking, she narrowed her eyes at Simone and began shouting angrily at her.

"I can't work with him! He is a disgusting pig! A horny Billy goat! He won't stop touching me, he gets himself all worked up and then he parades around in front of me. I just can't take it anymore! I quit! I want to go back to the states!" cried Jenna, shuddering at the very thought of Alexander.

Jenna cringed a little bit at her own ire, she felt bad about taking her anger out on Simone, but she was so shook up, she felt as if she hardly knew what she was doing!

"Touched you how? Are you saying that Alexander is sexually harassing you?" cried Simone, she gave Jenna a dubious look.

"It wasn't an accident, the way that he touched me...and the things that he said to me, I just don't think I can..."

"Jenna please...don't quit. I realize Alexander can be a bit difficult, but you and Adam are exactly what I have been looking for. You have no idea what we went through to bring you here. You being a minor and all," said Simone, giving her a sheepish smile. Her voice was soothing, but Jenna refused to be soothed. She couldn't remember ever being so angry in her entire life!

"A bit difficult! He's completely creeping me out! He is the most annoying, obnoxious and completely perverted guy I have ever met! I am tired of listening to his annoying sexual innuendo and I don't want him to ever touch me again!" cried Jenna, completely beside herself with her disgust for Alexander.

"Please Jenna, do not quit. I realize you are young and inexperienced, but soon you will realize, that's just how guys act. He probably just doesn't realize how young you are, I will have a talk with Alexander. I promise, if you have any further problems with him, Alexander will be out of the show," said Simone, pleading.

"Simone, I can't...he totally gives me the creeps," said Jenna, her face was contorted in disgust. She let out a frustrated sigh. She wasn't sure she could work with Alexander at all, he had completely shaken her.

"Please Jenna, you just can't quit. What would I do? It's too late to find replacements..."

"Simone, I'm sorry, but I can't work with Alexander. Maybe I should have never come here," sighed Jenna, her heart was still pounding nervously, Alexander had completely shaken her confidence.

"Jenna, I know you're young, but you are turning out to be a very beautiful woman. You might as well realize now, sometimes men act like complete morons around beautiful women. They can't help it, it's all that stupid testosterone," said Simone, giving her an earnest smile.

"I'm not completely naive, I've dealt with stupid, horny guys before," snapped Jenna.

"Then you realize, most guys are just a bunch of talk. They like talking dirty, making girls blush, then they go home, masturbate themselves into a frenzy and do the same thing over again tomorrow. Alexander is nothing but a big talker, he's not going to *do* anything. He's messing with you, he's just a testosterone loaded male who thinks he's such a ladies man. I guarantee, he's not going to cheat on Marika, her family is filthy rich!" said Simone.

"I'm sorry, I realize I'm going to mess up the whole show, but I can't do this," said Jenna, looking away in acute embarrassment.

"Jenna please, I need you. Trust me, Alexander is completely harmless. Guys like Alexander, they're all talk, he's just messing with you. He's not going to risk his entire career and a very lucrative marriage, to have sex with a fifteen year old girl," said Simone, shaking her head and rolling her eyes.

Jenna swallowed and chewed on her lower lip thoughtfully. That actually made sense. Though she still didn't trust Alexander, she truly had no desire to be anywhere near him, he had shaken her to her very core. "I don't know..."

"Please Jenna...what can I do to convince you to stay? What if I gave you and Adam the rest of the day off today? The two of you can go out and explore the city, relax a bit. I will talk to Alexander myself, and tomorrow we will start fresh," she pleaded.

Jenna gave her a dubious look, Simone's face looked completely earnest. "Simone, how can I possibly relax? He gives me this feeling that...I don't know..." Jenna bit her lower lip in anguish. It was weird, she wasn't quite sure if it was stress, but she just couldn't shake this feeling. It had invaded her entire body and for some reason, she couldn't really convey the depth of her apprehension to Simone. Something in the back of her mind was niggling at her consciousness, Alexander was dangerous. Was it was possible that she was just overreacting?

"Jenna, I know exactly how you feel, but unfortunately Alexander is not going to be the last guy who is going to act so obnoxiously around you. I fear soon you will have to fight off the men with a stick. Jenna please, I know you're overwhelmed, but go ahead, just take a little time out today. I realize this is a big change for you, being in a foreign country and facing the stress of being in a professional show and all. I promise, everything will feel different in the morning," said Simone, her eyes were pleading.

"I don't know if I can continue to work with him Simone. He's completely repulsive!" Jenna told her, sighing dramatically.

"Please Jenna...I will make him stop. I promise, you will have no further problems with Alexander," said Simone, giving her a reassuring smile.

Jenna sighed miserably, she really didn't want to go back to the states anyway, but if Alexander was determined to pursue her in this way, she wasn't sure if she could deal with it. She felt that she was much too inexperienced to deal with a man like Alexander. Matt had been her first, and only boyfriend, not to mention the fact that their relationship was still so new, it really hadn't progressed much past passionate kissing.

Besides, Matt and Jenna had been friends first. He had always been very patient and kind to her. She wasn't used to being approached with the finesse of a rabid dog,

"Okay, but Alexander is not to touch me again," Jenna told her, shuddering at the thought of Alexander's touch.

"I promise, Alexander will not give you any more problems," said Simone, taking her hand and squeezing it, reassuringly.

Jenna took a slow, deep breath. She wanted to believe that all her troubles with Alexander were over, but her sixth sense highly doubted it. He creeped her out, in a way she had never felt before. He literally made her skin crawl.

Jenna wasn't sure how she could possibly continue to maintain a professional relationship with Alexander. At this point, she could barely stand to look at him anymore. He was so arrogant, she was sure that Simone having a talk with him about his inappropriate behavior, wouldn't phase him in the least!

Besides, if there were another incident, she was sure that it wouldn't be Alexander and Marika who would be removed from the show. Why would the company send them home? They were Olympic gold medalists and the reigning World Champions, the show's headline act!

Jenna suspected if there were any further problems, it would be her and Adam, that would be going home. They had no World titles behind their names and they were virtually unknown in Europe! They had been brought in specifically because it was thought that their styles would mesh perfectly with Alexander and Marika.

Professionally, Jenna knew they were a good match with Alexander and Marika. She frowned, she had decided that she would have to deal with Alexander in her own way. Adam would be terribly disappointed if they were sent back to the states. It seemed silly to be sent home over something so trivial. Jenna sighed in resignation, she would have to find some way to tolerate his obnoxious behavior!

She was happy at least, that her and Adam were going to have the rest of the day off, to explore Paris. They were both dying to see the Eiffel Tower. Mr. Dumontier had instructed his limo driver to take the two of them anywhere they wanted to go!

Jean Marie Stanberry

CHAPTER FOURTEEN

When practice had ended, Alexander found himself in the company office. Jenna had stormed off the ice and never returned. He was pretty sure of the reason as to why he was now cooling his heels in the office. He had no doubt that Jenna had told Simone about their entire, slightly tawdry encounter.

Alexander shook his head numbly. He didn't know why Jenna was being so difficult. He'd made it absolutely clear today that he was done playing games. Being polite, befriending her and casually flirting with her hadn't worked. He had gone back to his room every day more frustrated at this infuriatingly coy seductress. Were all Americans this completely dense?.

Could she not see? He was not compatible with Marika, he was compatible with *her*. Up until today they had laughed together and flirted till his body had literally ached for her, yet she remained as distant as ever. Obviously, she was not in love with her partner Adam, their marriage was a ruse. It was crystal clear that they were only friends. Why was she pushing him away like this?

The door opened and Simone stepped in, nodding to him briefly.

"Mr. Peterov, thank you for coming," she said, walking around to sit behind the desk.

"Is there a problem?"

"I'm afraid there is Mr. Peterov. Miss Bruce is quite upset. She's lodged a formal complaint of sexual harassment against you," said Simone, her face was serious.

"Are you serious?" he cried, laughing heartily.

"I'm quite serious Mr. Peterov, this is something I cannot just overlook."

"I cannot believe it," said Alexander, his face looked perfectly shocked.

"Are you denying it?" asked Simone.

"I am quite stunned since I believe it is *I* who is being sexually harassed," said Alexander.

"Really?" Simone didn't look convinced at all.

"Yes, I mean I thought it was all accidental at first, she seems so innocent you know."

"Go on."

"Well she's always been a bit flirtatious, but she knows that I'm engaged to Marika, so I didn't take it very seriously. Sometimes she touches me, it seems accidental, but then I see the look on her face and I realize, it really isn't. Sometimes I can't help it...I get aroused," said Alexander, trying his best to look disturbed.

"Did you talk dirty to her?" asked Simone.

"I admit it I did, but she started it. What is a man like me to do? I guess I must admit, I enjoy the attention."

"Okay, here's the deal, Jenna Bruce is fifteen years old, a minor. She is off limits to you, do you understand?"

"What can I do? I think she wants me."

"I do not care. You are older, you must be the adult here. If she makes a move on you, you must keep your senses and put her off.

"What if I cannot?"

"You are testing my patience Mr. Peterov. If you cannot resist the charms of a fifteen year old little girl, I suggest you and your partner return to the Soviet Republic. I shall have no use for you."

"Understood," said Alexander, sighing in resignation.

He ambled casually out of the office, wondering what he should do now. Obviously, Simone did not buy his claim that he was the one that was being sexually harassed.

He was thinking...if he convinced everyone that he and Jenna were lovers, they couldn't possibly call it sexual harassment, could they?

He walked out the back exit of the building and lit a cigarette, he was standing there considering how he might accomplish his task when Marika suddenly appeared beside him looking agitated and angry.

"What is going on?" she snapped.

"Nothing, really," he told her casually taking a long drag of his cigarette.

"I do not believe you, Jenna stormed out of practice and did not return, next thing I know, you are in Simone's office. What did you *do* Alexander?"

"I did not do anything, it was her. Jenna made the moves on me," said Alexander, it was hard to conceal the smug smile that wanted to sneak onto his face. It required every ounce of self discipline in his body to keep his face smooth and emotionless.

"Made the moves on you? How?"

"She touched me, she talked dirty to me. She wants me," said Alexander, he couldn't look at Marika's face, he might start laughing. He looked down at the ground, like he was completely ashamed.

"That slut! I weel keel her!" cried Marika.

"She's just a kid, she didn't know any better. I told her that you and I were to be married in the fall. She didn't want to hear that, that's what made her so angry."

"So she stormed out of practice because you turned her down?"

"Yes, you know I love you Marika. I would not ruin our plans to marry just to have sex with a fifteen year old child. I'm not stupid."

"Oh, I'm so happy Alexander. I love you too," said Marika throwing her arms around him and kissing him.

They walked back to the hotel hand in hand. Alexander was pleased with himself. He had no idea he was such a skilled actor.

CHAPTER FIFTEEN

Mr. Dumontier had sent the company's limo to the rink to pick Jenna and Adam up. Before they knew it, they were whisked away to do a little sight seeing in Paris. It was a beautiful spring day. The sun was beating down through the trees as the limo wove through the crowded streets of Paris. The entire city seemed to be coming to life with all the bright, spring flowers. The budding trees were bending like dancers in the gusty breeze, all the flowering trees were scattering their petals into the brisk, spring wind.

Jenna smiled to herself as they drove along, it was definitely much too beautiful to be cooped up in an ice arena all day. She stared silently out through the dark tinted glass as they drove along.

She hadn't said much to Adam since they had gotten into the limo, he had been a little shocked when he found out that they had the

rest of the afternoon off. Jenna hadn't
offered him much of an explanation as to
why she'd stormed off the ice earlier this
morning. He knew something big was up,
why else would Simone have given them the
rest of the day off?

Jenna was nervous, she wasn't sure what
Adam would have to say about her little
melt down. He would probably think she
was being a big baby, getting all bent out of
shape like that, jeopardizing their careers by
storming out of practice without being
dismissed.

"So tell me. What happened back there
with Alexander?" he asked, as they watched
Paris speed by through the darkly tinted
glass. He was confused, as he had pretty
much missed it all. He only knew that
Alexander had done something to make her
very angry. Jenna bit her lower lip
nervously, she was afraid he wouldn't
understand.

She couldn't help it, she was finding all of
this very embarrassing! Jenna was only now
beginning to notice, that men were noticing
her. She guessed she wasn't handling it

very well either, but she almost wished that she were still just a little girl. Back when she had been twelve, the men just thought that she was just cute. Now the tables had turned and she was beginning to feel like an object of prey. For some reason, Alexander had set his sights on her as a sexual conquest. Jenna was not used to being looked at in that light, and she was not used to the loose sexual innuendo that adults used so freely. She knew her face was already bright pink with embarrassment just thinking about it.

"Well, it turns out that Alexander is a big horny toad! He can't keep his filthy hands off of me. He keeps touching me and making all these repulsive, suggestive comments. I just couldn't take any more, I'd had enough," said Jenna, tossing her hair indignantly. Adam was staring at her as anger washed over his face.

"Are you serious? Alexander made the moves on you? What an ass!" he cried, angrily. "What did you do? Did you tell him your *husband* is going to kick his ass?"

Jenna giggled, nervously. "No, but I made it perfectly clear that I want nothing to do with him, but he doesn't seem to care. It's like he never even heard a word I said. He's like twenty-two and engaged to Marika. She's completely convinced that I am going to steal him away from her. Ewww...like I could ever be attracted to that huge, hairy, sweaty...beast!"

"Well to hear Marika talk about him you'd think the man was a Greek God or something. She told me he's a *real* man," said Adam, rolling his eyes dramatically.

"Really? As compared to who? Oh please, you're a hundred times more attractive than that...Ogre. Marika is a complete nit wit!" said Jenna, shaking her head disgustedly.

"I think she's completely in love with him," said Adam.

"Good, I hope the little ninety pound moron marries him. He's nothing but a big, hairy, Neanderthal, as far as I'm concerned, I think they deserve each other," said Jenna, shuddering at the very thought of Alexander.

Jenna and Adam spent the entire afternoon touring the highlights of Paris. They'd had a wonderful day, touring museums and parks, eating lunch in a quaint bistro, though they had saved Jenna's must see landmark for their grand finale. Jenna couldn't wait to see the Eiffel tower, and their limo driver had told them to save it for the hour approaching sunset. There was nothing more romantic, than the Eiffel tower at sunset.

Jenna had to roll her eyes when he told them that. Obviously he thought that her and Adam were a couple, but it was okay. She was sure their view of the city would be completely stunning at sunset.

She glanced out the window and craned her neck to get a better view as she realized that they were now very near the Eiffel tower and the limo was pulling over to to the curb to let them out. In moments she was standing there gawking in awe at the tower looming above them.

"Up we go," said Adam, taking her by the hand, and leading her toward the tower. They went all the way up, as high as they could go. Then they stepped over to the railing to drink in the spectacular views that were unfolding all around them. Jenna giggled excitedly, she couldn't believe she was actually there, on top of the Eiffel tower. It was like a dream come true!

It was incredible! They could see for miles and the whipping wind was causing the tower to sway, ever so slightly. Jenna was completely enthralled by the views that were spreading out before them, she had never seen anything so beautiful in her life!

They were both enchanted by the views and neither of them seemed to be inclined to come back down as they stood up there, picking out landmarks in the city below and looking out across the countryside that was spreading out for miles around them.

Adam was just as enthralled as Jenna was, as he took in the amazing views. Jenna was smiling up at him, admiring the way the wind was whipping wildly through his thick, brown hair.

It was a warm, sunny day on the ground, but the daylight was fading quickly and up on the tower, the wind was colder than they had anticipated. Adam and Jenna were both wearing short sleeves, they had not been prepared for the cold wind up on the tower. They were both standing there, completely covered with goosebumps, their teeth chattering uncontrollably, but they were too enthralled by the magic of it all, to come back down.

"You're freezing, do you want to go back down?" Adam asked her finally, when he looked over and saw her standing there with her arms wrapped around her waist, her teeth chattering.

"I can't, it's too beautiful up here," she yelled to him over the whipping wind.

"Okay, but I'm going to have to keep you warm then," Adam told her, as he walked up behind her and slid his arms gently around her waist. Jenna smiled and leaned back contentedly, into his strong arms. It was heavenly. It was warmer because he was sheltering her from the wind, and strangely enough, it felt good to be held like that.

Suddenly, Jenna was feeling completely guilty. She was supposed to be in love with Matt. Yet here she was, on top of the Eiffel tower leaning into Adam's arms, like they were lovers or something. She felt guilty...but for some reason, she couldn't pull herself from his arms or tell him that she felt like it wasn't a good idea that he have his arms around her like that.

Jenna sighed and told herself that Adam was just being a good friend and trying to keep her warm. She decided that it wasn't any different than being at a competition. Adam had put his arms around her before, to warm her when they were on the ice. That's just how he was, he was a great guy! Jenna managed to shake off her guilt and continued to gaze out across the city, unable to drag her eyes from the views that stretched out for miles in front of them.

After she had stood there, in Adam's arms for about five minutes, with both of them staring silently out over Paris, Adam took her by the shoulders and turned her around slowly to face him.

Jenna had been in her own little world. She was stunned when she looked up into his eyes. He was smiling down at her and his eyes were locked on hers, very intently. Jenna was completely elated to be here in Paris, on top of the Eiffel tower, but Adam seemed strangely serious. His eyes seemed to be searching hers for a moment. She started to say something, but before she could speak, he had taken her into his arms and was kissing her.

The kiss started out gentle, and Jenna was way too surprised to even kiss him back. She was shocked, she wasn't sure what had come over him! In moments the kiss had grown deeper, and soon her heart was racing with excitement. No one had ever kissed her like that, except Matt...

Jenna was panicking...she wasn't exactly sure what to do. Her head was telling her to pull away, but her body was telling her exactly the opposite. It felt so good... Jenna kept her arms at her sides and nervously tried to ignore the fact that her heart was pounding and she was gasping to breathe.

Matt would be heartbroken if he knew, this was so wrong! Unfortunately, it didn't feel wrong. In fact, it was feeling better every second, until she had finally wrapped her arms around Adam's neck and was kissing him back with a passion she didn't even know existed in her.

Jenna wasn't sure how long the kiss lasted, much longer than a few moments, but not really long enough. Adam pulled away from her abruptly and she almost gasped with regret that the moment was over. Adam was backing away from her, his movements shaky, his eyes averted in shame.

Jenna attempted to regain her composure by fleeing to the railing on the opposite side of the tower. She desperately needed to put some space between her and Adam. She wasn't sure why he had kissed her, but she didn't want him to see how flushed her face was, or how she seemed to be gasping to catch her breath.

Jenna's heart was racing with a surge of adrenaline and she was fighting dizziness. Her entire body seemed to be awakening with a whole host of feelings that were completely foreign to her. Unfortunately, the elation she felt spreading throughout her body was quickly overridden by an overwhelming feeling of guilt.

"What was that?" cried Adam, his voice was laced with uncertainly. He was cautiously making his way toward Jenna, as she struggled to regain her composure.

Jenna was chewing nervously on her lower lip and her hands were clenched nervously on the railing. She stole a brief glance at Adam, who's face was nearly as red as her own, his breathing was labored and uneven. Jenna kept her eyes cast down, she could barely look at him, she felt so guilty. Jenna was struggling to collect her feelings...what had they done?

This was wrong, Adam was her best friend, he was Matt's best friend. For the past three years they'd worked closely together as friends and partners. There couldn't possibly be anything between them, yet Jenna was still struggling inwardly with a whole host of feelings she couldn't even begin to understand. She didn't want Adam to realize how shook up she was.

"I don't know...you started it," she told him quietly. Jenna was completely ashamed of herself. She still couldn't meet his eyes. Her heart was still pounding and her body was suddenly shaking with confusion. She was struggling to conceal it. She couldn't even imagine what had come over her. She wasn't sure why Adam had kissed her, but she had kissed him back, as passionately as she had ever kissed Matt. Jenna sighed in frustration...what was wrong with her?

"You finished it though, didn't you. What were you thinking? How do expect me to stay in the same room with you all summer and pretend that we're married, when you kiss me like that?" cried Adam, suddenly very upset. "That was definitely more than a best friend kiss."

Jenna glanced up at him numbly, completely stunned by his misplaced anger. She already felt bad enough, betraying Matt's trust like that. Besides, it was Adam who had kissed her! She couldn't help it that her own body had betrayed her and she had surrendered to his kiss so readily. At least, she thought she couldn't help it...

Jenna suddenly felt very defensive, this wasn't her fault! Why had Adam even kissed her in the first place? He knew the position they were in! He knew they had to stay in the same room together all summer. He knew this was a line they shouldn't cross!

Jenna shook her head miserably and glared at him. "Why are you so mad at me? You started it!"

"Because...I don't know...don't you realize I...I?" cried Adam, angrily.

"Realize what? It was you who...oh, never mind...I'm sorry Adam...really...it was nothing..." she mumbled, still visibly shaken by their unexpected kiss. She wasn't sure what to say to him, she was fumbling over the words. She didn't want to ruin their entire day by arguing with him. He was really the only friend she had, here in Paris. In fact, sometimes she thought he was the only friend she had in the whole world.

Marika's unkind words had shaken her, since that day she'd been worried. Would Matt find another girlfriend in Boston?

She'd seen lots of movies, she knew exactly what happened on college campuses.

Jenna was still struggling to breathe, she wasn't sure why Adam had kissed her in the first place, or why she had kissed him back. Her insides were all knotted up and she felt incredibly lost.

"It didn't seem like nothing..." said Adam cautiously, moving closer to her and trying to look into her eyes.

"I know...I said I'm sorry. I don't want to fight with you Adam. You're my best friend, I just don't want to ruin things between us..."

"It's too late...you've already aroused my curiosity," said Adam, tilting her chin up and gazing into her eyes.

"Your curiosity?"

"More or less. Besides, when you told me Alexander had touched you, it made me jealous, and I realized..."

"Adam no...don't say it."

"You can't tell me you didn't feel it too, there's something more, admit it," said Adam. The huskiness in his voice made her heart start pounding again.

"I can't Adam, this is wrong," she breathed, too shook up to meet his eyes.

"The paperwork says we're married," said Adam, flashing her a sly smile.

"Adam..." she said, squeezing her eyes shut and turning away from him. She didn't want to see his face. She didn't want to feel these feelings. They were best friends, they were too close. They couldn't become involved like this, it would be all wrong, it could never work.

"What would you tell Matt? asked Adam, as he walked slowly up behind her. He knew she was as shaken up by the kiss as he was.

"What?" Jenna asked, turning to face him, slowly. Her face was still red and burning with shame over the kiss. She was struggling to breathe normally. She couldn't concentrate...her emotions were going in a dozen different directions.

"What would you tell Matt, if you and I were to fall in love?" he asked, holding her face in his hands and finally managing to look into her eyes. Jenna closed her eyes and sighed. She did not want to have this conversation! Granted, she had kissed him back, but her and Adam could not fall in love. There were at least a hundred reasons why! Besides, Jenna was pretty sure she loved Matt. She couldn't possibly love them both, could she?

"Really Adam...I'm sorry. We shouldn't have done that. I want you to forget this ever happened," she told him, finally managing to remove herself from his grasp and take a shaky step away from him.

"No, I don't think I'll ever forget that moment. When I kissed you...you wanted me to kiss you. You still want me to kiss you, I can feel it," breathed Adam, his voice was deep and husky, making Jenna's heart pound with excitement at the very sound of it. Jenna took a slow, deep, breath. She couldn't let this go on. It would never work.

"Adam, I don't know why you kissed me, but I do know that I shouldn't have kissed you back. I guess I was just shook up over Alexander's bad behavior. I really don't know what's wrong with me. Maybe it's Paris," she said, walking slowly toward the opposite railing again. She was trying to put some space between her and Adam. She didn't feel comfortable with him standing right there next to her. Her resolve was weakened for some reason.

She could feel tears coming to her eyes, it had always been so easy before. There had been no attraction between the two of them. Adam had always been like a big brother to her. For some reason now, it seemed an effort to breathe, and she was feeling drawn to him in a way she had never felt before.

She was feeling overwhelmed because she knew she shouldn't have kissed him...but for some reason, she wanted to kiss him some more.

It was cold and windy on top of the tower, but she was suddenly feeling overly warm and uncomfortable.

"Adam please, we just can't..." she turned to face him again and she realized then, that he had followed her, and he was right there behind her. Without another word he took her into his arms and kissed her again.

This time, there was no denying that she wanted to be there. She wrapped her arms around his neck and he crushed her in his arms so tightly she could barely breathe. In moments, it seemed, her boyfriend Matt had been all but forgotten as she succumbed to the passionate kiss.

When the kiss was finally over, Adam pulled her into his arms and held her as they both gazed out across the city, neither of them wanting to speak. They stayed up there a long time in each other's arms. Jenna was lost...afraid to think, afraid to rationalize. She knew that her and Adam could never have the kind of relationship that was now filling her head.

She wasn't worried about what everyone here in Paris would think, they already thought that her and Adam were married. She was worried about her own, now very messed up, head. Would she be able to control these new feelings she was having for him, without ruining the friendship and professional partnership she cherished?

She let him hold her without moving or saying a word. What could she say, really? Jenna was afraid if they came down from the tower, to reality, it would be like waking up from a dream, and it would all be over.

They stayed up there in each other's arms and watched the sun set over Paris. When they finally came down, lights were coming on all over Paris and the stars were twinkling brightly above them.

When they returned to the limo, they were obviously both very uncomfortable. In fact, they didn't speak so much as a single word on the ride back to the hotel. Jenna was more confused than ever, about her life. What did the kiss mean? It had been barely two weeks ago that Adam had drunkenly confessed his love for her, on the night they arrived in Paris.

Jenna was relatively sure that Adam didn't remember any details of that night. He had been drinking with the other cast members in the lobby. In fact, he had so much alcohol in his system, she was sure he had no idea what he was even saying when he told her that he loved her. Maybe none of this was real. After their episode on the tower, Jenna worried how things would be between them.

She was anxious. They would have to spend the entire summer staying in the same room together, pretending to be married. They had spent the past two weeks sleeping in the same King sized bed, never touching each other. Adam had kept his word and been a complete gentleman. Jenna sighed miserably. This was only going to complicate matters.

Jenna couldn't help but wonder if Adam had plans for them to consummate their sham marriage. She wanted to believe that there wasn't anything more between her and Adam besides friendship and that her loyalties belonged to Matt, but now she wasn't so sure.

Marika was right, Boston was far away. She would be here all summer with Adam. Jenna wrung her hands nervously, her incident with Alexander had her completely messed up. She wasn't sure about anything at this point. What would she tell Matt, if her and Adam were to fall in love?

Jean Marie Stanberry

CHAPTER SIXTEEN

The next morning, Jenna and Adam had a light breakfast, then they rode their bicycles to the arena for practice. They had barely spoke to each other on their way home from the tower the night before. Not another word was said about the kiss. That night, they reluctantly slept together in the king sized bed, fully clothed, careful to keep enough distance between the two of them, so that they wouldn't touch. Neither of them seemed to be willing to bring up the subject of what had happened atop the Eiffel Tower. Jenna wasn't sure if she could last the entire summer in this strange, strained, relationship.

When they arrived at the ice arena, Jenna noticed immediately that Adam was different this morning. In fact, he seemed happier than she had ever seen him. Adam was not a morning person, he was usually quite moody when they first arrived on the ice.

On this morning though, he was greeting everyone and joking around. Of course, Jenna had serious misgivings about the source of his good mood. She was feeling guilty, she was suddenly fearing that Adam believed that their relationship had changed. Had it?

Jenna silently cursed herself for surrendering to Adam's kisses. She wasn't sure what was wrong with her, but his kiss had awakened something deep inside of her. Something that she didn't want to feel. Perhaps she had just been lonely, but she knew that the two of them could not become involved in a romantic relationship. It would be all wrong!

Adam's jovial mood had Jenna completely on edge. Marriage license or not, she wasn't ready for the direction their relationship seemed to be heading in. Of course, it wasn't long before everyone there at the rink noticed that Adam seemed to be like a new man. For a while, even Alexander seemed to keep a respectful distance from her. They had nearly made it through the entire practice without as much as a leering look or suggestive comment.

Jenna had spent most of the morning skating with Adam, but they had barely spoke at all as they honed their feature program. Claudia, their assistant choreographer, was busily directing them both, so it was easy to let the conversation slide. Besides, what would she even say to him? Their kiss the evening before had completely thrown her off. She felt like everything was all wrong between the two of them.

Simone arrived finally to take Adam to the other end of the ice to work with Marika. Jenna was shocked when Adam gathered her into his arms and pressed a quick kiss on her lips, something he had never done before. Jenna stared up at him in shock.

"See you in a little bit babe," he said, turning and skating toward the other end of the rink.

Jenna stood there numbly and watched as they skated away, not knowing if what she was feeling was relief or anxiety, now that she was finally separated from him.

Alexander watched their little exchange with a combination of shock and amusement. At first he worried that Adam had won, he seemed so elated this morning. Alexander couldn't help but be worried that Jenna and Adam had consummated their sham marriage last night. After the lame kiss though, he was wondering if the whole thing wasn't just some sort of an act. A show of dominance by Smyth to keep him away from Jenna.

Jenna was not such a good actress. Alexander decided he would approach her, just to feel out the situation. It was their turn to skate together anyway, he whispered seductively in her ear.

"That was a very cute touch. Did you have a good evening off, my darling? I couldn't help but notice, your *husband* seems very happy today," he whispered, flashing her a sly smile.

Jenna rolled her eyes at him and turned away. She had no desire to discuss her relationship status, with Alexander, of all people.

Not about to be deterred, Alexander skated around so he was standing in front of her again. He obviously wasn't about to let the matter drop. He folded his arms across his chest and gave her an arrogant smile.

You cannot fool me, my darling. Obviously, things have changed between you and Adam. Something happened last night, and I have a very good idea what it was. Mr. Smyth is, what do you Americans say? Not a morning person but on this particular morning, he seems, how do you Americans say it? Quite...satisfied. After an evening alone in Paris, I can only guess that the reason for his newfound happiness is that you have finally surrendered yourself to him and made him a very happy man," whispered Alexander, leering at her.

Jenna frowned and narrowed her eyes at him. "It is none of your business Alexander!" she snapped, turning to skate away. Unfortunately, Alexander grabbed her by the arm before she could escape. He jerked her roughly into his arms. Jenna's mouth dropped open in shock as she looked up into Alexander's face in acute surprise. Alexander was gazing down into her eyes with an amused smile on his face as he pulled her body against his own. Jenna narrowed her eyes at him and gave him a seething glare, he had no right to man handle her like that!

"I must admit, I am very surprised. I was under the impression that your marriage was, what you Americans call, a sham, and that you were a virgin. Seeing Adam today, I cannot help but wonder. I have not ever seen him so happy before. Now I am thinking, that since the two of you had an evening alone in the city, maybe the two of you were enchanted by the romance of Paris, and maybe this morning, you are no longer a virgin," said Alexander, raising his eyebrows at her, his voice was low and seductive.

Jenna shook her head numbly at him, she couldn't believe she was actually standing here listening to this.

She gave Alexander a disgusted glare and resisted the urge to tell him to take a flying leap. Then she saw, what she thought at the time, was the perfect opportunity to end Alexander's creepy infatuation with her.

She reasoned that it was possible Alexander wanted her because she was a virgin. Maybe if he thought she was no longer a virgin, he would no longer be interested in her. Maybe that was just part of his sick, twisted, game.

Jenna smiled secretively, the company had plenty of women for him to pursue. Right now, she was the only one that was completely off limits to him because of her age. She realized she was also most likely the only virgin. If she were to take away that one thing that had him so intrigued with her, maybe he would just leave her alone.

Jenna bit her lower lip anxiously. She had never been blessed with any acting skills, she feared he would see through her little white lie immediately. "Alexander, I guess I hadn't realized how perceptive you are..." she said, desperately struggling to keep her voice steady. "You are right, that is why Adam is so happy today, we are lovers now."

Alexander almost gasped, he hadn't expected that answer out of his shy little flower. He was trying to read her face. Was she serious, or was she just messing with him?

"Very interesting...these past several weeks I had come to the conclusion that there was no attraction between the two of you. He is like a cousin to you, is he not?" asked Alexander, stroking his chin thoughtfully.

Jenna was frowning at him, why did she feel the need to explain herself around Alexander? "I have always found Adam very attractive, we have been partners since I was twelve, I imagine it is hard for him to see me as a woman, and not a child," she told him, trying not to roll her eyes.

A sly smile was creeping to Alexander's lips, making her shiver a little bit, his demeanor just gave her the creeps. She couldn't help it.

"You are definitely turning into a very appealing woman, I fail to see how he's kept his hands off of you as long as he has," said Alexander, laughing a deep throaty laugh. Jenna jumped a little bit and took a step backwards. Alexander was making her very uncomfortable.

Alexander still wasn't convinced. She was obviously lying, she couldn't make eye contact with him and she was very jumpy.

"Tell me, did he make it good for you, or did he fumble around like a typically inept American?" asked Alexander, he was moving closer to her and flashing her a seductive smile.

"It was perfect," Jenna snapped, tossing her hair and turning away from him quickly. She didn't want him to see her face, she had never been any good at lying.

"I do not believe you. When you say perfect, are you trying to tell me, that you climaxed as well?" said Alexander, putting his hands gently on her shoulders. His voice was full of sarcasm.

Jenna frowned at him and gave him a blank stare. It was hard to carry on a conversation with a person, when you had no idea what on earth they were even talking about. Jenna's entire sexual education was derived from snippets of conversations she had overheard in locker rooms and most of that she really didn't understand either.

"No?" Alexander couldn't hide his amused smile. He had finally got her, she didn't even know what he was talking about. He was almost certain she had never had sex with Adam.

"I cannot believe that we are actually having this conversation," snapped Jenna, she finally had the vaguest inkling of what he was talking about and her face was feeling hot and pink, as her embarrassment became evident.

"You would know if you had one...an orgasm, that is. In fact, all you could probably think about, would be having another one. It's very addictive," said Alexander, smiling at her.

"Go away Alexander," snapped Jenna.

"Do not feel bad, if he did not do it for you. Not all men are skilled at giving their women such pleasure. I promise, one night with me and you will be begging me for more."

"Alexander, I told you no! Adam and I..."

"Do not be embarrassed my darling. Unless the man is nicely experienced, sometimes a woman's first time leaves much to be desired. I get the feeling that he was also a virgin. I am quite surprised he even knew what to do with his little boy toy," he turned Jenna slowly around to face him and she could see the mocking grin on his face. She was infuriated!

"Adam is not gay!" she cried, glaring angrily up into Alexander's eyes.

"My darling, I am well aware of that. Adam is quite obviously attracted to you. I just get the impression that the poor boy is miserably inexperienced. Maybe the reason you thought it was perfect, is that you just do not know any better. I can show you," said Alexander, gazing deeply into her eyes, a smile was tugging at the corner of his lips.

Jenna sighed miserably. Alexander didn't seem to care at all that she was, for all he knew, no longer a virgin. It was a nice try, but her little ploy hadn't worked. Alexander had now taken both her hands in his, and he was pulling her against his body seductively. Jenna tried to pull away from him, but he was much stronger than her. The fact that she was resisting him, only made him more determined.

"Adam is but a boy. You need a real man, an experienced man. I will show you," Alexander whispered, as he wrapped his arms around her and pressed his body seductively against hers.

He couldn't help himself, he wanted her in his arms so bad. The thought that Smyth had possibly had her first had made him incredibly jealous. He wished she would just give up this futile resistance and let him make love to her. He was't sure how much longer he could wait.

"Alexander, stop," cried Jenna as his hands roamed down her back, grabbing her buttocks tightly. Jenna was appalled and struggling in vain to pull away from him.

"I cannot stop, I love you."

"Go away, I don't want you to touch me!"

"Really? I am dying for you to touch me," Alexander breathed in her ear. He took her hand in his own and guided it down to massage the growing lump in his crotch.

Jenna gasped in surprise as Alexander boldly cupped her hand around the huge bulge in his warm up pants. He removed his hand from hers, but in her confusion Jenna's hand lingered there a moment, before she finally snatched it away uncomfortably, her face bright red with embarrassment.

"You are intrigued? Don't tell me you've never touched a man before?" chuckled Alexander, as he stared her down, boldly.

Alexander was very pleased. It was quite evident, she had never touched a man before. She was even more innocent than he had thought.

Jenna looked away, she couldn't hide her acute embarrassment, her cheeks were burning. She opened her mouth to speak, but nothing would come out. Honestly, she *was* intrigued, and completely mortified.

Her curiosity had gotten the better of her once again and her heart was suddenly racing with a surge of excitement.

It was true, she had never touched a man before. She was feeling completely guilty. Alexander hadn't forced her hand to linger there, but for some reason, she couldn't pull her hand away. The way Alexander's body had responded to her touch had been completely incredible, she'd felt him grow even larger with her touch. Jenna was feeling the strangest combination of shame and exhilaration, she kept her eyes averted in embarrassment, she couldn't even look at Alexander.

"Do not be shy my darling, I believe you should feel what you do to me. My body cannot help but respond to the proximity of your body. You must realize, it is uncomfortable to be so...aroused, yet unable to finish...you know what I mean..." he whispered into her ear, grinding his pelvis against her.

"Alexander, I didn't *do* anything!" she cried, she was still confused and obviously intrigued by his arousal.

"You do not have to *do* anything. My body cannot help but respond this way when you are near. I cannot help what I feel," said Alexander.

Jenna was still trying to struggle from his arms. She felt guilty that she had somehow aroused him. She just wanted to tell him she wasn't attracted to him in that way. She loved Matt.

"My darling Jenna, I have wanted to tell you for so long how I feel about you. I do not love Marika, I love you. Please tell me that you will give me a chance," said Alexander, whispering seductively in his Russian tinged voice. He was nuzzling her neck as she struggled uselessly to get out of his arms.

Jenna shuddered as she felt Alexander's hot breath in her ear. She just wanted to escape, her confused brain was spinning with feelings of shame and guilt over the fact that she had somehow aroused him, even though that had not been her intent.

She was puzzled, for some reason her own body was tingling with her own version of arousal. She wasn't sure why, she didn't care for Alexander at all, but unfortunately, there was something about his hard, muscular body and the way he had responded to her touch, that had left her feeling breathless and heady.

"Alexander, you are engaged to Marika and I am in a relationship with Adam, why can't you just leave me alone!" she cried, still struggling to be free of his arms.

"I have wanted you from the first moment I laid eyes on you. You are intrigued, now that you have touched me you want me too, you pulled your hand away because you are frightened. Do not be frightened of me," he whispered, his voice was silky and seductive.

"I don't want you," snapped Jenna, her voice was shaky and weak, she was trembling.

"We are destined to be together Jenna, not only on the ice, but in life as well. Besides, a man knows desire when he sees it, you are just too young and naive to realize what you want...what you need. Do not be frightened my darling Jenna. I am large, but I will take my time, you will like it," Alexander's hot breath in her ear made her shiver.

"Stop Alexander," she breathed, trying uselessly to peel Alexander's wandering hands off of her body.

"I cannot," Alexander was running his hands down her back as he pulled her closer in his arms in his quest to lewdly mold his body to her.

Jenna resisted the urge to scream. She didn't want Alexander touching her, but she also did not want to cause a huge scene in the arena. It was bad enough the rest of the cast thought she was just a naive little girl, but to be seen in such a compromising position with Alexander of all people, would be way too embarrassing!

Finally, Gail spied the two of them from where she was working across the ice with some of the other skaters, she began skating toward them as fast as she could.

"Alexander, stop it this instant!" she called to him.

Alexander gave Jenna an arrogant smile and released her. Then he turned around slowly to face Gail. His entire demeanor changed in an instant, as he flashed Gail puppy dog eyes and the earnest face of a Boy Scout.

"I am sorry Madame, it is not me. It is Jenna. I cannot work with her. She is teasing me, talking dirty to me. She wants me!" he cried, indignantly.

Jenna stared at him completely shocked, his demeanor had changed in the space of a second and she couldn't believe what she was hearing.

"No! I want you to keep your filthy hands off of me!" she cried angrily, but her voice was shaky and weak.

"That is not what you said a moment ago, you naughty girl," said Alexander, raising his eyebrows at her and giving her a seductive smile.

Jenna was already thoroughly shaken. She could only stare at him blankly. She was suddenly realizing that Alexander was trying to make it look like it was she, who had lead him on. Gail narrowed her eyes suspiciously at both of them, truly not sure who's side of the story to believe.

"I am warning you Alexander, one more incident, and you and your little fiancee will be out of here. Do I make myself perfectly clear?"

"I shall try Miss Gail...I am but a man. It is very hard to keep focused on my job, when she teases me like that," he said, looking at Gail very earnestly. "I cannot help it. The way she touches me, gets me all hot and bothered."

Gail was looking back and forth between Alexander's perfectly earnest face, and Jenna's face, which was currently wrinkled with confusion and embarrassment. She couldn't shake the feeling, she was guilty. Granted, Alexander had forced her hand to massage his crotch, but her hand had lingered there, fascinated by the feel of his swollen manhood, before she had the sense of mind to jerk her hand away.

Alexander had been right, she had never touched a man before. Her curiosity had gotten the best of her for just a moment, now she regretted it. It had excited her for the tiniest moment. Touching him so intimately had felt awkward at first, but his obvious response to her touch had been so incredible, it had delayed the urge to jerk her hand away. It was like nothing she had ever felt before, it was like the rest of Alexander, hard and unyielding. Intriguing and dangerous.

Gail shook her head miserably and skated away from them. Alexander gave Jenna a victorious smile as Gail turned away...he had just put doubt into her mind. Doubt that he was the aggressor in this relationship. Jenna's mouth had dropped open in shock, she was furious!

When Gail turned her back, Alexander licked his lips and smiled seductively at Jenna. He massaged his own crotch and took a few bold steps toward her, as he cocked one eyebrow arrogantly.

"Tonight you can touch me again...without my pants," he whispered in her ear.

Jenna gave him a disgusted glare and skated away. He was the most obnoxious and repulsive man she had ever met in her entire life! At this point, she wasn't sure if she could even maintain a professional relationship with him. She could barely stand to look at him. He gave her the willies!

From that moment on, Jenna went out of her way to avoid Alexander. Fortunately, the rest of their practices that week went without incident. For the most part, Alexander seemed to be a bit more focused on their skating, though Jenna was sure he hadn't given up yet.

Adam, Gail and Simone had all been keeping a close eye on Alexander. Though now it seemed Gail was convinced it was Jenna, who was pursuing Alexander, instead of the other way around. The very idea made Jenna completely livid!

Adam had been very angry when Jenna told him about the incident, though she didn't tell him that she had touched Alexander, nor had she told him that she had led Alexander to believe that the two of them had made love. She didn't want to give Adam any ideas. The two of them had not brought up their kiss atop the Eiffel tower since that night. Their relationship since then, had been strictly professional. Except for an occasional public kiss, which Jenna suspected Adam was doing strictly for Alexander's benefit, rather like a dog peeing on a bush to mark it's territory. Jenna never said a word about any of it.

CHAPTER SEVENTEEN

At the end of the week they were finished with their formal training for the shows and Jenna was happy that they would be able to relax a little bit. Their regular performances would begin this evening and they would have practices each afternoon, with performances to follow every evening.

They were booked for three weeks of sold out performances in Paris, then they would be off to Lyon. The shows were immensely popular in France, Jenna was very excited to start their tour.

The afternoon of their first Paris performance, they had their dress rehearsal and Alexander seemed to be back to his old ways. Every time they had to skate together, his hands seemed to wander everywhere, except where appropriate. Jenna was getting very irritated with him. Her seething glares were met with sly smiles from Alexander, which completely infuriated her! No one elsc seemed to notice Alexander's inappropriate behavior, and Jenna hated to be a big tattle tale, always running to Simone and Gail.

At the end of the number that featured both pairs, Jenna had to skate off the ice with Alexander. Alexander and Jenna skated off one side of the set, Marika and Adam skated off the other side of the huge set.

That afternoon Alexander skated off the ice right behind Jenna, just as always, but as soon as they had disappeared behind the black velvet curtain he had his arms around her and was nuzzling her neck, trailing kisses down her right shoulder.

"How are things with your lover Adam?" he crooned, as he turned her slowly around to face him. He was gazing seductively into her eyes, there in the dim light.

"Fine," growled Jenna, angrily trying to disentangle herself from his arms. She was panicking a little bit. The next act with all the back up skaters had already skated out on the ice. Marika and Adam had come through the curtains on the opposite side of the enormous set, so she was virtually alone with Alexander in the darkness.

Jenna was alarmed, she knew there was no one around to call out to if he actually tried something. Everyone else in the arena was busy doing their thing for the dress rehearsal, not to mention that the music for the next number was already blaring loudly throughout the arena.

"Is he keeping you satisfied, or do you need more?" he asked. Alexander's deep voice seemed to caress the words as his strong arms pulled her seductively against his body. Jenna cringed, she was anxiously trying to peel herself from his arms.

"Get your hands off of me Alexander, I don't need *anything* from you," she snapped angrily, flashing him a frown of distaste.

A panic was rising in her. The music was so loud, she knew if she screamed, no one would even hear her. She could only hope Adam would walk this way looking for her and not head straight back to the dressing rooms.

"Do you know what I cannot stop thinking about? Your legs. Every night I dream you are with me, with those long legs wrapped around me," breathed Alexander, his Russian tinged voice was silky and seductive.

"You can dream it all you want, but it's never going to happen," snapped Jenna, struggling to wiggle from his embrace.

"Oh my darling, why must you be so difficult? Never say never. Never is a very long time. You are coming around, it is only a matter of time before you want me just as much as I want you.

You are young and inexperienced, but you cannot help but be curious. I may have forced you to touch me, but your hand lingered there, long after I released it. Woman say that size doesn't matter, but they can't help but wonder..."

Jenna narrowed her eyes at him and drew in a deep breath. She struggled with him for a few moments and finally managed to pull one of her arms free. She was prepared to slap Alexander's smug face, but he caught both her wrists in his hands and raised his eyebrows at her, flashing her an amused smile.

"If you have a sudden urge to have your hands on me, I suggest you aim lower. I know we would both enjoy that more. Do you not think so? Go ahead Jenna, touch me...I will not mind," crooned Alexander, flashing her the tiniest, suggestive smile.

"I don't want to touch you, and I sure as hell don't want you to touch me," snapped Jenna.

Alexander guided her hand to his crotch and held it there so she couldn't pull her hand away. "Do you feel that! That is what you have done to me, without even trying. Do you think we can just ignore how we feel? Can you not see how overpowering our love is?" he breathed, as Jenna glared angrily at into his eyes.

Jenna was still struggling ineffectively to get away from him, but he was much too strong. Suddenly, he crushed her in his arms and kissed her.

He couldn't help it, he had waited so long and still she was resisting him. He just wanted to taste her sweet lips and run his hands across her body. He had waited weeks, he couldn't wait any longer. They were alone, the music was loud. His hands wandered across her breasts as he crushed his lips against hers.

Jenna struggled in vain to get away from him, as his lips moved unrelentingly over hers. He pressed his body against hers, making sure that she felt his obvious arousal.

Finally, he released her and stood there grinning at her in victory. Jenna was shaking uncontrollably as she stood there glaring at him angrily, she was furious.

"You cannot tell me now, that you do not want me. I could feel the heat...the longing," said Alexander, flashing her a seductive smile. Jenna was literally gasping to breathe, he knew she wanted him as much as he wanted her.

"No! I swear Alexander, don't you ever touch me again, or I will..." Jenna was gasping, trying to find the words, but she was too shook up.

"Or you will what? Make me so hot, I cannot stand it? Do not worry...it is already done," said Alexander, his voice was deep and velvety. He reached out to take her into his arms again but she pushed him away. She thought about running away, but she was wearing skates, she wouldn't make it very far. Alexander laughed that deep throaty laugh again. Jenna swallowed anxiously, she was completely on edge.

"You resist me now, but your mouth was sweet and yielding, just like the rest of you will be soon. You and I, we will be together in time. I keep forgetting...I have all summer to make you mine. You are young, you need to be courted. I realize you do not know what to expect because you have not had a real lover before. I will teach you, you will like it," he said, smiling at her, there in the dim light.

Jenna was completely incensed! Now she really wanted to slap him, but Alexander once again caught both of her wrists in his hands and held her as she stood there shaking with rage.

"No darling...lovers do not hit each other. Our love is passionate enough..." he whispered, in his silky, Russian tinged voice.

"You bastard, I mean it, leave me alone Alexander!" she cried, jerking her wrist from his hand as she spun around quickly and headed toward the other side of the backstage area where she would find Adam.

Jenna's heart was racing wildly with fear and she was so angry she could barely see straight! She was nearly running toward the other side of the backstage area. She could not believe the nerve of Alexander, basically forcing himself on her like that, then babbling all that crap about love. The man was nothing but a horny billy goat as far as she was concerned!

She came tearing around the back side of the large set and almost ran right into Marika in her haste. Jenna still had her skate guards in her hand because she'd been too flustered to stop and put them on. She was breathing heavily from her panic and she was sure she looked completely stunned to see Marika standing there, with her arms folded impatiently across her chest.

"What is going on?" cried Marika, she was glaring at Jenna suspiciously in the dim light.

"Nothing!" snapped Jenna, she was still struggling to breathe. She knew her face was flushed with embarrassment and her voice was shaky and weak. Her entire body was trembling with the adrenaline that had been infused into it.

She really just wanted to get to Adam. Alexander had her completely shook up, and she had no desire to be in a confrontation with Marika. Jenna anxiously tried to push past her, but Marika had already decided that something big was up. She grabbed Jenna by the wrist and glared at her, as they stood there, face to face, in the dim, backstage light.

"Hmmmpt...your lipstick is all messed up. What have you been up to?"

"Nothing, let me go!" snapped Jenna, her shame and embarrassment had rendered her completely unable to meet Marika's angry gaze.

"I don't know exactly what is going on, but I know you lust after Alexander," said Marika, jerking Jenna closer to her and glaring angrily into her eyes.

"I do not lust after Alexander," breathed Jenna, trying to keep her voice at a reasonable tone.

"You made the moves on him...you kissed him!" cried Marika, her voice rising in anger.

Jenna's lower lip was quivering and she was on the verge of bursting into tears. She was so shook up, she couldn't even speak.

"Filthy whore! Keep your hands and your lips off of him. He is mine!" cried Marika, obviously beside herself with anger.

"It is that disgusting pig, who will not keep his hands off of me!" cried Jenna, angrily.

"You are lying! I will kill you!" cried Marika, suddenly lunging at her, like a tiger lunging at it's prey. Jenna was stunned to suddenly be involved in a cat fight with a tiny woman who barely weighed ninety pounds. Marika was completely enraged, grabbing at her and desperately trying to pull her hair.

Jenna could hear the ripping of fabric as they both fell to the floor in a frenzied scuffle. Marika was clawing recklessly at her. Jenna was so surprised by the attack, it was all she could do to simply defend herself against Marika's unexpected assault.

They were both on the floor wrestling furiously and before long Simone came racing around the corner of the set, followed by Adam and Alexander, who had somehow heard Marika's shrill screams over the blaring music. Marika was tiny, but she was feisty! Jenna actually had to fight back just to protect herself, Marika meant business!

"What is going on?" cried Simone, surprised and angered to see the two of them on the floor fighting like that. She was standing there glaring at them, with her hands on her hips.

Jenna looked up at Simone from where she lay on the floor. She was completely disheveled. Her costume was essentially shredded and her hair was a complete mess, as Marika had been trying to pull it out in handfuls. It had taken all of her energy just to keep Marika's skate blades away from her, otherwise her entire body would have been cut to shreds right now.

"She attacked me!" cried Jenna, getting up from the floor slowly and pointing at Marika. She was still slightly dazed by the intensity of the attack.

Marika was glaring at Jenna angrily. "She has kissed my Alexander, she wants him! The leetle beembo has been trying to take him away from me since she got here! She is trying to seduce him!"

Simone spun around and gave Alexander a surprised glare. She'd already lectured him about staying away from Jenna. He was standing there grinning broadly at them, much to Jenna's chagrin, her lipstick was still smudged all over his lips.

Alexander said nothing, he merely shrugged casually and flashed Simone a guilty smile. Then he carelessly wiped the lipstick off with the back of his hand. Simone's mouth dropped open in shock, as he raised his eyebrows at Jenna and gave her a knowing smile.

Jenna gasped and narrowed her eyes at him, he had set her up! He had done all this for Simone's benefit. He was trying to make Jenna look like the aggressor, and he was deliberately trying to make it look like the two of them were having some sort of affair! Jenna was furious!

"Simone please...it is Alexander, he won't keep his hands off of me. He accosted me the moment we came off the ice," Jenna cried, though she was suddenly sure that she was the one who looked thoroughly guilty, regardless of what had really happened.

"I accosted *you*? Unfortunately, I cannot hide what your wandering hands have done to me," crooned Alexander, raising his eyebrows at her and giving her a seductive smile.

Simone's eyes got wide as she noticed the bulge in Alexander's pants. She started to say something, but Alexander flashed her a coy smile and shrugged in mock embarrassment.

Unable to hide her anger any longer, Marika glared at Jenna and took an aggressive step toward her. Alexander reached out and grabbed her by the arm, as Jenna's mouth dropped open in shock, as the implied meaning of Alexander's words finally sunk in. Jenna looked away in embarrassment, her face a bright shade of crimson.

Simone rolled her eyes and shook her head miserably. "Enough already! I do not know what is going on between the two of you, but keep it out of my dress rehearsals and performances. I really do not care what goes on in the off hours, that is your business. When you are on the ice, you keep it strictly professional. Comprenez-vous?" snapped Simone, glaring at them both very seriously.

"Simone I..." Jenna's voice was fading away to nothing, she was sure it was she who looked completely guilty. Alexander had put in an Oscar winning performance.

"Enough I said! I am disgusted, I do not want to hear anymore," cried Simone, turning on her heel and stalking away.

Jenna sighed and fought back tears. Now it seemed that Simone was convinced that her and Alexander were having some sort of an affair and Alexander had done a fabulous job convincing her that she was the one who had instigated it all!

Marika was fighting anger as well, Alexander was holding her back, lest the cat fight ensue again...

"Slut! Alexander is mine, if I see you weet heem again I weel keel you!" snapped Marika, her face consumed with hatred.

Jenna couldn't speak, Alexander had skillfully made her look like the aggressor, she was completely shocked.

Adam was stunned into silence as well and was standing there staring at Jenna in shock. Jenna started to say something, but she was so upset she couldn't even manage to speak. She shook her head miserably and headed toward the dressing room. What could she say? It was completely obvious to her, that no one would ever believe her side of the story anyway!

CHAPTER EIGHTEEN

That evening when they were finally back in their room, Adam demanded that Jenna tell him exactly what was going on between her and Alexander. He, much like Simone, had been completely convinced by Alexander's lies. She told him everything, but she could tell by the dubious look he gave her he didn't believe a word of it. Jenna was distressed that Alexander had apparently even convinced Adam, that the two of them were having an affair.

Unfortunately, Alexander was a very skilled actor. He could be quite convincing when necessary. At this point in her life, Jenna was inexperienced in dealing with men at all, let alone manipulators like Alexander. She cursed herself for being so naive, at this point, she rued the day she had even come to Paris. She wondered if she should just go straight to Mr. Dumontier now, and tell him she wanted to go home to Hans and Carolina.

Jenna spoke with Carolina almost daily on the phone. Carolina had become like an adoptive mother to Jenna, she was much closer to Jenna than her own mother. Jenna longed to confide in Carolina during one of their conversations, but she couldn't. She felt everything that had happened there in Paris was her fault. Alexander making the moves on her, Adam inexplicably kissing her...what kind of crazy signals was she sending out?

When Jenna talked to her real mother, she only got even more discouraged, though speaking to her mother could do that to a person. She felt so alone, she just wanted someone to understand...she wasn't all those things Marika had called her, she hadn't asked for any of this.

"Mom...can I ask you something?" Jenna was hesitant, she and her mother had never been close, and of course, her mother had almost never been helpful, but who else could she possibly confide in?

"Oh God, it's not about sex, is it?" groaned her mother. Jenna sighed, she could almost see the look of displeasure on her mother's face. It was probably why she was in this predicament in the first place. She knew nothing about sex, except what she had picked up in a few random conversations she'd overheard. Hans had lectured her about guys being testosterone loaded, horn dogs but other than that, she was completely clueless.

"It's Alexander Peterov...you know, he's the gold medalist from the Olympics..." said Jenna, hesitating. She wasn't sure how to address this issue, it was so embarrassing!

"Holy crap! You're having sex with Peterov? He's completely gorgeous, the man is like a muscle bound God! I can only imagine how big his..."

"No!" snapped Jenna, feeling her face turning red, almost instantly. "We're not a couple! I need your advice, he's sexually harassing me."

"Sexually harassing you? How?"

"When it started, it seemed innocent, he would touch me, sometimes he would talk dirty to me. I never encouraged him, but it's been getting worse..."

"How so?"

Every time we're together...oh my God, how do I say this?"

"Forget I'm your mother and just spit it out. Don't forget, I've been in your shoes. I traveled with the London ballet," said her mother. Unfortunately, that didn't make Jenna feel any better. She'd heard tales of her mother's travels in Europe.

"It's just embarrassing mother. Whenever we are together he gets a hard on," Jenna couldn't believe she'd just said that to her own mother, but it was the truth. How could her mother help her, if she didn't know what was going on?

"I don't know why you're so embarrassed about that. It's perfectly normal for a young man to become aroused when they are with a beautiful young woman, it's all that testosterone, they can't help it."

"This is just so embarrassing."

"Did you touch him?"

"I did one time, it wasn't my fault, he made me..."

"Was he huge? Of course he was, I've heard that Russian men are best endowed men on the planet..."

"Mother!" cried Jenna, hardly able to believe that her own mother had said such a thing.

"Jenna really, Peterov is an Olympic gold medalist. Why are you stubbornly clinging to your virginity when you've got a man who is obviously dying screw your brains out with his huge Russian penis. I mean, talk about a golden opportunity."

"What?" breathed Jenna, she was literally shuddering in disgust. Of all the things she hd expected her mother to say, that was definitely not one of them. Though sometimes she forgot, her mother was not like a mother at all, there was seriously something wrong with her.

Her mother let out a strange, almost evil, laugh that made Jenna cringe anxiously.

"Jenna, physically you may only be fifteen years old, but mentally you are much older. Perhaps hooking up with an older guy is exactly what you need. You're never going to be compatible with a boy your own age. Men are so much slower to mature, if you were to date someone your own age, what on earth would the two of you even talk about? What would be the attraction, besides sex?"

Jenna sighed miserably, she couldn't even speak for the moment she was so embarrassed. Why did she ever stupidly confide in her mother?

"I realize it may sound a bit callous, but you're finally learning what makes the world go round...sex. Don't be afraid of it, use it to your advantage! Peterov is a man and therefore, a slave to his penis. Like it or not, you are becoming a woman Jenna, you will have a power over all these hapless morons, you just have to know how to use it," said her mother.

"What?" asked Jenna, none of this was making sense to her.

"What I'm saying is, you have the upper hand in this game of life. You're pretty, you have what all men want, a pretty face, long legs. You just have to learn how to use it. If this guy wants you, make him work for it."

"But I don't like him, he gives me the creeps," said Jenna, cringing.

"You don't have to *like* him. Men use woman all the time. If you can use Peterov to get something you want, do it. You're only young once. Imagine the possibilities...he's a world champion, a gold medalist. Hell, every woman in the world probably wants this guy. If you were to be linked to him, think of the publicity! The press would eat it up and it would make you desirable to every other guy..."

"Mother, I'm fifteen years old..."

"Don't be a complete moron, what difference does it make? Besides, nobody has to know that. You've been given a great opportunity Jenna, don't completely screw it up like you screwed up the Olympics. Don't make the biggest mistake of your life by playing the innocent little virgin when your sexuality will take you so much further. God gave you my good looks, I pray you don't waste them," snapped her mother.

Jenna sighed in distress, she was discouraged, her mother hadn't been helpful at all! She was tired of playing these games. She was not interested in Alexander at all and she was growing weary of trying to dodge him all the time. Lately it seemed, he always seemed to show up wherever she was. At this point, she was scared to be alone with him, he was totally creeping her out and she did not want to end up in another cat fight with Marika!

Over the next several weeks Jenna found herself completely torn. At times, she had seriously considered quitting the show and going home to Hans and Carolina. It was obvious to her, that coming here to Paris had been a huge mistake.

It didn't seem fair to though, to abandon the show at this point. If Jenna were to leave the show, Adam would have to leave too, that would leave a huge hole in the show. Simone and Gail had put their heart and soul into this production, it just didn't seem fair to abandon them, after they had worked so hard.

Jean Marie Stanberry

CHAPTER NINETEEN

Three weeks of performances in Paris seemed to go by very quickly. Unfortunately, Alexander's bad behavior seemed to be escalating with each passing day, and though Jenna made every effort to avoid being alone with him, their paths seemed to cross more frequently than she was comfortable with.

During dress rehearsals, when Alexander and Jenna had to skate off the ice together at the end of the combined pairs number, she had resorted to pushing her way through the crowd of back up skaters as they were leaving the ice, just so she wouldn't have to be alone in the shadows with Alexander. Then she would sprint to the dressing room, before he could catch up to her!

In the meantime, Alexander had been quite busy weaving his web of deception. He had been spreading rumors about the two of them throughout the cast. It wasn't long before his lies had infiltrated the entire cast, soon they were all completely convinced that Alexander and Jenna were having quite the covert affair. Even Adam had heard the rumors and was completely convinced that Jenna was planning to ditch him for his rival, the Olympic gold medalist. He was hurt and he had grown distant and quiet.

Apparently, the rumors had been circling the cast for weeks, but Jenna had been completely oblivious to the scandalous talk. Though looking back, she guessed there would be no reason for anyone to repeat the rumors to her. Still, she was completely shocked when her friend Colin finally let the cat out of the bag.

That afternoon, as they were leaving their dress rehearsal, Jenna walked out the back door with Colin and she was distressed to see that Adam's bike was already gone. He hadn't bothered to wait for her. Jenna sighed miserably.

"I can't believe he just left without saying anything to me," she said, staring blankly at the nearly empty bike rack.

"Not to worry Jenna. I imagine he's just a bit jealous, not to mention the fact, that his feelings have most likely been hurt. He hasn't been himself the past few weeks you know, with everything that has been going on, but I am quite certain he will bounce back splendidly," said Colin, pulling his bike from the rack.

"Jealous? Jealous of what?" asked Jenna, staring at Colin completely stunned. What did Adam have to be jealous of?

"Well, jealous of Alexander of course. There's no question about it, it does reflect badly on Adam as well. I mean, for all intensive purposes Adam is supposed to be your husband, yet you and Alexander are...well, at least that's what he's been telling everyone...that the two of you..." Colin was stumbling over the words, as he suddenly realized that it was all a lie.

"What has Alexander been saying?" asked Jenna, biting her lip nervously. She wasn't sure she wanted to hear Colin say it.

"It's all a bloody lie isn't it?" cried Colin, as a look of shock washed across his face. Jenna sighed and shook her head miserably.

"God...he's told everyone that we're sleeping together, hasn't he?" she gasped, shaking her head disgustedly.

Colin nodded, his face was contorted with shame.

"You believed it!" cried Jenna, barely able to contain her shock.

"I didn't want to believe it. I couldn't imagine what you would see in such a...I'm sorry...he's rather convincing, it seems," said Colin, frowning.

"Do you know what I have been going through the past several weeks? He won't keep his hands off of me, and the things he says to me...oh my God! Colin what can I do? I can hardly stand to look at him anymore. He totally gives me the creeps!" she cried, hardly able to stomach the fact that most likely, everyone in the company, believed Alexander's bogus lies.

"If he's been sexually harassing you, then you need to tell someone in the company, like Simone or Gail," said Colin.

"They know, though Alexander has managed to turn it all around. They think it's all my fault...that I'm trying to seduce him," she said, shaking her head miserably.

"I'd heard that you already did...I am ashamed to admit that I actually believed that rubbish," said Colin, frowning.

Jenna felt like crying. Now everyone in the entire company thought that her and Alexander were having an affair and he had pretty much made it look like she was the one who was pursuing him! Even Adam was convinced that it was true and he was apparently upset with her.

Jenna was struggling with despair, she didn't want to abandon the show, but she wasn't sure how much longer she could put up with Alexander. He took advantage of every single second they were alone, and during every dress rehearsal, he felt the need to talk dirty to her, in Russian. This made her very glad she couldn't understand a word he was saying. To top everything off, whenever Marika looked at her, Jenna got the distinct feeling that this tiny woman was secretly plotting her death!

****

Alexander was battling his own frustration over the situation. He had been working on Jenna for weeks and she seemed to be no closer to giving in to him than ever. He wasn't sure what was holding things up. He knew she was close, but something was holding her back. It wasn't her partner Adam, since Alexander began spreading rumors that he and Jenna were lovers, Adam had become distant and moody. Alexander had to smile, it was at the very least, good to know that Adam wasn't getting any either.

Alexander was at a loss as to what to do next. Jenna hadn't budged an inch on her feelings for him. In fact, she'd be avoiding him lately. He was now wondering if he would have to use a bit of force, just to show her what she was missing. It was why he had started the rumors. If the rest of the cast was convinced that they were already lovers, they would never believe her if she told them he had forced himself on her.

Of course, he didn't *want* to force himself on her, but she was being so coy lately. He knew she was intrigued by his desire for her. Maybe that's what she wanted. Maybe that was her game...

****

That evening they skated their final performance in Paris to a sold out crowd. During the finale, Jenna could tell that her left skate blade was getting loose. After the final curtain call she skated off the ice and hurried to the dressing room. When she unlaced her skates she realized that one screw was completely missing and two screws were loose. Jenna started wandering around backstage looking for Dion, their prop master. Dion took care of everything like that. He would have an extra screw, and he would have her skates fixed up for her in no time.

She was finally able to track him down and he took her skates and told her he would fix them and return them to her tomorrow.

When Jenna returned to the dressing room finally, she realized nearly everyone had left for the evening, even all of the back up skaters were already gone. It was Saturday night, most of the skaters were older and had probably left to spend the rest of the evening in clubs that had dancing. Jenna hurried to get dressed and anxiously hoped that Adam would still be out back waiting for her.

When she came out the backstage door, she stopped short. She looked around quickly and realized that only two bicycles remained there in the stand. Hers and Alexander's...

Jenna glanced around quickly, hoping that maybe Alexander was still inside. In seconds, her hope evaporated. She could see Alexander standing there in the shadows, he was leaning against the concrete wall, smoking a cigarette. When he saw her, he dropped the cigarette on the concrete and ground it out deliberately with his foot.

Jenna chewed nervously on her lower lip as he sauntered slowly towards her. Jenna shivered and drew in a shaky breath when she saw his arrogant smile. Alexander was the last person she wanted to be alone with, in the dark backstreets of Paris.

Unfortunately, running away was not an option. Alexander's big, blocky body was blocking her only exit from the alley, she had no desire to run the other direction, deeper into the dark alley. The rink was essentially deserted now, if she went back inside, she would be no safer in there, than she was now, here in the alley.

Jenna rolled her eyes at him and marched over to pull her bike from the rack. She was irritated that no one had waited for her, and she was scared. Her heart was pounding irregularly and she was struggling to breathe. She had no idea what Alexander might try, now that they were truly alone.

Jenna was attempting to pull her bike, clumsily from the rack when Alexander walked over and stepped in front of her, smiling at her seductively.

"My darling, don't be in such a hurry to leave, the night is young. In a few moments the rink will be completely deserted and you and I will have the entire place to ourselves," he told her, flashing her a sly smile.

"If you think I want to spend any time alone with you, you must be completely delusional! Simone has already told you that I am off limits to you! You are engaged to Marika! Go back to the hotel and your fiancee and leave me alone! Stop trying to convince the entire world that we are having an affair," Jenna cried, completely annoyed with him. She drew in a deep, shaky breath and hoped that Alexander couldn't tell how frightened she was, standing there in the dark alley.

"Marika is a cold fish. You are the one I want," said Alexander, taking a bold step toward her.

"I've told you to leave me alone Alexander!"

"I truly cannot, my darling. You do realize that you are here because of me. It was I who pushed Mr. Dumontier's hand to bring you here, despite the fact that you are only fifteen years old.

Are you so naive you believe that he would bring you all the way to Paris on your talent alone? A relative newcomer, after your scandalous failure in the Olympics? Really my darling, don't kid yourself. I pled your case quite passionately, though I truly could care less about *skating* with you," said Alexander with a bit of a chuckle.

"If you so much as lay a hand on me I will call the Police! This is sexual harassment, if I turn you in to Mr. Dumontier, you and Marika will be fired," cried Jenna, though she was perfectly sure that no one in the company would take her claims seriously.

"You have sexually harassed me as well, everyone in the company has seen it. Touching me, getting me all hot and bothered. Does that make you feel powerful Jenna? Teasing a man like me and then walking away?" asked Alexander, his voice was silky and taunting.

"I never did that!"snapped Jenna.

"Oh, so angry! How about Adam? Did you tease him as well? Did you make him so hot he couldn't stand it, and then walk away? Is that why he's been so cool and distant lately? Maybe the stress of sharing a bed with a woman who is nothing but a tease is just too much for him," seethed Alexander, flashing her the tiniest bit of an amused smile.

"You have no idea what you are talking about!" snapped Jenna. She was angry. Angry at Adam for leaving without her, and she was angry because she was, once again, alone with Alexander.

"Face it Jenna, you've played it cool and aloof much too long, perhaps Adam is done waiting for you. A man can only handle so much rejection...before he moves on," said Alexander.

Jenna was staring at him, shaking her head numbly. He was completely insane.

"I would never leave you though...I would wait for you forever. I think you know that," said Alexander, his voice was strong and earnest, but warning bells were going off in Jenna's head. Alexander was dangerous...

"Of course, you need to grow up a bit. I know what I want, but you are just a silly young girl who has no idea what love really is. You have no idea how special it can be between a man and a woman. You are too young and frightened to realize that passion between a man and a woman is to be revered, not feared," said Alexander.

Jenna sighed and took a slow, deep breath. She didn't know how anything Alexander said could sound reasonable, but for some reason, it did. She felt confused, she wished she were strong enough to confide in Carolina. How was she supposed to know what was right and wrong? She had been pretty much abandoned by her own parents, she really knew nothing about real relationships.

"Really Alexander, the two of us can never be together. I should go," said Jenna, her voice quivering with obvious discomfort.

"I want to hear the truth from you, why can we never be together?"asked Alexander.

"I told you before Alexander. I have a boyfriend. Matt and I..."

"Matt is not here in Paris. Matt is far away, perhaps he is with another woman right now. You do not know, do you?"

Jenna drew in a deep shaky breath, he was right. There were no promises between her and Matt, they were not engaged. Matthew would meet many women at college...

"I know Matt, he wouldn't..."

"All men have *needs* Jenna. Sometimes we cannot help ourselves. Perhaps this Matthew loves you, but tell me, what would he do if a woman aroused him, the way that you've aroused me so many times?"

"Alexander, I have to go," she snapped.

Alexander was making her very nervous. She didn't want to be alone with him in this dark, back alley. He was messing with her mind and she suddenly had the urge to break down and cry. She felt so lost and alone here, she knew now that she should have gone back to the states immediately, staying here had been incredibly naive of her.

"Where do you plan to run off to? Are you going to run back to Smyth, the very one who deserted you tonight?" he taunted.

Jenna nodded emotionlessly. Adam *had* abandoned her, and it hurt her. Alexander shook his head, obviously disgusted.

"I guess you will never learn. I find myself completely flabbergasted by how stupid and blind you are. Can you not see? It is I, who loves you. When you kissed me, I was the happiest man in the world...I guess I should have known, the heartless little ice princess was just playing with me, leading me on," said Alexander, looking away, his face was filled with anguish.

Jenna sighed miserably. She didn't know how Alexander could make her feel bad for him, but he did. "Alexander..."

"You already know what you do to me. How long can we keep denying these feelings, they are so strong? Can you not see, that my entire body aches for you?" the silky calm of Alexander's voice, suddenly sent a shiver down her spine as he leaned toward her, wrapping both his hands around the handlebars of her bicycle. He stared into her eyes and gave her an sardonic smile. Jenna shivered imperceptibly. Alexander was messing with her head. This wasn't love, it was some sort of creepy obsession.

"Alexander really, I just want you leave me alone," snapped Jenna, still anxiously trying to pull the bicycle from his hands.

She couldn't help it, her voice had a crescendo of panic in it. Alexander's eyes drifted over her her cooly. She was suddenly sure that he had not missed the panic in her voice.

"My sweet Jenna, do not be frightened my darling, the last thing I want is to hurt you. I only wish to make beautiful love to you," he told her in his silky, Russian tinged, voice.

"No Alexander...I told you a million times. I don't feel the same way about you!" cried Jenna. She was desperately trying to calm her racing, now completely overloaded brain. Alexander was not listening to her, his delusional brain thought the feeling was mutual. Jenna was trying desperately to hold herself together and not dissolve into a panic. She glared into his eyes defiantly.

"Why do you feel the desire to play these games? I am a World Champion, everywhere I go women want me, they do not send me away. I can give you pleasure you have never experienced. I know you want me, I could feel your desire the day I kissed you backstage. You wanted me so badly your body was shaking," said Alexander, flashing her a satisfied smile.

"I was shaking because I was scared. Desire is a mutual thing, you were forcing yourself on me," she cried, her voice was now shaking, much like her body. She felt as if she could barely breathe.

"Is this what American women do? Deny their feelings, pretend they do not have needs?"

"I've told you Alexander, I'm not attracted to you, why can't you leave me alone!" snapped Jenna.

"Unfortunately, some women have no idea what they want. You, my darling, are one of those woman. You claim to have a boyfriend in Boston, perhaps it is true, but I know you have already betrayed him with Adam. What you have with Adam is a marriage of convenience, there is no passion. He is perhaps attracted to you, but you my darling, can do so much better.

I do know that something has happened between the two of you, but I am certain that he has not yet made love to you. Perhaps you are frightened that it would change your relationship. I am telling you it would. You would be disappointed in the sex and your casual friendship would be over forever. Is that what you want Jenna?"

"Alexander..."

"If Matthew were to learn of your indiscretions against him, even if they seemed innocent at the time, do you actually think he would trust you again? Could you tell him what you and Adam have done? Would he still love you?"asked Alexander gazing deeply into her eyes.

Jenna was suddenly trembling, she didn't want to react to his accusation, but her face was suddenly burning with shame, it was true, she had betrayed Matt. Even though her and Adam had never slept together, the betrayal was the same. Matt would be heartbroken if he knew that she had kissed Adam the way she had, that night on the Eiffel Tower.

"Please Alexander, just leave me alone," cried Jenna. She was suddenly fighting tears.

"You are afraid? Please my darling, there is nothing to be afraid of, there is nothing more beautiful than the passion between a man and a woman. I promise, I will be a complete gentleman," he told her, still smiling at her seductively.

"Alexander, I told you, I am not really attracted to you. We have to work together, you are engaged," she snapped.

"Why do you deny me this? When I kissed you, your lips were hungry for more. When you touched me you were embarrassed, but your hand lingered there...you could not help your curiosity," said Alexander, raising his eyebrows at her, daring her to deny it.

Jenna sighed, completely exasperated, she couldn't help the curiosity that had overwhelmed her that day. Unfortunately, Alexander was very observant, Jenna had no doubt that he would use this tiny indiscretion against her the rest of the summer.

"Alexander, this is ridiculous, you're not listening to me! There is nothing between us, there can never be anything between us!" snapped Jenna.

"You are wrong, we are so much alike, you and I. It is why we were inexplicably drawn to each other, I believe we are soul mates. Our circumstances were so similar..."

"What circumstances?" cried Jenna. She was finding herself completely unnerved by his attempts to manipulate her. It seemed unfair. It was just so easy for him.

"I know our childhoods were very similar. They were lonely...unhappy. I am aware that you were essentially abandoned by your parents. Your own father was too busy to deal with you," said Alexander.

"That's not true," snapped Jenna.

"My darling, months ago I overheard Mr. Dumontier on the phone with your father. I wanted you here so badly with me. I suggested that your father fake your marriage to Adam. I knew it was a long shot. What parent sends their young daughter to Europe without an adult chaperone? But your father barely hesitated.

It seems your mother has some serious issues...it's the only reason you're here, in a faked marriage, living a ruse. It is nothing to be ashamed of. It's not *your* fault, apparently your father already has his hands quite full with your mother..."

Jenna gasped, how could he possibly know?

"After she was hospitalized for her nervous breakdown your life was never the same, was it? You got your mother back eventually, but someone had to be the responsible one...it was you wasn't it?"

Jenna's lower lip was quivering, she wanted to cry, but the tears wouldn't come. How could he know all of this? No one was supposed to know...

"Then Hans Grimaldi came along and took you away from all that and he became more than your coach didn't he? You finally had a father."

"Alexander stop," breathed Jenna, a tear had finally rolled down her cheek at the mention of Hans' name. She missed him so badly she could barely stand it. She just wanted to go back to Chicago, back to Hans and Carolina.

"Did it not feel good to finally have someone to love you? That is all I want Jenna. I want someone to love me," said Alexander looking into her eyes very earnestly.

Jenna chewed on her lower lip in a desperate attempt to stem the tears that were threatening to come bursting from her eyes,

Alexander had found her weak spot and she didn't want him to realize it.

"It was the same for me, when I was younger. My parents sent me to Moscow when I was just six, to train on the ice. There were eight children, sending me to Moscow was godsend for my parents, one less mouth to feed. Of course I was lonely...I was just a baby, all alone. I had no friends...." said Alexander, taking a cautious step toward her.

"What about Marika?" asked Jenna, her heart was pounding with guilt and she wasn't sure why.

"Marika came later...unfortunately most of my childhood was spent there in Moscow. A lonely child, living there in the dormitory, till my coach took me to her bedroom when I was just twelve years old..."

"What?" cried Jenna, the anguished tone in his voice seemed to tug at her heartstrings.

"I know it seems very shocking that a grown woman would take a mere boy to her bedroom, but she was lonely. What could I do? I truly had no one. So she used me to fulfill her needs. I knew it was wrong, but I really had no choice, I was barely old enough to even know what was going on..."

"Are you telling me this woman had sex with you? When you were twelve years old?," cried Jenna, completely horrified. Now she was beginning to understand why Alexander was so completely inappropriate, why her youth didn't seem to bother him at all.

"I was afraid at first, it seemed so unnatural. She told me she was making me into a brave little man, but my family was deeply religious. I feared God was going to strike me dead for our sins. We weren't married and she was an adult and I was just a child. I called my parents and told them what had happened. I wanted them to come get me, but of course, they didn't care. Perhaps they didn't even believe me. I had food and a roof over my head, they told me I had no reason to complain...I imagine that is true..."

"But you were just a boy!" cried Jenna, now finding herself angry at Alexander's parents.

"I imagine some things make you stronger...a survivor. I was much like you, desperate for my parents approval..."

"Wait...how did you know?"

"So young and so driven...and for what? You truly have no one to love you. Your relationships are superficial. You waste your life, not being loved, not loving others. You are shallow and distant, you cannot help it, you are damaged...afraid to let others into your heart," said Alexander, with a little shrug.

"I'm not...shallow and distant!" cried Jenna, though as she said the words, she felt that maybe Alexander was right.

"Perhaps you think me too forward, but I blame it on my passion. After many years of neglect by my own parents, I choose to love freely. Life is too short Jenna. Do not deny yourself happiness," said Alexander, giving her a little smile.

Jenna bit her lower lip to stem it's sudden quivering. She suddenly felt like crying.

"Do not cry my darling, I understand your pain, I have felt this same pain," said Alexander, holding his arms open to her.

Jenna took a deep, shaky breath. For some reason she longed to go to him, to have him hold her while she cried. Jenna tried to shake off her confusion, he was like a wolf in sheep's clothing and her brain was telling her that this was all an act. Unfortunately, her heart was telling her she had nowhere else to turn. Adam had abandoned her tonight, just like her own parents had abandoned her.

Jenna took one shaky step toward him, Alexander just nodded in encouragement and she fell into his arms sobbing. Alexander held her for a long time while she cried in his arms. She was so confused, she felt as if there was no one in the world she could trust, not even her own parents.

Alexander took her face in his hands and kissed her tenderly. The kiss was so gentle, Jenna was caught off guard. In moments, she felt herself kissing him back, despite her better judgement. As the kiss grew more passionate, she began to have second thoughts, obviously Alexander had found her weak spot, he was playing her.

"Alexander, I have to go," she said, pulling away nervously.

"Do not go, let me kiss you some more," said Alexander, kissing her again, more deeply.

Jenna felt her entire body succumb to the passionate kiss. Alexander looked deeply into her eyes as he brushed his knuckles softly across her cheek. Jenna felt a shudder of desire rush throughout her entire body. This was insane, how could Alexander's kisses arouse such feelings in her, when up to this moment, she didn't even like him?

She was wrapped in Alexander's strong embrace and the kiss felt so good, Jenna was forgetting all her misgivings about Alexander. She kissed him back, tentatively at first, then eagerly, as he plunged his tongue into her mouth suggestively and wrapped his arms around her even tighter.

Jenna could feel her heart accelerating as the kiss deepened, her entire body seemed to be coming to life.

As Alexander's hands began to roam across her body, Jenna realized what was happening. Alexander was using her own insecurities against her. He had exploited her loneliness and fear. He was engaged to Marika, yet he was here, making the moves on her...Jenna knew this wasn't right!

"Wait Alexander...we can't do this. You are engaged to Marika." she gasped, trying to catch her breath. Alexander groaned with desire as Jenna, tried to pull away and peel his wandering hands from her body.

"Yes, it was all arranged, but I do not love her, I love *you*," he whispered into her ear.

Jenna was fighting tears, in her entire life no one had ever told her that they loved her, except Adam...and he'd been drunk...

Jenna struggled to breathe. Her entire body seemed to be on fire, infused with a strange combination of adrenaline and desire. All she had ever wanted was someone to love her. Did Alexander truly love her, or was this all just a lie?

"Alexander, I know you would never jeopardize your relationship with Marika. Just let me go!" snapped Jenna, trying to pull herself from his arms.

"I swear, I would do whatever you want. Please, I cannot marry Marika," breathed Alexander, his face was completely earnest.

"What? Why can't you marry Marika?" snapped Jenna, glaring at him.

"It is an arranged marriage. I had no choice, I do not love her," said Alexander, looking into her eyes very earnestly.

"Then just tell her!" snapped Jenna, she didn't know how that could possibly be so hard.

"She knows," said Alexander, with a sigh.

"You told her that you don't love her, yet she still wants to marry you!" cried Jenna, it seemed insane, but Marika and Alexander were from another culture, a culture completely foreign to her, she guessed things were very different there, in the Soviet Union.

"Marriage is not always about love, in other cultures. I guess her family is most interested in the athletic babies we could make together," said Alexander.

Jenna shook her head numbly. She had heard of that at least, people picking spouses all on the basis of their physical characteristics, hoping to genetically enhance their family line.

"You should just call it off, if that's how you feel," said Jenna, beginning to feel very uncomfortable. She was still in Alexander's arms and he was looking into her eyes with an expression that was so contrite, she almost felt sorry for him.

"I cannot call it off, I am trapped like a rat," said Alexander, frowning.

Jenna took a deep shaky breath. "Alexander, I'm sorry, I feel like I'm not thinking rationally right now. I need to go."

"No do not go Jenna. Please, you have to help me," cried Alexander, his face was suddenly stricken.

Jenna was frowning, not really sure what was going on. Alexander looked completely devastated. "What do you want from me?"

"I want to marry you," said Alexander, his face was perfectly serious, yet Jenna wanted to burst out in hysterical laughter. They were not even friends, they were co-workers with a very strained relationship. Why on earth would he want to marry her? The very thought was insane.

"What?"

"Jenna, you need me as much as I need you. You are alone, your family doesn't want you. After your summer here, what will you do? Return to these people who do not love you? I love you. I am a World Champion. Think about it, if we were to marry, return to the states and become partners, perhaps next year we would be World Champions together."

"Alexander...I..." Jenna wasn't sure what to say, her head was spinning, she was suddenly so confused.

"When I return to the Soviet Union this fall they will force me to marry her, but if..." his voice seemed to fade away to nothing, he seemed so consumed with emotion.

"If what!" cried Jenna, she was actually getting annoyed. Why was Alexander pursuing her like this, and why was he suddenly professing to be in love with her?

"If another woman is pregnant with my child, they will not force me to marry Marika. The man should marry the woman who is carrying his child," said Alexander, wiping away a tear.

"Alexander, I'm fifteen years old. I'm not ready to have a child," cried Jenna.

"I cannot marry Marika, we are not compatible at all. On the ice, we are magic. If we marry, my life will be ruined forever. I cannot stand the thought," cried Alexander.

"I'm sorry Alexander, I do not feel the same way about you," said Jenna, trying to pull herself from his arms. Alexander wrapped his arms around her tighter.

"You will, I promise. It will be perfect, just let me show you," said Alexander, looking into her eyes.

"Alexander please, I can't," said Jenna.

"Just tell me you love me too," said Alexander, taking her face in his hands and kissing her tenderly.

Jenna jerked herself from his arms and reached for her bike in the rack. "I don't love you Alexander, I'm leaving," snapped Jenna.

Alexander reached out and clamped his hand on her wrist and jerked her roughly toward him. The bike crashed to the pavement as Alexander pulled her violently against his chest.

"I swear, I am done playing games with you," he scowled angrily. Jenna drew in a shocked breath and looked up at Alexander as he pulled her forcibly into his arms. Jenna's mouth dropped open in shock, his dark eyes were cold and determined looking. Jenna struggled anxiously to breathe. Her first instinct was to scream, but it would be of no use, there was no one nearby.

She was trapped here, in this deserted back alley. The traffic from the street out front, and the loud music drifting out of the nearby clubs would drown out her screams. Besides, she knew, whenever she was truly scared she was simply incapable of screaming loudly. Her frightened voice would fade away to nothing. She'd had countless nightmares over her lifetime about screaming, and absolutely nothing coming out of her mouth!

Jenna's heart was pounding with fear and she was shaking uncontrollably. She knew she was no match for Alexander, he was strong as an ox. He would simply overpower her and do what he wanted.

"You have teased me enough, it is time for for you to give me what I have waited most patiently for," growled Alexander, he was suddenly crushing her in his arms. He molded his body to hers and whispered something into her ear in Russian. She shivered when she felt his hot breath in her ear. Jenna was struggling to get out of his arms, but he was much too strong.

In moments, his lips were moving over hers and he was playfully nibbling at her lips, seductively trying to persuade her to part her lips and allow his tongue in. Jenna was frightened, she could barely breathe as he pressed his body suggestively against hers. Unfortunately, her struggling was useless, he was just too strong!

Jenna pressed her lips together tightly as he tried to force his tongue into her mouth. In moments, Alexander had backed her into the corner and pushed her up against the concrete wall, where he was now lewdly grinding his pelvis against her.

"Why are you suddenly so cold to me, when moments ago your sweet lips were threatening to devour me?"

"You know this is wrong Alexander," breathed Jenna.

"Relax my darling, I will not let Marika kill you," panted Alexander, as he dragged his mouth from her lips and ardently began trailing kisses down the right side of her neck.

"We can't Alexander, this was a mistake," said Jenna, rueing the second she had fallen for his bogus lies.

"No, you kissed me back, you want me," he breathed, pressing his body seductively against hers.

"It was wrong, you are engaged...Marika will..."

"Marika will marry someone else. Besides, *you* are the one I cannot stop thinking about," panted Alexander.

"Please Alexander, stop," cried Jenna. She couldn't move, she was pinned against the wall, Alexander was hastily unbuttoning her shirt, trailing kisses down her chest toward her right breast.

"They are small, but nice, no?" breathed Alexander. He pushed her bra strap off her shoulder and dropped his head down, drawing her nipple into his mouth. Jenna gasped and shuddered involuntarily as Alexander rolled her nipple between his teeth and darted his tongue across it gently.

It seemed insane, but Alexander seemed to be awakening feelings inside her, she had never experienced before.

"Please don't," moaned Jenna, in moments her entire body was trembling with a strange desire she had never felt before.

"Do not deny us this Jenna, admit it, you need this as much as I do," Alexander's, hot breath in her ear caused Jenna to shiver as he buried his face in her neck, playfully nibbling, causing her body to shudder with pleasure.

Jenna was still trying to push him away, she wanted to push him away, but his touch was arousing her in a way she had never felt before. It was completely insane, her body seemed helpless to Alexander's practiced touch. He knew exactly what he was doing and Jenna felt as if her entire body was on fire. She was so inexperienced, even

Matthew had never even attempted the things Alexander was doing to her now. Jenna knew it was wrong, but she felt strangely heady, and completely out of control.

"Alexander," she gasped. It was the only word that her mouth could utter. Her knees were feeling weak as he lowered his head and drew her nipple into his mouth again, sending an electric current, coursing through her body. Jenna could barely breathe, the feeling was so all consuming.

Jenna was trying desperately to regain her focus, but Alexander's lips had claimed her mouth again with an overpowering kiss. When her lips finally parted, he plunged his tongue deep inside her mouth. Jenna felt all of her resolve melting away as his hands roamed across her body, caressing and massaging her until she couldn't take it any more.

Jenna felt an overwhelming sense of guilt at the feelings that were rocketing through her body right now...it was completely insane. She couldn't help it, her body seemed to be on autopilot as Alexander greedily pushed her shirt off her shoulders, his mouth moving from one breast to the other. Jenna's entire body seemed to be glowing with a whole host of feelings she had never experienced before. Alexander's hands drifted down to lift her skirt.

"No," she gasped.

"Yes," breathed Alexander, pressing her against the concrete wall even harder. In just moments, he was lifting her skirt and sneaking his hand into her panties, his long fingers were working to spread her apart and probe her, deep inside.

"No Alexander, stop," gasped Jenna. No one had ever touched her like that before and her body was suddenly shuddering uncontrollably, she could barely catch her breath. Alexander knew exactly what he was doing.

"I cannot stop. You are so wet...you want me too," he gasped, nibbling on her earlobe, as he worked his fingers deeper inside her. Jenna gasped involuntarily.

"That's it my darling, just relax, let me show you what you've been missing," whispered Alexander. Jenna was still struggling with him, but it only made Alexander plunge his fingers in deeper, taunting and twisting within her.

"Alexander, I can't...Marika..." gasped Jenna, her heart was racing, it was an effort just to breathe.

Alexander's hand had fixated on a tiny, fleshy spot between her legs. He massaged it relentlessly and Jenna was bucking involuntarily, not sure if what she was feeling was pleasure or pain. An involuntary sigh escaped her lips as Alexander continued to caress this intimate place between her legs.

"Your body is telling me otherwise my darling, relax and let me take you over the edge," breathed Alexander, sliding his fingers deep inside her again.

Jenna gasped and let out an anguished cry. She felt guilty, but she suddenly wanted him to take her over the edge, she could fight no longer. Her heart was racing from the adrenaline that had been infused into it. Alexander had massaged her into a frenzy. She had never felt anything like this before, her legs were so weak, she could barely stand, her body was shuddering involuntarily as Alexander pushed his fingers into her, as deep as they would go. Jenna's body collapsed against Alexander's, twitching uncontrollably, as she gasped to catch her breath.

"That's it my darling, I told you, you would like it," crooned Alexander. Jenna's body was still shuddering uncontrollably as she collapsed in Alexander's arms, he was basically holding her up, her legs were like jello. Jenna couldn't think, her brain was completely useless. Her entire body seemed to be on fire. She had never felt like this before, she didn't want it to stop, but this was Alexander. What had just happened? Jenna felt her face growing red with shame and guilt, how did Alexander manage to arouse these feelings in her?

"Now it is my turn," said Alexander, fumbling to unbuckle his jeans.

"No, Alexander...don't, not like this," breathed Jenna, uselessly trying to wiggle out of his arms.

"What do you mean...not like this? You are ready, I can feel it," he breathed, seductively.

"I can't I'm a virgin...and Marika..."

"I know...but you are ready. Do not worry, I will go slow, I will not hurt you. Marika is all but forgotten, just like Matthew," gasped Alexander, still trying to unbuckle his jeans with one hand.

"No Alexander, we can't."

"I cannot stop now, I need this, I have waited for many weeks. You cannot deny, you need it as much as I do," he gasped, dropping his head down and drawing her nipple into his mouth, causing Jenna to gasp and shudder uncontrollably.

"Alexander...please," she panted, just wanting him to go away. But Alexander misunderstood, he had finally escaped from the bonds of his bluejeans, and he was determined to seek his own release.

"I know my darling, I cannot wait any longer either."

"Alexander no," she cried, trying to push him away.

"Yes," he breathed, his fingers spreading her to receive him.

"Are you really going to force yourself on me?" cried Jenna, hardly able to believe that a man with any self respect would do such a thing.

"Force is a bit of a harsh word. Yes, I am doing a bit of persuading, and it is working. Have you ever heard the saying, you cannot rape the willing? Some girls want it like this, they need the very suggestion of danger. They want to be taken, it's exciting for them," breathed Alexander.

"Alexander, I think you need to go back to hotel and talk to Marika. I just feel like..."

"I know exactly how you feel. Right now, you are slightly ahead of the game, it is time for you to slow down and let Alexander catch up to you. Do not worry that it is your first time, it will be good, I have already brought you to your climax, it is my turn. You want it, and I am very willing to give it you," said Alexander, grinding his pelvis against her.

"No Alexander," cried Jenna. Though she wasn't sure how she could possibly get away from him now, she was pinned against the wall. She was essentially trapped, her face was red with shame. As much as she wanted to deny it, Alexander's touch had aroused her, her body had responded to his touch, thus arousing Alexander even more. Jenna felt guilty, she felt as if she had shamelessly led him on, now she wanted to deny him what he wanted so badly.

"I know, you are scared, because you can feel how large I am, do not worry Jenna. You are ready...my fingers are wet with your desire," whispered Alexander, lifting his fingers to his lips and licking them seductively.

****

Alexander was considering what would be the best way to do this. He had really hoped that their first lovemaking would happen someplace a little less tawdry than a back alley, but he'd wanted to touch her so bad. When he did touch her, her response had been enough to drive him completely insane.

Once he had her in his arms he couldn't make himself stop, he had brought her to an orgasm and feeling her body shudder with pleasure had made him so hot, he could barely even think right now. He knew she was a virgin and he needed to be gentle, but right now he could barely control himself.

****

Jenna was trembling, she couldn't help it, she was frightened. She couldn't hide her own desire, but she had never asked for any of this. She had been struggling to get away from Alexander, but she knew he would overpower her eventually. His hot breath in her ear, sent a shiver down her spine. Jenna was silently panicking as he pressed his body against hers.

Just then, the backstage door opened and bathed the back alley in a pocket of bright light. Jenna was surprised to see their friend Rainier walk out the door, whistling softly to himself.

"Rainier!" she cried, when she saw him. He looked up, startled to see her there in Alexander's arms. In his surprise, Alexander had let go of Jenna, and she had ran to Rainier's side the second she was free.

"Bonsoir," said Rainier, obviously startled that Jenna had bolted out of the shadows and was now clinging desperately to his arm. He was eyeing them both warily. He was uncomfortable, he was well aware of what he had interrupted, there in the dark alley.

He had heard the rumors, Alexander and Jenna were lovers, but both in relationships with others. It was no wonder he had caught them back here in the alley, it wasn't like they could go back to either of their rooms and do it.

Alexander had not moved away from the wall, he remained there in the shadows, hiding his obvious arousal and panting and glaring at Rainier arrogantly. He wanted to throw a fit and curse, he'd been so close.

Jenna was at Rainier's side, literally gasping to breathe. She was sure that Rainier, like everyone else in the cast, believed all the rumors that Alexander had been spreading about the two of them.

Alexander had not said a word, but was still glaring intently at Rainier, slowly catching his breath, as Jenna clung nervously to Rainier's arm. He was desperately trying to come up with a plan.

"You walked to the arena tonight?" Jenna asked Rainier anxiously. Obviously, his bike wasn't there in the rack. Jenna's voice had broke with fear as she spoke, she was suddenly feeling faint.

"Yes..." said Rainier, not really sure why Jenna was here, clinging to his arm. He couldn't even make eye contact with her, he was completely embarrassed. He couldn't help it, when he'd opened the backstage door, he hadn't been looking to get an eyeful, but he had seen more than enough to know exactly what he had interrupted.

He had been caught completely off guard as he walked out the stage door. He hadn't expected to see Jenna backed up against the wall with her skirt bunched up around her waist, her blouse gaping open. Of course, Alexander was fully aroused and obviously more than ready to enter her.

His first instinct was to turn around and go back into the rink, but everything had happened so quickly. When he opened the stage door, Jenna had appeared at his side so quickly, he really hadn't had time to absorb everything.

It was common knowledge throughout the cast that Alexander and Jenna were lovers. Alexander bragged about it all the time. Rainier wasn't sure why Alexander had pursued Jenna the way he had. Sure, she was pretty enough, but she was skinny with tiny breasts, like an adolescent. Besides, her and Adam were officially married, even though Rainier suspected that was some sort of scam.

For some reason, Alexander was completely obsessed, he may have been engaged to Marika, but the stories he told were all about Jenna. Rainier didn't know Jenna very well at all, she seemed quiet and shy when she was separated from her partner Adam, but she was apparently wild in the bedroom, at least, according to Alexander she was.

At this moment, Rainier was so embarrassed, he couldn't even look Jenna in the eye, knowing what he knew about her. Insatiable, that was how Alexander described her. Alexander bragged that they had sex practically everywhere in the ice arena, including on the ice. In fact, she was so out of control, she had probably urged Alexander to do her in the alley. She would have got her wish if he hadn't walked out when he did.

Now she was standing here next to him, trembling and clutching his arm tightly. Her shirt was gaping open slightly, affording him the slightest view of her breasts. They were small, but her nipples were dark pink and puckered up tight, like little rosebuds. The rest of her body was tight and muscular, and she had shapely, long legs, probably the best legs he had ever seen.

Rainier was soon fighting his own arousal as he snuck another glance into her open shirt. He couldn't help but be intrigued. Her nipples were standing out, tight and engorged, just begging to be touched. He shook his head miserably, Alexander was a lucky bastard.

Rainier glanced over at Alexander, who had still not regained his composure. He had managed to tuck himself discretely back into his pants, but the poor bastard was still panting, and fighting to catch his breath, they had been so close...Rainier almost chuckled, it served him right, Alexander was engaged. Marika was probably waiting for him right now, and here he was, in a dark back alley cheating on his fiancee with his lover!

Alexander's mind was reeling, trying to come up with a plan. If Jenna left with Rainier, she would tell him how he'd tried to force himself on her, despite the fact that her body had practically been begging him to just give it to her. It was her head that was still screwed up. He was willing her to just walk away from Rainier. They would find a way to be together and she would love him, Alexander knew she would...

Rainier glanced down at Jenna, who was still trembling. In fact, she looked completely mortified. He had to stifle a smile, she had probably never been caught in the act before. That kind of stuff embarrassed women, but to men it was like a badge of honor! Rainier looked her over casually, wondering why she had gravitated to him the way she had. Why didn't they just wave him away and keep going?

Alexander smiled with a sudden idea.

"Jenna, I know what you are trying to do, but not tonight my darling. I am not quite ready to share you with another man," said Alexander, barely able to conceal his smug smile for his own genius.

Rainier flashed him a quizzical look. Alexander almost chuckled, that had certainly aroused Rainier's curiosity.

"I'm sorry Mr. Maxim, Jenna is quite anxious, but I myself am not quite ready to fulfill her little fantasy of being with two men at one time. I hope you understand," crooned Alexander, never taking his eyes off of Jenna.

Jenna was trembling, she wanted to say something, but she couldn't seem to form any words as a look of understanding flashed across Rainier's face.

"Oh," said Rainier, he was suddenly acutely embarrassed. He was now carefully trying to peel Jenna off his arm, but she had a death grip on him.

"No Alexander," she managed to mumble.

"My darling, I know you are disappointed but my heart will not allow it at this time. Perhaps we could just let him watch this time."

Rainier couldn't help it, his heart was suddenly pounding with a bit of excitement. Jenna was still clinging to his arm and gasping to breathe.

"I'm sorry I startled you. Alexander is just teasing, do you mind if I walk back to the hotel with you?" asked Jenna, her voice breaking with fear.

Alexander glared at her angrily, he couldn't believe it, she was practically throwing herself at Rainier.

"Jenna, don't do this. I know what you are trying to do. If you seduce Rainier..."

"Alexander!" cried Jenna. She was trying to ease herself away from Alexander without any violence. She wanted to convince Rainier that she was injured and not able to ride her bike back to the hotel, but Alexander was trying to make it look as if she were recruiting him for a threesome, if she could just get away from Alexander...

Rainier looked over at Alexander who narrowed his eyes at him. Rainier felt his heart accelerate with a bit of anxiety, maybe he had stepped in the middle of something he had no business being in.

"Umm, I think I should just go," said Rainier, glancing over at Alexander nervously.

"No, Rainier! I fear I injured myself tonight and cannot ride my bike back to the hotel," Jenna lied. She looked up into Rainier's eyes and gave him a half hearted smile.

Rainier flashed her a dubious look. He looked over at Alexander, who was glaring at him with a vengeance. Something was a bit off, but he wasn't sure what.

"You want to walk back with me?" breathed Rainier, he was nervous. Something was definitely off. What would Jenna Bruce want from him? He wasn't gay, but he sure wasn't a ladies man, like Alexander.

"Yes," breathed Jenna, forcing her voice to sound normal.

"Are you okay? Do you need me to call you a cab?" he asked, playing into her little ruse, his face full of concern. He was still nervous, she didn't look like she was in pain, she did look...distressed. Alexander was glaring at him with narrowed eyes, he should probably just walk away.

"I'm fine to walk," she said, she was struggling to keep her voice steady. She was dangerously close to breaking down in tears, she was so stressed out.

"Umm, I feel as if I have interrupted a private moment, I should really go," said Rainier, looking around nervously. Whatever Jenna wanted from him, Alexander was not happy about it. He really wasn't up for an ass kicking tonight.

"No, please," snapped Jenna, gripping his arm even tighter. She gazed up at him with pleading eyes.

Rainier sighed miserably, how could he possibly tell her no? Alexander was still there in the shadows, glaring at him. What was going on with Jenna?

"As you wish," said Rainier, giving her a slight nod She gave him a fake smile as she clung tightly to his arm.

Rainier nodded to Alexander nervously, wondering exactly what was going on. He knew Jenna was not injured...they'd been totally getting it on. Why wouldn't they just send him on his way and get back to business?

Jenna was clinging to Rainier's arm, silently praying that Alexander would just let them go, that he wouldn't try to start something with Rainier. Jenna was watching Alexander warily as they turned to walk down the gangway that would take them to the front of the building.

She was almost holding her breath she was so worried that he would just attack her, even though Rainier was there as a witness.

Alexander had told her before, he always got what he wanted. Jenna wondered what happened when others defied his wishes.

"I will see you in the morning darling, I hope you feel better," said Alexander, his voice was a mask of forced cheerfulness. He gave them both an arrogant nod as he watched them walk away. Jenna was so frightened, she couldn't even look at him, as she walked away on Rainier's arm. She was tensed, nervously anticipating Alexander's attack, she couldn't relax until they reached the street out front.

Rainier couldn't help it, he was nervous as well. Alexander was watching them intently and he was obviously angry, so he was guessing that his leaving with Jenna, had not been part of the plan. What exactly, was he doing strolling away with Jenna, when obviously, Alexander wasn't done with her yet?

Rainier peeked at Alexander over his shoulder, he looked ready to blow, he was so angry. Jenna was nervous and shaky. It was odd, at first he'd thought her odd demeanor was a result of being interrupted in the act, now Rainier was not quite sure what was going on.

Jenna was fighting hysteria. She was anxiously making small talk with Rainier, knowing that he probably thought that she had gone completely bonkers. Jenna turned and looked cautiously down the gangway to see Alexander still standing there staring them down, as they strolled away from him, his face was a mask of barely concealed rage.

CHAPTER TWENTY

Alexander was furious. He had been so close, then stupid Rainier had to come out the back door and ruin everything. Alexander shook his head disgustedly. Jenna would tell Rainier all the tawdry details and then he would be back in Simone's office again, accused of sexual harassment.

He was tired of Jenna being such a tease, she wanted him. He knew she did. She had writhed in his arms as he skillfully brought her to an orgasm, but the selfish little slut refused to return the favor.

He silently reprimanded himself for thinking that. He knew she was young and frightened, but he had never desired anyone so powerfully in his entire life. He had fallen in love with her. She didn't believe him, but he would convince her. He wanted to make love to her so bad, he would do just about anything to make sure it wouldn't be painful for her, though he was beginning to think no matter what he did, it was still going to be painful.

Women had been coming on to him as long as he could remember, he'd never actually pursued a woman himself. He'd never been with a virgin before, even Marika had been with another before him.

Alexander was worried, every woman he'd ever been with had told him he was huge. He could tell that Jenna had never been touched by another man, he could barely fit his thick fingers inside her. He worried no matter how ready she was, it was going to be painful

He worried what Jenna was telling Rainier right now. Alexander was panicked, if Jenna and Rainier went to Simone and told her that he had tried to rape her, he would be sent home immediately. Suddenly, he had a fabulous idea, he jumped on his bike and raced back to the hotel.

He ditched his bike in the rack and headed for Simone's office, he had to hurry before she left for the night. He approached the door and forced his face to look completely anguished. He lifted his hand and knocked on the door.

"Come in," called Simone.

Alexander walked into the office to see her sitting behind her desk sifting through a stack of papers.

"May I talk to you for a moment," asked Alexander, forcing his voice to break with emotion.

Simone took one look at his devastated face and her heart contorted for him, he looked on the verge of tears.

"What is it Alexander?"

"Oh Simone, I don't know what I'm going to do," cried Alexander, working it with everything he had. He had even managed to work up a few tears.

"Please tell me."

"It is Jenna," he sobbed, clutching his chest dramatically.

"Alexander, what have you done?" gasped Simone, suddenly fearing the worst. He was definitely obsessed with her, that much was obvious. Hopefully, he hadn't done anything stupid.

"It was not me. Oh God, I'm not even sure I can talk about this," cried Alexander. He was practically sobbing now and he was infinitely pleased with his own acting talent.

"Tell me, what has happened," said Simone, Alexander seemed on the verge of a complete breakdown, she had never seen him so completely devastated.

"Jenna and I are lovers, it has been going on for weeks now," said Alexander.

Simone cringed, she had suspected that they were a bit more than friends, but she had nothing to support that theory. Jenna had accused Alexander of sexually harassing her, he had claimed the harassment was mutual. Up to this point, she really didn't know who to believe.

"Go on," said Simone.

"I love her more than anything, I was planning to leave Marika and marry Jenna, but but for her, I am not enough," said Alexander, still sobbing softly.

"What do you mean?"

"She wants more than me. She wants other men. I try to keep her satisfied, but tonight after our performance, I..."

Alexander couldn't seem to go on, he was now crying like a baby as Simone stared at him curiously.

"Please Mr. Peterov, how can I help you, if I do not know what is upsetting you?

"I'm sorry, I just can't get those horrible images out of my head!" cried Alexander.

"Alexander..."

"I walked out the backstage door and Jenna was there in the alley. She was doing it with Rainier Maxim," sniffled Alexander.

He looked up at Simone's face which was now contorted with disgust. He almost lost his focus and laughed, but he managed to be able to channel a few more tears in a last ditch effort to bring Simone around to his side.

"They were having sex?" cried Simone.

"Yes," cried Alexander, sobbing some more. Simone handed him a tissue and he wiped his eyes and blew his nose loudly.

Simone was didn't know what to do. Alexander was so upset, but there was really nothing she could do. Unfortunately this type of thing happened all the time. There really wasn't any rules that forbid cast members from hooking up, though she was worried about Jenna. She was a minor and their entire ruse hinged on the fact that she was married to her partner Adam.

Poor Adam had not been himself lately, now she knew why. If Jenna was truly as wild as Alexander had painted her to be, she would be difficult to control and with her being a minor, it could lead to quite the scandal. Simone knew she must do whatever it took to minimize the effect this had on the rest of the cast.

Simone looked over at Alexander who was still sobbing softly.

"I will deal with Miss Bruce. Please go on to your room. I imagine your "fiancee" is wondering where you are," snapped Simone.

Alexander stood up and headed for the door. He was completely ecstatic, but his body language remained that of a man completely broken. He was nearly coming unglued at the thought of the illusion he had created.

Maybe after he and Jenna were married and he was a US citizen he would have a future as a Hollywood actor, he was quite obviously brilliant.

Jean Marie Stanberry

CHAPTER TWENTY ONE

Rainier and Jenna walked slowly back to the hotel, Rainier was walking slowly for her benefit, as Jenna was feigning a Charlie horse in her calf. Though now that she was away from Alexander, she really wanted to sprint as fast as she could.

Rainier and Jenna had walked nearly four blocks, Jenna had been talking non stop, small talk the entire way. Finally, Rainier could take it no more, he stopped and turned to her, giving her a curious look.

"Jenna, tell me. What is really going on?" he asked, he looked into her eyes earnestly.

Jenna fought the urge to break down in tears. Her placid facade was dissolving rapidly.

"Rainier, I was so happy to see you, I was so scared, I was trapped there in the alley, Alexander was going to force himself on me."

"What?" cried Rainier, that wasn't what he had expected at all.

"Alexander and I are not a couple. I know he has been spreading rumors that we are having an affair, but that is all a lie.

He was waiting for me when I came out of the arena tonight. I was afraid of what he was going to do, with the two of us alone," Jenna sighed in frustration and looked over at Rainier to see if he was even buying her story so far. Alexander was so convincing, no one ever seemed to believe her. Rainier looked completely shocked.

"I know everyone is convinced that the two of us are having an affair, but I think he is the most repulsive, disgusting man I have ever met. He won't keep his hands off of me. He was going to force himself on me...if you had not come out the door when you did...well..." Jenna couldn't finish, she was still completely freaked out. She had barely escaped.

"I know, I saw. If Alexander is sexually harassing you, you must tell Simone and Gail. The entire company is convinced that the two of you are lovers," said Rainier, looking at her earnestly.

"I know, Rainier. I've told Simone and Gail, but Alexander is very good. He can twist things around, and he's such a good actor, most times I end up so confused, I can't even tell my side of the story. Besides, Alexander is so convincing. He has everyone convinced that we are lovers, and that I am to blame for all of this. That it was I, who seduced him," she told him cringing, the very thought made her nauseated.

Rainier put his arm around her and tried his best to comfort her as he walked her the rest of the way back to their hotel. They walked slowly, talking the entire way. By the time they arrived Jenna was happy that at least one person in the Company believed her side of the story.

Rainier walked her through the lobby. He told her that he had plans to meet some of the rest of the cast in the hotel bar for drinks. She bid him good evening, he hugged her and kissed her on the forehead, then he headed toward the hotel bar to meet the others. Jenna turned to walk to the elevators. As she turned, she saw Simone standing there, not twenty five feet away from her, near the elevators. She was staring at Jenna with a shocked look on her face.

"Bonsoir," said Jenna, giving her a bewildered look. She was not sure why Simone was staring at her like that. Jenna felt like she was not thinking straight, she was still messed up over her encounter with Alexander.

"I would not have believed it, had I not seen it myself," seethed Simone, still staring at her, looking completely stunned.

"What?" asked Jenna, staring at her now completely perplexed.

"Come with me to the office, right now! We are going to straighten this out tonight, if it kills me!" exclaimed Simone, grabbing her hand and pulling her unceremoniously toward the office. Jenna was trailing along behind her, she was completely baffled as to why Simone was acting so strangely.

Simone dragged her, almost forcibly to the office, then she flipped on the lights, pulled out a cigarette and lit it immediately. She pointed to one of the chairs.

"Sit!" she demanded, taking a long drag of her cigarette, as she began pacing the room like a caged tiger. Jenna was staring at her completely perplexed, she had never seen Simone agitated like this. She had no idea why Simone would be behaving this way. She seemed to be very angry about something, though Jenna had no idea what it could be.

Simone stopped her agitated pacing of the room and suddenly turned to give Jenna a harsh glare. Jenna shivered under her intense scrutiny. What had she done?

"I was not happy when Mr. Dumontier brought a minor into the Company. I was worried...about trouble. He promised me, there would be no trouble. I had my doubts initially, but I did not think it would be you, that would be causing the trouble. You always seemed so sweet and innocent!" exclaimed Simone angrily, as she turned and resumed her restless pacing of the room.

Jenna was staring at her completed mortified, she had no idea what she was talking about. "I beg your pardon?" asked Jenna, her face was contorted in confusion.

"Miss Bruce, please do not mistake me for a complete idiot! I do not have the patience for this tonight. I have not been completely blind to what has been happening behind my back over the past several weeks.

For your information, Alexander has been here, in this office for the past twenty minutes bawling his eyes out!" cried Simone, slamming both of her palms down on the desk angrily, causing Jenna to jump involuntarily.

Jenna was still staring at her oddly. She was completely perplexed. She had no idea what Simone was talking about. She had shrunk down in the chair, completely bewildered by Simone's anger, which for some reason, was focused on her.

"I do not know what you think you are up to, but I will not have a little slut like you, disrupting my entire show. You may be enjoying the power you seem to have over these men, but I am disgusted by your antics. Your little games are disrupting the entire cast!" cried Simone, taking another long drag on her cigarette and glaring at Jenna disgustedly.

"Simone, I don't know what Alexander has told you, but he is lying. The two of us are not having an affair, he..." Jenna didn't get to finish. Simone slammed both of her palms down on the desk angrily once more. A stack of papers tumbled off the other side of the desk onto the floor. Jenna slid down in her chair uneasily. She was suddenly afraid Simone might strike her, she seemed so angry. She had never seen Simone like this before!

"Alexander has just been in my office for the past twenty minutes, crying hysterically, because he is upset that you have dumped him for Rainier. Initially, I didn't buy a word of it. Alexander can be a bit melodramatic at times. Then I saw your emotional little encounter with Rainier in the lobby and I realized it was all true...you have been deceiving me!"

"Simone...no," breathed Jenna, staring at her in shock.

"I must admit, you are very good. You tried to make it look like Alexander was harassing you, but it was you, who was pursuing him! Now it seems, you have dumped Alexander and seduced Rainier! I will not tolerate this type of behavior, especially from you, a minor! Do you realize the trouble you could cause for these men, with you being a minor?"

Jenna sat up in her chair abruptly, completely horrified that Simone believed that her and Alexander had truly been having an affair, and now Simone believed that she had seduced Rainier, it was completely ridiculous!

"Simone, no! Rainier was just walking me back to the hotel...I..."

"I saw the two of you smooching in the lobby. I am not completely clueless to what is going on around here!" snapped Simone, narrowing her eyes at Jenna.

"Please Simone, Rainier and I weren't smooching..."

"What about Adam? Have you even thought about what you are doing to him! I mean, he was so happy, but lately...well, I'm sure he knows what's going on. I swear the whole show is just going to fall apart!" cried Simone, who was now ranting loudly.

"Please Simone, if you could just hear me out."

"No, I cannot take it anymore! I will talk to Mr. Dumontier in the morning and you and Adam will be out of the show!" cried Simone, still more angry than Jenna had ever seen her. Simone had her back to her now, she refused to even look at Jenna, she was so angry.

"No Simone, please listen to me..." Jenna was choking back tears. She wondered how everything could have gotten so badly out of hand. Jenna wanted her to hear her side of the story, but she was too angry to even listen.

"Get out!" cried Simone, turning and pointing to the door, her voice was nearing hysteria. Jenna jumped up from the chair, tears were coming to her eyes. She felt as if she could barely breathe.

"Simone..." whimpered Jenna softly, she took a step toward her, desperate to have Simone hear her side of the story.

"Out!" cried Simone. Jenna hesitated, then ran out the door with tears streaming down her face. This was a nightmare and she had no idea what to do. Simone was so angry, Jenna knew she would never believe her, over Alexander. Especially, since he was so convincing and he had gotten to her first.

Jenna ran blindly out into the hallway and nearly ran right into Mr. Dumontier and Rainier, who were both on their way to the office.

"What is going on?" cried Mr. Dumontier. He was obviously surprised to see her standing there in the hallway, with tears streaming down her face.

"She's kicking me out of the show," Jenna whimpered brokenly, she could barely speak at all, she was so upset.

"She is kicking you out of the show? Why in the hell is she doing that? cried Mr. Dumontier, looking completely baffled.

"She thinks I...she...thinks..." Jenna could only cry and snort, she couldn't bring herself to tell him the awful story. Mr. Dumontier took her by the hand and dragged her back toward the office. Jenna was almost afraid to go in, Simone was so angry with her. She was afraid that the very sight of her, would cause Simone to go off the deep end!

The three of them barged right into the office. Mr. Dumontier was leading the way, dragging Jenna along behind him, with Rainier trailing along in their wake. Simone was still sitting there at her desk, gulping down a drink and smoking, yet another cigarette. She looked stunned to see Mr. Dumontier barging into the room, with Rainier and Jenna.

"Miss Aubiere, what in God's name is going on?" he cried, looking at her quizzically, his tone was abrupt and businesslike.

"Francois, I'm glad you're here. I cannot deal with Miss Bruce anymore, she is disrupting my entire show," Simone sighed dramatically. "Mr. Peterov was just in here for twenty minutes, bawling like a baby. It appears that not only did Miss Bruce seduce Alexander several weeks ago, and break up his relationship with Marika, but now she has seduced Rainier and she has apparently dumped Peterov like last week's garbage," said Simone, taking another long drag on her cigarette. She rolled her eyes and glared at Jenna as if she were a disgusting animal or something.

"I am afraid you have it all wrong Miss Aubiere. I have just been speaking to Rainier. He came and found me after he apparently saved Miss Bruce from a very compromising situation tonight. Mr. Peterov has been lying. He has been spreading the rumors, he is the one that has been harassing Miss Bruce. Rainier brought Miss Bruce back to the hotel tonight because he feared for her safety. It is Alexander that is the danger here," said Mr. Dumontier, looking at Simone confidently, his arms folded across his chest.

"Oh please! I know that Jenna and Peterov are having an affair!" cried Simone, she stood up abruptly, and stood face to face with Mr. Dumontier.

"How do you know this?" he asked.

"I have seen them together! Just the other afternoon I had to break up a little cat fight, between Jenna and Marika. Marika was so angry, I thought she might kill Miss Bruce. I cannot say that I blame her. It was obvious to everyone what was going on. They both looked completely guilty, her lipstick was on his lips! It is affecting my rehearsals Francois, the two of them could barely keep their hands off of each other."

"Besides, Mr. Smyth has not been himself either. Who could blame him, his supposed wife, can't keep her hands off of Alexander! It is affecting the entire cast. Now she's seduced Rainier, thank God the rest of them are all gay!" she cried, shaking her head miserably. "You haven't had her too, have you Francois?"

Mr. Dumontier shot her a look, he was obviously very angry. Jenna's mouth was dropped open in shock, she couldn't believe Simone could actually say such a thing. Mr. Dumontier turned to Rainier. "Mr. Maxim, would you please walk Miss Bruce to her room, to ensure she makes it back there safely? I need to speak with Miss Aubiere alone," said Mr. Dumontier, his voice was pleasant, but strained.

"Oui Monsieur," said Rainier, he offered his arm to Jenna and escorted her from the room. Jenna left hesitantly, she was worried about where the conversation would head, with her out of the room. She wasn't sure how much of Simone's little outburst Mr. Dumontier actually believed. She was actually horrified that Simone believed Alexander, though he was very good at making her look like the guilty one.

Rainier escorted Jenna to her room. When they reached the doorway he took both of her hands in his. "Do not worry Jenna. Mr. Dumontier is a very fair man. He does not believe for a moment, that you and Alexander are having an affair. Everything will be fine. Bonsoir Mademoiselle,"

Rainier kissed her lightly on the cheek, then he turned and headed back toward the elevators. Jenna stood there and watched him walk away, still in shock over everything that had happened tonight.

As she watched Rainier walk away, Adam suddenly flung open the door of their room.

"Where the hell have you been!" he cried. "Was that Rainier?" he asked peering down the hall after him.

Jenna could suddenly feel the tears coming to her eyes again. She took a deep breath and pushed past him into the room. The TV was blaring loudly in French. She sighed, she really didn't want to repeat the entire story again to Adam. Jenna really just wanted to cry herself to sleep. This entire day had been a nightmare!

"Yes, that was Rainier, and no, I'm not having an affair with him!" Jenna cried, sarcastically. She flopped down on the sofa dramatically. Adam switched off the TV and turned to look at her very seriously.

"You need to tell me exactly what is going on! Where the hell have you been? I was worried about you! Were you with Alexander? Marika was looking for him and she's totally pissed!" cried Adam, angrily.

"If you would have just waited for me tonight I wouldn't be in this huge mess right now!" cried Jenna. She was fighting back tears and she felt as if she could hardly breathe, she was so upset!

"I *did* wait for you. I waited like twenty minutes. It couldn't possibly have taken you that long to get dressed. Everyone else was long gone. I finally decided that you had run off with Alexander. I'm not stupid, I know what's going on. The guys have been talking about it for weeks! I knew for sure when I saw him hanging around out back. I knew he was waiting for you, his little *nymphomaniac*!" snapped Adam, sarcastically. He raised his eyebrows at her, as he awaited her response.

"What? I don't even know what that is, but Alexander and I are not sleeping together," snapped Jenna.

"That's not what I heard," he snapped, rolling his eyes miserably.

"It's not what you think Adam. Alexander started the rumors. Tonight I was running late because I had to find Dion. My skate blade was loose and I was missing a screw. When I came out the back door to leave tonight, you were gone, and Alexander was waiting there to accost me!" Jenna cried, angrily.

"Did you get one?" asked Adam sarcastically.

"Get one what?"

"A screw! snapped Adam, that's what Alexander was waiting for right?"

"Adam would you please just listen to me,"cried Jenna.

"I swear, I don't know what's going on between the two of you," said Adam, shaking his head miserably.

"It's just like I've been telling you Adam. Alexander has been harassing me, he's been spreading the rumors," cried Jenna, ready to break down in tears.

"I know, I've heard them all!"

"Everything he's told the crew is lies Adam. He's been stalking me, tonight he cornered me in the alley, we were alone and he...he touched me," she cried.

"Oh my God, I can't listen to this!" cried Adam.

"Adam it was wrong, he told me lots of lies...I guess for a while I believed him. I just feel so alone here, and when you didn't wait for me, I was hurt. He held me while I cried...

Then I don't know what happened, I was scared, I was trying to get away from him. But then, oh God, I'm so stupid. I don't know why I even listen to anything that comes out of that man's mouth, it's just so easy for him to manipulate me. I feel like he's the rational voice in my irrational brain. What is wrong with me Adam?"

"Jenna just stop! I told you I don't want to hear this!" cried Adam.

"Adam please listen to me, we didn't do it. But he wanted to. Maybe at one point I wanted to, I don't know, I was just so confused, I couldn't think. I finally realized what was happening...he was playing on my emotions and fears. He told me that he loves me, but...please Adam, don't leave me alone with him, I don't want him to touch me anymore! I was trapped, I couldn't get away, I think he planned to force himself on me," cried Jenna, her voice raising involuntarily in despair.

"Wait...you think Alexander was going to rape you?" cried Adam, suddenly very upset.

"Well, he really just wants me to say yes, but that's never going to happen," said Jenna, biting her lower lip anxiously. Adam was suddenly pacing the room.

"So what does Rainier have to do with all of this?" he asked, his voice bordering on sarcasm. He was staring at Jenna very seriously.

"Alexander was waiting for me tonight. I was all alone, I couldn't get away from him...I was really scared. Then Rainier came out the back door, thank God. I didn't even realize he was still there, since the only bikes that were still in the rack were mine and Alexander's. Fortunately for me, Rainier had walked to the rink...I lied, I told him that I'd been injured, that I couldn't ride my bike back to the hotel, just so I could walk with him. I was so scared that Alexander would try something..." Jenna was fighting back tears.

"Alexander let us leave, he didn't give us any trouble. On the way back to the hotel I told Rainier everything. It took us quite a while to walk back...I was so upset. Apparently Alexander rode his bike right back to the hotel and went directly to Simone. He cried in her office and told her that the two of us had been having an affair. He told her he was upset because I had dumped him for Rainier," Adam was staring at her, in shock.

"I guess she wouldn't have believed him, but she saw me walk into the hotel with Rainier...he was trying to comfort me, but

Simone thought that Rainier and I had..."
Jenna sighed miserably. She could barely
continue, she was so upset. Adam was
watching her carefully, trying to decide if he
believed her, or not.

"So you are saying that Simone thinks that
you and Rainier are lovers."

"Yes, when Simone saw Rainier and I
together in the lobby, she pretty much
flipped out! She was calling me a slut, she
wanted to kick us out of the show..." Jenna
was ranting on.

"Shit! She wants to kick us out of the
show?" cried Adam.

"Rainier talked to Mr. Dumontier, he's
talking to Simone right now. Mr.
Dumontier asked Rainier to walk me back to
my room..." She suddenly couldn't talk any
more. She started sobbing uncontrollably.
Adam took her in his arms and held her
while she cried. He held her for quite a
while, then he smiled at her sheepishly.

"I'm sorry I didn't believe you before. I don't know what I was thinking," said Adam.

Jenna felt so safe in Adam's arms, she didn't want him to let her go. She'd been so stressed out lately. She was too upset to talk anymore. Jenna wrapped her arms around his waist tightly, not wanting him to let her go.

"Adam, I love you," she whispered nervously.

"Jenna please, not now..."

"I mean it Adam. Alexander told me I am distant and shallow, and he's right. I've been pushing you away, and I'm sorry."

"It's okay, I understand. When we got here to Paris, I think we were both a little overwhelmed. It was just too much, too soon," said Adam, suddenly feeling nervous.

"I'm sorry Adam, I pushed you away," said Jenna, looking up into his eyes earnestly.

"Jenna really, it's okay."

"No it's not. This is all my fault. Maybe you were right about our relationship, about people not buying it. Maybe if Alexander believed we were a couple, he wouldn't be pursuing me like this," sighed Jenna.

"Jenna, you can't blame yourself..."

"I was scared when you made the moves on me. I thought if we did...you know...what you wanted, it would ruin our relationship, but I'm not scared anymore."

"What?"

"Adam, you're the one I want, when I was with Alexander all I could think about was you..."

"Whoa, whoa, whoa!" cried Adam, pushing her away nervously. Over the past several weeks he had been struggling with his feelings for her, he had finally resigned himself to the fact that her and Alexander were lovers and now she was here, throwing herself at him, what the hell?

Now Jenna was stepping closer to him, wrapping her arms around his neck and kissing him. "Please don't push me away Adam, I love you."

Adam was frowning, it was not what he needed to hear right now. He nervously peeled her arms from around his neck. They were were best friends, destined to spend the entire summer together, once they crossed the line, it would be impossible to get back their easy friendship. He knew he had to distance himself from her a bit, he was worried that their screwed up emotions might get the best of them, then it would be impossible to start over.

"Jenna this is not fair...I was convinced that you and Alexander were an item. I had to force myself to get over it. Now that Alexander has you all hot and bothered, you want me to finish it. Sorry, but that whole scenario does nothing for me." snapped Adam angrily.

Jenna sighed uncomfortably and gave him a dejected glare. She did love Adam, she had always loved him, but now she was afraid that her own raging hormones had caused her to make a complete fool of herself.

"So sorry, now you know exactly how Alexander and I have *both* been feeling," said Adam, his voice was laced with sarcasm.

Jenna bit her lower lip, she suddenly felt like crying. She hadn't meant for any of this to happen.

Adam was smiling at her as if she was the most hilarious little girl he had ever met, she didn't think any of this was funny at all. She was worried about the meeting that was still going on in Simone's office and she wondered if everyone else in the company was convinced that her and Alexander were having an affair.

Jenna didn't like being the center of speculation and gossip, and she didn't like her career hanging in the balance like this. She was afraid that her and Adam were going to get kicked out of the show, and it would be all her fault.

That evening, Mr. Dumontier and Simone talked and worked everything out. When they talked to Jenna the following day, they promised her that she would have no further problems with Alexander. Even as young and naive as she was at the time, Jenna had her doubts about that. Alexander wasn't one to back down, simply because he had been told to do so. He was arrogant and felt like he was entitled to take whatever it was he wanted. Unfortunately what he wanted, was her...

How was she to know, that things were only going to get worse?

CHAPTER TWENTY TWO

Alexander returned to his room feeling strangely exhilarated. He had been so close tonight. Jenna had writhed in his arms, her body responding to his touch with a passion he had only dreamed about. He felt as if their fate was sealed. He was destined to make love to this woman. She was destined to become pregnant with his child. When Jenna was finally carrying his child, there was no way Marika's family could force him to marry her.

He unlocked the door to his room expecting Marika to be fast asleep, instead she was waiting for him. It was well after midnight, but apparently Marika knew exactly what was going on, and she was not happy.

"Where have you been? It is late," she snapped, when she saw him standing there in the doorway.

"I was out," said Alexander. He was not in the mood to deal with Marika. He wanted to go to sleep and dream that he had actually finished his deed.

"Did you do it?"

"Did I do what?"cried Alexander, now thoroughly irritated.

"Did you fuck her?"

"No."

"Why not?"

"Maybe I want our first time to perfect," seethed Alexander.

Marika laughed an evil callous laugh. "Perfect?"

"Just because *you* are a cold frigid bitch doesn't mean she has to hate the thought of my touch," snapped Alexander.

"You were not the only one that was forced into this betrothal Alexander. Perhaps I just love someone else," snapped Marika.

"Then maybe you should follow your destiny and be with this man. I know I was not your first. This man you love, was he your first?"

Marika nodded in embarrassment.

"Why are you with me, when obviously you love someone else?"

"I have to marry you Alexander. I can never be with the man I love."

"I do not understand, why not?"

"The man is my cousin," whispered Marika quietly.

Jean Marie Stanberry

CHAPTER TWENTY THREE

The following night was their last night in Paris. The Theater Company was hosting a huge catered dinner for the entire cast and crew as a celebration to kick off the rest of their European tour. The party was at a charming little cafe on the Seine, just a few short blocks from their hotel.

Alexander had big plans for their last night in Paris. He wasn't sure why Jenna was still being so resistant to him, it was obvious her body wanted him. In fact, her response to his touch had turned him on even more. It was all he really wanted, a passionate woman who would enjoy sex as much as he did.

Unfortunately, he had gotten a little out of control last night. He was afraid he might have frightened Jenna, he would apologize for trying to force himself on her and tell her that he loved her, he couldn't help it.

He had been thinking a lot about their situation. Jenna needed him as much as he needed her. When they finished their tour with the company, why would she possibly want to go home to her parents? It was obvious they didn't care for her at all. They had created a huge scam just to be rid of her for the entire summer, leaving their young daughter to basically fend for herself in Europe. What kind of parents did that?

He himself was facing marriage to a woman he did not love, a woman he could barely tolerate. If Jenna were to "accidentally" get pregnant with his child, there would be no way Marika's parents would be able to force him to marry her. He had finally decided, the sooner Jenna was carrying his child, the better. He had gotten a taste of freedom while he was here in Paris and there was no way now he could go back to the Soviet Union and his shabby little flat on the 12th floor.

He wanted to be an American citizen, he would be the envy of everyone, with his leggy blonde wife with the enchanting smile. He would have his own house and their children could play in the backyard, they could have a puppy. They would go on wonderful vacations to Paris and London and New York, it would be perfect.

He couldn't wait to make Jenna his wife, he didn't have a clue as to why she was being so difficult.

Unfortunately, dinner that night turned out to be a complete fiasco. Alexander was seated with the "stars" at the front of the cafe, wedged between Marika and Maria Gastineau, an alcoholic, bulimic mess of a woman who seemed to have her heart set on seducing him.

Months ago he would have probably took her up on her sly invitation, but now she just didn't appeal to him. She was French and quite beautiful, but Alexander had no desire to spend any time alone with Marina. She was the embodiment of the phrase "rode hard and put away wet".

Jenna was seated in the back corner of the cramped cafe, she had ended up far from Alexander, seated in between Adam and Luc Dupre. Luc Dupre had been invited to their party mainly because he was one of the sons of the man who owned the chain of hotels the company stayed in while they were in France.

Alexander was not happy about the seating arrangements. He just wanted to be near Jenna and he wanted Jenna far from Dupre. The man was way too good looking and he seemed to be quite infatuated with Jenna, which only made Alexander more restless and agitated.

Alexander almost growled when he snuck a look at them. That ass Luc Dupre was busy flirting with his future fiancee. He resisted the urge to go back there and say something to him, he didn't want to cause a scene their last night in Paris. It seemed to be fine, Jenna was conversing politely with him, but it was obvious that she was not interested in Luc Dupre.

Alexander was relieved, but the next time his eyes drifted to their table in the back of the cafe, Dupre had moved his chair even closer to Jenna and he had his arm draped familiarly across the back of her chair.

Alexander took a slow deep breath in an effort to get his anger under control, this man had a lot of nerve! The more he watched them together the angrier he got. As the night went on, they seemed to be really hitting it off.

Finally, he could take it no more, his heart was aching. He loved Jenna, why was she laughing and smiling at Dupre? Why was she letting him sit so close? Why was she smiling into his eyes like that? He was obviously completely enchanted with her, but Jenna...Jenna was his! Alexander walked over to her table and slid up behind her chair.

"You look so beautiful tonight, I've missed you. Why don't you ditch this loser and come find me later," he whispered in her ear.

"I don't think so," snapped Jenna, flashing him a seething glare.

Alexander's heart was suddenly filled with pain. Why was she acting like this? He flashed her a confident smile before he headed back to his own table, even though his heart suddenly felt like it had been trampled on. Adam and Dupre were both glaring at him.

"What did he say?" asked Adam.

"Nothing, he's lost his freaking mind," snapped Jenna, she was nervously watching Alexander walk away.

"Is he bothering you?" asked Luc Dupre, in his thick French accent.

"I'm not sure *bothering* is the correct word," said Jenna, rolling her eyes.

Alexander didn't hear what transpired after that, he was already too far away and the room was too loud with many conversations. He didn't care what Jenna said, he had already planted the seed in Dupre's head that he had designs on Jenna.

He returned to his table and sat down, Marika was already glaring at him with narrowed eyes.

"What are you planning with de slut?" she seethed.

"None of your business," snapped Alexander, unable to take his eyes off the party at the table he had just left.

"I told you, she is trouble. She is stupid, she will be pregnant the first time you do it and then you will be stuck."

"That's exactly what I'm counting on," said Alexander, flashing her an evil smile.

"That is what you want, to get the little American slut pregnant? Why?"

"Why not? She is attractive and talented. If we are even half as compatible in the bedroom as we are on the ice, I could have a new wife *and* a new partner. God knows you and I are not compatible in the bedroom."

"Sex is not everything, you and I are World Champions and Olympic gold medalists together, do you really want to ruin what the two of us have together?"

"I am not happy and I doubt you are happy either. Why should we put off the inevitable when it is obvious we are not compatible?" said Alexander, shrugging slightly.

"You are a moron, it will not be the fairytale you think Alexander. Jenna Bruce is nothing but a child and her family is a bigger mess than your own, do you really see any sort of a future with her?"

"Of course I do. She may be young, but she is passionate, about her skating career and her life, we are perfect for each other," said Alexander.

"If you feel that way you had better get in line, it looks as if the Frenchman is determined to have her first, and she seems much more receptive to him than she does to you," said Marika, flashing him a mocking grin.

Alexander's eyes drifted over to the table where Jenna sat with Luc Dupre. Adam had given up and was talking to someone else. But Dupre had moved in for the kill, he had moved his body so close to Jenna's their knees were touching. Alexander's face turned steely with anger as he saw Luc Dupre smiling into Jenna's eyes. She didn't seem to mind his close proximity at all as he reached up and brushed a stray lock of hair off of her face.

Alexander felt his heart constrict with anger. What was wrong with her? She was actually flirting back. He narrowed his eyes as he saw Jenna laughing at something Dupre had said and smiling into his eyes with adoration.

Marika laughed a loud, callous laugh when she saw Alexander's angry expression. "Well she might be pregnant by morning, but not with *your* baby I fear."

"Shut up," snapped Alexander, unable to take his eyes off the scene that was unfolding at the table across the cafe.

"My poor Alexander, I really feel for you. I do believe she wants him as much as he wants her. Oh look, he's pouring her a glass of champagne, I believe her fate is sealed. I guess you my dear, are just out of luck," crooned Marika, flashing him a smug smile.

Alexander was completely consumed with a strange mixture of anger and desire. It took every ounce of self restraint he had in his body to remain at his table and finish his dinner, when he really wanted to spirit Jenna out of that restaurant and get her far away from Luc Dupre.

Alexander took a long sip of his wine. Why was she flirting with him like that? As the night wore on, he couldn't take his eyes off the two of them. Dupre seemed to be quite enamored with her and Jenna was smiling coyly and laughing at all his lame stories. It truly did seem that Jenna might leave with Luc Dupre at the end of the evening.

How could she flirt with Dupre, when she loved him? Alexander was sure she loved him.

Marika was completely disgusted with him, he had been so consumed by jealously he could do nothing but stare blankly at Jenna and Dupre. Marika had finally left the party with friends when he refused to even speak to her. She had enjoyed teasing him about his failure, but he had eventually tuned her out, all his attention was focused on Jenna and Luc.

Alexander was getting more and more agitated as the night went on. He was angry and he was feeling rejected. His heart was filled with sorrow. He had started drinking in an effort to numb his broken heart. When he had polished off the last of the bottle of wine on the table, he got up and headed out of the cafe.

He staggered out to the street and lit a cigarette. He needed to think, to form a plan. His head was spinning a bit from the wine, but the cool air felt refreshing. His heart was aching, he had been trying to convince Jenna of his love for her, but for some reason she was resisting him.

Why was she flirting with Dupre like that? What could she possibly see in him? Did she really desire Dupre, or was she trying to make him jealous? Of course, that had to be it, thought Alexander as he ambled restlessly through the dark streets of Paris.

Luc Dupre was nothing but a spoiled French playboy, what could Jenna possibly see in him? He on the other hand, was a star, an Olympic gold medalist. Jenna was young and insecure, she was trying to prove to him that she was attractive to other men, it was nothing but a silly game.

As Alexander walked along, a light rain began to fall. He pulled the collar of his jacket up around his neck and quickened his pace a bit. He hated the way women played games, they did whatever they could just to get attention, it was infuriating.

He had so hoped to spend the evening alone with Jenna, now it seemed as if she might leave the party with the Frenchman. Alexander racked his brain to come up with a plan.

He had finally arrived back at the hotel. His room was dark and quiet. He walked over to the console just inside the door and poured himself a vodka. He was still angry that Jenna was playing games with him. How dare she lead him on like that and then flirt with Dupre, right in front of him like that.

He looked down to see his vodka glass was once again empty so he poured himself another. He heard the ding of the elevator as it stopped at his floor. He ran over to the door and flung it open to see if it was Jenna.

Damn, it was a housekeeper. Maybe Jenna wouldn't be back at all. What if Dupre had plied her with champagne and took her back to his place? What if he was making love to her right now? Alexander picked up a vase of fresh flowers and flung them across the room. The vase hit the wall and broke with a crash.

Alexander was shaking with rage, he was pacing the room nervously and his brain seemed to be spinning in so many different directions he couldn't form a complete thought. He walked over to the window and looked out over Paris as he took a long sip of his vodka.

He needed to calm himself down and formulate a plan, something he could never do in this agitated stare. He took another long sip of his vodka, hoping the alcohol could calm his fragile nerves.

When Jenna got back to the hotel he would invite her to his room, maybe he would be able to entice her into having a drink with him. He had bought champagne as a celebration of their last night in Paris. With any luck she would already be semi intoxicated, thanks to Luc Dupre. If she was a bit buzzed from the alcohol, that would make it that much easier to seduce her.

At least Adam wouldn't be leaving the party any time soon. Alexander already formulated a plan to keep him out of the way. It had been amazingly cheap to line up two prostitutes to keep him busy for the rest of the night.

Alexander stood in front of the mirror in the entry and looked at his reflection. He looked good, what woman would be able to resist him? He took off his shirt and flexed his muscles admiring the way he looked in the mirror.

If he came to the door with no shirt on, she might be intrigued, he thought...no maybe naked, he thought with a smile.

No, that might scare her, she was young and inexperienced, he didn't want her to run away screaming. She was inexperienced but she was curious, if he could just arouse her curiosity somehow...

The elevator dinged again, Alexander ran over and flung the door open to see if it was Jenna. He startled the bellman, who was bringing a stack of packages up to the room across the hall.

"Sorry," said Alexander, sheepishly closing the door.

He took a deep breath, he needed to settle down, he was *way* too keyed up, he needed to think, to plan what he was going to do when Jenna got here.

He poured another glass of vodka to calm his nerves. He paced the room trying to calm himself, he just felt jumpy, on edge.

He walked over to the mirror and looked at his reflection again. Tonight was the night, if he couldn't romance her in Paris it was probably never going to happen. It had been many weeks now and he had been so close last night. Her body had wanted him, but still she had pushed him away. He was convinced she was too young and too naive to know what she needed.

Alexander suddenly had an idea, he walked into the bathroom and took one of the big fluffy towels off the shelf. He slid off his pants and shorts and wrapped the towel around his waist, admiring his reflection in the mirror. Yes, this was the look. It made his muscular torso and arms look magnificent. Yes, he thought, when Jenna saw him, there would be no way she would ever refuse him.

He got hard just thinking about the way Jenna had shuddered in his arms. She was beautiful, passionate and actually capable of having an orgasm, he couldn't wait for them to come as one. He began pacing the room nervously once again, she should have been here by now. What if Dupre had taken her home with him?

Alexander shook the idea from his head, that would be preposterous. She was perfect for him, they were meant to be together.

He picked up the bottle of champagne that was sitting on the marble topped table in the entry. He wasn't a fan of champagne, but maybe he could persuade Jenna to drink some, it might loosen her inhibitions a bit.

The elevator dinged once again and Alexander bolted for the door. It was Jenna...

Jean Marie Stanberry

CHAPTER TWENTY FOUR

It was their last night in Paris, at dinner, it seemed, there were way too many people crammed into the smallish cafe. Jenna was seated in a cramped corner near the back of the cafe between Adam, and a very attractive gentleman who claimed to be the owner of their hotel.

Jenna gave the gentleman her standard fake smile, when he told her that. She seriously doubted that this man could be the owner of their hotel. It seemed as if he couldn't be much older than Adam and he was an impossible flirt. Jenna had seen him many evenings at the hotel, working at the front desk. He always seemed to be watching her from afar. His name was Luc Dupre, and he seemed to want to monopolize her attention during every moment of dinner.

Mr. Dupre was very charming, Jenna had to give him that much. He was tall and athletic looking, and he had these incredible, electric blue eyes that caught her attention right away. Though Jenna thought he was completely gorgeous, though she was relatively sure she really wasn't interested in dating some spoiled rich, Frenchman. Of course officially, she couldn't date anyone. As far as the outside world knew, Jenna and Adam were a married couple.

As the evening wore on, sitting between Luc and Adam had begun to wear on Jenna's fragile nerves. They were both vying for her attention and it was becoming quite tiresome.

Luc had spent most of the evening with his arm draped familiarly over the back of her chair, which made her quite uncomfortable, and seemed to infuriate Adam. He had also reached out and taken her hand several times, in an attempt to kiss it, but she managed to snatch it from his grip before he was able to lift it to his lips. Jenna didn't want him to have any indication she might be interested in spending any time with him after dinner. She already had one unwelcome stalker too many!

When dinner was almost over, Jenna had nearly reached her limit with Mr. Dupre's unwelcome flirting. She was prepared to tell him "Bonsoir", when Alexander suddenly slid up behind her chair and whispered seductively in her ear.

Jenna shuddered and resisted the urge to roll her eyes as he slipped away. Alexander did not seem to realize, hell would freeze over, before she would *ever* go looking for him. The very thought of being anywhere near him sent a cold shiver down her spine!

Jenna decided she would turn all her attention to Mr. Dupre. She reasoned that maybe if Alexander saw her flirting with Luc, he would get the clue that she was not interested in him in the least. Luc was attractive and he seemed to be a nice enough guy. He was very smart and they actually seemed to have quite a bit in common. He seemed to be completely delighted by Jenna's sudden, undivided attention.

Jenna couldn't help but feel a little bit guilty for shamelessly flirting with him like that, but she would be leaving for Lyon in the morning, she reasoned, she would probably never see Mr. Dupre again.

The mere fact that she was smiling at him and laughing at his lame jokes had caused Luc Dupre to scoot his chair even closer to Jenna's. He was very charming and he had the most amazing eyes Jenna had ever seen, she couldn't help but be a bit caught up in the spell he seemed to be casting over her.

He had poured her a champagne, Jenna wasn't sure she should drink it. Alexander wasn't far away, and he hadn't taken his eyes off of her all night. She didn't want to encounter him later, in an impaired state.

She had only meant to take a small sip, but before long she had drank the entire glass and Luc Dupre had poured her another. Someone was taking snapshots and Adam was calling to her to come over and get in the picture. When she stood up, she almost slid back down into her chair she was so light headed.

After the impromptu photo session ended, Jenna returned to the table. Much to her surprise, Luc Dupre pulled her onto his lap and kissed her. In her slightly drunken state Jenna didn't kiss him back, but she didn't push him away either. She was too shocked.

He looked deeply into her eyes and smiled at her. Jenna had to look away quickly, she was panicking. What had she done?

Obviously Luc Dupre had feelings for her, she was suddenly feeling incredibly guilty for leading him on the way she had.

Jenna was beginning to wonder what was wrong with her. Here she was sitting in the lap of a man she barely knew, when she was supposedly married to Adam. To top things off, Alexander who had recently proclaimed his love for her, was glaring angrily at her from across the room. This entire night had turned out to be a complete fiasco!

Just after midnight, Jenna could feel her body seriously winding down. The entire company had spent the day sightseeing and they would be catching the train for Lyon at 6 am, she knew she needed to get some sleep.

Luc had already reluctantly bid her Bonsoir, earlier in the evening, as he had commitments to attend to and couldn't stay. She was glancing around casually for Adam, to see if he was ready to leave.

Jenna could see him standing near the back of the cafe, he had two gorgeous women draped on either arm and they were involved in some deep conversation. He was laughing and talking animatedly, and the women looked quite entertained by whatever amusing story he was telling them. He certainly didn't look ready to leave!

Jenna sighed, she couldn't really pull him away from his little fan club, he looked like he was having a fabulous time. She really didn't want to make Adam leave, just because she was ready to leave. Jenna already felt bad that Adam had to spend much of his time babysitting her. She didn't want him to be resentful of her, he was her best friend and she loved him.

After Jenna had scanned the room and decided that there was no one else around she could walk back to the hotel with, she finally decided to just walk back alone. She wasn't worried, it was a beautiful night and it was relatively safe to be walking alone in this district of Paris, at this hour.

Jenna walked the few short blocks alone. She strolled along leisurely and admired the lights shining on the Seine and the music that was drifting out of all the little clubs and cafes along the way.

Jenna smiled as she heard the laughter and conversations drifting out of the clubs she passed. There were lovers strolling along the sidewalks in the cloud dappled moonlight. An old man passed her walking a tiny dog, he was whistling cheerfully and he gave her a friendly nod as they passed. Jenna was smiling when she finally climbed the stairs of her hotel. She was definitely going to miss Paris. It truly was, the most charming city in the world!

It was late and the hotel lobby was nearly deserted. Jenna rode the elevator up to the fourth floor, blissfully tired and alone in her thoughts. She ambled slowly down the hallway, distractedly digging in her purse for her room key. When she was halfway to her room, she heard a Russian tinged voice call out her name.

Jenna looked up, startled to see Alexander standing there in the doorway of his hotel room. He was smiling seductively at her, and he looked as if he had been expecting her to come along at any moment. Jenna glared at him and rolled her eyes disgustedly.

"Hello Jenna. All alone? Come celebrate our last night in Paris with me," he told her, flashing her a sly smile.

Jenna narrowed her eyes at him. He was standing there, posed seductively in the doorway. Jenna grimaced as she realized he was completely naked, except for a towel around his waist. He was obviously quite intoxicated as he stood there smiling at her, holding a bottle of champagne.

Jenna cringed and looked away, she thought he looked like a Yeti standing there, he was so big and hairy. She wanted to tell him he was so disgusting, there was no way she would ever even consider spending the night with him, but she thought it was best to try to get along. Jenna and Alexander had a professional relationship to maintain. The two of them had to work together every single day, Jenna thought it was best that she not completely piss him off.

She resisted the urge to roll her eyes, then she gave him her best fake smile. Maybe if he thought she wasn't really alone, if he believed that Adam was right behind her, he would back off...he was obviously very drunk.

"Actually, I'm not alone. Adam will be up in just a moment. I'm tired, I really just want to go to bed," she said, then she cringed and cursed herself when she thought of how Alexander might interpret her own words. It was the wrong thing to say to a horny toad like him.

"Then I will take you to bed with me. It will be good, you will see," he said, flashing her another seductive smile. He almost laughed out loud, Adam would not be right along, he had two pre paid prostitutes who had been instructed to keep him occupied and do whatever he wanted.

Jenna just wanted to scream at him! He just didn't get it. "No Alexander, I'm not interested! You've been told to stay away from me," she snapped nervously.

Jenna shook her head miserably and continued to walk toward her room with as much confidence as she could exude. She was now ruing her decision to have a glass of champagne with Luc Dupre, she was still feeling a bit tipsy and she didn't want Alexander to have any indication that she might be a bit impaired.

"Please my darling. I wanted to apologize for my bad behavior last night. You are not ready to take our relationship to the next level, I am sorry I tried to rush you."

At this point, Jenna was beginning to panic a little bit. Adam would not be right along. She was suddenly painfully aware, that it could be a very long time before Adam returned to their room.

To make matters worse, this entire block of rooms was rented by the Theater Company, most of the other skaters were still out for the evening. Of course, they were all older than her, so most of them had gone out for the evening, to clubs that had dancing. Jenna was realizing miserably, if Alexander pushed her into a confrontation, she would most likely be forced to face him all alone...the entire floor was most likely deserted.

"You've forgotten one key point Alexander. You and I are not *in* a relationship. I'm going to my room, Adam will be right along," she snapped nervously.

"Adam is not coming," seethed Alexander, in a harsh tone that caused Jenna to shiver and stop in her tracks. She turned around slowly and glared at him.

"What?"

"I have made arrangements for his time to be otherwise occupied. I do not believe he will be back for quite some time," Alexander smiled, as Jenna slowly met his eyes.

"What have you done?" cried Jenna, she was suddenly afraid that he had done something sinister to Adam.

"Do not worry about your *husband*, he is perfectly fine. I knew if I wanted to spend any time with you, I must divert his attention from you, it was easy enough.

I know that American guys only want to get laid. I arranged a sure thing for him, a trio, or threesome, as you Americans say. The two women I hired, will keep him quite satisfied for the rest of the night, since it seems that any more, he can scarcely let you out of his sight," said Alexander, flashing her a wicked smile. Jenna was staring at him in shock as she realized that Alexander, had once again, set her up. She shivered imperceptibly as his words finally sunk in.

"I have been planning this, our last night in Paris together, all day. I wanted it to be perfect. I had been a bit worried that the annoying Frenchman would ruin everything and take you home with him tonight. He was so enchanted with you. I was afraid he would impress you with his expensive sports car and whisk you away for the rest of the evening. Fortunately, I do believe he was a bit put off when he finally realized how young you are. Believe it or not, your tender age does not bother me at all. Besides, I can tell you want me as badly as I want you," Alexander went on, flashing her a suggestive smile. Jenna grimaced distastefully.

"I don't want you Alexander. Leave me alone!" Jenna scowled angrily. Her heart was suddenly pounding in fear at the dark realization that she was, once again, alone with Alexander.

"I do not believe you. The last time we were together you melted in my arms. I felt you shudder with pleasure," he crooned, leering at her suggestively.

"I told you, that was a mistake! I've never been touched like that and..." Jenna hesitated, she wasn't sure what she had meant to say to him, but she was sure he would turn it around to suit himself anyway.

"How can something so wonderful be a mistake? You cannot deny it, your body wants me, but your head is confused Come in my sweet Jenna, let me kiss you some more," said Alexander smiling and bowing to her regally. Urging her to enter his room.

"No Alexander!" she snapped, angrily.

He smiled and shook his head, suddenly amused. "Why do you make this so difficult for me? You want to tease me? Make me beg? Please darling, I promise, this time will be even better than the last."

Jenna was standing there staring him down, suddenly shaking with a strange combination of fear and rage. She was struggling inwardly to calm herself. She didn't want Alexander to realize how scared she was, she was sure that he would somehow use her fear against her.

"I know exactly what is going on. I saw you with the Frenchman, Luc Dupre. I saw the way you were looking at him, flirting with him. This Frenchman, you desire him do you not?"

"Alexander just leave me alone," snapped Jenna. Alexander was bordering on agitation and she just wanted to get back to the safety of her room.

"Yes, that is it. It is the rich playboy you want. I see, now Alexander is not good enough for you. Of course I understand, he is a bit younger, more polished. Perhaps more your type, at least socially. I imagine most women would find him quite attractive, but if you will allow me, I will show you that I can give you more. I believe you will appreciate the fact, that size does matter," said Alexander, raising his eyebrows suggestively at her.

Jenna gave him her best look of disgust. She had a moment of panic, what if Alexander followed her to her room?

Jenna stood there for a moment her brain reeling with indecision, she thought about heading back to the elevators, but she decided it would be safer to head toward her room. She certainly didn't want to be alone in the elevator with him. Besides, he'd obviously been drinking and he was only wearing a towel. She was pretty sure he would never follow her all the way down the hall to her room. She was almost certain he was much too plowed to make it that far anyway.

"Do yourself a favor and just sleep it off Alexander," she called to him as she turned abruptly and headed for her room.

"You will be sorry!" he called down the hall after her.

Jenna just waved to him over her shoulder and continued down the hall to her room. She was suddenly spooked by his odd demeanor. She was so intimidated right now, her pace had at least doubled, in her haste to get back to her room.

She could almost feel the hair on the back of her neck standing up, as she hurriedly fumbled with her key to open the door of her hotel room.

Alexander watched as Jenna walked away, she seemed confident enough, but he could tell she was on edge. His own head was spinning from the combination of his own overwhelming desire for her and the large amount of alcohol he'd consumed which seemed to be suppressing the rational part of his brain. He'd tried to apologize and she had rudely blown him off, he was suddenly very angry. Why was she being such a cold hearted bitch?

Jenna's heart was suddenly pounding with anxiety, and an overwhelming sense of impending doom. Her worst fears were realized as she rushed to close the door behind her. She was knocked violently to the ground by the door being flung open. Alexander had kicked it in, before she managed to lock it behind her.

He stormed into the room, panting and angry. He was angry, he was tired of playing these childish games. Jenna didn't seem to be taking him seriously, he had a plan, a plan for them to be together. She was ruining everything!

His heart was pounding with rage as he closed the door behind him and locked it with a resounding click. As he turned around and saw her sprawled on the floor, her shock with the situation was evident. Alexander couldn't help it, a diabolical smile was slowly crossing his face. Jenna had been controlling him, but she was not going to be in control anymore. He was now in control and the feeling was amazing.

Jenna's heart nearly stopped when she looked up and saw him standing there, his eyes raking over her cooly.

Jenna was still sprawled on the floor, slightly disorientated by how quickly he'd forced his way into the room. She could feel her heart suddenly accelerating in fear, and she began crawling backwards, in a desperate attempt to get away from him.

"Let us just get one thing straight Miss Bruce, you do not tell me no, ever! Do you understand? I am done playing games with you," he snarled angrily. He strode over to her, reached down and jerked her up from the floor.

Jenna was shaking uncontrollably as he pulled her to her feet. She managed to scream, despite the fact that she was so scared, she could barely pull any air into her lungs.

Alexander jerked her into his arms and clamped his hand over her mouth roughly. He was almost sure there was no one nearby, but he didn't want any concerned citizens calling the police, at least not till he was finished with her.

Jenna was frightened, Alexander was furious. Jenna was struggling to get free from his arms, but in an instant he had taken the champagne bottle he still held in his hand, and broke it on the entry table.

He pulled her forcibly against his body with his other arm so he could whisper in her ear. His Russian tinged voice was silky and calm. A shiver ran down Jenna's spine as she felt him pressing the sharp edge of the broken champagne bottle to her neck. She choked back a sob and willed herself to stay strong and not break down crying. She would not go down without a fight.

"You will behave yourself, and do exactly as I say. One more sound out of you and I will slit your throat, so help me God," he seethed, pressing the glass even tighter, against her throat.

Jenna struggled to breathe as the adrenaline surged through her body, raising her heart rate alarmingly high and causing her to feel hot and dizzy. Alexander's strong arms were holding her against his body like a prisoner, her body was tensed against his and suddenly, she was too scared to even breathe.

Jenna was frozen in fear, she could feel the sharp edge of the glass, pressed against the skin of her neck by Alexander's, not so steady hand. She felt dizzy, she'd been holding her breath anxiously, as she was afraid to move at all.

"Please Alexander, don't do this. You're a World Champion and Olympic gold medalist, is this really how you want to be remembered by your fans? Desperate and out of control?" she whispered.

Alexander was completely plowed, she feared one false move, and Alexander might accidentally slit her throat. He was obviously completely intoxicated and desperate, she was frightened and trembling, it was a dangerous combination.

"My darling Jenna, I am very much in control at at the moment. I have endured enough of your rejection, your lies, and your games. You are not married to Smyth as you claimed to be, you speak of a boyfriend, I doubt even exists, even your own parents want nothing to do with you. You truly have no one. Why must you keep putting me off, when you know you will give in to me eventually?" he whispered into her ear.

"I will never give in to you," seethed Jenna.

"Really? Then there is truly no reason for us to wait another moment, is there? seethed Alexander, turning her around and glaring into her eyes.

"Are you really that stupid Alexander, do you think you can rape me and actually get away with it?" snapped Jenna. She thought if she could convey to him how despicable that would be, he would back off.

Alexander chuckled a bit. She was still harping on that sexual harassment bullshit. Did she not realize? The entire cast thought that they were lovers, he could do what he wanted, what he needed so badly and no one would even care!

"Admit it Jenna, we were meant to be together. My touch aroused you, I felt your climax. It was so beautiful," he whispered into her ear, his hot breath sent another icy shiver down her spine.

"Alexander, I wasn't lying, I have a boyfriend, and you have Marika," Jenna breathed, her heart seemed to be thundering in her ears. She was struggling, uselessly, to calm herself.

"Enough of this talk. I have waited many weeks. I do not want to wait any longer," seethed Alexander. All this talking was making his head spin. The proximity of her body was making him so hot he could barely stand it.

"Just let me go Alexander, please..." Jenna's voice was full of desperation, it seemed to be fading away to nothing.

"I felt your desire for me...you cannot deny it. Tonight darling, we will come as one," he whispered into her ear.

Alexander's hand was still at her throat, pressing the glass firmly, reminding her that no matter what she said, it was Alexander who was in control. Jenna knew she could never overpower him, she could only try to reason with him. At this point he seemed past reason. Jenna's legs were weak and her head was spinning with thoughts of what Alexander planned to do to her.

"Alexander, this is all a mistake. You are very drunk, just leave now and I promise I won't tell anyone...we can forget all about this," whispered Jenna, she willed her voice to be strong, but when the words left her mouth, they were nothing but a desperate whisper.

Alexander chuckled, a strange evil laugh. "If I could leave, I would, but my body will no longer let me ignore what it needs so badly," he whispered into her ear, in his silky, calm voice. "I have told you before what I want, it is time for you to stop teasing me, and give it to me."

"I have not been teasing you," Jenna whispered angrily. She shrank away in disgust as his stale breath washed across her face, he smelled of vodka and cigarettes.

"Oh you teased me, with those seductive glances, and those legs...and when you kissed me...I could only dream that every inch of your body tasted as sweet as your lips," said Alexander, his throaty voice seemed to caress the words. Jenna was still struggling to get free of his arms. He was holding her roughly, like a prisoner. Jenna's panic was increasing by the moment.

"Alexander, I did not kiss you! You forced yourself on me!" cried Jenna, her voice shaking with the tears she could barely suppress, this was a nightmare!

"I cannot help what I feel, every day we are on the ice together, our bodies touching intimately, with nothing but the thin fabric between us, our bodies longing to be joined together..."

"Alexander, please get out of my room, you are completely delusional!"

"I believe it is you, who is delusional...I felt your desire, we are destined to be together. You are destined to be my wife and have my babies. They will be such beautiful babies, with stunning blue eyes, like their mommy,"crooned Alexander.

"Alexander, I don't want babies. I'm too young, my career has just begun," breathed Jenna.

Alexander laughed a strange drunken laugh. "Perhaps just one for now then. Think about it, I can become an American citizen, you and I can be partners on the ice as well. We mesh so well on the ice, I have no doubt that we will be perfect together in the bedroom as well. Face it Jenna, you want my love...you need it."

"Alexander, I'm sorry I kissed you, that was a mistake, this is all a mistake..." breathed Jenna, her fear was consuming her, she was realizing Alexander would never leave until he got what he had come for.

Alexander looked into her eyes. Why did she insist that this was all a mistake. He loved her, she would love him too, if she would only give him a chance. She was making him angry, she was going to need a bit more persuading.

If Jenna wanted to play mind games, then so be it, thought Alexander. He would show her exactly who was in charge, and he would get his way. He would not make love to her until she agreed, if she told him yes, it could not possibly be considered rape.

"Regardless, I have told you I am done waiting, you can make this easy, or you can make it hard, just remember, I am in charge here," with that, he took the broken champagne bottle and pressed the glass into the skin of her neck, to make his point.

Jenna winced as she felt the glass pierce her skin, soon, she could feel the blood trickling down her neck, in a tiny river of red. She could feel the warmth of it, as it flowed from her body and soaked through the front of her dress.

Jenna choked back a sob and fought to maintain her composure, having a complete breakdown would not help matters at all.

"Do not cry my darling Jenna, I do not wish to hurt you. Do not fight me, just relax and let me do what I want. I think you might enjoy it," Alexander breathed seductively into her ear, as he pulled her tightly against his body and molded his pelvis to hers, making sure she could feel the evidence of his arousal.

"Alexander...no..."breathed Jenna, she could barely speak and she was fighting tears.

"Do you feel why you must not tell me no?" he snarled, grinding his pelvis against her. Then he threw her down on the bed angrily.

Jenna bounced roughly across the bed, then she rolled off the other side, in a clumsy attempt to escape. Unfortunately, her options were limited, she could only head for the door, or the balcony. Alexander was a big guy, he could cross the large room in just five steps. It turned out, he was not quite as inebriated as she had originally thought. Perhaps it had all been an act, in an effort to get her to let her guard down. Jenna felt stupid for falling right into his little set-up.

Her clumsy attempt to escape had only infuriated Alexander more. Jenna had made it just two steps to the door before he had caught her in his arms again. His face was red and he was literally snarling at her as he crushed his massive arms around her.

"You cannot escape Jenna, God help me, I will kill you if you try again," he snapped, as he flung her back onto the bed. Jenna's mind was racing desperately and Alexander was towering over her completely naked, as the towel he had been wearing, was now long gone.

Jenna considered her options. Alexander was fast, she was sure she could never make it to the door. Jumping off the balcony would mean crashing four stories to the sidewalk below, that would mean multiple broken bones, though that almost seemed like a better option than taking her chances here, with Alexander.

Jenna was struggling to breathe, Alexander had now moved to the foot of the bed, he was prowling toward her slowly, like a predator moving toward his prey. Jenna swallowed convulsively as she tried to concentrate and come up with a plan. Her eyes drifted slowly to the balcony door.

"You can try it, but I promise you will never make it," crooned Alexander, flashing her an amused smile. Jenna's heart faltered as she realized he still had the champagne bottle weapon in his hand. Jenna watched numbly as he wiped her blood carelessly, on the bedspread.

Alexander was climbing on top of her, straddling her, his powerful knees were soon locked on her hips. He wanted to make sure she could not make another break for the door.

"Please Alexander, don't do this. When Simone finds out what you've done, she will kick you and Marika out of the show," Jenna gasped, her voice was barely a desperate whisper, she was so scared. She didn't know why she was trying to reason with Alexander, it was obvious, he was well past reason at this point.

"You will shut up and give yourself to me now!" he snarled, leaning over her and smiling darkly into her eyes. Jenna looked away, she was trying to evade the panic that was washing over her body. Alexander was completely out of control.

"I will never give myself to you," seethed Jenna. It was an empty threat, she couldn't even move at the moment, his knees were locked on her hips and his hands gripped her wrists so tightly, she felt as if the circulation was being cut off.

Alexander released her wrists and sat up, assessing her carefully for a few seconds. An evil smile crossed his face and he held the broken champagne bottle out in front of her face. Jenna drew in an anxious breath as he pressed the jagged glass of the broken champagne bottle to her neck again, and emotionlessly watched her blood flow as he drew the makeshift blade across the skin of the opposite side of her neck.

"I do not like the word...never..." he seethed, his voice was so stern and cold, Jenna's heart was pounding with anxiety. This was it. Alexander had completely lost his mind...he was going to kill her.

Jenna shuddered brokenly, as she felt the warmth of her own blood running down her neck. She knew at that moment, that this was more than a drunken misunderstanding. Alexander was really going to kill her. Alexander was systematically torturing her...controlling her.

This was like a nightmare her body refused to wake up from, her entire body was trembling, and she was desperately trying to avoid surrendering to the hysteria that was threatening to overtake her body.

She was loosing the will to fight, the pain in her wrists was searing. Alexander was leaning over her, staring into her eyes with an arrogant, evil smile. Jenna closed her eyes so she wouldn't have to see him towering over her like that. She was stunned when he suddenly slapped her face so hard, she was sure the imprint of his hand was left behind on her cheek.

"Open your eyes and look at me. I want you to see how large I am. See that...more like a bull than a man," he grunted.

Jenna opened her eyes and gave him her best look of disgust. "You're completely disgusting," she seethed.

"You said nothing of the sort, when I had you moaning with pleasure yesterday, you selfish slut. Do you not realize? I have already established us as lovers with the rest of the cast, you can tell Simone and the rest of the cast any lame story you want, but they will never believe you. If I do what I want tonight, no one will care. You can call the police, but they will never believe that you didn't want it," Alexander told her, emotionlessly.

"I'm a minor Alexander, just fifteen years old," Jenna managed to breathe.

"Yes, you are just fifteen, but would you dare tell the police that? They would deport you, send you home to your crazy mother in an instant, is that what you want? No, I know you don't want that Jenna. Your mother would make your life completely miserable. Perhaps it is better to simply let Alexander have his way with you. I promise, you will enjoy every second of our lovemaking," crooned Alexander, flashing her a sly smile.

Jenna stared at him in shock. Alexander had left no stone unturned, he was completely evil.

"Come on darling. Enough with the games, you know you want it. Touch it," he bellowed, finally sliding off of her and pulling her up to a sitting position. Jenna was suddenly sitting there in front of him in the bed. Her hands were cramping as the blood returned to them, painfully. Her sudden change of position had made her dizzy, she was struggling to make herself focus. Jenna felt as if she was failing miserably, the terror of the situation was overtaking her.

Alexander's face was suddenly only inches from her own. "Don't just sit there you stupid slut, touch it! Tell me that you have never had a man so large."

Jenna stared at him numbly, her overwhelmed mind was uselessly trying to focus. Jenna suddenly realized he no longer had the glass in his hand. She was sure this was probably her only chance to catch him off guard, she knew she had to do something.

Jenna punched him squarely in the nose, as hard as she could, hoping she would, at the very least, break his nose. Her fist connected with his nose, and Jenna could feel the bone crunch with a satisfying snap.

In Alexander's surprise, she was able to roll off the bed and run for the door. He was only hindered for a moment, Alexander had caught Jenna by one arm before she could manage to unlock the door. Jenna swung around and punched him again with her free hand, hitting him in the right eye this time.

Alexander was completely enraged! He grabbed both of her arms as she tried to fight him and shoved her violently up against the wall, pinning her wrists on both sides of her head. Jenna's head hit the wall with so much force, she actually saw spots before her eyes.

Alexander was gripping her wrists tightly and was now pressing her into the wall with all his body weight. Jenna winced at the the searing pain of his massive hands locked on her wrists.

Jenna was fighting to breathe as the hysteria threatened to overtake her. Alexander's nose had already started to swell and a trickle of blood coursed it's way from his nose to his lip. He was glaring angrily into her eyes. Jenna was panting breathlessly and glaring back at him. She wanted to make sure he knew, she wasn't about to go down without a fight.

"You crazy American bitch, you didn't tell me you liked it rough," snarled Alexander, his face was now just inches from her own.

"Let me go Alexander," Jenna managed to whimper, the pain was overwhelming. He was pressing her wrists and her shoulder blades into the wall. Her head was throbbing, it had hit the wall so hard.

"My sweet Jenna, I told you what I wanted. You are being very difficult," he gave her a wink and smiled seductively.

"Please Alexander, just leave now...I promise, we can forget all about this," breathed Jenna.

Jenna was feeling light headed, either from the alcohol or the fact that she had been holding her breath as his hot breath washed over her face. She was feeling defeated, there was no reasoning with him and her energy was waning, she knew there was no possible way she could overpower him and escape.

Alexander's face was still only inches from her own as he glared at her with dark, angry eyes. His face was red and the veins in his neck were bulging out like garden hoses. Jenna was trembling as he held her pressed against the wall. At this point, she was sure that he was going to rape her and then kill her. In any case, she wasn't going to make it easy for him!

"My darling, I cannot just forget about this, and I cannot wait any longer. Everyone knows we are lovers, perhaps things just got a bit, what is it you Americans say? Kinky," said Alexander, smiling darkly into her eyes.

He twisted her arms behind her roughly, then he flung her back onto the bed. Jenna bounced across the bed hard, hitting the headboard with the top of her head. She winced in pain, she'd already been dizzy from the first blow to her head.

Before she knew it, Alexander was on top of her again. He was staring darkly into her eyes. Jenna was shaking uncontrollably and fighting the urge to break down crying.

"Do you think I am not up for a fight? You are a skinny girl, and I am a big strong man. Just let me do what I want and no one will get hurt. There is no point in resisting me. I told you, I will have you one way or another," boomed Alexander.

Alexander had the broken champagne bottle in his hand again, Jenna's heart faltered as she caught a glance of it. The sight of the dark glass glinting in the light sent a shiver racing down her spine. Her heart accelerated at the thought that he was going to kill her right now. Jenna held her breath as the light reflected off the makeshift weapon.

"One of us is overdressed," seethed Alexander, as he reached out and grabbed the front of her dress and cut it from top to bottom in one smooth motion. He pulled the fabric back and his eyes wandered up and down her now, nearly naked body. Then he sawed through the fabric of her bra and pulled that away too. Jenna was trembling in fear.

"Do you like it this way Jenna? Is this how it has to be for you, with the man in complete control? Do you need to be taken?" he breathed, his smile was mocking, as a touch of sarcasm snuck into his voice.

"I've told you no, are you really going to stoop to this level and rape me?" Jenna was shaking so violently, she could barely speak.

"I have stooped to *your* level. I am about to commit a crime almost as heinous as one you have perpetrated. I have endured your flirting, your teasing and your lies.
Everyone here already believes that we have been intimate. What have you got to lose Jenna?"

"I have not been leading you on, I am sorry if it seemed that way..."

"I am merely playing along with the game that you started. I know what women want. All women want to be pursued. They want to be desired...taken. I even know what *you* want.

I know you have to pretend you are married to Adam, or risk deportation. I also know that your sham marriage has never been consummated.

Your own family doesn't want you. You are completely alone, you need me. We could be a couple as easily as you and Adam, on and off the ice," said Alexander, looking deeply into her eyes.

"If this is what you want Alexander, you have to give me time, I..."

"I have given you plenty of time! You have been playing me. I refused to be played any longer!"

My little Jenna has been putting up a quite a fight. I expected you to give in to me long ago willingly, but you are such a silly young girl, you know nothing about desire. Desire cannot be turned on and off like a switch, especially an all consuming desire. It is a shame it had to come down to this.

You told me you have a boyfriend in Boston. A boyfriend who has never touched you the way I have touched you," Alexander's face was inches from her own, he was staring darkly into her eyes. Jenna's heart was pounding so hard, it threatened to burst from her chest. She struggled to breathe. The weight of Alexander's body on her chest was crushing her.

"Mathew is..." Jenna was fighting to take a breath, she was so weak, the words just wouldn't come.

"Enough about your darling Matthew!" snapped Alexander, glaring into her eyes. "You are a player Jenna, you play men! You played me with the expertise of someone much older. It makes me wonder, are you not as innocent as you let on?

I just wanted you to want me. To look at me the way you looked at the Frenchman tonight. But it is too late to make amends now, you have hurt me with your childish games."

Jenna swallowed nervously. She had never been a player, but she'd certainly been one tonight. Her plan to flirt with Luc Dupre, in an effort to push away Alexander, had backfired miserably. In fact, it may have been what had pushed Alexander over the edge tonight.

"What about Marika, how can you be with me, if you are betrothed to Marika?" asked Jenna, struggling to keep her voice from faltering.

"Marika and I have been betrothed for a year. It seemed to be a good match at first, we are partners on the ice, so our families of course, believed we were suitable to marry. She comes from a good family, they are very rich. Unfortunately, our off ice relationship is not as pleasing.

I guess you could say, she does nothing for me sexually. She is as cold in the bedroom, as she is on the ice.

She was overindulged as a child and nothing but trinkets can make her happy. Apparently, there is nothing in life that gives that woman pleasure, nothing that makes her smile. I need to be with someone who lights the fire in my heart, someone who will enjoy my attentions," said Alexander, he was leaning closer to her, his face was just inches from her own.

"Alexander, I am not that person. Really, why are you doing this?" breathed Jenna, she felt like her heart was wearing her out with it's furious beating. She was slowly wearing down, but she refused to surrender to him.

"Like I told you before...it was I, who had you brought here. I knew the two of us would be magic on the ice together, but I could really care less about skating with you. I was more interested in your porcelain skin and your beautiful legs. How was I to know you'd turn out to be nothing but a snotty little cock tease?" Alexander told her, as he seductively pressed his body against hers.

"I never led you on Alexander," breathed Jenna, the weight of his body was making it hard for her to breathe.

"That is right, I forgot. You would not even give me the time of day. Alexander is not good enough for you. What is wrong with you? I am a World Champion, everywhere I go, women want me. Who are you, to just push me away?" his voice was suddenly raising in distress. Jenna bit her lip nervously, he was getting agitated again, she desperately tried to defuse him.

"I'm sorry Alexander, you were right. I was scared because I don't know what to expect...with a real lover."

"Don't you see Jenna, it's too late for your little cock tease games. You had your chance, I watched you, I saw how you used every man around you, to keep me away.

You hurt me Jenna, flirting with Rainier, throwing yourself at Dupre. It was quite amusing, the stupid bastards all thought they were so special that you were paying attention to them. They actually thought they had a chance with the little ice princess. Well, now you are going to pay attention to *me*," seethed Alexander, pressing the glass to her neck once again.

Jenna held her breath nervously as he gazed down at her, his eyes searching hers intently. She couldn't say a word, she was too scared to speak.

"What is the matter? Suddenly you have nothing to say? Are you not going to call me a horny goat? That one is my favorite, go ahead Jenna say it," said Alexander, his voice was cold and mocking. Jenna shivered involuntarily as he loomed over her.

"Alexander...please..."

"Oh my love...you do not have to beg any more. I am going to give it to you," said Alexander, a sly smile was crossing his face.

Jenna gave him a stoney glare, she couldn't make herself speak. Her throat was so dry it felt like sandpaper, she was ready to dissolve into a panic. Her entire body was burning with the adrenaline that had been transfused into it with her overwhelming fear. Both of Alexander's hands were locked on her wrists and she couldn't even struggle with him anymore, she was slowly loosing this battle.

Alexander suddenly released her wrists and sat up abruptly. The blood was rushing back into her hands suddenly, causing them to cramp and feel like they were suddenly on fire. Alexander was still straddling her body, towering over her with a sardonic grin on his face.

Jenna swallowed anxiously, he had the glass in his hand, he was turning it in the light, watching the light reflect off it's sharp facets. He was eerily calm, as he watched her fighting to breathe. She wanted to struggle with him, to get away, but her entire body was suddenly useless. She couldn't move at all.

"You are a stubborn one, my darling Jenna. A control freak, I guess you could say. I could think of nothing else but you, with those blue eyes and your long legs. You were always the one in control, leading me on every day, touching me, letting me touch you, but never giving me what I really want," breathed Alexander, a far away smile on his lips.

"I'm....I'm, sorry..."Jenna panted, she could barely get the words out, she couldn't draw in a full breath.

"You were right about one thing Jenna, a gentleman would never force himself on a lady. That is why I am going to give you a choice, so that you may still have a bit of control in our little relationship," he said, running his finger seductively over the primitive blade he held in his hand.

Jenna was trembling as his dark eyes glinted down at her. She was gasping to breathe as her entire body quivered uselessly.

"Now listen carefully darling, the choice is me, or the blade. Which one do you think will feel better?"

Jenna swallowed and shook her head numbly, she couldn't speak at all. Her teeth were chattering and her heart was beating furiously in anticipation. He leaned over her, gazing into her eyes with a suggestive smile. Jenna was fighting back tears.

"What do you say my darling? Is a hot Russian bull sounding better to you now? This blade might just ruin you for life...you *do* know what I plan to do with it, do you not?" he seethed, turning the blade over in the light and letting the light bounce off it's sharp facets. Alexander's face was bright red and covered with a thin sheen of perspiration. He chuckled to himself, then he slowly and deliberately pressed the glass against her neck again.

Jenna gasped as he pressed the makeshift blade into her skin, dangerously close to her carotid. She was too frightened to move, she was struggling merely to breathe, she couldn't make a sound.

Jenna could feel the glass pressing deeper and deeper into the skin of her neck, her brain commanded her mouth to scream, but nothing would come out, but a panicked rush of air.

Alexander was trembling as he drew the primitive blade shakily across her skin. It would be so easy to end their pain right now. It had made him insane with jealousy, seeing her with Luc Dupre. He was now sure he could never let another man have her. His heart was pounding with indecision, should he kill her now, or just scare her a bit?

Jenna wanted to scream, but she couldn't, she was completely overcome with terror. All that came out of her mouth was an anguished sob as she felt the blade penetrate the soft skin on her neck. Soon she felt the warmth of more of her own blood flowing down her neck. Jenna looked up to see Alexander's eyes were now full of tears. The panic was overtaking her body, he was going to kill her now!

"Alexander don't...please," she managed to whisper.

Alexander had tears flowing down his cheeks. He felt as if he was having some sort of mental breakdown. He was suddenly consumed with feelings of anger and an overwhelming desire.

He loved her, but she refused to see it. At this moment he wanted to hurt her, he wanted to pay her back for all the pain she had inflicted on him. If he couldn't have her, no one could. His heart was aching from the pain, tears were streaming down his cheeks from the emotion.

Jenna was struggling to maintain consciousness, her body was ready to surrender to a panicked faint and Alexander had suddenly dissolved into a rage. He had the glass in his hand and was now slashing at her angrily. Jenna could feel him stabbing her repeatedly in the chest, the neck, the shoulder, wherever the blows seemed to land.

After the first few stabs, it seemed there was no more pain, only the eerie feeling that she was barely clinging to consciousness. Finally, the senseless stabbing stopped. Alexander's face was just inches from her own, he was panting, as his hot breath washed over her. He flashed her a sardonic grin as he held the blade in front of her face.

"How does it feel? Do you like the pain? Is this what you want to feel inside you?"

Jenna was shaking her head numbly she couldn't speak she was so consumed with terror.

"Tell me my darling, what do you want?"

Jenna wanted to say something...anything, but she couldn't make her mouth form any words.

"Tell me now darling, do you want Alexander or the blade," he whispered. Jenna shivered, that was what he wanted. He wanted permission...the arrogant jerk assumed it wouldn't really be rape, if she told him, yes. Jenna shuddered a little bit when she thought about that.

She was trembling so badly she could barely speak. "I...I..."

Alexander's entire body was shaking as well. His heart was pounding with an adrenaline rush. He just wanted to hear her say it.

"Think hard before you make your decision. The wrong decision surely has dire consequences..."

Jenna looked up into his cold, dark eyes, she knew that physically, she couldn't fight him anymore. She seemed to be teetering on the brink of consciousness. It was probably best to just let him do it and get it over with. With any luck, maybe she wouldn't even remember it.

"Please, not the glass, just do what you have to do," she managed to whimper.

"Hmmm, I am not sure I like your response..."

"What?" Jenna was feeling dizzy, it was hard to focus.

"I just wish you could have managed a little more enthusiasm," said Alexander, his voice was mocking.

Jenna drew in a deep shaky breath, she was afraid to make him angry again, he might start stabbing her again, this time he might not stop till she was dead.

"I'm sorry, I'm just scared. I'm afraid you might be too much man for me, Alexander," she managed to squeak out with the minimal amount of air she was able to draw into her lungs. "You were right, I've never been with a man."

"Finally...I hear the truth. I just need *more*," said Alexander, his voice was taunting. He wanted her to surrender to him completely.

"What? I...I don't know what to do," breathed Jenna.

"Tell me you want me," seethed Alexander, his arrogant smile was distant and deeply disturbing to Jenna.

Jenna struggled to take a deep breath, she was tired of playing these games. Why wouldn't her body cooperate and just pass out?

"Try to be convincing Jenna, I still have a weapon in my hand," said Alexander, flashing her a sly smile.

Jenna swallowed, her mouth was so dry she could barely breathe, let alone speak. No matter what she said, Alexander was not going to be satisfied. She had essentially been born without acting skills. Anything she said, was going to sound fake and rehearsed.

"Oh for God's sake, just do it Alexander," she wailed.

"Is that the attitude you want to have with me? Really Jenna, I am not afraid to use this." seethed Alexander, holding the glass up in front of her face. "Somehow I don't think the pain will be half as good as what I have to offer. Or do you like the pain?

Jenna shivered when she thought about what he might do with the that glass. The thought was horrifying, she needed to play along, even though she wasn't sure that was actually possible.

"No please, not the glass."

"Then tell me what you want."

"I want *you* Alexander," crooned Jenna, trying her best to sound convincing. She was suddenly in survival mode, doing whatever he wanted just seemed like her only option right now.

"How much do you want me?" his voice was silky and seductive. He was playing the game, Jenna was struggling to play along.

"I never wanted anyone so badly in my life," breathed Jenna. The lies were coming easier now, she just wanted this ordeal to end. It was beginning to seem like she had been trapped in this room with Alexander forever. She felt as if she were hovering on the edge of consciousness, but her body wouldn't cooperate and succumb to the darkness.

"Now, tell me you love me," breathed Alexander, his voice was low and seductive.

"I love you," mouthed Jenna, her voice sounded hollow and emotionless, but Alexander still seemed moved by her words.

Alexander took her face in his hands and kissed her, Jenna couldn't help but be surprised, the kiss was almost gentle. As the kiss intensified, his hands roamed across her body and he was passionately trying to shove his tongue into her mouth. He tasted like a stale combination of vodka and cigarettes, Jenna kept her lips clamped shut.

"This will be much easier for you, if you just relax," whispered Alexander, grinding his pelvis against her.

Jenna cringed, this was going to be awful, there was no possible way she could relax. She'd heard the rumors, the first time was painful...Alexander was huge!

Alexander was towering over her, his face was bright red and the perspiration was rolling from his temples. Jenna was still shaking uncontrollably, but she was suddenly angry, this wasn't how her first time was supposed to be. It was supposed to be perfect...how dare Alexander take that away from her. She took a deep, shaky breath, she glared into Alexander's eyes as she drew her legs up, and kneed Alexander in the groin as hard as she could. As weak as she was, she'd got him good, he rolled off the bed, groaning in agony. Jenna jumped up and made a break for the door.

Unfortunately, she hadn't completely incapacitated him, she had only infuriated him more. As she reached the door, Alexander grabbed a handful of her hair and jerked her back toward him. Jenna fell backwards in surprise, and he had his arms around her, before she could unlock the door and escape.

Alexander was laughing a strange, evil laugh as he swept her up into his arms and stared down into her eyes with a diabolical smile. Jenna was panting with fear and exertion from her run to the door.

"I told you, I am done playing games with you," he seethed. Jenna shivered when she saw the depth of his rage, he threw her roughly onto the bed. He was angry, she was still playing games, avoiding him. Jenna could hear her own heartbeat echoing loudly in her ears. She was panting and trembling as Alexander stalked toward her.

Before she knew it, Alexander was climbing on top of her again in a final attempt to subdue her. He was staring down into her eyes, his own dark eyes seemed far away and lifeless. He was angry, angry enough to wring the life out of her with his bare hands.

Something inside of Alexander had finally snapped, he was no longer a man, he was a monster. He seemed to be infused with superhuman strength as his hands were now encircling her neck and they seemed to be wringing the very life from her.

Jenna was panicking, she couldn't breathe at all. She had her hands on his wrists, trying desperately to peel his hands from her throat, but she couldn't, her hands were slippery with her own blood.

Alexander was leaning over her, his hands wrapped around her neck, stemming the flow of blood through her carotids. In a few moments she would pass out, it would disable her enough that she couldn't fight him. Maybe she wouldn't even feel the pain when he finally broke through her tiny, virginal passage. At this moment,

Alexander was so angry he couldn't even see straight. He couldn't believe Jenna, it was still resisting him. He was done waiting!

Jenna couldn't speak, the weight of his body on her chest seemed immense. His hands were slowly closing off her airway, she was panicking as she struggled in vain to peel his hands from her throat.

The panic was completely overwhelming as she struggled merely to breathe. Alexander was strangling her, she was dizzy, and her vision was growing dimmer by the second. Alexander was leaning over her, this thumbs poised over her trachea, ready to crush it, with very little effort on his part. He was speaking to her, but his voice seemed to be cutting out, she was so close to passing out, she couldn't breathe at all, the air hunger was all consuming.

Jenna could feel her body finally succumbing to the darkness when abruptly, Alexander sat up and removed his hands from her neck. Jenna gasped in relief and finally sucked in a deep breath. The room was spinning and she was gasping to breathe. She was still struggling to take a deep breath as Alexander ripped her panties off wedged his knee between her legs. Jenna was so weak, she couldn't even struggle as he slid his hand between her legs and forced one long finger inside of her.

Jenna gasped in discomfort, it wasn't like the last time Alexander had touched her, it was forceful, violent. Jenna was struggling to remain emotionless, but tears were sliding down her cheeks. The room seemed to be growing dimmer by the second and it seemed to be tilting at a crazy angle.

"Oh so tight...this is going to be a challenge," breathed Alexander, callously pushing another finger inside of her.

Jenna was barely conscious, and the entire room seemed to be spinning. She wanted to say something, anything to make him stop, but she still couldn't manage to get a deep enough breath. She felt like crying but the tears wouldn't come either, her eyes kept sliding closed and she knew that soon she would pass out, in fact, it would almost be a relief.

Jenna was teetering on the brink of unconsciousness, sounds were fading, except for her own heartbeat which seemed to be roaring in her ears. Jenna forced her eyes open as she felt Alexander slide one hand under her buttocks, then he lifted her hips off the bed. Jenna felt a surge of panic as Alexander used his other hand to guide himself between her legs.

Jenna squeezed her eyes closed again, as if that could protect her frazzled brain from what was happening. Alexander wasted no time, the look on his face was determined as he forced the thick tip inside her, but it seemed as if he'd hit a brick wall. Alexander grunted determinedly as he tried to push himself deeper inside her. Jenna let out a sob of pain as he began to brutally ram into her.

Jenna wiggled uncomfortably as Alexander drove into her again and again. Jenna squeezed her eyes closed and hoped it would be over soon. In just moments, he had stopped.

Jenna opened her eyes cautiously, hoping that was all there was to it. Alexander's face looked anguished, he was cursing adamantly in Russian, Jenna was completely perplexed. She assumed he would be happy, but she was young and inexperienced, she didn't realize that things weren't exactly working out for Alexander.

Alexander was cursing under his breath. This was the worst nightmare ever! He had dreamed about this moment for weeks and he finally gets his chance and her freaking hymen is like a steel plate or something. Alexander sighed miserably, he would have to try something else.

Jenna almost breathed a sigh of relief as Alexander finally withdrew, but unfortunately, Alexander hadn't given up yet. Jenna was just too overcome with fear to realize what was going on. Alexander chuckled a bit and gave her a sardonic smile.

"I fear this is going to be harder than I anticipated."

Jenna swallowed convulsively, her mouth was so dry, she couldn't speak at all. At this point, none of this even seemed real anymore, Jenna longed to slip into the dreamlike state she was teetering on the edge of.

Alexander was determined, he plunged his fingers into her again, as she gasped and groaned uncomfortably.

"Do not worry my darling, Alexander loves a challenge," he seethed, as he seemed to be stretching her with his fingers. Alexander changed position slightly, lifted her hips even higher and begin ramming into her once again. Jenna finally cried out in pain, as he plunged full length, inside her.

The searing pain was all consuming, Jenna felt as if Alexander had ripped through her insides. Jenna was sobbing, she prayed that Alexander would just finish, and then leave her alone.

Alexander groaned with relief when he finally managed to force his way through her hymen. This wasn't going to take long, she was so tight and he had been on edge for so long. He was desperate to impregnate her, if it didn't happen tonight, there was a good chance she would never let him touch her again.

Jenna was glad that once the initial pain subsided, it was only unpleasant, at best. Her entire body was shaking from the initial pain and the adrenaline that had been infused into her body. Alexander was still on top of her, thrusting determinedly, saying things in Russian she was glad she couldn't understand. She just wanted this ordeal to end.

Alexander thought he heard someone in the hallway but it didn't matter, his climax was seconds away, if they were discovered now, his seed would be buried deep inside her. He prayed she would become pregnant with his child. Maybe she would realize *he* was the one she wanted...not Luc Dupre.

Jenna had nearly succumbed to the darkness, her brain was drifting out of the hell that was the real world and into the cool, beckoning darkness. She snapped to attention when she thought she heard a noise at the door, but Alexander's voice broke her concentration.

"Here is what you need my darling." he gasped, moving his body even faster as his breathing increased to short quick gasps.

Jenna could barely breathe, but she gave him her best look of disgust anyway.

"Just imagine, if by chance, I get you pregnant tonight, your father will be very angry. He will force me to marry you," panted Alexander, a slight smile coming to his lips as he continued to drive into her relentlessly.

Jenna shuddered brokenly, she'd forgotten about Alexander's weird plan for the two of them to marry. Up to this moment, she had only been worried about loosing her virginity to Alexander, she'd never even considered the possibility that she might become pregnant! That would be a nightmare to end all nightmares!

Alexander mistakenly took her shudder of distaste for an orgasm and he smiled into her eyes.

"That's it my darling, I told you, you would like it," he crooned.

Jenna tuned him out, her mind was still turning with the possibility of her getting pregnant from this ordeal. Was that what they did in the Soviet Union? Forced women to marry the man who had raped them? Jenna shuddered again at the thought. Her father was definitely not father of the year material, but she was sure he would never force her to marry Alexander.

Jenna heard a fumbling at the door and a click that seemed to echo through the room, her heart was almost racing with relief. In seconds, the hotel room door swung open, at that very moment Alexander let out an animalistic groan and threw his head back as his body shuddered uncontrollably. He collapsed on top of her, his face contorted in ecstasy, as he finally climaxed. Jenna's eyes moved to the door, to see Adam standing there staring at the two of them, his face consumed with shock. At that moment, fate finally granted Jenna her wish and she fainted.

CHAPTER TWENTY FIVE

Adam stood there completely motionless, as his mind struggled to process the disturbing scene in front of him. He was completely bewildered, he had hurried back to the hotel when he realized Jenna had left the party without him.

He had been worried about her walking back to the hotel alone. He was now standing here, shaking his head in confusion, it hadn't even occurred to him that she had left with Alexander...

He was standing there staring numbly, seemingly unable to move. He was completely overwhelmed with shock. When he opened the door he saw them on the bed, with Alexander obviously, in his moment of glory. Adam couldn't help but be angry, Jenna had told him she wasn't attracted to Alexander at all...so why?

Of course, he'd been hearing the rumors about Jenna and Alexander for weeks, but they seemed like just that, rumors... He had never expected to come back to their hotel room and find the two of them in bed together. He was shaking his head numbly, obviously Jenna had completely lost her mind!

Alexander was panting and covered with sweat, as he looked up and saw Adam standing there in the doorway. He almost burst out in hysterical laughter. Adam the poor bastard, looked so shocked.

Alexander let out a satisfied laugh, rolled off of Jenna, and turned to face his very confused and bewildered adversary. Alexander gave Adam a arrogant smile as he stood to approach him, he could tell Adam was completely shocked as to what he was witnessing.

Adam was acutely embarrassed. He wanted to back out of the room, he didn't want to see what he was seeing, but for some reason he was frozen in place. Jenna had lied to him, she had told him that the rumors were completely untrue. Now

Alexander was in front of him, completely naked, approaching him slowly, a satisfied smile was spreading across face. That was when Adam noticed the blood...

Suddenly, his heart was pounding with anxiety. There was so much blood...what in God's name, had Alexander done? Something was wrong...Jenna was still sprawled limply on the bed, she hadn't moved at all and her entire body seemed to be covered in blood.

Adam gasped, and took a tentative step toward the bed. He thought Jenna might be dead, she seemed so pale and lifeless. He stared at her for a moment till she finally drew in a shallow breath, though it seemed to be quite an effort. She wasn't dead, but she didn't look so good. Adam was panicking, should he go to her, or kick Alexander's ass?

Alexander gave Adam a sly smile as he swaggered slowly toward him. Adam felt a shiver travel down the length of his spine when he finally got his first good look at him. Alexander looked absolutely hideous, he was completely naked and smeared with

blood from head to toe. Adam was
hesitating, still not sure what had happened
here. Alexander's expression was cold and
arrogant, Adam couldn't even speak...

"I am very sorry Mr. Smyth, but it seems
you've missed all the fun," said Alexander,
in a voice that was silky with malice.

"What have you done to her, Alexander?"
cried Adam, his voice breaking with
emotion.

"I seriously doubt you are that naive Mr.
Smyth. I mean, you *were* lucky enough to
witness our big finish. It was pretty
spectacular, was it not?"

Adam was standing there shaking his head
numbly. This was all wrong...

"In case you were wondering, she was a
virgin, but she's not anymore. We had a bit
of a rough time of it, but you know what
they say...no pain, no gain," he teased,
flashing Adam an evil smile.

Adam was approaching them slowly, he
was suddenly very worried about Jenna,

since he'd entered the room she hadn't moved at all. He just wanted to check on her, make sure she was okay, there was so much blood. "Is she okay?"

"Of course, she's okay. I just gave her what every woman wants, ten inches of pure pleasure," laughed Alexander.

"Why is there so much blood? What did you do to her?" cried Adam, finally reaching Jenna. He reached for her wrist, found a thready pulse and let out a sigh of relief. Jenna's eyes fluttered open. Adam's heart accelerated nervously when he noticed that it appeared that Jenna had been stabbed, seemingly dozens of times.

"I finally gave her what she has needed for so long."

"She's been stabbed. You stabbed her?" cried Adam, his face was incredulous. It was obvious he still wasn't quite sure what had happened in this room.

"It was nothing but a silly game. She just required a bit of...ummm...foreplay, I

believe you Americans call it," said
Alexander.

"I'll kill you, you bastard," seethed Adam,
lunging at him.

Jenna could finally breathe again. The air
had rushed, almost forcefully into her lungs
as Alexander jumped up from the bed to
face Adam. Jenna felt as if she couldn't
move, her eyes were moving around the
room, but her body seemed useless. For the
longest moment, she wasn't even sure where
she was. It seemed as if she had been
awakened from a terrible nightmare. As the
seconds ticked away it became apparent that
this was not a dream, it was a real life
nightmare!

Jenna's eyes drifted around the room
numbly, not really knowing where she was,
or what she was doing there. She felt
strangely detached and dizzy. Her vision
was slowly returning, but everything seemed
to be veiled in a thin fog, she was vaguely
aware that Alexander was there in her hotel
room, and he was now fighting with Adam.
Jenna struggled to shake off her confusion.

As the blood began to slowly return to her oxygen starved brain, a second wave of terror washed over her. Alexander had meant to kill her, now he was going to kill Adam. Jenna knew she needed to call for help. Her body was so weak and shocky, she could barely drag herself to the bedside table and the phone. She lifted her hand to pick up the receiver and was shocked to see that her hand was covered in blood.

Jenna gasped, as her eyes trailed down the rest of her body to see that all her clothing was slashed and nearly torn off of her, and she was completely covered in blood. Though she seemed to be teetering on the edge of consciousness, she was suddenly snapped back to reality and somehow, she managed to call security.

In a matter of moments it seemed, the room was full of security guards. Before she knew what was happening, she was sitting on the bed with a blanket wrapped around her, as the Police arrived and removed Alexander from the room in handcuffs.

Jean Marie Stanberry

CHAPTER TWENTY SIX

Alexander was handcuffed in the back of a police vehicle, but he wasn't upset. He wanted to laugh with joy. He had won, he had finally won!

His entire body was shaking, but not because he was completely naked under the rough, gray blanket they had draped over him, but because the adrenaline from his attack on Jenna was finally wearing off. It hadn't gone was smoothly as he'd planned, but it had been the most intense orgasm he had ever experienced.

He frowned slightly as he thought about the scene he had just left behind. Maybe something was wrong with him, he had not been himself, he had been completely out of control.

He hadn't even realized it until he was being led out of the room in handcuffs. The room did look like a crime scene. It had never occurred to him how violent the scene looked until he was walking away and finally saw all the blood. The thought almost brought him to tears. That was all Jenna's blood, he had hurt her.

Now that the adrenaline was wearing off he was feeling very guilty. He had been completely consumed with jealousy and anger. In fact, at one point he had been so close to slitting her throat, he had actually almost done it.

Now Alexander was filled with remorse over the fact that he had hurt her. She had begged him to stop, but he couldn't, he had *wanted* to hurt her. Her pale skin had been completely covered with blood. He had her blood smeared all over him from head to toe. Alexander shuddered in disgust, there was no question, he was in serious trouble. How could he possibly explain away the horrifying scene he had just left behind?

All he could really do now was rack his brain to come up some sort of explanation. He wasn't some crazed lunatic, he was a World Champion and Olympic gold medalist. He couldn't really deny what he had done to Jenna, that much was obvious. He'd been completely out of control, he'd used the broken champagne bottle as a weapon to terrorize her and control her.

He felt bad that he'd gotten so out of control, but it had made him feel so powerful at the time, he couldn't help himself. She had been controlling him for so long, it had been very liberating when he finally had complete control over her.

Alexander was suddenly worried, how could he possibly explain all of this away? He would be arrested and Jenna would probably never speak to him again.

When they arrived at the police station he expected to be booked in like a common criminal, but the detective there recognized him immediately as the Olympic gold medalist who was in Paris to skate in the ice show. He told Alexander he could hang out in his office with him. That way he wouldn't be put into one of the holding cells with the common drunks and the petty thieves.

Not only was Alexander able to avoid getting thrown into a holding cell, but the detective told him he could make as many phone calls as he wanted as he hung out there in the office. After Alexander had called his coach, his lawyer and Marika's very influential family, he had one more phone call to make.

He pulled the crumpled piece of paper out of his wallet. He had found this number one afternoon when Simone had left him waiting in her office. He had riffled through Jenna's files and found the phone number for her parents. He had thought her mother at least, might offer him a bit of leverage against her very stubborn daughter.

He dialed the phone and was ecstatic when her mother answered on the second ring.

"Mrs. Bruce?"

"Yes?"

"This is Alexander Peterov. You don't know me, but I am skating in the show in Paris with your daughter Jenna."

"Yes, you're the Olympic gold medalist," said Jenna's mother.

"That's right," said Alexander.

"I have to warn you, I already know a bit about what is going on there. Jenna had called me and told me that you had been sexually harassing her, is that true?"

Alexander sighed, he had been hoping to recruit her mother to his side. From the stories he had heard about her, she seemed to be a bit of a lose cannon, easy to manipulate, but apparently Jenna had gotten to her first.

"I am in love with your daughter. I think we are compatible both on and off the ice. I want to marry her but she has just been resisting me, she has some delusions about some guy named Matthew."

"Matthew Thayer? The guy is away at college in Boston, I'm sure he has a girlfriend there by now. Besides I'm very intrigued by what you've brought up. Before she left for Paris I was hoping to find Jenna another partner, but she was resistant to the idea. I'm not sure how she did it, but she managed to sabotage my attempts to find her a new coach and a partner. I am very intrigued that you feel you are so compatible with her. I mean you're an

Olympic gold medalist, that would be perfect," crooned Jenna's mother.

"I couldn't agree more," said Alexander.

"The coach I tried to enlist didn't want Jenna, since she's so tall, she was afraid she would grow more and outgrow her partner. You're a pretty big guy, right?"

"Yes, I am very large. I do not believe there is any risk of Jenna outgrowing me. If Jenna and I were to marry, I could defect to the states, we could train there and be partners on the ice. I have no doubt I could be on the podium with her at the Olympics in four years," said Alexander. He could feel she was close to biting, now all he had to do was reel her in.

"The Olympics, that would be fabulous," cried Jenna's mother. "What do you need from me?"

"Well Jenna has been quite stubborn. I've been working on her for weeks yet she still refuses to even give me the time of day."

"You want me to convince her to go out with you?"

"No, I imagine it's too late for that," breathed Alexander. How do you explain to a woman that you've just raped her daughter and you would really appreciate it, if she would talk her into not pressing charges.

"What?"

"There was a bit of an incident tonight. It was our last night in Paris and I wanted to spend some time with her, alone."

"Go on."

"Like I said, I love her, I want to marry her, but she has been very stubborn. She's been stringing me along for weeks, teasing me. I just couldn't take it any longer," whined Alexander.

"So you are saying you forced yourself on her?" asked her mother. She didn't seem upset, she seemed amazingly removed.

"I'm ashamed to admit that I did," said Alexander.

"She plans to press charges then?"

"I don't know, I haven't had the chance to talk to her about it, they took me to the police station. I love her, I want to marry her," sobbed Alexander.

"I understand how difficult she can be. I will do whatever I can to help you avoid criminal charges Mr. Peterov. When are you thinking for a wedding?"

"As soon as possible," said Alexander, it was hard for him to conceal his smug grin. Jenna's mother was completely on his side. He had no doubt that her mother would tell whatever lies necessary to keep him out of jail. She was a typical stage mother, she would do anything so that her daughter could have the perfect partner and achieve her goals of fame and fortune.

Alexander hung up the phone completely pleased with himself. He may be in jail for the moment, but there was no way he was going to be charged with anything. He may have temporarily lost his mind, but it was Jenna who was going to come out looking like the crazy one, and he would look like the hero when he offered to marry her.

Jean Marie Stanberry

CHAPTER TWENTY SEVEN

Jenna was completely disorientated, there were just too many people in the room. As the minutes ticked by, her disorientation was slowly wearing off and she was shaking uncontrollably, as her mind slowly and painfully returned to reality.

Jenna was hovering in a strange state of semi consciousness. She appeared to be fully awake, but her brain seemed to have completely shut down, she couldn't seem to process what had happened, nor what was currently going on in this hotel room. Jenna looked up numbly at the medics who had arrived to take her to the hospital. They had taken her vital signs, started an IV and they were loading her onto a stretcher, when she suddenly began to panic. Where was Adam?

"What are you doing?" she asked, looking up at the medics, she was squinting to make her eyes focus, but their faces continued to fade in and out of the thick mist.

"We are taking you to the hospital, you are going into shock, you have lost quite a bit of blood," said one of the medics.

"Blood!" exclaimed Jenna, sitting up and looking at the medics, completely shocked.

"Please Mademoiselle, lay back down, you've been cut up and stabbed many times. You are in shock, we must get you to the hospital," said the medic, he pushed her gently back down and continued to wheel the stretcher toward the doorway.

"Adam, I need Adam," Jenna managed to cry before they removed her from the room.

"Just relax, you are going to be fine. He cannot come with us, he is busy with the detectives," the medic told her, his strong French accent seemed to throw Jenna off for a moment, she was having trouble concentrating. There were so many voices in the room, it was overwhelming.

"Adam!" cried Jenna, sitting up and looking around the room desperately. Her heart was suddenly pounding anxiously again, she couldn't let them take her, not without Adam.

"Andre, give her the sedative," snapped the medic at the foot of the stretcher.

"The detective wants to talk to her, if I give it, she'll be completely useless!" cried the other medic, he had his hand on her wrist and was trying without success, to make Jenna lay down on the stretcher.

"She's already useless. Give it, they can talk to her in the morning, her blood pressure is too low, we need to be on our way!"

The man rolled his eyes and pulled a syringe out of his pocket. They were speaking in French, but even as devastated as Jenna was, she could still understand every word they were saying. Why were they going to drug her?

Jenna was panicking, and struggling with the man as he tried to access her arm that had the IV in it.

"I'm just going to give you some medicine to help you relax," said the medic, finally straightening her arm. He pulled the needle sheath off with his teeth as he struggled to hold her still with his other hand.

"No, I don't want any medicine!" cried Jenna, still desperately looking around the room for Adam. It was difficult, something was wrong with her vision, she already felt dizzy and there were dozens of people in the room. It was hard to concentrate.

"Please Mademoiselle, we must have a doctor see you immediately," said the medic, moving quickly to the head of the bed to help his partner restrain her.

Jenna was wrestling furiously with them. She wasn't sure what they were up to, but there was no way she was going with them. She panicked when she saw the medic with the syringe in his hand, she had no idea what he planned to inject into her IV, but as far as she was concerned, it wasn't happening.

She finally managed to pull her right arm free, then she ripped her IV out. There was now even more blood everywhere, and both medics were cursing adamantly in French.

Jenna's eyes were now darting nervously around the crowded room, where was Adam? Sometime terrible had happened and she needed him. She was frightened. She had no desire to go to the hospital and be checked out by, God knows who. She was embarrassed enough for all these people to see her in this state, nearly naked and severely compromised. No one had asked what had happened to her yet, though Jenna was aware that it was most likely painfully obvious to everyone.

The medics realized they had been given an impossible task. Jenna refused to let them anywhere near her, they finally withdrew to the corner of the room after their pleas to convince Jenna to go to the hospital, fell on deaf ears.

Jenna couldn't help it, her fear had completely overwhelmed her. Initially, she had been tempted to go with them, till they told her Adam would have to stay behind.

Hell would freeze over before she left this room without Adam. He was her best friend, perhaps her only friend. People came in and out of her life frequently, Adam had been her constant companion for the last three years.

Hans and his wife Carolina had taken her in and been the only parent figures she had known for the last three years. Her own parents had essentially dropped her off in St. Louis and abandoned her. Jenna fought back tears wishing that Carolina was here to hold her and tell her that everything would be all right, but of course, that would be a downright lie...

A police detective had finally taken control of the scene, he wrapped Jenna in her blanket and moved her to the narrow sofa so he could question her, as the rest of the detectives worked the room. Jenna, still covered in her own blood, was swaddled in the blanket with her arms wrapped around her legs in a tight little ball. Jenna was desperately trying to hold herself together and not having much success. Simone was sitting there beside her on the sofa with her arms wrapped around her tightly. She was rocking Jenna like a baby.

As the evening wore on, the room seemed to swell with a whole host of people milling in and out of the room. Before long, the hotel manager is there in the room, he is very apologetic and offering Jenna and Adam another room for their last night in Paris. Jenna could only nod her head at him lamely, her mind couldn't absorb anything at this point, she was completely overwhelmed.

Just moments after that, Luc Dupre and his brother Nicolas arrived in a show of support for her. Luc looked completely devastated. When he saw her sitting there on the sofa wrapped in her cocoon of blankets, he hurried over to her and knelt down in front of her taking her face into his hands and kissing both her cheeks tenderly.

"Oh Mon Cheri, I am so sorry. I never should have left you," he murmured. He was so distraught he had tears in his eyes.

Jenna would have burst into tears at that very moment if she'd had any emotion left in her body, but at this point, she almost felt like an outsider. The strange mix of emotions that was playing out in this room had no effect on her, she felt strangely detached.

She had completely tuned out Luc as he continued to murmur encouraging words into her ear. Why was he even here? Why were all these people here?

Luc's brother Nicholas finally came over and placed his hand on Luc's shoulder and gave Jenna a gentle smile.

"I think perhaps we should go and give Jenna some space. Besides, the police need to do their job," said Nicolas.

Luc nodded as he clasped Jenna's hand tightly. He kissed her hand one final time and reluctantly told her good night. Jenna sighed miserably, and wondered if the whole world would be present when she finally lost the last shreds of her sanity.

Everyone in the room, it seems, is talking to her, but she is so confused and upset, she can barely comprehend anything anyone is saying. The voices are nothing but an unintelligible jumble of words, the voices seem detached and far away.

Jenna feels like she is trapped in a strange nightmare. She is sitting there on the sofa in a daze, unable to stop the persistent shaking of her entire body. The images of Alexander towering over her seem to be burned into her brain, but for some reason, she cannot come up with a clear picture as to what has happened.

A Police detective is sitting in a chair across from her, speaking to her in a deep monotone voice, but she is so emotionally overwrought, she cannot concentrate on anything the man is asking her.

Simone and Gail are both sitting next to her on the sofa fussing anxiously over her. Gail has brought her a cup of hot tea, but she is shaking so badly, she can't even raise the cup to her lips. Simone is nervously smoothing her hair and patting her arm, which wasn't easing Jenna's distress anymore than it was easing her own.

"So Miss Bruce, how did this all begin? Did you invite Mr. Peterov to your room?" the Police detective asked. Jenna stared at him, completely confused. At this point, she still wasn't exactly sure what had happened. Her brain was basically a slideshow of troubling graphic images, but she couldn't seem to make herself focus enough to get a complete picture of what had happened to her. It seemed as if she had been awakened from a horrible nightmare, though she was getting the feeling that none of this had been a nightmare. It was all too real!

Jenna glanced distractedly across the room and saw another Police officer standing there, he was wearing latex gloves and was carefully folding her shredded, blood soaked dress and putting it into a paper bag. She looked over at the bed, another officer was closely examining the tangled white sheets that seemed to be completely covered in her blood as well. Jenna shivered and looked away...the scene was so troubling. Was that *all* her blood?

"There's so much blood...whaa, what happened?" She was shaking uncontrollably, it seemed an effort to form a complete thought. Her body felt battered and drained, but she was too numb to feel any pain. She glanced over at the bed again, with it's tangled, blood stained, sheets. Her lower lip started quivering and she reached for Simone's hand, and gripped it desperately.

"Detective, must you question her right now? She is shaking like a leaf, I really don't think it's a good idea," said Simone, glaring at the Detective, her arms were wrapped around Jenna protectively as she continued to rock her anxiously.

"I should have waited for Adam...where's Adam?" asked Jenna, numbly.

Jenna was suddenly looking desperately around the room for Adam. There were too many faces there, all vaguely familiar yet strange faces. The faces all had a haunted look about them. Expressionless, not friend, not foe, just faces. She glanced around anxiously till she finally saw Adam, he was standing by the French doors that led out to the little balcony. He was being questioned by another Police officer.

Jenna bit her lower lip to avoid the tears that were threatening to come rushing from her eyes. Adam's clothes were torn and his lip was bleeding. She suddenly felt an overwhelming sense of guilt over the fact that Adam had gotten hurt, most likely defending her. Jenna stood up disjointedly to walk over to him, she had to tell him she was sorry...that she'd never meant for him to be dragged into this nightmare.

"Miss Bruce, please..." said the detective, following her across the room. He couldn't get her to stay focused for more than a minute at a time.

"But Adam...he's bleeding...it's all my fault," said Jenna, her voice was distant and emotionless.

"Please sit down Jenna, we'll take care of Adam," said Gail, gently taking her by the arm and leading her back to the sofa.

"Owww..."said Jenna, pulling her arm away. That's when she noticed the bruises. Both of her forearms were bruised nearly from her wrist to her elbow. Jenna hadn't even seen the bruises on her neck yet. She was standing there, staring numbly at the bruises, still not able to comprehend what had happened to her.

The detective approached her again and sat her gently on the sofa again. "Miss Bruce. I really need you to tell me what happened tonight," said the detective. "Did you let Mr. Peterov into your room? Were the two of you in a relationship?"

Jenna struggled to take in a deep breath. Whatever had happened here was horrible, but her brain refused to focus. Alexander had been there, she was covered with blood, the bed was strewn with bloodstained sheets.

"What?"breathed Jenna, shaking her head miserably. Did he say relationship?

"Miss Bruce, please try to focus. Were you and Mr. Peterov involved? Can you tell me about your relationship?"

"There was no *relationship*..." the word almost made her burst out in maniacal laughter.

Jenna closed her eyes, trying to remember how this nightmare had began. Her brain was trying to protect her, it was trying to shut down and protect her from the shock that was inevitable. She grasped Simone's hand tightly. She was suddenly feeling faint, then she realized she had been holding her breath for some reason. Jenna took a slow, deep breath and tried to concentrate.

"Miss Bruce...I know how hard this is for you," said the detective. He was staring at her, his face was concerned.

"I'd been doing everything I could to avoid him, but Alexander was waiting for me tonight..." Jenna struggled to breathe as the memories came tumbling into her consciousness like a hellish nightmare. "He knew Adam wasn't with me, he knew..."

Jenna wasn't sure what she wanted to say, but suddenly she knew exactly what Alexander had done to her, she could see every second of his violent assault as the horrifying memories came tumbling back into her consciousness. She wasn't sure she could tell the Detective what Alexander had done to her, it was so demeaning.

Alexander had emotionally and physically violated her and the very thought made her want to break down and cry, but the tears just wouldn't come, she felt so empty and lost.

She was sure everyone in the room knew exactly what had happened to her, it was completely obvious. Of all the people who had been in and out of this room, this detective was the only one who had made eye contact with her, the others had all averted their eyes in embarrassment.

"I know this is very hard for you Ms. Bruce but you need to tell me what happened here tonight," said the Detective, looking at her very seriously. Jenna chewed on her lower lip in a lame attempt to make it stop it's ceaseless shaking.

Jenna finally let out a distressed sigh, there was no doubt in her mind what had happened to her, the troubling slideshow in her brain refused to shut off.

"Alexander Peterov forced his way into this room and raped me," she squeaked, her voice was barely a shaky whisper, the detective had to strain to hear it, there were so many other voices in the room.

Jenna looked down again at the bruises on her arms and finally broke down crying. It was the first time all night that she had actually allowed herself to cry, and soon it seemed as if she might never be able to stop crying

CHAPTER TWENTY EIGHT

Detective Bellinger sat across the table from Alexander Peterov watching him carefully. The only sound in the stark, white interrogation room was the annoying sound of Alexander casually strumming his fingers on the table.

Bellinger was astounded, for a man who had just committed, what appeared to be, a very brutal rape. Mr. Peterov seemed to be quite placid and calm. Alexander was sitting across the table from him, calmly sipping coffee from a styrofoam cup, waiting for the moment Bellinger asked to hear his story.

Bellinger sighed, Alexander Peterov was impossible to read. He didn't seem upset, guilty, angry or any of the other emotions a man might be right now. In fact, if it weren't for the gray pajama-like outfit he was wearing, it might appear that he was here for a job interview. He looked barely phased to be confined in this interrogation room with the detective.

Bellinger hoped this was all a strange misunderstanding, it would be a shame to have to put the man in jail. He was the reigning World Champion in pairs figure skating and he had just won the gold medal in the Olympics. He was a superstar, it seemed inconceivable that someone of his elite status would stoop to something so chilling as brutally raping a coworker.

"Mr. Peterov, would you like to tell me what happened tonight?" asked Detective Bellinger.

Alexander sighed miserably and gave him an embarrassed frown. "I fear things got a bit out of hand, I am embarrassed to admit," said Alexander, looking quite humbled.

"How so?"

"Well, in our quest to keep things exciting, I fear we might have gotten a little crazy and possibly scared Jenna's poor husband half to death," said Alexander, stifling a bit of an amused smile.

"Please go on, I fear I do not understand Mr. Peterov.

"Jenna and I are lovers. It has been going on for many weeks now. Unfortunately, we both have ties to others, so it has all been quite covert. I am engaged to my partner, she is married to hers. We cannot help the feelings we have for each other..."

"So you and Ms. Bruce have been having an affair," said the Detective, writing furiously on his notepad.

"I hate to call it an affair, that sounds so scandalous. I prefer to say that we are in love, deeply in love. I could not get enough of her, nor could she get enough of me. Whenever we could sneak off together, we did. Of course, we both felt guilty for cheating on our partners, but what could we do? Marika and I are gold medalists and World Champions together, to break that union...well, it would not be possible. A secret relationship was the only way."

"Mr. Peterov, the scene I walked into tonight seemed very violent, not something I would expect of lovers deeply in love," said the Detective, giving Peterov a dubious glare.

"That is what is so embarrassing, I must admit, we were both completely out of control," said Alexander, looking away and shaking his head miserably.

"May I speak freely Detective?" asked Alexander, choking back a sob.

"Certainly, I insist."

"What you witnessed tonight was the result of a crazy sexual game, that unfortunately, got a little out of hand," said Alexander, shrugging slightly at the Detective.

"A sexual game?"

"Jenna is, I guess most men would say, insatiable. She craves sex constantly and she loves anything dangerous or out of the ordinary. You know, like having sex in public places, she adores the thrill of possibly being caught in the act.

In fact, another cast member Rainier Maxim, caught us in the act, just the other night in the alley, outside the ice rink. You could speak with him, in case you have your doubts," said Alexander, infinitely pleased with the way things were working out. He'd never planned to have so many witnesses.

"Believe me, I will be checking out everything you tell me Mr. Peterov. This incident will not be taken lightly," said the Detective.

"I would expect nothing less Detective. That is why I am offering you my full cooperation."

"Thank you Mr. Peterov, please go on."

"Well, Mr. Maxim got quite an eyeful the other night, he was very embarrassed about it. As you might guess, that really turned Jenna on. In fact, that little incident last night got her so excited, she immediately began to plan our last night in Paris. She wanted us to sneak away from the party and have sex in the room she shared with her husband. The thrill of Adam possibly walking in and catching us in the act, was something that excited her immensely," said Alexander, barely able to hide his smile, he was an amazing genius!

"Do go on."

"We were at a party to celebrate our last night in Paris. I knew she was planning to take me back to her room, what I didn't realize was she was also planning to make me very jealous," said Alexander, it was a struggle to hide his smug smile from the Detective.

"Make you jealous, why would she do that?"

"So I would be angry...angry enough to force myself on her. It was a big game to her, she knows I have a terrible jealous streak. When I see that another man wants her I can't help but become very jealous, especially when she flirts with them. When she flirted with other men, we quarreled. The fighting would often be passionate, but the make up sex was so intense, neither of us could get enough of it.

She knew how much I loved her, and how easy it is to make me jealous. Lots of men flirt with Jenna, but when she flirts with them...well, I can barely stand it. Last night, she spent the entire evening flirting with Luc

Dupre, one of the owners of our hotel. In fact, I was so convinced by her flirting, I feared she might actually leave the party with the man. So of course, I was extremely jealous..."

"Mr. Smyth, was he jealous as well?"

"I believe he was at first, it was a struggle, both men vying for her attention, but soon Adam became bored. I believe he left the party with two women who claimed to be big fans of his, he seemed quite happy with their attention," said Alexander, flashing the man a sly smile.

"Then what happened?"

"Well, like I said, Jenna was so convincing in her attentions to Luc Dupre, I feared she was going to leave the party with him. Ask anyone, she was all over him! It wasn't long before I could not take it anymore, my heart was aching, so I left the party. Just after midnight there was a knock at my door, it was Jenna. She told me to come to her room and bring champagne," said Alexander.

"Did you?"

"Of course, I did. My anger was in no way, enough to overcome my need for her. Besides, Jenna has a way of controlling me, she can always make me do exactly what she wants. I arrived at her room a few minutes later. Unfortunately, it is not in my character to forgive and forget, so of course, there was a confrontation."

"What did you say?"

"I told her I was surprised that she wasn't screwing Dupre, she seemed so hell bent on getting him into her bed," snapped Alexander, angrily.

"What did she say to that?"

"She told me that she had tired of me, she thought that Mr. Dupre was very handsome."

"I imagine that made you angry?"

"Of course it did. I called her a whore and threatened to expose our affair to her husband," said Alexander, stifling a bit of a smile.

"What did she say to that?"

"She told me I wouldn't dare, then she tried to slam the door in my face, but I kicked it in. I didn't want her to shut me out, we needed to talk this out. I loved her, if she was just using me for sex, then I wanted to know."

"What did she say?"

"She told me that she wanted Dupre, he had been interested in her as well, but he was put off by the fact that she was married. Apparently, he was not willing to pursue a married woman," said Alexander, distastefully.

"Did that make you angry?"

"Of course it made me angry, how could she want Dupre? Jenna told me that she loves me. We are perfect for each other..."Alexander sniffled and wiped away a tear.

"I am very sorry Mr. Peterov, can you tell me what happened next?"

"I told her that I loved her, that she was the only one I wanted, that's when it started..."

"What started?"

"This, this, nightmare! She told me I was lying, that I didn't love her. I told her I loved her more than anything," wailed Alexander, choking back a sob.

"What did she say to that?"

"She told me I was an idiot, that she could never possibly be faithful to one man. She told me she had screwed not only Rainier, but our sound manager and several other members of the cast, I was completely horrified," breathed Alexander, infinitely pleased with his own acting ability.

"You thought that you were the only one?"

"She had told me I was the only one. I mean, sure, I knew she was married, I knew that her and Adam had sex, but she told me it was very infrequent, and not all that satisfying for her," Alexander sighed in despair.

"Then what happened?"

"I called her a slut and I slapped her," said Alexander, looking completely ashamed.

"You hit her?"

"I know, it's horrible. But I couldn't help it. I was angry and I was hurting so bad. I'd had no idea she'd slept with all those men."

"Did she hit you back?"

"She just stared at me a few moments, like she couldn't believe I had hit her. I was scared, I thought it was over between us," wailed Alexander.

"Go on."

"Then I recognized the look on her face, she wasn't angry, she was completely turned on. The argument intensified. It got a bit physical, when I tried to subdue her, for her own good, she hit me, I think she broke my nose. Soon, I began to realize that we were playing a game. She'd made me jealous on purpose, and now she was doing everything possible to make me angry.

My anger began to come out in a sexual kind of way and it excited us both. The struggling and the name calling was making me so hot, I was ready, but she kept putting me off, doing things to make me angry, so that the fighting never really ended.

Finally, she broke the champagne bottle and threatened to slit my throat with it. I took it away from her and held it to her neck, just to get her to settle down a bit...I had never seen her out of control like this. We were both a little crazy, I ended up cutting her neck a little bit, accidentally. It wasn't deep, but as soon as she saw the blood, she was completely turned on. I didn't want to hurt her, but she wanted me to cut her more..." Alexander managed to sob and tears were soon coursing down his face.

"So you cut her more..."

"We were both so out of control, she just kept pushing me, demanding more and when we finally did it...well...it was intense. Unfortunately, Mr. Smyth walked in and of course, it did look bad. I imagine to an outsider it looked scary as hell, but you're a police officer, I imagine you've seen all kinds of things, here in Paris. I'm sure you realize, for some couples it's a constant struggle, just to keep things exciting.

Detective Bellinger nodded. He had seen a lot of bizarre things over the many years he'd been an officer. It did seem amazing the amount of women who required the suggestion of violence with sex, just to have a freaking orgasm.

Maybe it came from the Victorian beliefs that women were't supposed to enjoy sex. It seemed odd, but Bellinger had no doubt that Alexander was telling the truth. This was not a rape, but merely a couple who was obsessed with sex, they had to keep raising the bar just to keep their interest, eventually, things just got a bit out of hand.

Detective Bellinger looked down at his notes in boredom, there was no crime here, just two lovers who had been overcome with passion and jealousy.

CHAPTER TWENTY NINE

Jenna started crying uncontrollably again, as Gail and Simone tried uselessly to comfort her. The male detective finally gave up and brought in a female detective to question her. The female detective was cold and businesslike, Jenna didn't care for her at all. When the rest of the detectives had finished their collection of evidence, the woman ushered them all out of the room.

The female detective didn't speak the best English and Jenna of course, felt as if she were completely out of her mind, so communication was a bit of an issue. Adam had finally been allowed to come to her and she was clinging to him desperately, like a baby monkey.

"He should go," said the woman, waving her hand at Adam. "There are things I need to ask you of a personal nature, you may not want him to hear."

"No! I want him to stay, I have no secrets," Jenna told her, clinging to Adam's arm, possessively. She was certain Adam knew full well what had happened to her. Hell would freeze over before she let go of his arm, she could not bare to let go of him for a single second, she was still so frightened.

"As you wish. Just so you know, we will also need some swabs, for the sexual assault kit," said the woman, eyeing her seriously.

"Fine," snapped Jenna, sharply.

"We will arrange for you to go to the hospital, they will need to run some tests. You know, to check for semen, make sure you are not pregnant, and to check for sexually transmitted diseases."

Jenna gasped, this was the worst nightmare ever. Even if she were pregnant with Alexander's baby, she would *never* marry him! Hell would freeze over first!

"Ms. Bruce, I'm guessing by all the blood on the sheets, he did manage to penetrate you," said the woman nonchalantly, never taking her eyes off of her clipboard.

Jenna glared at her distastefully and struggled to take a deep breath. It was weird how a police officer could make it all sound so clinical. She crossed her legs uneasily, the word penetrate almost sounded gentle, compared to what Alexander had done to her.

Jenna glanced over at Adam who looked completely horrified. Jenna was now wondering if perhaps, she should have sent him away for this interrogation, but she suspected he knew anyway. Her motives for keeping him with her were purely selfish. Adam was all she had, she needed him!

"Yes," she said, nodding her head grimly. Jenna shuddered and numbly shook off the images of Alexander looming over her, the very thought made tears come to her eyes again. It wasn't supposed to happen this way, it just wasn't fair! Jenna had dreamed that someday Matthew would be her first. Jenna wondered, when Matt found out what Alexander had done, would he even want her now? What was Adam thinking right now? Did he think this was all her fault? She realized the woman was speaking to her again, she hadn't heard a word, she'd been lost in her own thoughts.

"What?"

"I said, did he climax?" asked the woman.

Jenna flashed her a look of distaste. She suddenly felt the urge to vomit. It was the one horrifying image she couldn't seem to get out of her mind, it seemed to haunt her. Jenna bit her lower lip miserably and snuck a look at Adam. His face was expressionless as he sat there, staring off into space.

"I warned you these questions would be of a personal nature, do you still want him here?" asked the woman, pointing to Adam.

Jenna nodded her head emotionlessly and grasped Adam's arm even tighter. "Yes, he climaxed, she sighed. I don't understand, why does it even matter?"

"Rape is not always about arousal and sex, sometimes it is just about domination and violence. The scene here appears to be quite violent. Sometimes rape is merely an outlet for uncontrollable rage."

"Alexander has been sexually harassing me for weeks, he was told to stay away from me..."

"Did you climax?"

"Are you completely insane?"

"Just answer the question Ms. Bruce," snapped the woman.

Jenna gave the woman a disturbed glare, she felt completely naive, her sexual education was so sparse. Was climax the same thing as orgasm? Would that mean that she had somehow enjoyed it?

"If you are asking was it pleasurable...I guess I just find it insane that anyone could find being violently raped pleasurable," snapped Jenna.

"Everyone responds differently. It would not be abnormal for a woman who was raped by a friend or coworker to have some sort of a...ahhh, how shall I say it, a response. When it comes to co workers, often these women secretly long for these men to make the moves on them," said the woman, eyeing her arrogantly.

"I do not know what French women fantasize about, but I did not secretly long for Alexander to violently rape me!"

"I am sorry, it just seems that you appear to be holding yourself together quite well. But as I said, each victim is different, some women shut down completely, they cannot even speak. Some claim to have no memory of the event at all, which many times is a blessing. Some women cannot help their physical response to the, ummm, stimulation, I guess you could say. They have feelings of guilt about their response to their attacker."

"No, there was no response! I couldn't wait to have his sweaty body off of me," snapped Jenna, she looked over at Adam, he looked away quickly, his face was red with embarrassment.

"This next question is going to sound a bit cold," said the woman. Jenna nodded in resignation. To her, all the questions sounded cold and emotionless.

"Did he penetrate you with anything other than his penis or his hands? You know, like an inanimate object," said the woman, her tone was so businesslike, Jenna had to fight the irrational urge to burst out in maniacal laughter. This entire interview was almost as disturbing as the actual rape!

Adam was staring down at the floor emotionlessly, Jenna felt selfish for having him here, but she couldn't help it, she needed him.

"Inanimate object?" breathed Jenna, wondering exactly where this conversation was heading. It seemed to be heading in a direction she didn't like at all.

"For instance, a baseball bat, a gun barrel, a bottle," said the woman, barely looking up from her pad she was scribbling on.

Jenna shuddered and felt her stomach contort, as the horror of what Alexander had done to her replayed in her brain again and again. It was finally over, but for the longest time her ordeal seemed as if it would never end, why did her brain have to keep replaying it over and over again?

"Why would you ask such a thing?" cried Jenna, her voice breaking. The very thought sent a shiver down her spine!

"Like I said Ms. Bruce, sometimes rape is about violence. Penetrating a woman with another object prior to the actual rape is a show of control by the man. Sometimes it is merely a final attempt to terrorize her, sometimes it is meant to hurt her or damage her in some way," said the woman, causing Jenna to shudder uncontrollably.

"Oh my God," cried Jenna, her face was red with embarrassment, poor Adam looked as if he wanted to crawl into a cave somewhere.

"Well?"

"He didn't actually do it, but he threatened to," breathed Jenna, the thought was so terrifying, she could barely speak, she was beginning to feel dizzy again.

"Threatened to penetrate you with what?" asked the woman, her demeanor was distant, Jenna guessed she had to be that way, to deal with all the horrors she saw on her job every day.

Jenna chewed on her lower lip and looked warily at Adam, she didn't want to have this conversation in front of him, but she still couldn't let go of him. He was her best friend, they told each other everything!

"The broken champagne bottle, the one he stabbed me with. He threatened to ruin me for life," said Jenna, sighing disgustedly.

Adam stood up abruptly and ran into the bathroom and vomited. Luckily, the female detective finally decided Jenna had been subjected to enough questioning for one night, she brought the medics in to take Jenna to the hospital.

After what seemed like another assault on her battle scarred body, Jenna was finally released from the hospital. She had received 24 random stitches, and she felt as if every orifice of her body had been swabbed and probed. Unfortunately, it was too soon to tell if she had gotten pregnant from her ordeal.

It was well after five a.m. when Jenna and Adam were finally settled in their new room, which was not the honeymoon suite, so this time, it did have two beds. Jenna had taken a long, hot shower letting the water run over her, taking all the blood and the last traces of Alexander away down the drain. Jenna was exhausted, but she was way too shook up and upset to sleep.

CHAPTER THIRTY

The morning after Alexander's violent attack, the rest of the Company left Paris to continue their tour in Lyon. Jenna and Adam were pretty much forced to stay behind and spend the entire day at the Police station. Jenna was completely miserable, she felt as if she'd told her story over and over again, to whomever would listen, but still she felt the entire police force was eyeing her suspiciously, as if she were the one who had committed the crime.

Of course, she had no idea what Alexander had already told them. She was sure that he was standing by his story, that the two of them had been having a torrid affair for weeks now.

The detective and the Police Chief himself, had already interviewed Alexander and they were both frustrated that their stories came nowhere near matching.

"I do not understand why you insist on pressing charges. The two of you were lovers!" cried the Police Chief, barely able to conceal his impatience with her.

"We were not lovers, he raped me! He had been sexually harassing me for weeks!" cried Jenna, angrily.

The Police Chief rolled his eyes distastefully.

"Vraiment? I know that you let him into your room, there was no forced entry into the room. I know that the two of you quarreled, perhaps things just got a little out of hand," said the Police Chief, shaking his head miserably.

"A little out of hand! He stabbed me, he was going to kill me!" cried Jenna, completely horrified that everyone seemed to be taking Alexander's side.

"I am sorry, but I have a hard time calling this rape when everyone, including your own husband, was aware that you were having some sort of an inappropriate relationship with Peterov," snapped the Police Chief, his face was perfectly serious.

Jenna could feel tears coming to her eyes again. Adam believed her side of the story now, but even he, had believed Alexander's lies until he walked into the hotel room and witnessed the aftermath of Alexander's violent attack.

Jenna was struggling to say anything, this was completely insane. Their conversation was interrupted when another officer came to the door and motioned for the Police Chief to step outside. Jenna took a deep breath and sighed in relief, she couldn't wait for the scrutiny to end. She felt more like the criminal than the victim in this interrogation.

In about five minutes, the Police Chief returned to the room, he was smiling broadly as he sat down at the table across from her.

"I have good news," he said, his eyes twinkling with delight.

Jenna merely nodded, her emotions were stretched so thin, she couldn't even speak, she didn't want to hope that her ordeal might be close to ending.

"Mr. Peterov is very worried about how all this will look when it comes out to the public. He stands by his statement that the sex was consensual, but he is feeling very guilty that you might have been hurt in the heat of the moment and he is quite upset that you are still angry with him this morning. He wanted me to tell you no matter what, he still loves you," said the Police Chief.

Jenna's mouth dropped open in shock. Upset that she was still angry with him? She wanted to scream at the top of her lungs! Alexander was a brilliant actor, he would never let go of the illusion that the two of them were lovers!

"In fact, Alexander himself had to be taken to the hospital with a mental breakdown this morning," said the Police Chief.

Jenna was frowning at him. Alexander would have a mental breakdown when hell froze over, she was certain he didn't feel one ounce of guilt!

"Like I said, he stands by his statement that the sex was consensual, but he feels guilty that things seemed so violent. He told us how you had made him jealous by flirting with Mr. Dupre. He told us that your attraction to Dupre had made him quite angry. The two of you argued and things had got a bit physical. He told us that he really didn't mean for things to get so out of hand," said the Chief.

"Oh my God!" cried Jenna, unable to believe that everyone was buying this crap.

"He wants to make things right. He wants to marry you in exchange for all the charges being dropped," said the Police Chief, smiling at her, as if this were the happy ending she had been hoping for.

"Are you freaking kidding me? That bastard!" cried Jenna, standing up abruptly. Could they not see that this was the prank to end all pranks for Alexander? He was still playing the game. In fact, he may never stop playing the game, ever! Jenna's entire body had started shaking again, she was so upset.

"I believe he's being quite generous, I mean it's not necessary for him to marry you, unless of course, you are pregnant."

"I pray to God I'm not pregnant! The last thing in the world I want is the spawn of that evil bastard growing inside me!" cried Jenna, tears were streaming down her face. She wanted justice, not ridiculous marriage proposals!

The Police Chief was eyeing her as if she had completely lost her mind. He seemed to think it was a perfectly good idea that she marry the heartless bastard who had raped her and stabbed her repeatedly.

"So do you agree?" asked the Police Chief, flashing her an excited smile.

"No, I do not agree!" cried Jenna, perfectly certain that her sanity was leaving her. "First thing, I believe you are already aware, I'm already married to Adam, second thing, I don't want Alexander anywhere near me, comprendez vous?"

"Maybe you should wait, before you make so hasty a decision. What about your husband Adam, how does he feel about all of this? Is he keeping you? Sometimes the husbands...they get a little put off by the whole thing," said the Police Chief, frowning.

"A little put off? Do you think I'm not completely creeped out by this whole ordeal...you're worried about my husband!" cried Jenna, she was shaking her head disgustedly.

Jenna was stunned when a clerk stuck his head into the tiny room and informed her that her lawyer had arrived. Jenna gave the police chief a slight shrug, she hadn't been anticipating a lawyer showing up, she didn't even know any lawyers in France. In moments, the door swung open and a tall, stunning blonde woman was standing in the doorway smiling at her.

Jenna was staring at the woman in disbelief, she was wearing a charcoal business suit and her hair was pinned up in an elegant chignon, she was completely gorgeous! She introduced herself as Solange DeRousse, Mr. Dumontier had hired her to help Jenna prosecute Alexander. Jenna sighed in relief, finally she had someone on her side!

Solange spoke with Jenna at length, she was sympathetic but realistic. She had already met with Alexander's lawyers, so she had already heard Alexander's side of the story and though she suspected he was lying, he was a skilled actor and he had covered his tracks well. If this went to trial, it would be Alexander's word, against Jenna's. After Solange heard Jenna's story, she advised her to push for assault and battery with a deadly weapons charge and just drop the charges of rape.

"Drop the charges of rape? Are you completely mad?" cried Jenna, staring at her in awe. Jenna was angry, she had no intention of dropping any of the charges! Alexander had forced himself on her and raped her, how dare this woman advise her to drop the rape charges!

Solange tried calm Jenna. She wanted to reinforce her reasoning for dropping that particular charge.

"You tell me what you want Jenna, because the decisions we make today will make or break your skating career," said Solange.

"What do you mean?"

"Well, Mr. Dumontier tells me that you are just fifteen years old, is that right?"

"Yes," said Jenna, her heart was already pounding nervously.

"Unlike the U.S., the age of consent in France, is fifteen, so I cannot pursue this as statutory rape, which would make things much easier. Though the scene appears quite violent, there were no witnesses to the actual attack, so it will basically be Alexander's word against yours, and frankly, Mr. Peterov tells a more convincing story," said Solange.

"Solange, I swear, I'm telling the truth," sighed Jenna.

"I have no doubt that you are the one who is being truthful, unfortunately, Alexander has a lot of people convinced that the two of you have been having an affair for many weeks now. Right now, no one in this Police station, save you and I, are aware that you are just fifteen years old and living here in France under the guise of a sham marriage.

Pursuing rape charges against Alexander will most likely, cause all this to come out at the trial, ending up with your deportation, and the unfortunate end of your career with the European Theater Company," said Solange.

Jenna sighed miserably, not only did Alexander rape her, but now she would not have any sort of justice, or so it seemed.

"So basically, you are saying we cannot prosecute Alexander on rape charges," said Jenna, sagging in defeat.

"We can, I am just making you aware now, of the huge can of worms we will be opening up. Your entire life will be placed under a microscope. When the courts discover your age and your fake marriage, it just may ruin your skating career. I say we prosecute him on assault and battery charges," said Solange.

"I don't think you realize what Alexander did to me! He sexually harassed me for weeks, he convinced everyone I knew, including my own partner, that the two of us were having an affair, then he forced himself into my room and raped me. Now this morning, he has offered to marry me, in exchange for me dropping all the charges against him!" cried Jenna.

"Have you ever heard the saying that insanity and brilliance are closely linked? I do not doubt anything that you have told me Jenna, but Alexander, is a man of calculated genius. He has already thought of everything. I almost believe he had a plan in place before he raped you." said Solange, with a frown.

Jenna sighed miserably, it was true, Alexander had told her that no one would ever believe her, he had already stacked the deck in his own favor.

Solange handed Jenna a stack of papers that had been given to her by Alexander's lawyers. Jenna shook her head miserably as she read page after page of eyewitness accounts collected by the defense. They were sworn statements from various people who had supposedly seen her flirting with, not only Alexander, but also Rainier and Luc Dupre.

Now, people who had heard both sides of the story, were wavering, they had no idea who to believe, Alexander was so convincing! Jenna was livid that everyone thought that Alexander was her lover, a man they all supposed was just another conquest for her. She was fifteen years old, she wasn't some experienced seductress!

"Okay," said Jenna, handing the stack of papers back to Solange, shaking her head miserably. "I admit it, I did spend the entire evening flirting with Luc Dupre, but I never, ever, did anything to lead Alexander on. In fact, I did everything I could, to try to end his creepy obsession with me. And Rainier...Rainier and I are only friends. Rainier is a complete gentleman, he walked me back to the hotel one of the other times Alexander was going to attack me! He was trying to protect me!"

"Unfortunately, Alexander himself has sworn under oath that you did more than flirt. He has told the investigators that you made him jealous by sleeping with, not only Dupre, but Rainier Maxim, your show's lighting manager, Claude Dumonde, and three other minor players in your show's cast. Of course they've all denied these allegations but so far, they've all been too shook up by the questioning to actually pass a lie detector test. Unfortunately, things are not looking good," said Solange.

"Oh my God, Alexander is trying to completely destroy me. If I'm such a slut, why on earth would he offer to marry me?"

"His desire to make amends with you, despite your supposed infidelity makes him appear quite gallant to the police department. Besides, marrying an American would be his ticket out of the Soviet Union, did he ever mention that to you?"

"Oh my God, cried Jenna. He did. He told me he was trapped and I was his only way out."

The grand scheme of Alexander's deception was suddenly falling into place in her mind.

"Desperate men do desperate things. At this point, it doesn't matter what the truth is, we only have to minimize the damage that has already been done by all these unfounded rumors. You must realize, his lawyers are going to do whatever they can, to make you look like the biggest slut who ever lived!

As far as these men are all concerned, it is always the fault of the woman. Even if the only reason they can come up with, is that you were just too beautiful. Apparently being attractive, gives men the right to turn into crazed lunatics and attack you." said Solange, rolling her eyes miserably.

"If it was truly just about attraction. I could almost understand it. This wasn't just about sex Solange, it was a creepy obsession, I endured the sexual harassment for weeks. As for the rape, which all the men here in the Police Department are sure was consensual. He tortured me! Can they not see that? I'm covered with bruises, he cut me and stabbed me multiple times. If Adam had not come back when he did, I might be dead! How can they possibly justify that?" Jenna was angry, she knew she would never get justice with Alexander.

"I do not believe his intent was to kill you. You are strong and independent, Alexander recognized that right away. The only way he could get you to give in to his demands, was to terrorize you and overpower you. The physical dominance he used was not so much to hurt you, as to break you down emotionally.

Alexander's defense will testify that most of your wounds were superficial. The deeper wounds, Alexander has already admitted were quite accidental besides, he is the one who has a broken nose and two black eyes...it has earned him a great deal of sympathy...from the Police," said Solange, bracing herself for Jenna's retort.

"Of course, I broke his nose! I was basically fighting for my life, he had me convinced he was going to murder me!" cried Jenna.

"I am sorry, my hands are tied, besides Adam, there are no other witnesses, so it is basically your word against his. Unfortunately, Adam arrived at the end he was not witness to the beginning of your ordeal, which would be more helpful to our case.

Of course, Alexander has told everyone that you invited him to your room. Unfortunately, our backs are against the wall, the police found no evidence that he forced his way in. The lock on the door wasn't broken. There was a footprint on the door, but Alexander has explained that away as well, he told the police that the two of you were arguing. He was jealous of your attentions to Luc Dupre. Soon, the argument got physical and that led to rough sex. As for the cutting, he told his lawyers the first cut was an accident but it turned you on so much, that things got out of control after that. He's explained the entire ordeal away as a sexual game and unfortunately, all the men here believe him...if it goes to a jury trial, I have no doubt the outcome will be the same..."

Jenna frowned, she felt so stupid, she had believed that Alexander was too inebriated to follow her all the way to her room, the lock on the door wasn't broken because he'd forced his way in before she even got the door shut.

"The Police have questioned the entire cast and crew. Unfortunately, there were only a couple of people they spoke with that weren't completely convinced that the two of you were having an affair. It is no wonder, Alexander is probably the most gifted actor I have ever met. When I questioned him, he was able to break down in tears at the drop of a hat. Especially when he goes on and on about how much he still loves you," said Solange, with a frown.

Jenna sighed and frowned too. She never thought it would be possible that she would end up looking like the "bad guy" in all this, but she was apparently wrong. Jenna still couldn't talk about any of this without breaking down in tears, but apparently all the police officers just thought they were tears of guilt...for shamelessly leading Alexander on for all those weeks.

"So I will never get any justice, that's what you are saying," snapped Jenna, angrily.

"No, not for the rape...I'm sorry..." said Solange.

After what seemed like the longest day ever, Jenna and Adam were finally back in their hotel room later that evening, watching TV and trying to relax. They both felt like they'd been put through the wringer. They both felt like they were the ones that had committed a crime!

Jenna had been getting discouraged with all of their questioning because no one seemed to be concerned about the truth. It seemed all they wanted to do was discredit her and Adam so they wouldn't have to prosecute Alexander. Even the Police Chief himself had told her multiple times that Alexander was a World Champion and he felt terrible that she was going to ruin his career!

Jenna wondered if Alexander had murdered her, would it still be her fault that Alexander had ruined his career? These people were all morons as far as she was concerned! Jenna was still a walking bundle of nerves. She still expected Alexander to burst through the door at any minute and attempt to finish her off. Jenna realized that Alexander was in Police custody, but they seemed to be so sympathetic with him, she almost expected them to just let him go!

That evening Jenna and Adam were sitting there on the couch watching an episode of Happy Days in French, when there was a tentative knock on the door. Jenna was like a zombie, there was no way she was going to get up and answer the door. Adam got up reluctantly and answered the door.

"Jenna, it's for you," said Adam, his voice had an edge of sarcasm in it.

Jenna frowned, hoping that it wasn't another Police detective or someone like that. She was done with the interrogations for one day. Jenna was beginning to feel more like the criminal than the victim. She turned around to see who was standing there in the doorway.

Jenna was stunned to see it was Luc Dupre. He smiled at her from the doorway, he was holding a huge bouquet of flowers. Jenna resisted the urge to roll her eyes, she stood up and walked curiously over to the door. What could Luc Dupre possibly want?

"Bonjour Jenna. I just came to check on you. I have been very worried about you," he said, holding the flowers out to her.

"Thank you," said Jenna, taking the flowers from him and giving him an odd look.

"Um...I just wanted to let you know...if you need anything..." he was looking down at the floor, he seemed to be at a loss for words.

Jenna was staring at him with a blank look on her face wondering why he had come here, then she remembered something that Solange had mentioned to her. Solange had told her she might be able to sue the hotel, for not taking better security measures. Jenna had completely dismissed the idea. She knew, what happened to her, was in no way, the fault of the hotel, though she imagined that Luc had come to her room tonight, to smooth things over, to head off such a lawsuit.

"It's okay Luc, you don't have to worry, I'm not going to sue the hotel," she said, almost rolling her eyes. Jenna had thought the idea was crazy when Solange had suggested the possibility to her, she didn't want money. She wanted justice!

"I am not here because I think you are going to sue the hotel. I am here because I am finding myself drawn to you. I enjoyed talking to you at dinner. The two of us have a lot in common. I was devastated when I was called back to the hotel last night. I feel terrible that your time in Paris had to end so badly," said Luc. He gave her a sincere looking smile.

Adam was standing there next to her, he rolled his eyes and ambled back over and flopped down on the couch. Jenna was standing there staring at Luc with a puzzled look on her face. It only took a few moments for her frazzled brain to register what was going on here. Luc was standing shyly in the doorway, smiling broadly at her and Jenna was realizing that in her quest to keep herself surrounded by men that were not Alexander, she had now attracted the attention of Luc Dupre.

Jenna was silently rueing her own naivety, she hated to hurt anyone. She had assumed that Luc was nothing but a rich, French playboy, accustomed to flirting with women all the time, but never really forming any serious feelings for them. Jenna had assumed that like many other guys she had met, his intent was to take her home with him at the end of the evening, when that didn't happen, she assumed that she would travel on to Lyon and he would forget all about her.

"Um...I appreciate you coming by Luc, but Adam and I will be leaving for Lyon in the morning and..."

"I know," said Luc. "I just wanted to know if I could see you again...sometime."

Jenna almost sighed in frustration. She had only flirted with him in a fruitless attempt keep Alexander away.

"Luc...I'm sorry that I flirted with you like that. I thought that if Alexander was convinced that I was interested in you...well the truth is, I should have never flirted with you in the first place, I'm married," she told him breathlessly, nodding toward Adam on the couch.

"Well, I happen to know that the whole marriage thing between you and Mr. Smyth is nothing but an illusion," said Luc, flashing her a sly smile.

Jenna's jaw dropped and Adam suddenly jumped back up from the couch and darted toward them. Jenna couldn't even speak, she was staring at Luc in shock...no one outside the Company knew that their marriage was a scam, except maybe Solange, and her parents. It was something that could never be public knowledge, otherwise her career with the European Theater Company would be over! Jenna was desperately racking her brain, trying to figure out how he could have found out. This was a nightmare!

"How did you find this out?" cried Adam, his face was stunned, he looked as if he was panicking.

"You just told me," said Luc, with a sly smile. "It was just a little theory I had. You just confirmed it."

"Luc, you cannot tell anyone!" breathed Jenna, still in shock.

"I am not going to tell anyone. The last thing I want, is to have you deported. I just wanted you to know, if you need anything let me know. I know what everyone is trying to make this look like..." he told her, gently.

Jenna sighed, she could feel the tears coming to her eyes again. This was a nightmare, she wondered why she had even come to Paris in the first place. Jenna looked away in embarrassment. She was not the person everyone thought that she was, but she had stupidly put herself in this position. She was rueing her decision to go along with all of this, and pretend she was much older than she really was.

"Don't worry Jenna...I know the truth..."he said, looking into her eyes meaningfully. His piercing blue eyes seemed to make her heart pound nervously. Jenna took a deep breath, and a careful step away from him, he was standing much too close to her.

"Luc, I..." Jenna felt bad. She had led Luc on and she wanted to apologize for flirting with him. She wanted to tell him she really wasn't interested in him like that, but she couldn't seem to find the words.

"You do not have to explain, I understand...you did what you had to do," he said, nodding to her. "Au revoir Mon Cheri," he said, taking her hand and kissing it, then he gave Adam a little bow and he turned and headed down the hall.

"Au revoir," said Jenna, her voice was faint and rough with emotion as she watched him walk away down the hall, her face was a mask of confusion.

Jenna closed the door and walked back into the room, she was shaking her head slowly in confusion as she set the bouquet of flowers down on the marble topped table behind the sofa. Adam was snickering as she approached the sofa and flopped down on it.

"Don't worry, I'll let you tell Matt you have a new boyfriend," said Adam, a sly smile creeping across his face.

"Shut up," she snapped. Jenna folded her arms over her chest and pouted. This mess just got worse and worse.

"I must say, he is a much better catch than Alexander," said Adam, flashing her a devilish smile.

"Any man in the world would be a much better catch than Alexander," seethed Jenna, angrily.

"You do realize, his family owns the chain of hotels we stay in, here in France, don't you?" asked Adam, flashing her another sly smile.

"They do?" she asked, looking at him incredulously.

"Yep, I shouldn't be surprised if he showed up in Lyon, just to try to see you again. You had better be nice to him though, he could refuse to let us stay in his hotels, now that he knows we're not legal. Although I get the distinct impression he is more than okay with the fact that you and I are not married. Ahhh...I can't help but feel bad for the guy, he's just another hopeless victim of your flirting," said Adam, with a little laugh.

"I feel bad. I *did* flirt with him, but he didn't really seem like the kind of guy that was really serious. I mean...I figured we'd go on to Lyon and I'd never see him again," said Jenna.

"We can only hope that they don't call him as a witness for Alexander, if he gets on the stand and tells the jury you flirted with him and he was attracted to you, it's going to look really bad, especially since you are supposed to be married to me!" said Adam, frowning.

Jenna sighed miserably, knowing Adam was absolutely right. Her entire life was being examined under a microscope right now. She couldn't wait for the scrutiny to end...

Jean Marie Stanberry

CHAPTER THIRTY ONE

Jenna was beginning to wonder if her and Adam would ever get out of Paris. They had been planning to leave for Lyon this morning, but the police called Jenna in for more questioning. Mademoiselle DeRousse picked her up at the hotel and drove her to the police station.

They were led into the "conference room" which was really a very stark white, industrially furnished, interrogation room. They were told that there was a new investigator on the case, and he would be in to speak to them soon. Jenna was nervously chewing her nails, she expected the worst. So far, everyone here had treated her as if she were the real criminal and she had brought this all on herself. Jenna expected today to be more of the same.

A clerk brought Jenna and Solange both coffees and about five minutes later, the new investigator walked in. He was tall and refined looking in his dark, pinstriped suit. He was wearing a navy, paisley silk tie. His perfectly groomed, dark brown hair was peppered with silver and his grayish blue eyes seemed to light up the entire room. Jenna almost rolled her eyes the moment he walked in the door. This guy didn't look like a detective, he looked like a movie star. She almost groaned, she pretty much expected today to go exactly as yesterday had.

"Good morning ladies, I'm Detective Garnier, thank you for coming this morning," he told them in his smooth, velvety voice. Jenna resisted the urge to roll her eyes and sat there patiently with her hands folded in her lap.

Detective Garnier spoke exclusively with Ms. DeRousse for a few moments. Jenna was staring blankly at the stark, white wall. She had pretty much tuned them out. It seemed to her that everyone was more worried about Alexander's fate than hers. She was patiently waiting for the interrogation of the victim to begin. Everyone seemed so convinced that she was the guilty one.

Jenna just wanted this nightmare to be over, she'd been completely humiliated and she was tired of talking about it. She'd hoped to go on to Lyon today so they could resume their practices with the company. She was afraid if they didn't show up for practice soon, they would be edited out of the show and she would be sent home to her parents.

"All right Miss Bruce, I realize that you have been asked a lot of these questions before, so please just bear with me," said the Detective, giving her a wry smile.

Jenna sighed and gave him a resigned nod.

"Tell me, what was your relationship with Mr. Peterov," asked the Detective.

"We were co-workers," she sighed.

"How long have you known Mr. Peterov?" asked Detective Garnier, looking up and assessing her cooly.

"Adam and I arrived in Paris on April 19th, I met Alexander the next day, at rehearsal on the 20th," said Jenna.

"So would you say that you and Mr. Peterov had to work closely together?" he asked.

"Unfortunately, yes."

"Why do you say it like that? Unfortunately?"

"The first week of practices, everything seemed fine, Alexander seemed very nice, polite even. The second week is when Alexander began sexually harassing me. It started out slowly, it seemed almost accidental at first.

As the weeks went on, things began to escalate. Soon, whenever we had to work together he was constantly touching me, talking dirty to me," Jenna told him distastefully.

"Did you ask him to stop?" asked the Detective.

"Of course I did! I did everything I could think of to let him know I did not want to be the object of his attention!" cried Jenna.

"When his behavior escalated, did you communicate your concerns to the company's management? Did you file a formal complaint?"

"I communicated my concerns to anyone who would listen! In fact, I had threatened to quit and return to Chicago. I had spoke with both Simone and Gail about it, and later Rainier and Mr. Dumontier knew as well," she told him.

"And what did the Company do to remedy the problem?" asked Detective Garnier.

"No one took it seriously. They didn't really see Alexander as a threat, they thought he was just a horny guy who was shooting his mouth off," said Jenna, rolling her eyes miserably.

"The company told you this?"

"More or less. I was told that they had a talk with him, several talks as a matter of fact. He was told if he didn't stop harassing me, he and Marika would be cut from the show," said Jenna.

"Can you tell me me, in your own words, exactly what happened that night that you *claim* Alexander raped you?" asked the Detective.

Jenna cringed when she heard the slight inflection of sarcasm in his voice. He already didn't believe her, what was the point in pouring her heart out once again, when obviously, he thought this was all a joke?

"Can you tell me, in all honesty, that you will believe anything I say, after hearing Alexander's own award worthy performance?" snapped Jenna angrily.

"I cannot help but be surprised by your cynicism Miss Bruce, I have not given you any reason to doubt me, have I?" asked the Detective, his face completely stunned.

"I would greet your questions with the utmost respect, had I not already been treated with disdain and contempt by the rest of your department. Your entire department seems to believe it was Alexander, not I who was wronged. I guess I feel I have no other outlet, but to be cynical of your reception," said Jenna.

"You must know, the deck has been stacked against you from the start.. Everything you've told us, has already been refuted by others. The only other witness...your husband, can only hope to save his own reputation," said the Detective, cringing at the sight of Jenna's angered face.

"I admit Alexander did quite skillfully stack the deck against me but..."

"Wait, let me just show you this," said the Detective, pulling several sheets of notes from his briefcase and handing them to her.

"What is this?" she demanded.

"These are sworn statements, all from people we interviewed who believe that you and Alexander are currently having an affair," he said.

Jenna frowned and reluctantly took the sheets of paper from his hand. Her eyes scanned the list in boredom. Of course, nearly every member of the cast was on this list, it was no more than she expected. Then a name jumped out at her that made her entire body convulse in anxiety.

"My mother! You spoke with my mother and she told you that she thought that Alexander and I were having an affair!" cried Jenna, tears coming to her eyes.

"To be sure, she actually volunteered the information. She worried that your relationship with Mr. Smyth was less than satisfying for you, she told us that the two of you had discussed it by phone," said the detective.

"Detective, my mother is crazy. I'm not sure why I ever called her in the first place, but I certainly did not call her to tell her that I was having a covert affair with Alexander."

"She seemed perfectly lucid when I spoke with her. Why would she lie about such a thing? I mean you *are* her daughter, wouldn't she at least try to protect you?" asked Mr. Garnier, his face was suddenly wrinkled with confusion.

"I guess I should have expected this, she's detested me from the moment she found out she was pregnant with me. Looking back now, I realize how stupid it was, for me to ask her advice. Alexander had been sexually harassing me, and I'm not sure why, but I imagined my own mother might help me to deal with it. Do you think that is too much to ask Detective? All I wanted was someone who cares about me, someone who might offer me some guidance."

Detective Garnier looked uncomfortable, but said nothing, he was waiting for her to elaborate.

"I forget that my own mother is not really like a mother at all, she thought that I should welcome Alexander's attentions, since he is a world champion. She thought it would be good publicity, to have my name linked with his, she...oh no...she wouldn't...." breathed Jenna, it was all becoming crystal clear to her. Her own mother had betrayed her.

"Are you saying that your mother lied to us?"

"I'm saying that my mother would like nothing more, than to have me forever out of her way. Even if that meant I be unhappily married to Alexander. She coveted his status as a World Champion, she would have been quite happy to see our names linked, even in a scandal such as this," said Jenna, shaking her head miserably.

"So your mother lied in the hope that you might, in the heat of the scandal, marry Mr. Peterov?"

"I imagine she hoped he would come up with a proposal, to smooth over the ensuing scandal, since I managed to live through his attack," snapped Jenna.

"Miss Bruce, most of your stab wounds were not deep. I do not believe his intent was to murder you. I must defer to your slightly disagreeable personality...perhaps you drove the man to violence."

Jenna stood up, completely enraged. "My personality has never been disagreeable until I came here, to this small minded and admittedly biased police department! Including the Chief, the entire department has been hell bent since my arrival here, on proving Alexander's innocence and making me look like the criminal!

Alexander raped me and I still bare the bruises and the stitches from his attack. We were not lovers, but even if we had been, you tell me what in your very small minds allows him to attack me like that and not be punished. I fought him to the point of exhaustion and still he won, how does that make me the criminal, sir?"

Solange had been very quiet till this moment, she gasped and stood up as well, afraid that Jenna had enraged the detective.

"Jenna please, contain yourself," she cried.

The detective sighed. "I am very sorry. I feel the entire department has been biased by all Alexander's claims of sexual games and a desire for danger. You are right, had you been in a relationship and he violently attacked you, it could not be justified."

"Thank you Detective, and that being said, let me tell you again that the only relationship between Alexander and I was our professional relationship, which was growing more and more strained as time went on.

Before that night, there were several other episodes, where he attempted to force himself on me. I'm guessing in the hopes of being discovered, so that he might reinforce the illusion that the two of us were having an affair. I assure you that I only tried to discourage Alexander's advances, I never led him on."

"Tell me about your marriage to Adam. My information here says that you were married this spring...in Chicago?"

"Yes," she breathed...she hated to lie, even though she wasn't officially under oath.

"I find that very odd, because I contacted the Cook County department of records, it seems they have no official record of your marriage," said the Detective, giving her an arrogant nod.

"We weren't married in Cook County, we were married in Lake County," Jenna told him, her heart was suddenly faltering nervously.

"Well Miss Bruce, perhaps I forgot to mention that not only did I contact Cook County, but also the counties of Lake, DuPage, Kane, Kendall, McHenry and Dekalb," said the Detective, looking at her very seriously.

Jenna sighed and looked down at the table anxiously. If it came out that she was a minor and her marriage to Adam had been faked, she'd most likely be deported back to the states and her career with the European Theater Company would be over.

"I've been doing quite a bit of research, in fact, I haven't slept in more than twenty four hours. I've been working like crazy trying to figure all of this out. So far, I have figured out that you are not really married, and you are not even close to being eighteen. I am still trying to figure out why the company would do that to you. To me, it seems ridiculous to ask a fifteen year old girl to fake a marriage to her partner just so she can skate in an ice show. Did they not care about your welfare at all?" cried the Detective, incredulously.

"It wasn't the really the company...it was my parents that did it actually. My father, I'm guessing. I didn't even realize what they had done till we arrived here in Paris," said Jenna, still looking down at the table, she couldn't bring herself to look up at him.

"Your own parents faked your marriage?" he asked, he seemed genuinely concerned.

Jenna nodded her head grimly. She had known as soon as she found out about it, that this was a huge mistake. It was too late now...the damage was done.

"It seems so odd that they would do such a thing, according to my research, your parents are both professional people. Your father is a college professor, and your mother is Lydia Gray, the famous dancer right?" asked the detective, shaking his head slowly in disbelief.

Jenna nodded her head again. She couldn't bring herself to talk about her strange, dysfunctional family. She was sure if everything was falling apart, the way she thought it was falling apart, she'd be going back to Chicago sometime soon. Of course, her parents would be angry that she had allowed their little scheme to fall apart!

"What could have possessed them to cook up such a an elaborate hoax? I mean if you were my daughter, there is no way..."

"You must understand Detective Garnier, my parents never wanted children in the first place. Their *careers* are their lives. My mother's pregnancy and my subsequent birth was a tragic little mistake. I essentially crashed their party. They really don't care to have me around.

I've pretty much lived with my coach Hans and his wife Carolina in St. Louis since I was twelve, before that, I lived mostly with my grandparents. My parents could really care less what happened to me. I'm quite certain they worked out a very lucrative deal with Mr. Dumontier.

Since I'm a minor I don't collect a regular paycheck like the rest of the cast, I merely get a stipend. I imagine the bulk of my pay is going straight into my parent's bank account. Having me shipped off to Europe for the summer and being paid handsomely for it, was probably a dream come true for them."

The detective was staring at her with a shocked look on his face. Jenna shrugged slightly. She had somehow gotten used to the insanity that surrounded her family.

"Tell me, what exactly is your relationship with Mr. Smyth?" asked the detective, who suddenly looked like he was getting a headache, as he rubbed his temples and squinted at her.

"He's my best friend and my skating partner, I've been with him for the past three years, since I was twelve and he was fifteen," she told him.

"Are the two of you sleeping together?" he asked, not even looking up from the legal pad he was scribbling on.

"No! It's not like that between Adam and I." Jenna cried, indignantly.

"Are you saying you are not lovers now, or not ever?" he asked, still writing furiously on his pad.

"Not ever," she told him, rolling her eyes disgustedly.

"Is he gay?" he asked, looking up at her curiously.

"No!" Jenna cried. She bit her lip and cringed a bit at her harsh tone. It was beginning to become a sore subject for her. She was tired of everyone assuming that there was something was wrong with them because they weren't screwing like a couple of rabbits!

"It is just that he's eighteen years old and...well, I cannot imagine how hard it would be for him to..." said the detective.

"It *has* been hard for us detective, we were basically thrown into this situation without any warning. I didn't really mean that it wasn't a possibility...someday. The truth is, before Alexander, I had never...well, you know...and... Well, I sure as hell hadn't planned on a creep like Alexander being my first! Adam is a great guy, if anybody deserved a chance, it would be him..."

"Are you saying that you were a virgin when Mr. Peterov raped you?" cried Detective Garnier, his face was suddenly ashen and contorted in shock.

"Yes," said Jenna, trying to steady her voice. She was on the verge of breaking down in tears again, and she was tired of crying about this over and over again, she just wanted this nightmare to end!

"The doctor at the hospital had hinted that you were a virgin in his report, but that part of his examination was thought to be a mistake. Since you claimed to be married to Mr. Smyth, no one here was willing to believe that you were actually a virgin. You are quite serious...you've never had sex with Mr. Smyth?"

"No, it's never been like that for Adam and I. Though recently things have been changing...I guess there have been times when I have found myself attracted to him."

"So you want him, but he doesn't want you," said Detective Garnier, still not looking up from him notepad.

"If you would please let me finish Detective Garnier...I guess I'm not really sure what either of us want. There have been several incidents...where things happened..."

"What kind of things?"

"Things that just don't happen between best friends...I have a boyfriend in Boston, and I never had any reason to think that Adam and I might...." Jenna hesitated, this all seemed way too intimate to get into with a complete stranger, but who else could she confide in, certainly not her own mother!

"Please, go on."

"Our first night in Paris, the stupid company put us in the honeymoon suite. Instead of a room with two double beds like I expected, there was just the one king size bed. After we arrived we'd spent the entire evening at a reception to welcome the new cast. There was lots of drinking. Adam

ended up getting completely plastered,"
Jenna told him.

"And?"

"When we got back to our room that night,
I was shocked. I had realized they were
going to put us in the same room, it's just
that I had expected our room to have two
beds, not just that one. Adam was not
himself...like I told you..he'd had too much
to drink."

"Did the two of you quarrel?" asked the
detective.

"No, it was the alcohol...he started talking
nonsense. Since the company was
presenting us to everyone as a married
couple, he wanted to consummate our
marriage," Jenna told the detective, she
could feel her cheeks getting hot and pink
with embarrassment. She'd never told
anyone but Colin about that night. She'd
never even told Adam all the details, he'd be
horrified if he knew!

"Did he try to force himself on you?"
asked the Detective.

"I had been worried about that, but he was so drunk he eventually passed out. Then I left the room and spent the night with Colin, I figured that was the safest thing to do...since Colin *is* gay." she told him.

"Wait, you spent the night with Colin Anders?" asked the detective, raising his eyebrows at her.

"Yes, don't look at me like that, it wasn't like that at all. I've already told you that he's gay...we're friends," snapped Jenna.

"Did anyone see you leaving his room in the morning?" asked the detective.

Jenna frowned. "I don't think so. What difference does it make?"

"I am only trying to head off any rumors that might come up," said Detective Garnier, looking at her seriously. "Adding another name to the list of possible sexual partners would only make things worse.

"There is a list of possible sexual partners?" Jenna cried, completely shocked by the disgusting possibility.

"Not on my desk, but I can guarantee the defense attorneys are compiling one. Alexander is painting you as a slut to justify his rage. You know, poor Alexander was head over heels in love, but Jenna was toying with him, sleeping with whomever she could, just to make him jealous," said Detective Garnier.

Jenna shook her head miserably, once again she was beginning to feel more like the criminal than the victim.

"I told you, Colin never laid a hand on me, he's gay," snapped Jenna, disgustedly.

"It makes no difference, many of the gay ones go either way. I still don't want the possibility of his name showing up on some list," said Detective Garnier, scribbling something on his pad.

Jenna sighed miserably, she thought this detective had a lot of nerve, he didn't even know them.

"Colin is a wonderful friend, I will not have you speaking of him like that!" she cried

"I'm not trying to insult him, I'm merely being realistic. So are you certain that no one saw you with him?" asked Detective Garnier, his voice rising with irritation.

"I don't think anyone saw me coming out of his room that morning. I guess I really can't be sure. I wasn't being sneaky about it, so I really wasn't paying attention," said Jenna, with a little shrug.

"You and Mr. Anders must be quite close, he was one of the few people in the company that wasn't completely convinced that Mr. Peterov and you were having an affair," said Detective Garnier, he leaned back in his chair and stretched.

"That's right, besides Adam, Colin is my best friend in the Company, he knew exactly what was going on," Jenna told him.

"He also knew your marriage was a sham?" asked the detective.

"Yes," Jenna nodded her head again.

"Alexander knew it as well?" he asked.

Jenna frowned, the detective continued to scribble notes.

"Alexander knew that the marriage was a scam...he thought that Adam and I were lovers," said Jenna.

"Really? Why did he think that you and Adam were lovers? Just because the two of you slept in the same room together?"

"No...because I told him," said Jenna, staring down at the laminate table top.

"Why did you tell him such a thing? Were you trying to make him jealous?" asked Garnier, still scribbling on his notepad.

"It was faulty reasoning. I thought that maybe Alexander just wanted me because I was a virgin," she sighed miserably. "I thought that maybe if he were convinced that Adam and I were lovers, he wouldn't want me anymore...he would back off."

"That line of reasoning didn't work out then."

"No," Jenna shook her head miserably.

"Well regardless, I imagine you will be heading back to the states soon. When this faked marriage comes out in the trial, you do know that the authorities will most likely send you back to the states, don't you?" he asked, grimly.

"Please Detective Garnier, I can't go back there. Does this really all have to come out in the trial?" Jenna cried, she was suddenly trying not to hyperventilate, she did not want to go back to Chicago!

"Do you think it would be ethical, for me to ignore what I know and let you stay here under the guise of a sham marriage?" he asked, staring at her incredulously.

Jenna was suddenly panicking! "What if Adam and I *really* got married? Could I stay?" cried Jenna, she could barely catch her breath all of a sudden.

"Miss Bruce, please relax. Under the circumstances, don't you think it's best you just go home to your parents. You've just been through a terrible ordeal, you don't really want to get married, you're fifteen," said detective Garnier, staring at her oddly.

"I would do it, if it would keep me from being sent home to my parents," she told him blandly, though there was a lot of things she would do, to avoid being sent home to her parents.

"I am sure you are exaggerating, could it really be that bad, to be sent home to your parents?" he stared at her, he was hardly convinced.

"Mr. Garnier, there are things in life that are worse than a fifteen year old being on her own in Paris. Besides, it's not like I'm a runaway out on the street. I'm with the Company, if it weren't for Alexander, no one would even know the truth right now. All of Europe is convinced that Adam is my husband. Most people don't even guess, or seem to care that I am only fifteen years old," she told him with a shrug.

"I guess if we could avoid a trial...work out a deal with Peterov and his lawyers." said Garnier, thoughtfully.

Jenna frowned, she was now certain that her staying in Europe was going to entail Alexander somehow getting off scott free for what he'd done to her. Though Jenna really wasn't about to give up the rest of her tour and go back to Chicago for the rest of the summer.

"What will happen then? Will he get any jail time?" cried Jenna. "He not only raped me, but I'm certain he intended to kill me, Detective Garnier. He needs to be punished!"

"We're only going to deal with his lawyers, not drop all the charges. Unfortunately, the rape charge would be the one charge least likely to stick and hardest to prove. His lawyers will essentially do whatever it takes to discredit you. They will drag your name through the mud, all in an attempt to make all this look consensual. My suggestion is we go for assault and battery with a deadly weapon, we give him a privacy clause, maybe a suspended sentence..."

Jenna closed her eyes and rubbed her temples, now it seemed that she was fighting a headache as well. The thought of them just letting Alexander out of jail was totally shaking her up. Jenna just wanted him behind bars, where he could never touch her again!

"And what do I stand to gain from this?" she asked, she couldn't help it, the sarcasm was sneaking into her voice. She felt like Alexander had already won.

"Privacy essentially. No one will dissect your life and discover that you are here in Europe under the guise of a sham marriage, with faked paperwork. You will get to stay on with the Theater Company and finish your season."

Jenna looked down and studied the fake woodgrain of the table. She was torn, she wanted to stay on with the company, but she also wanted Alexander in jail forever. Somehow giving Alexander any sort of a break just didn't seem right. She sighed miserably.

"Why don't we all take a little break. You and Mademoiselle DeRousse can go have some lunch, we'll meet back here at one o'clock and you can let me know what you've decided."

Jenna nodded numbly, her stomach had been growling, but she'd been ignoring it. She'd skipped breakfast because she was too nervous to eat anything. She had decided that throwing up on a police detective was never a good idea.

Jean Marie Stanberry

CHAPTER THIRTY TWO

Jenna and Solange walked to a little cafe at the end of the block. While they were waiting for their food, Jenna excused herself and ran to the restroom in the back of the cafe. When she came out, there were two huge men standing there, just outside the door. Jenna felt a bit uncomfortable when neither of the men moved at all so she could walk past. Jenna looked up in confusion, realizing that the men were looming over her, assessing her cooly.

Jenna was froze in place, it seemed odd that they were just standing there staring at her like that. A gentleman would step aside and let her pass. Jenna was suddenly alarmed and shrinking away from the two huge men, she felt anxious and claustrophobic with them towering over her like that.

The larger, and apparently older man, finally spoke as Jenna stared up at them, numbly.

"Jennalise Bruce?" he asked. He had a deep, booming voice, and a thick Russian accent.

"Who wants to know?" asked Jenna, taking a deep breath and eyeing them both suspiciously. She was having a bad feeling about this.

Without warning, the shorter, stockier, man suddenly grabbed both Jenna's arms and shoved her roughly against the plaster wall. The force of the blow took her breath away, and she was too stunned to scream.

"Who we are, is not your concern," said the man, as he leaned closer to her, his stubbly face was just inches from her own. Jenna drew in a shaky breath and glared at the man.

"We have come to make you a very lucrative deal," said the older man, who was suddenly eyeing her with an amused smile.

"I don't make deals with strangers," said Jenna, forcing her voice to sound confident. She was suddenly acutely aware that this man was crushing her into the wall, in much the same way Alexander had, her wrists were searing from the pain of his unforgiving grip. Jenna was trying to calm herself and not hyperventilate.

"I think you should listen to what we have to say," seethed the stubbly faced man, in her face. Jenna looked into his cold, dark eyes as he calmly crushed her into the wall. She was struggling to focus and not dissolve into a panic. His breath on her face was unpleasant and making her eyes burn. Jenna was frowning distastefully.

"I think you should get off of me before I scream. You are hurting me," snapped Jenna, her heart was accelerating as the adrenaline coursed through her body, she was struggling to keep her voice calm.

The man released her with a little shove. Jenna stood there for a moment, rubbing her wrists, which were still bruised from her encounter with Alexander. Jenna glanced slowly up at both men looming over her, she knew she couldn't get past them if she tried. She also knew that Alexander had sent them. Jenna sighed miserably, Alexander was in police custody, yet she still wasn't safe from him.

"We are offering you twenty thousand dollars American, to drop all charges against Alexander," said the older man, eyeing her arrogantly.

"Twenty thousand dollars?" she mouthed, her eyes were wide. Jenna could hardly believe they were actually serious.

The older man opened a duffle bag and showed her the stacks of bills inside. Jenna was staring into the bag in shock. She had never seen that much money before. She was stunned. She wondered who these men were and why Alexander's innocence was so important to them.

"Who are you?" she demanded, assessing them both cooly.

"That is none of your concern," said the younger man, the one that had roughed her up.

"Like I told you before, I don't make deals with strangers," Jenna told them, refusing to be bullied by them.

"Refusing us would be a grave mistake Miss Bruce. Let us just say that your life depends on it," said the older man, flashing her a toothy grin. Jenna grimaced and drew in a stunned breath. She was already glancing around slowly, trying to figure out how she could throw the two of them off, and escape. She was sure it wouldn't be easy, she was getting the impression that these two men were professional thugs, they had probably seen just about everything in their careers.

"I'm sorry but I don't take very kindly to threats," said Jenna, narrowing her eyes at him.

"Well, let us just call it an agreement then. Here are the terms of our little agreement," said the older man, eyeing her very seriously. "You will tell the Police this was all a mistake. You will tell them that you and Alexander were lovers, despite the fact that he was engaged to Marika. Your little affair went on for a while, then

Alexander soon began to realize that he truly did love Marika, thus he attempted to end your little affair.

You of course, did not want it to end. That evening you seduced Alexander and you staged the rape to punish him for breaking it off with you. You will tell the police you wish to drop all the charges and clear Alexander's name," said the man.

Jenna was staring at them incredulously, she was suddenly struggling to breathe. This was complete insanity!

"No...this is insane..." Jenna told them numbly, though she was vaguely aware that they may not be happy with her answer.

"Yes, you must clear Alexander's name." said the older man, taking a bold step toward her. "You must drop all the charges. We will make it twenty five thousand."

"No!" cried Jenna, she was suddenly starting to panic. What if these two men didn't just let her walk away? She had no idea who they were, or why they had come to her in Alexander's behalf. They were both stepping closer to her, towering over her and she was shrinking away from them. Jenna was suddenly afraid of what was going to happen next. Would they grab her and drag her out of the cafe, or just whack her, right here, outside the restrooms?

Jenna was shrinking against the cold plaster wall, desperately trying to come up with a get-away plan. Her heart was pounding in fear and her entire body was tensing with the burst of adrenaline her brain was infusing into her body.

"Excusez-moi!" said a tiny voice, from behind the men. Both men turned in unison to see a tiny, little old woman who apparently wanted to get past them, and into the restroom. Both men's attention was momentarily diverted.

Jenna almost breathed a sigh of relief. She smiled sweetly at her. "Je pars," said Jenna, as she stepped out of her way so she could pass. The woman nodded regally to Jenna as she stepped between her and the two men so that she could walk into the restroom. Jenna used the momentary diversion to run down the narrow hallway and back to her table in the now, somewhat crowded, cafe.

"What?" cried Solange, as Jenna skidded dramatically up to the table, looking as if there was a ghost chasing her.

"There's two men back there, they grabbed me and..."

"Have you completely lost your mind?" cried Solange looking at her as if she were crazy. Just then, the two Russian men walked out into the restaurant and started looking around the room casually. Jenna froze, she was afraid to breathe.

Jenna silently wondered if they would even worry that the cafe was crowded with witnesses and just grab her and run out the door with her. She assumed that since she had refused their money, they would attempt to silence her in other ways.

The taller man caught her eye, then he merely nodded to her, then he walked out the door as the shorter, stubbly faced man followed him calmly. Jenna was shaking uncontrollably as she watched them walk out the door and into the street.

"Who the hell were those men?" cried Solange, she actually looked scared, as she watched them walk out of the cafe.

"I don't know, they were Russian...they offered me twenty thousand dollars to drop all the charges against Alexander," said Jenna, her voice was suddenly weak and shaky.

"Oh my God, you did not take it did you? The money?" cried Solange, her face was completely stunned.

"No...they wanted me to tell the police that it was all a big mistake, that Alexander and I had been having an affair the whole time. That he tried to break up with me, and I was the one that went off the deep end and set him up to make it look like he tried to rape and kill me, just to get him into trouble," said Jenna, shaking her head miserably.

"Who were they? Friends, family, some government agency?" she asked, her eyes were still wide.

"I don't know, I just know the younger one man handled me. I think I was lucky to get away. They had me trapped back there, a tiny little old lady came along and needed to pass by, it diverted their attention for a second, and I ran away!"

"You do know if you drop all the charges now, they will make you look like a complete ass," said Solange.

"I have no intention on dropping all the charges. I don't want my sham marriage exposed, and for that, I am willing to deal with his lawyers. For privacy clauses or whatever, but I will not drop all the charges.

Alexander is evil, I saw the coldness in his eyes. He will do this again, if not to me, then someone else. I don't want that on my conscience." Jenna told her.

Jenna and Solange finished their lunch, but Jenna only picked at her meal, she was so shook up. She walked with Solange back to the police station, but she was nervous and jumpy as they walked down the street. Paris would never seem warm and welcoming to her again. Jenna scanned the faces on the street nervously for the Russian Mafia guys, or whatever they were. Whoever they were, they scared the hell out of her, but she would not be dealing with them, not for twenty thousand dollars, not even for twenty five thousand dollars.

They returned to the conference room and Solange told Detective Garnier that they wanted to try and make a deal with Alexander's lawyers. Jenna was just anxious to put this all behind her. She wanted to go on to Lyon and finish her season with the Company.

Solange and Detective Garnier wrote everything out to be sent to Alexander's lawyers. Then Solange brought Jenna back to the hotel. All they had to do now, was just wait and see if their terms would be accepted by Alexander and his lawyers.

When Jenna got back to the hotel, she flopped down on the couch and turned on the TV. She laid there staring at the TV but not really seeing anything on the screen, she was still a complete mess! She still hadn't recovered from Alexander's attack, yet she was forced to spend two full days in a Police station being treated like she was the one who was the criminal, now she had the Russian Mafia, or whatever the hell they were, showing up trying to bribe her to let Alexander off the hook for his crimes.

Later that evening, Jenna and Adam ate dinner at the hotel and spent their evening just ambling around the streets of Paris. Jenna was silently praying that their deal would be accepted by Alexander's lawyers so that her and Adam could leave for Lyon. She was tired of hanging out in Paris without the rest of the company, only Mr. Dumontier had stayed behind to wait for them.

As they were walking back up the stairs of the hotel Jenna heard a voice calling her name. She turned to see Solange DeRousse running up the stairs behind them. Jenna stopped and waited for her to catch up to them.

"Jenna, I have been trying all evening to get a hold of you. Alexander's lawyers have accepted our conditions. You and Adam are free to leave for Lyon tomorrow if you'd like," she cried excitedly.

Jenna sighed with relief, she felt as if a tremendous weight had been lifted from her chest. She smiled and hugged Solange. It wasn't what Alexander deserved, but at least her career was still intact. That's all she really cared about, at this point.

They walked into the hotel and sat down on one of the secluded sofas in the lobby.

"This is a good thing, the privacy clause will also protect you. The media will know nothing about the incident, or any court proceedings after today. Access to any records about your marriage or anything else in your private life are off limits, so that can never be dragged into court at a later date," said Solange.

Jenna let out a sigh of relief. The scam was still going to go on, and she wouldn't have to go home to Chicago. That was enough to make her happy.

"Thank you Solange, for everything," said Jenna.

"I sincerely hope everything works out for you. You are very talented," said Solange.

Jenna hugged Solange warmly, burying her face in the soft cashmere of her sweater. Solange patted her on the back uncomfortably, she had not expected Jenna to be so emotional.

Only Jenna realized that the Russian mafia guys had just walked into the lobby and were looking around carefully.

Jenna didn't want them to realize she was right there, practically in front of them.

When Jenna finally released Solange the men were gone. Jenna looked around anxiously afraid that the men were intent on running off with her in an attempt to silence her. Jenna took an uneasy breath, she couldn't wait to get out of Paris.

CHAPTER THIRTY THREE

The next morning, they were finally on their way to Lyon. Jenna breathed a sigh of relief as their limo finally pulled away from the curb. Alexander was still in the hospital after his "breakdown", and Jenna was happy that she had escaped the hotel without seeing, or being assaulted by the Russian Mafia guys again.

The rest of the cast had left for Lyon two days ago by train. Mr. Dumontier had stayed behind with Jenna and Adam, and the three of them were traveling to Lyon in the company limo.

Jenna pretended to read most of the way, even though reading in the car made her nauseated. She was extremely uncomfortable being in the limo with Mr. Dumontier. Adam slept most of the way, which is what he always did anytime they traveled by car, train, plane, etc.

They arrived at their gorgeous hotel in Lyon to find the marriage scam was still on, in full force. They had once again, been placed in the honeymoon suite since officially, they were newlyweds. Adam and Jenna's fake marriage certificate showed that they had been married the first weekend in April, shortly before they arrived in Paris.

Jenna rolled her eyes as she looked around at their honeymoon suite. Adam glanced at her and immediately began laughing hysterically. The room was gorgeous, it was decorated in pale champagne silks on the windows and bed, with thick wool rugs.

Once again, there was a bottle of champagne in a silver bucket on the entryway table, and a beautiful bouquet of peach colored roses. The card on the champagne read: Welcome to Lyon, enjoy-the management. The card on the roses read: I have been counting the moments till I would see your smile again, Luc Dupre.

Jenna read the card on the flowers and then dropped it onto the table in shock. She sighed miserably, Luc's budding infatuation with her was not going to help them at all to pull off their ongoing marriage scam!

Adam saw the look on Jenna's face, he ambled over, picked the card up and read it. He rolled his eyes and let out a hearty laugh. "Man, he's got it bad...I better go find him and kick his ass! You're my wife, I will not tolerate this type of behavior!"

"Don't be angry with Luc, it's my fault. Please, just let it go. I'll talk to him," said Jenna, giving him a shrug.

"No...he just needs to back off. He's going to screw everything up!" cried Adam. He opened the door and stormed out into the hallway as Jenna watched him with a frown. She didn't even try to go after him, once Adam decided to do something, there was no changing his mind, unfortunately, it was one trait that they both shared.

Adam stormed angrily down to the lobby and walked up to the front desk. The woman at the desk saw him storming up to her angrily. She narrowed her eyes at him briefly, then she gave him a dazzling smile, in an effort to diffuse his fowl mood.

"How may I help you?" she asked.

"I need to talk to Luc Dupre immediately," said Adam, the displeasure was evident on his face.

"Luc Dupre is not available at the moment, would you like to speak to Nicolas Dupre?" asked the woman.

"I imagine that will have to do," said Adam, with a nod of his head.

The woman spoke on the phone for a moment, then she escorted him to a suite of offices behind the front desk. Adam was escorted into a large, ornately furnished office. There was a man seated at the large burl wood desk. He had his back to the door as he flipped through a planner and spoke on the phone. He heard the footsteps and turned around and smiled at them. He gestured to Adam to take a seat and the woman turned and left the room without a word.

Adam sat there eyeing Nicolas Dupre suspiciously. Mr. Dupre was young, probably in his early twenties. He had dark, wavy, hair and he was wearing an expensive, gray, wool suit. He was speaking reassuringly in French, to whomever was on the other end of the phone line.

Nicolas finished his phone call and then he turned his complete attention to Adam with a smile.

"Hello Mr. Smyth, I am Nicolas Dupre, what can I do for you?" he asked, standing to shake Adam's hand. Adam hesitated briefly as Nicolas shook his hand and smiled at him with straight white teeth.

"I don't believe I told that woman my name. How did you know who I was?" asked Adam, slightly baffled.

"We have never been formally introduced, but I recognize you as Jenna Bruce's partner. I saw you in her room, the night I was summoned urgently back to the hotel, because a heinous crime had been committed there. I am pleased to see that your lip is healing nicely," said Nicolas Dupre.

Adam touched his lip, self consciously. He didn't remember Mr. Dupre coming to the room that night, but most of that night had been reduced to a blur of horrifying memories that he'd just as soon block from his mind forever!

"Don't be so surprised Mr. Smyth, I not only do I know who you are, but I have a pretty good idea, as to why you are here," said Nicolas, giving him a sly smile.

"You do? Well by all means, please enlighten me," said Adam, his voice raising with sarcasm.

"Well, are you, or are you not, the man who is supposedly married to the young lady my younger brother is currently fixated on?" asked Nicolas.

"Damn you're good," said Adam, shaking his head in amazement.

"Unfortunately, I've heard of little else in the past several weeks. The lovely Miss Bruce, Luc is completely enchanted with her. Believe it or not, I told him not to send the flowers, but he obviously did so anyway," said Nicolas, rolling his eyes.

"What do you mean supposedly married?" asked Adam.

"What is it you say in America? The jig is up?" said Nicolas, with an amused laugh.

"Fair enough Mr. Dupre, you've found me out. I need to beg for your discretion. If our little white lie was found out, Jenna would be sent back to the States immediately. It is imperative that you keep our secret," said Adam, looking at him very seriously.

"I realize that, rest assured your secret is safe with me. I was lucky enough to catch the show in Paris, I admire the two of you too much to have you sent back to the states. Besides, my brother would never forgive me. He is quite smitten, I must say.

As you have probably realized by now, Luc is very observant, when there is something he has an interest in.

He noticed Jenna immediately and was attracted to her. When he first saw her, he believed she was trapped in a troubled marriage, then he began to realize, there really was no marriage at all. It was at your company's farewell to Paris party, that he actually fell head over heels in love with her.

Before that night he had only seen her from afar, he'd not had the opportunity to spend any time with her. By the end of the evening she had stolen his heart completely. He found her to be quite intelligent and they both seemed to share a passion for music and literature. He had never before met a woman he had been so compatible with, he was quite stunned to find out that she was only fifteen years old.

As observant as he is, he could see right away that the two of you were not a married couple. Actually, I think we are quite lucky she is only fifteen years old. I do believe if she were older, we might have a serious problem on our hands. I would guess that keeping Luc away from her then, might not be so easy," said Nicolas, with a sly smile.

"If she were eighteen I wouldn't be in this dilemma in the first place. Please, tell your brother to back off. Jenna is not available. As far as anyone here in Europe is concerned we are married. Comprenez vou?" said Adam staring at him very seriously.

"Oui," said Nicolas, giving him a sly smile...

CHAPTER THIRTY FOUR

Jenna was anxiously watching the clock, her and Adam were due to be on the ice in five minutes. Jenna was dressed and ready, but Adam had run off. She was guessing it was to bawl out Luc Dupre for sending her flowers. Adam was as worried as Jenna was, that Luc Dupre's sudden interest in her, would cause their little marriage scam to come crashing down. Jenna paced the room nervously, as she waited for Adam to return. It was their first day back with the company, Jenna didn't want to be late for their practice.

Suddenly, Adam burst through the door. Jenna searched his face, but she couldn't tell from his expression how things had went with Luc. Jenna felt bad, this mess was essentially all her fault. She realized now, she should have never flirted with Luc that night at the party. It seemed as if everything she did, always came back later to bite her in the butt.

"Did you find Luc?" she asked, trying to hide her amusement.

"No, but I spoke with his brother, Nicolas. I think we've come to an understanding," said Adam, giving her a wry smile.

"We're going to be late for practice," Jenna told him.

"You know what? After all you've been through, I think you're entitled to be a little late. Besides, how else can you make a grand entrance?" asked Adam, giving her a gentle smile. He took her hand and kissed it. Jenna gave him a shy smile.

Adam hurried to get dressed and they arrived on the ice, a full ten minutes late. Jenna was embarrassed, she was never late, ever!

The entire cast was grouped in one corner of the rink and Simone and Gail were busy talking to them, someone in the group noticed Adam and Jenna were skating toward them and every single person in the group turned around and applauded for them.

Everyone was clapping and smiling at them as they approached and Jenna was nearly moved to tears by the emotion of it. Her face was suddenly red with embarrassment. She wondered, what had the rest of the cast had been told? She knew they hadn't been left completely in the dark about what had happened, as Marika and Alexander had been removed from the cast.

Everyone was coming up to Jenna and hugging her, welcoming her back and finally the emotion was just too much, and the tears began rolling down her cheeks. It hadn't been till recently that Jenna felt like anyone cared about her and the emotion was overwhelming. She had spent her entire childhood as an unwanted child, it hadn't been until she had moved in with Hans and Carolina that she had actually felt loved.

In a few moments Jenna was finally standing in front of Simone. Simone threw her arms around Jenna and squeezed her so tightly she could barely breathe. Simone was sobbing and whispering how sorry she was for not believing her. Jenna backed away from her numbly, she hadn't expected her return to the company to be so emotional.

The group finally got to work and after about fifteen minutes Jenna realized that the company's headline skater, Maria Gastineau was not there on the ice with them. Jenna was looking around curiously, wondering where she could possibly be. Of course, the dual pairs act was out now so Adam and Jenna were going to fill in the gap by doing their regular short program, the one they had used at the Nationals in Miami.

Jenna had skated to the side of the ice to get a drink of water. When Colin saw her standing there, he skated over to her. He hugged her for the second time this morning. Jenna clung to him as her emotions got the best of her once again, she didn't want to let go of him, she felt like she might start crying again. Of everyone in the company, Colin was her best friend besides Adam.

"I missed you so much," he said, as he squeezed her tightly. "Are you okay? Can I do anything for you?"

Jenna did her best to give him a brave smile. She just wanted to put all this behind her. She didn't want to discuss it anymore, she wanted to pretend that none of this had ever happened!

"I'm better now that I'm here, back with the people I love. Dealing with the police made me feel like I was the criminal!" she told him.

"I still can't believe it!" cried Colin. "Oh honey, look at your neck." Colin touched her neck tenderly. It was hideous! Jenna had bruises encircling her entire neck from where Alexander had tried to strangle her. Her forearms were bruised from her wrists to her elbows. Jenna swallowed convulsively and tried to block the images of that night that were tumbling into her defeated brain.

"The stab wounds are even more hideous," said Jenna, sighing as the tears seemed to automatically come to her eyes once again. She wiped them away angrily.

"I am sorry I upset you my angel. I am just thankful that you are still alive, I am hoping that you soon get the news that you have not gotten pregnant because of your ordeal. That would be a nightmare," said Colin, looking into her eyes earnestly.

Jenna looked away in embarrassment, Colin was such a good soul, she just wanted to throw herself into his arms and sob, but she had cried enough about this fiasco. Besides, the entire company was on the ice right now, she just wanted to maintain her composure. She didn't want anyone under the impression that she was an emotional mess who just needed to be sent home to her parents.

"Colin please, I don't want to talk about it anymore. It's over..." she told him, her voice breaking with emotion.

"I am very sorry my sweet," he said, putting his arms around her and holding her tightly.

"Where is Maria?" asked Jenna, she was still stunned that she didn't seem to be around at all.

"She passed out, the first afternoon we were back on the ice. We had only been on the ice maybe fifteen minutes. She's been hospitalized. No one has officially told us what is wrong with her, but I have heard the rumors...complications from anorexia..."

Jenna frowned and nodded grimly. It was certainly a reasonable explanation, Maria did seem to be much too thin. She had never personally seen her eat a thing. Jenna wasn't surprised that she was possibly anorexic. There was always a lot of pressure to stay thin when you were a skater or a dancer.

"Colin!" cried Gail, from across the rink.

They both looked up to see Gail skating toward them.

"She is married Colin, knock it off," said Gail with a smile, when she saw Jenna in his arms.

"I cannot help it, I love her so much!" said Colin, teasing her with a smile.

"You have work to do...you, young man, are getting a second number, we have holes to fill," cried Gail.

"Oh goody!" said Colin, sarcastically as he skated away with Gail.

The practice went pretty well, as messed up as Jenna was feeling. She felt like a robot who was merely going through the motions. She felt like she had lost all her personality on the ice. She knew Adam was worried about her, he didn't like it when she wasn't herself. Gail and Simone were desperately trying to fill the holes in the show left by the sudden departures of Maria, Marika and Alexander.

The following day, it seemed as if the entire show was destined to fall apart. It was Colin, who was now missing. It seems that his father had a massive heart attack during the night and he was on his way back to England to be with him.

Gail and Simone were completely beside themselves with worry, the entire show was falling apart! They had just over forty eight hours till the opening performance.

Simone was frantic, she knew she had to make something of her faltering cast. All three headline acts were now toast! This was a nightmare! Not only had she lost the World Champions, Marika and Alexander, but now she had also lost Colin, her Olympic Gold Medalist and Maria, a French National Champion. All that remained of the Premier cast was Rainier, Greg, Angelina and of course, Adam and Jenna. Jenna feared she was pretty much useless, she felt as if she was nothing more than a zombie on ice skates!

Jenna was stunned when Simone assembled the entire cast and told them she was reworking the entire show. They all stared blankly at her, there was no time to rework the entire show! She explained that she had an idea to take an old opera, "The King of the Gypsies" and make it into an elaborate dance on ice. The company had done another program with Gypsies about five years prior, so the costumes would not be a problem, they could just have them sent down from Paris and have them altered.

Jenna had to admit, the music was beautiful, but she wasn't sure how they could do all this in less than 48 hours. The entire cast threw themselves into the project, they worked long, hard hours and on Friday night they were actually ready. They would open their newest show, The King of the Gypsies.

Jenna loved the music, but she was worried that the show's patrons would be a little overwhelmed by all the violence in the tragic opera, it was not exactly, an uplifting story. Like Jenna's own life, it was a story of love and obsession gone awry. Most of the premiere cast ended up murdered, at some point, before the end of the show. Though the music was haunting and beautiful, the patrons of the company usually preferred the jaunty upbeat numbers, the kind of thing you would whistle to yourself on your way home.

Jenna didn't really care anyway, her mood was essentially dark, despite the amount of violence in the show. She was happy enough, her character the Princess, spent most of the show in despair after the murders of her husband and her father on her wedding night, which was followed by her being kidnapped by the King of the

Gypsies. It was not hard for Jenna to get into character. She felt as if she had already lived every emotion the Princess was feeling.

Especially, when she is forced to marry the King of the Gypsies whom she detests! Jenna didn't have to fake the sorrow that the Princess was feeling over the deaths of her husband and her father, who were both murdered by gypsies. Jenna had finally decided that this was all for the best. A happy, cheerful, show might not have worked out for her at this point. It's hard to skate around with a fake smile on your face when you were basically struggling, just to go on with life.

Opening night in Lyon went well. The show ran for two weeks in Lyon, then another two weeks in Marseille. Though the shows had done well, it had not been the blockbuster, sold out performances that Mr. Dumontier had hoped for and he was a bit disappointed by the audience's cool response to their performances. The cast would be leaving for Switzerland in two days and Jenna hoped with all her heart that the shows would do better there.

Unfortunately, they seemed destined to fail. The show was just way too dark, Jenna had heard the comments from the patrons as they were leaving the arena, despite the talent of the cast and the beauty of the music, the plot of the old opera was just too dismal, it left people feeling sad.

When Jenna arrived at practice their last day in Marseille, Gail and Mr. Dumontier were there, but Simone was missing. Gail was obviously upset and looked as if she had been crying. Mr. Dumontier gathered the entire cast at the edge of the ice to speak to them.

Jenna clutched Adam's hand nervously as they stood there at the edge of the ice. Something big was up, and she was having a bad feeling about this.

"There will be some changes made to the show," said Mr. Dumontier, as he addressed the cast. They were all standing there staring at him, completely dumbfounded.

"As you are probably aware, we did not get the best reviews in Lyon and Marseille with our new show, The King of the

Gypsies. I realize that Madame Aubiere did not have a lot to work with, as things seemed to be falling apart there for a while. I have been working hard to replace the holes in our Premier cast and I hope that all of you will be happy with the choices I have made."

Jenna took in a deep breath and stared at him in horror. Her heart was heavy as she suddenly realized what was going on. He had fired Simone, she was sure of it! Jenna could already feel the tears coming to her eyes...

Jenna felt bad, it hadn't been Simone's fault that they had lost four people from the Premier cast in the space of just four days. She had done her best to keep the show on track. Jenna suddenly felt horrible.

"In light of some serious concerns our board had for Miss Aubiere's recent mental status, she has been relieved of her duties and we have hired a new lead choreographer for the show," said Mr. Dumontier, as the entire cast gasped in disbelief.

"The Board members not only had concerns about Miss Aubiere, but also some serious concerns about the show and it's appropriateness. Most of the board members felt that the entire show was way too melancholy, with too much violence, not the kind of family oriented entertainment our patrons are clamoring for."

"They also felt that it was in poor taste for Simone to cast Miss Bruce in a role where she is brutally kidnapped by Gypsies and forcibly married to the Gypsy King...given her recent bad experience, here in France," said Mr. Dumontier, grimly.

Adam shot a surprised look at Jenna. She shrugged at him and grimaced. She had never voiced any concerns about her role in The King of the Gypsies. She had not complained to Mr. Dumontier, or anyone. She had been happy enough to leave what happened in Paris behind and to return to the show. Being back to work was a welcome diversion for her. All the tragedy and death in the show had barely phased her. In fact, it had strangely matched her own dark mood.

"I would like to introduce you to your new lead choreographer, Tom Singleton," said Mr. Dumontier as the man skated out onto the ice. The man was British and he was tall and thin with a receding hairline. When Mr. Dumontier explained his qualifications, Jenna was impressed. She knew by his stunning resume, that Tom Singleton was not only a very accomplished choreographer, but she had no doubt that he would be able to take on any role in the show, including the star skater, none the less, and blow everyone away if necessary.

The man immediately began speaking to the group, he seemed like a nice enough guy, but Jenna could barely concentrate on anything the man was saying, she was so upset that Simone had been fired!

Jenna had pretty much tuned out his entire speech until he said something that made her snap back to attention.

"Our series of shows in Switzerland have been cancelled, unfortunately, our new show is going to be quite a large production, it will take more preparation time than we have allowed. We will resume with our new show on schedule, in Italy. The best news is that our two headline skaters, Colin and Maria will be rejoining us," he told them excitedly.

Jenna smiled and breathed a sigh of relief. She had missed Colin so much. Other than Adam, she was closest to Colin, though recently, she had become very close to Rainier as well.

"I have also recruited another set of pairs skaters for the show, the pair is from Switzerland, they will be joining us beginning tomorrow so that we can have a combined pairs number again. I have also hired another female skater. Her name is Nicole Varenne, she is also from Switzerland."

Jenna was happy, at least, that Tom seemed to embrace the combined pairs act. It truly was a good idea, as long as Alexander and Marika weren't involved.

Tom jumped right in and begin working with everyone, busily teaching everyone their new acts for the show. Simone had been a great choreographer, but Jenna was now realizing that Tom was a complete genius! He had a very creative mind and an ear for music. He had the entire show choreographed in a matter of hours.

Jenna knew she was going to love the new show and it wasn't hard for her to learn the programs, she was already familiar with all the music.

They were doing clips from a variety of Broadway shows. Jenna's mother was the founder and lead choreographer of Chicago's Broadway review. Jenna had literally grown up there in the theater, she knew every Broadway show backwards and forwards.

That evening after dinner, Jenna and Adam were getting on the elevator to head back up to their room, when Jenna heard a familiar British voice behind her.

"Is that my favorite girl?" he cried.

She turned around and saw Colin standing there. She was so excited to see him, she ran to him and threw her arms around him in a big bear hug. He squeezed her and kissed her on the cheek.

"How have you been my love? I missed you so much!" he cried, holding her away from him and looking her over carefully.

"I missed you too Colin," said Jenna, squeezing him again and sighing contentedly. Tears of joy were coming to her eyes, but Adam was rolling his eyes in boredom at their emotional little reunion.

"I have been very worried about you, my love. I am glad to see that your bruises are finally gone," he said, touching her neck gently.

Jenna shivered involuntarily at the very thought of Alexander. In reality, she hadn't made much progress in getting over that night. The placid facade that everyone saw, didn't reveal any of the fear and anguish she was still feeling over the attack.

Colin had to leave so quickly to be with his father, she really hadn't had much time to talk with him about it. She had talked to Adam about the incident some, but there was still too much tension between them. She just didn't feel comfortable pouring her heart out to him. Besides, she got the idea he was almost more screwed up about everything than she was.

Simone had been her closest confident, yet Simone had been overcome with tremendous guilt. She pretty much felt responsible for Alexander's attack, since Jenna had asked for her help and she had pretty much believed Alexander's lies over Jenna's pleas for help. Poor Simone had felt so incredibly guilty, it had led to her emotional unraveling. Jenna had seen it coming in the weeks after they had left Paris, but she had been too consumed with her own screwed up emotions to try and help her, or do anything about it!

"You've lost some weight, have you been eating?" exclaimed Colin, as he looked her over carefully.

"Sometimes I can't..." Jenna bit her lip anxiously, she wasn't really any closer to being over this than she had been, weeks ago.

"Please darling...we've already had one cast member hospitalized with an eating disorder, we cannot make it two. I know it is going to take time for you to get over this...I am here for you my love."

Jenna was suddenly fighting back tears again, hearing Colin's emotional plea was almost too much for her. "I was so sorry to hear about your father," she said, trying selfishly, to move the focus off of herself for a moment. Colin's father had died the day after he had arrived in England.

"At least I got to say goodbye to him before he died. He didn't suffer, he had his family all around him. I hope someday I die so dignified a death," said Colin, thoughtfully.

Jenna squeezed both his hands and smiled up at him. He always had a positive take on everything. That's why she had missed him so much. She had no doubt that he would come up with something positive that had came from her little ordeal with Alexander, though she had no idea what it could possibly be.

"What did you eat for dinner tonight?" asked Colin, looking at her seriously.

Jenna gave him a blank stare, she couldn't even remember, she was living her entire life in a daze. She remembered going to dinner, but she had no clue what she had eaten.

"She basically just picked at a shrimp salad," said Adam, rolling his eyes. Jenna frowned, Adam had already given her countless lectures about her eating, or lack of it. She couldn't help it, everything seemed to taste like dirt, she had no appetite.

"That settles it, you're coming with me for desert. I know how much you like cheesecake, and I know a chef that makes a perfect one," Colin smiling at her.

"Colin, I'm tired and..."

"I'll hear no excuses, you are coming with me, like it or not. Besides, I haven't spent any time with you in an eternity, it seems," said Colin.

Jenna sighed and nodded to him as he offered his arm to her. She spent the rest of the evening with Colin, eating the most sinfully delicious cheesecake, she had ever eaten. She was glad that Colin had pressed her to join him. He was quite a comedian and kept her laughing all evening. She felt quite refreshed when she finally returned to her room just after ten.

The next morning they had their first full cast, practice. Colin was back on the ice entertaining everyone with his crazy antics. Maria was there. She didn't look any meatier, but she did seem to look healthier than the last time Jenna had seen her.

The Swiss pair that would replace Alexander and Marika had arrived last night. Their names were Philippe and Cerise. So far, they seemed to be very nice, although Jenna was being very cautious. She had thought that Alexander was very nice at first, as well. Jenna felt as if she couldn't trust her own judgement anymore. Philippe was tall and thin with dark brown hair, and a slightly receding hairline, even though he was only twenty six years old.

Cerise was small and blonde with a beautiful smile.

Jenna decided that working with Philippe and Cerise was a thousand times better than working with Marika and Alexander. She didn't think that Philippe and Cerise were an item, but if they were, at least Cerise didn't feel the need to come to her and tell her to keep her hands off her boyfriend. Cerise and Jenna got along very well!

Tom had arranged a huge production and it turned out to be the biggest hit the Company had ever had! The Broadway style show proved to be a big hit and it was completely sold out everywhere they traveled.

Jenna felt like she was finally starting to recover from her incident with Alexander and she finally felt like she fit in with the rest of the cast. She was still the youngest member of the cast, and the only minor. Though she was still closest to Adam and Colin, she had also forged strong friendships with the rest of the premier cast and she felt like they all belonged together.

The one exception was Maria, she was not really close to anyone in the cast and Jenna was sure that she was still battling anorexia. Nicole, the newest cast member, was the shy and retiring member of the cast. She was small, with long brown hair and big brown eyes. She was completely gorgeous, Jenna was beginning to think that Adam had a little bit of a crush on her. At the end of every performance it seemed, he was always there at her side talking to her, while she smiled shyly at him.

Unfortunately, he could do little more than flirt with Nicole. Officially, Adam and Jenna were still married. Adam had spent a lot of time while they were in France keeping Luc Dupre out of their practices and as far away from Jenna, as he could manage. Luckily, Luc had went away to college in England finally, so he hadn't been around lately. Now it was just Adam's affection for Nicole that threatened to blow their sham marriage out of the water.

Though Jenna missed Simone greatly. She admired their new choreographer Tom, and had become quite close to him. He adored

Jenna and she loved him like a father, since her own father really didn't want her around.

   The rest of the summer passed by uneventfully. Jenna and Adam had a great time. They were excited to get to travel to so many beautiful places and meet so many wonderful people. They had been all over Europe making stops in Brussels, Salzburg, Rome, and then finally London, though by September, Jenna was pretty much done with all of this and ready to return to the states and begin a new competitive season.

Jean Marie Stanberry

CHAPTER THIRTY FIVE

Spending the entire summer skating had paid off immensely! Jenna and Adam returned to Chicago to resume their training with their coach Hans. Jenna immersed herself in her training and her studies. She hoped to pursue a degree in law after she graduated and she had the grades to get her into any college she wanted.

Despite the fact that Matt was far away in Boston, they managed to resume their long distance romance. Matt had been very understanding of her ordeal. Jenna was lucky enough to spend Christmas vacation with Matt and his family on their family vacation to the Caribbean.

Jenna had been relieved that Matt seemed as unwilling to bring up the subject of Alexander as she was, at first. Unfortunately, she knew it would come up eventually. She just wondered if their fragile relationship could survive this cruel blow.

Matt knew what had happened, but Jenna was too emotionally scarred to go into any detail about her ordeal. Her wounds from Alexander's violent attack had healed into small, white, scars on her chest and arms. A subtle reminder of the all consuming rage, that Alexander had unleashed on her, as he stabbed her multiple times.

Jenna and Matthew were sitting on the beach, watching as the sun slid below the horizon. They were holding hands, Matthew was mindlessly rubbing his thumb over a small scar on her arm, Jenna jerked her arm away, her face was pink with embarrassment.

"Are you *ever* going to talk about it Jenna? I know you are embarrassed about it, but it wasn't your fault...what Alexander did. These are the scars of anger, not love. I love you, I just want you to trust me. I just feel like you're shutting me out. I just want to be there for you," said Matt, looking into her eyes earnestly.

"I know Matt, I'm sorry. It's not that I can't talk to you about it. I can't talk to anybody about it. For so long everyone blamed me for the attack, I still feel guilty about it, like there was something else I should have done. I keep playing everything out in my mind, wondering what else I should have done to prevent it, I just feel so stupid..."

"Jenna no man has a right to rape you, no matter what. You are not to blame, it is Alexander who is at fault. You have to put this behind you, realize that there are just bad people out there," said Matthew.

Jenna sighed miserably. Matt was a great guy, she knew that he loved her, but she also knew there was no way he could ever comprehend the horror of what had happened to her. Jenna felt as if she'd been ruined forever.

She loved Matt and she enjoyed spending time with him, but she wondered if the romance they shared before she left for Paris would ever be rekindled. Alexander had hurt her so bad she couldn't imagine ever letting Matthew or anyone else for that matter, ever touch her again.

They'd kissed many times while they were away in St. Kitts, but Jenna always felt the need to pull away early and limit the kiss. Jenna was too frightened to let Matt touch her, if their kisses progressed and she felt Matt's hands roaming, she would always push him away. She was attracted to Matt and she hoped that someday their relationship would progress into more, but she was afraid if she aroused him, he would turn into a crazed monster, just like Alexander.

At the end of their vacation, Jenna returned to Chicago and Matthew returned to Boston. Matthew's parents seemed happy enough and invited to her come back with them in March, when they brought Matt down for spring break. Jenna thanked them and told them that would be great, but she had her doubts that Matt would still want her for his girlfriend. Jenna hoped that Matt wasn't too frustrated by her attempts to distance herself from him, but she couldn't help it. She wasn't the same person who had got on that plane back in April.

Jenna worried that by spring break Matt would have found a girlfriend that was much more receptive to his attentions. He was young and gorgeous, why would he waste his time on someone as damaged as she was?

The competitive season went quite well. Jenna and Adam worked hard all season honing their programs, and all their hard work paid off. They ended up placing second at the Nationals and they were excited that they had qualified to go to the World Championships in Copenhagen, Denmark.

As they planned for their trip to the World Championships, Jenna was almost relieved when Hans announced to her that he had forbid Matt to come along with them. He thought it would be best for Jenna's concentration, if Matt stayed behind.

Jenna was happy to hear this news. She was going to be screwed up enough, she didn't need Matt there, reminding her that she had become distant and shallow. She knew that Matt needed more from her, she just wasn't sure that she could ever give it to him.

Jenna and Adam trained hard in the weeks leading up to the Worlds. The training and the hard work leading up to the Worlds didn't bother Jenna, but as they boarded their plane to fly to Denmark, she began to get very anxious. It wasn't anxiety about performing, or being away in a foreign country that was bothering her. In fact, the only thing that Jenna couldn't seem to get out of her mind, was the fact that she knew they would be competing against Alexander and Marika.

As a result of the plea bargain, Alexander had plead guilty to lesser charges and had spent barely any time in jail. Of course, he and Marika were the reigning World Champions and they were having another stellar season. Jenna wasn't looking forward to being in the same country as Alexander, let alone the same ice arena. She was filled with trepidation about the whole trip, and it seemed as if nothing could relieve her anxiety.

Hans had told her, if he had anything to say about it, Alexander wouldn't get anywhere near her, still, Jenna had a bad feeling about all of this. Alexander had violently attacked her, being in the same ice arena with him, was a situation she really didn't want to put herself in.

Jenna tried her best to relax and put all her fears behind her, but it was almost impossible. Alexander had got off with barely a slap on the wrist, and the privacy clause had minimized the scandal that would have filled the European newspapers. Though most of the scandal had been swept under the rug, the rumors had continued to fly. For months Jenna had endured the raised eyebrows and whisperings of cruel people who couldn't possibly have a clue as to what she had suffered at the hands of Alexander.

Jenna had ignored the rumors as much as possible, but she couldn't help hearing the the snippets of whispered gossip as she passed through crowds.

"They had a torrid affair." "She broke his heart." "Terrible slut." was murmured, even though most times she was still in earshot. Jenna would take a deep breath and do her best to keep smiling, even though the gossips always seemed to take Alexander's side. He had certainly done his PR work.

After his hospitalization for "a breakdown", Alexander courted the media with his story of true love and heartbreak. He told them he had been deeply in love with Jenna, but she had broke his heart and returned to the states with Adam. He even did a tearful interview on TV asking Jenna to forgive him and come back to him. Jenna jumped up from the couch and left the room the moment Alexander's face appeared on the TV screen.

Adam and Hans had begun to fear that Alexander was suffering from some sort of mental disorder, after Jenna returned to Chicago, Alexander had tried to phone her multiple times, but Hans had been screening her calls. Hans angrily told him to leave her alone, but Alexander did not seem inclined to obey his wishes. Letters and packages arrived by the dozens, but Hans tossed them all unopened, into the trash.

They arrived in Copenhagen a full seventy two hours early, to rest and do a bit of sight seeing. Jenna didn't do much sight seeing, she was tired and suffering from jet lag. Outwardly she appeared serene, though truly, she was almost completely paralyzed with fear at the thought that Alexander was somewhere nearby.

The following day Jenna and Adam skated their compulsories, which were fine, but they'd ended up ranked 7th, which was quite disappointing. Jenna had to blame herself and the difficulties she was having, making herself focus on her skating. She'd managed to completely avoid any confrontations with Alexander and Marika though, which she considered a good thing.

Luckily, Alexander and Marika were quite easy to spot, of course they were the reigning World Champions, and they had recently been married in the fall, so it seemed as if they always had a news crew following them around.

Tomorrow night they would be performing their short program. Jenna felt bad that her and Adam had done so poorly in the compulsories. Compulsories were not their strong point anyway, but she knew her messed up mental status had caused their performance to suffer.

Jenna knew they would have to give a perfect performance tonight if they were going to gain enough ground to stand on the podium during the medal ceremony on Friday night. Jenna was determined to clear her mind and skate a perfect program tonight.

Jenna had watched some of the other skaters during their practices and she knew that their routine was one of the most technically difficult and she felt that if they could ace it, her and Adam could come from behind and take the gold medal.

They were in the last group of four pairs to perform. Alexander and Marika would be the first of their group to perform. Jenna had seen them briefly in their warm up when all eight of them were on the ice at the same time. Jenna and Adam were busy working on their newest lifts during the warm up, so Jenna had done her best to ignore them.

She hadn't even looked in Alexander's direction.

Marika and Alexander had noticed her presence on the ice though. Alexander had tried very hard to make eye contact with Jenna, and Marika had skated very close to Jenna and flashed her a seething glare. When the short warm up was over, Hans had tucked Jenna and Adam away in a private area so that they could stretch and finish warming up. He really had no desire to have them watch the other couples skate their programs.

When the last of the previous three couples finally took to the ice, Hans came to get them. Jenna and Adam arrived in the arena, just as the couple before them was leaving the ice, they took to the ice for a quick warm up as the other couple awaited their scores. Jenna was jubilant as the scores were called out, they were pretty lame. This last couple must have made some big mistakes.

The announcer called out their names and Jenna and Adam skated to their places on the ice. Jenna took a deep breath and tried to calm herself. Her heart was pounding anxiously, she was suddenly overcome with fear, over the fact that Alexander was somewhere in that arena, probably watching her right now!

Adam gave her a reassuring smile and squeezed her hand. The music started and Jenna managed to put everything out of her mind and just skate. Jenna immersed herself in the music and their program. When the music finally ended, she was ecstatic! She had made it through the entire routine and everything had seemed perfect, even their side by side spins, which was, by far her biggest weakness. Jenna was breathing a silent sigh of relief as they took their bows in front of the huge crowd. Adam was bursting with excitement as they both waved to the crowd and then skated around picking up a few of the flowers that were now falling down like rain, onto the ice.

Jenna and Adam skated over to Hans, who was so excited, he was jumping up and down like a madman. They had given the performance of a lifetime, and he was beside himself with joy. He was sure that they would be going home with a gold medal on Friday night.

They sat in the "kiss and cry" area and listened as their scores were announced. They were overcome with joy and relief as the announcer read them out, they were almost perfect, bringing them up to second place. Jenna was completely overjoyed! It would be quite an accomplishment to go home with the silver medal after being to far behind in the compulsories. They waved jubilantly to the crowd as they left the arena. The three of them were riding high on adrenaline from the near perfect scores.

Jenna was ecstatic, but exhausted by the emotional roller coaster she'd been on since their arrival in Copenhagen. She was elated that they had been able to move up from seventh place, to second. Now, the only thing that stood between them and the gold medal was Alexander and Marika, and just two tenths of a point.

The three of them were waving to the crowd excitedly as they headed for the exit of the ice arena. Jenna was surprised and dismayed to find they were suddenly surrounded by dozens of reporters. The reporters were all shoving their microphones into their faces and they all seemed to be shouting out questions at the same time.

Jenna was so surprised and overwhelmed by the sudden pandemonium, she could barely understand anything, any of them were shouting at her. Hans was angrily trying to wave them away, when Jenna suddenly realized that they weren't there to question them about their outstanding performance, they had all approached them to harass Jenna about her relationship with Alexander.

"What do you think about the Soviets being in first place?" "Miss Bruce, have you spoke with Alexander since you arrived in Copenhagen?" "What are your feelings on his plea bargain?" They were all firing questions at her and she was suddenly completely overwhelmed, she hadn't expected any of this.

They continued to push through the unrelenting crowd, when they were nearly to the exit, a network reporter stepped in front of Jenna, nearly jamming his microphone up her nose. His cameraman rudely jostled Hans and Adam out of the way with his heavy equipment, effectively separating her from Hans and Adam.

"Jenna Bruce, what are your feelings about the fact that Alexander Peterov, a man you say violently attacked you, was able to get himself a plea bargain and manage to compete in the World Championships this season?" asked the reporter, Jenna was cringing away from the microphone he was intent on cramming between her lips.

"I have no comment," she told the man sharply. Jenna was craning her neck, trying to see where Hans and Adam had been shoved off to. She didn't like being separated from them in the growing crowd. She was tired and ready to go back to her room, but the man wasn't getting the hint, as he continued trailing along behind her.

"What can you tell me about your involvement with Alexander Peterov, and the criminal charges he had to face in Paris?" asked the reporter, refusing to get his annoying microphone out of her face.

Jenna was suddenly standing there staring at him with her mouth hanging open. She was completely stunned. She had hoped that this was all behind her. She had given all her statements, Alexander had faced and been convicted of reduced charges. He was free while he awaited his sentencing, why was this even an issue?

Jenna had been forbidden by the French courts to even speak of the details. It was a sealed case. There was a privacy clause, supposedly to protect them both from the negative publicity. That little stunt had apparently not worked. Here she was, facing the negative publicity head on, and suddenly she could not see Hans and Adam anywhere nearby, she was panicking silently as the crowd swelled around her, threatening to swallow her up.

Jenna shivered involuntarily. She knew that Alexander was here in this ice arena somewhere. He'd been allowed to compete, even though it was possible he would have to return to France at some point for his sentencing.

"He and his partner told us that he had to face battery and attempted rape charges in Paris. While he contends that the two of you were involved in a consensual sexual relationship that went on for several months," said the reporter, Jenna glared at him. He had apparently already spoke to Alexander and Marika. She wanted nothing more than to slap that smug smile right off his face.

Jenna narrowed her eyes at the man. "I suggest you get your facts straight. It was assault and battery with a deadly weapon. He was convicted of those charges...there were witnesses," said Jenna, nearly shuddering at the thought that Alexander was most likely there in that arena somewhere. "I'm sorry, it's a sealed case, neither of us are at liberty to discuss it with the media," she told the man abruptly.

Jenna was scanning the crowd anxiously for Hans and Adam. She had not seen Alexander and Marika perform, but she knew that Alexander was lurking out there in the arena somewhere. She was suddenly creeped out, she didn't want Alexander anywhere near her!

The arena was loud and teaming with people, and every reporter in the building it seemed, was shoving their way directly toward her. Jenna kept looking around frantically, trying to catch a glimpse of Hans and Adam. Finally, she spotted them, about fifty feet away, they were trapped by other reporters.

She started pushing her way through the crowd, desperately trying to make her way to Hans and Adam. It made her nervous being separated from them. Jenna was still shook up over the possibility that Alexander might be there in the arena somewhere. The annoying reporter was still following her, trying to interview her, despite the fact that she was ignoring him.

"He had witnesses also...to the affair, including your own mother," said the reporter, as he pushed through the throngs of people, right behind her.

Jenna whipped around to face the man. She just wanted to punch him, she was suddenly so angry. Who would have thought that her own mother would betray her like that? Who's parents would have sent a minor away to Paris without a guardian in the first place? Jenna's face was red with anger as she looked down at her clenched fist. If she punched this reporter, she would once again, be made out to be the bad guy. She just wanted everyone to leave her alone.

"That is probably why he was convicted in the first place, lack of any creditable witness. Certainly you've heard my mother has her issues, so she is not what anyone would consider a reliable witness. Maybe one of your film crew could pull up the clips from the Nationals a year ago, and show them to you. That way you could see first hand, what a wonderful person my mother is. You could see how she reacts when things don't go exactly her way!" snapped Jenna, feeling incredibly guilty to be bad mouthing her own mother, even though her mother would never miss out on an opportunity to bad mouth her.

The man had been momentarily stunned by her unexpectedly candid comments, but there were other reporters shouting out questions at her as she pushed past them. Jenna just tuned them out. She wanted out of that arena, and she wanted to be beside Hans and Adam. Suddenly, a familiar voice whispered in her ear from behind her. The very sound of that voice sent a cold shiver down her spine.

"Have you missed me, as much as I missed you?" the voice whispered in a taunting tone, with a chilling Russian accent.

Jenna whirled around to find Alexander standing there directly behind her. His hand was locked on her wrist before she even realized what was happening. Jenna was suddenly panicking! The crowd had driven even more space between her and the others. Now, here she was standing face to face with Alexander. She was so scared she could barely breathe.

Jenna swallowed convulsively and slowly looked up into his dark eyes. She was sure her heart stopped for a moment. A sardonic grin was crossing his face and she immediately felt the blood in her veins turn as cold as ice. The crowd was surging all around them like an ocean tide, and she was drowning in it.

Jenna was struggling to stay afloat it seemed, but the surging crowd was consuming her, jostling her even closer to Alexander. She was literally bouncing off of his chest as the crowd continued to surge all around them. Jenna felt like she was trapped in a horrible nightmare, the monotonous drone of the hundreds of voices all around them was overpowering, she was slowly surrendering to her overwhelming panic.

Jenna's first instinct was to run away, but Alexander obviously had no intention of letting that happen. Not to mention it would be highly improbable in this tightly packed crowd anyway. She was staring down in shock, at Alexander's hand locked on her wrist. His knuckles were white as he jerked her even closer to him, he was gazing down into her eyes with an evil smile.

Jenna was struggling to breathe, her brain was consumed with fear and her body was beginning to shake involuntarily. She looked over at Hans and Adam, but the surging crowd was pushing them even further away, still. She was struggling to quell the overwhelming panic that was suddenly rising in her chest. Jenna and Alexander were not alone, but she still knew she was not safe, she would never be safe from Alexander.

"What do you want?" she cried, over the din of the crowd. She was staring at him with contempt. Normally, she would have thought it would be much safer to be in a crowd with Alexander, than alone with him, but Alexander was very calculating. He never did anything without a plan.

Jenna suddenly felt like she was at the center of a crazed mob, as soon as Alexander attacked and started to tear her up, the crowd would join right in and help him to completely destroy her. She was sure whatever humiliation Alexander had planned for her was best accomplished in the midst of this tightly packed crowd. Maybe the media was a large factor too. Jenna frowned, of course he would do whatever it took to use the media to his advantage too. Her heart was pounding furiously, she forced herself to focus and breathe.

Alexander was so close to her now, she could feel his hot breath on her face as he jerked her against his chest. Jenna held her breath, expecting the worst. Her hand was numb, his fingers were like a vise clamped on her wrist. She looked up at him with her eyes narrowed at him defiantly.

"I already got exactly what I wanted, unfortunately, once is not enough. You feel the same way, do you not?" Alexander's voice was silky with malice as he flashed her an evil grin. Jenna shuddered and fought the hysteria that threatened to overtake her entire body.

"You're completely disgusting."

"You cannot deny that we are perfect together. I was very disappointed when I found out you were not pregnant. If you had been, I would have broke off my engagement to Marika for you," said Alexander, flashing her a seductive smile.

"I never would have married you, regardless if I were carrying your child or not," seethed Jenna.

"Do you really believe your parents would let you carry a bastard child to term. They'd convince you, in their special way to marry me. Besides, since you never returned any of my calls, I spoke to your lovely mother many times. She understands how much I love you. She believes my side of the story, that we were lovers, but things just got a little out of control...

"Alexander stop.." wailed Jenna, the thought that her own parents had conspired behind her back had nearly brought her to her emotional breaking point. She just wanted out of the arena and away from Alexander, she was trembling and fighting tears.

"I know...it's heartbreaking that our love had to end. It is too late now. I am married to Marika, you missed your chance to marry the man of your dreams," crooned Alexander in his silky Russian tinged voice.

"Alexander please, just leave me alone."

"You couldn't convince anyone it was rape, could you, you little slut? You wanted it."

Jenna was trembling, she couldn't even speak, she just wanted this nightmare to be over.

"You wanted it then and you still want it, don't you? What does Adam think of his little whore now? Or was he glad that I had you first?"

"You're completely disgusting, leave me alone Alexander."

"It is your fault, you have ruined my life. This is not over," he whispered. Jenna shivered at the sound of his voice in her ear.

Jenna looked up at him quizzically. She had ruined his life? She wanted to tell him how awful he was, how he had ruined her life, how she couldn't get over the fear of him trying to strangle her to death. Unfortunately, Jenna couldn't say anything, she couldn't even breathe. Without warning, he pulled her forcibly into his arms and kissed her. Cameras were flashing all around them and the crowd erupted into cheers!

The entire time he was kissing her, she was struggling uselessly to get out of his arms, but he was too strong. His arms were wrapped around her so tightly she could barely breathe, as his lips moved aggressively over hers. Jenna fought to pull herself from his arms.

Adam was standing about fifty feet away. He could hear the cheers of the crowd and he was struggling to see what was going on from where he was standing. The surging crowd seemed to be pushing him and Hans even further away, still.

Jenna was still putting up a futile struggle, anxious to get out of Alexander's arms. She knew she was stuck there till Alexander was done with her, unless someone else stepped in and whacked him on the head with a two by four or something. Unfortunately, no one seemed to have the sense of mind to do that.

Reporters and photographers were all surging toward them like a rising tide, pushing them even closer together. Everyone, it seemed, was anxious to know exactly what was going on between the two of them. Every photographer in the arena was suddenly tripping over each other in their haste to get a shot of the unexpected kiss.

Finally, Alexander broke off the kiss and looked darkly into Jenna's eyes. She fought off a fresh new wave of panic, her entire body had begun shaking uncontrollably and her legs were in serious danger of buckling beneath her. Jenna drew in a shaky breath and angrily tried to pull herself from his arms.

"That was a nice kiss. It's a shame you have to be so difficult all the time," he said, smiling down at her, as she continued to struggle uselessly to get out of his arms.

Jenna was furious. She couldn't stand for Alexander to touch her at all, let alone kiss her like that!

"Now that was a photo opportunity if I ever saw one! Now the entire world will know the truth...we were in love! I believe the world will suspect that you *still* love me, despite our odd circumstances. I am so sorry my darling Jenna, I am afraid that you and Adam will have to settle for the silver medal, this go round. The gold medal is already spoken for. I will take it back to Russia for you, and I will will kiss it every night and pretend I am kissing you."

He released her finally, giving her an arrogant smile. Then he turned, without another word and began speaking to the very first reporter that approached him.

Jenna was angry and disgusted that he had touched her at all. She felt dirty and violated by his kiss, which she was quite certain now, was staged for the media. Unfortunately, she was much too stunned to actually do anything. She was standing there shaking, completely dumbfounded and she could hear Alexander talking to some reporters just a few feet away.

"As you can tell, she is still in love with me, despite the fact that I am now married. Unfortunately, it is impossible for me to resist her charms, especially when she throws herself at me like that..." he was telling the reporters as he smiled and waved to everyone in the crowd, a huge smile was plastered across his lips.

Jenna shuddered and began to claw her way frantically through the crowd in an effort to reach Hans and Adam. She was so desperate to get away from Alexander, she didn't even try to talk to any reporters and give her side of the story.

Jenna wasn't sure she was even capable of speaking to reporters at this point, she doubted any of them would care anyway. They all wanted a sensational story, she didn't have a sensational story to tell. She would just be disputing everything Alexander said, and his charming "love story".

Jenna was finally able to push her way through the crowd to Hans and Adam. When she reached them, she flung herself into Hans' arms and burst into tears as soon as she reached him. Hans and Adam both put their arms around her and walked her out of the arena and back to her room.

Adam had seen Alexander's little stunt. He was sure it had been some sort of set-up. He was sure that Alexander had planned the whole thing, in a lame effort to prove to the entire world that the two of them had been in love and had an affair.

He was sure that Alexander planned to make Jenna look like a jilted lover who could not get over him, and was still hopelessly in love with him. That way, Alexander would been seen by the public as the victim, not be the vicious monster who had brutally attacked her. Adam was furious!

Hans had been way too short to see what was going on through the dense crowd. He too, thought it was some sort of publicity stunt. He felt bad that Alexander had been able to get to Jenna like that. He was also worried, he was certain that all this would come back to bite them in the butt, in the publicity department.

Jenna went back to her hotel room that night and tried to relax. Unfortunately, she didn't sleep well at all. Alexander's presence in the immediate area had her completely on edge. The hotel management had assured her that the location of her room would be kept confidential, but still, she kept expecting Alexander to come bursting through the door at any moment.

Jenna could barely relax, let alone sleep. When Adam, Hans and Jenna arrived on the ice at six thirty a.m. the following morning, all three of them were moody. It seemed as if none of them had slept well that night.

Their practice went well enough, considering, and Jenna was confident that they could, at the very least, hold on to their second place spot. Hans offered to take Adam and Jenna to a renowned cafe that was just at the end of the block for lunch, but Jenna wasn't hungry. She felt like a zombie and she decided it would be best if she just went back to her room and took a short nap, something she rarely did.

Jenna returned to her room and snuggled under the covers for a short nap. She was awakened with a start, by the phone ringing.

"Hello?" she mumbled sleepily.

"Jenna Bruce?" asked the female voice on the other end of the line.

"Yes?"

"This Pamela Barrett, I'm the overseas affiliate for NBC. I was wondering if you would be free to do an interview this afternoon?" she asked.

"You'll have to speak with my coach Hans, he coordinates everything for Adam and I," Jenna told the woman, sleepily.

"I don't need to interview both of you, it's just you I'd like to speak to," said the woman.

"Why just me?" Jenna asked suspiciously. She had thought that maybe they were interviewing them because they were now in second place, but she was beginning to suspect that this interview wasn't even about their skating.

"I plan to do a feature story and I wanted to get your thoughts on this whole reunion thing. I mean you and Alexander have been apart for months, he was married in the meantime, now it looks as if the two of you are getting back together..."

"Alexander and I were never together," Jenna cried angrily.

"Well I just spoke to Alexander and he said..."

"I don't care what Alexander told you, the two of us were never in a relationship, therefore, we can never get back together! He raped me and attempted to murder me, I can barely stand to look at him!" she cried angrily. Jenna grimaced as she realized she had probably just violated the privacy agreement she had signed, but Alexander had obviously violated it also, so she couldn't be too upset with herself.

"Well, the photos I saw, seem to be telling a different story," said the woman, her voice was laced with sarcasm.

"What photos?" demanded Jenna.

"Get yourself a copy of any American newspaper, the pictures are everywhere!" snapped the woman.

Jenna was so stunned, she slammed down the phone and headed for the door of her room. Her hair was all disheveled from her nap, but she didn't care. She headed for the hotel lobby and walked straight up to the concierge.

"Do you have any American newspapers?" asked Jenna, trying to keep her voice within a reasonable octave.

"I have The US News, and you are on the front page," said the man smiling at her. He obviously thought it was a good thing. Jenna was getting the sinking feeling it was going to be quite bad.

The man held the newspaper out to her and she snatched it from his hands, greedily. There she was, in a front page, full color photo, wrapped in Alexander's arms. Jenna stared in horror at the picture, apparently her struggling with Alexander only made their kiss look all the more passionate. She sighed miserably, in the camera's eye it truly looked as if her and Alexander couldn't keep their hands off of each other. She took a deep breath and tried to calm her furiously beating heart. Jenna wanted to scream, why was this happening?

"Jenna?" she heard Adam's tentative voice behind her.

She spun around and stared at him in shock. She was numbly trying to hand the newspaper back to the man at the concierge desk. Jenna suddenly felt faint. She felt as if she were trapped in a crazy nightmare and there was no way for her to escape.

"I'm sorry Jenna, I was just coming to tell you," said Adam, his face was grim. Jenna was silently staring at him, she couldn't speak.

He took her by the arm and started to lead her toward the elevators. Jenna was completely numb, she could only trail along with him. She was sure he knew she was close to completely loosing it and he wanted to make sure she could do it in the privacy of her own room. Jenna let him lead her along, unable to utter so much as a single word.

Adam led her onto the elevator without another word, just as the elevator doors were closing an elegantly dressed woman squeezed in and gave Jenna and Adam a smile. Adam gave her his standard fake smile, while Jenna never even looked up at her, as she clung desperately to Adam's arm. Jenna felt as if she were teetering on the brink of insanity, and all it took was a tiny nudge to send her right over the edge.

"Hey, you guys are the American pairs skaters, Bruce and Smyth!" cried the woman, smiling in recognition.

"Yes," said Adam, nodding his head curtly.

"Wow, I'm a big fan of yours! Miss Bruce, I am so happy that you and your boyfriend were able to work things out and get back together again. I saw the pictures and the news clip...very romantic!" said the woman, with a smile.

Jenna stared at her numbly, she was very close to screaming like a crazed lunatic, but the doors of the elevator opened and she seized the opportunity and leapt out. Jenna was not even sure what floor they had arrived on. She only knew she couldn't stand there and pretend to be civil to that woman any more. She couldn't believe that this was happening to her. Why was everyone taking Alexander's side?

Adam jumped out of the elevator and followed her as she wandered aimlessly down the hallway. "Jenna," he said, walking along behind her. "This isn't our floor."

Jenna turned around and saw him standing there, looking at her defeatedly. He knew how upset Jenna was, and he wasn't sure what to do for her. Jenna took one look at him and burst into tears. He took her into his arms and she stood there sobbing for a good, solid five minutes.

When she finally finished crying she felt amazingly refreshed. Adam led her back to the elevator and took her up to her room.

"Can you stay?" asked Jenna, when she saw him standing there in the doorway. He looked uncomfortable, but she really didn't want him to leave. She didn't want to be alone.

He nodded grimly and walked over to the sofa and sat down.

"Just so you know, Hans is pretty upset," he said, blandly.

"This is not my fault Adam. I'm upset too," she said, glaring at him with a stunned look on her face.

"Hans is worried about the pictures. I guess now that he's seen the pictures, he doesn't believe your side of the story."

"What?"

"I'm sorry Jenna,they look so convincing...I imagine anyone who wasn't there might be convinced that you and Alexander were truly lovers. I mean, he spent months crying his eyes out in all those interviews," said Adam, quietly. He stood up and walked over to the window and looked out over the streets of Copenhagen, he couldn't look her in the eye, for some reason.

"What are you trying to say Adam? Do you and Hans think I'm actually having an affair with Alexander?" Jenna cried angrily.

"Jenna, you know I don't, but Hans wasn't there...in France. He can't understand how this could have happened. He doesn't understand how evil and calculating Alexander is..."

"Oh my God!" cried Jenna, sighing miserably. She stood up and began pacing the room like a caged tiger. She had only recently turned sixteen but still, the press and the public seemed to think she was some sort of accomplished seductress. She thought it was perfectly ridiculous that everyone seemed to think it was her, who was controlling Alexander, causing him to be unfaithful to his wife. Jenna frowned distastefully, she felt like her name would be indelibly linked to Alexander's in the eyes of the public and she could barely even tolerate the thought of him!

"Jenna please, can you just settle down. We're going to work this out," said Adam, taking hold of her shoulders and looking into her eyes earnestly.

"I can't just settle down, we have to do something! Hans has to call a news conference and meet with the press. We need to set the record straight," Jenna told him, even though she was relatively sure she wasn't capable of meeting with the press at this point.

"No, Alexander is totally screwing with you. He's messing with your head so we totally fuck up our program tonight. You can't take the bait, you can't fall for it!" said Adam.

"What can I do? I don't want everyone to believe the two of us are truly having an affair," cried Jenna.

"Hans wants you to stay away from the press. Don't confirm or deny anything. Alexander wants you to get all upset and go off the deep end. He's so convincing, and the photos...well, they look quite convincing too. If you go to the press and try to deny everything they will all think you've completely lost your marbles. Hans wants you to stay out of the spotlight and just let all this dissolve on it's own," said Adam, cringing. He already knew what her opinion of this plan was going to be.

"Just let all this dissolve! cried Jenna, angrily. You must be completely mad! I don't want anyone, for a single second, to believe that Alexander and I are lovers, is that perfectly clear, Adam? I don't care how convincing the photos look, because that bastard forced himself on me, and if I could have gotten an arm free I would have slapped him so hard, his head would have spun around!" cried Jenna, her voice rising an entire octave in distress.

"Jenna I know, okay. We're at a disadvantage here, he's been courting the press all day with his bogus stories, it's too late for you to come along now and deny everything," said Adam.

Jenna was standing there glaring at him with her arms folded over her chest. She was trying desperately to digest all of this nonsense, but she felt as if her emotions were going in a dozen different directions. She wasn't sure if she should cry, laugh hysterically, or scream like a banshee.

The phone started ringing and Adam walked over and answered it. Jenna could hear an angry male voice on the other end of the line. She assumed it was Hans.

"What? Of course not, don't be ridiculous. No, it's not like that at all. Sure here she is," said Adam, rolling his eyes and handing her the phone. "It's Matt."

Jenna took the phone from him numbly. She was getting a bad feeling about all of this.

"Hello?"

"When were you going to tell *me* you were resuming your affair with Peterov? Or maybe you've just moved on to Adam, who is already conveniently in your hotel room" cried Matt. Despite the strange overseas delay on the line, there was no mistaking his anger.

"Matt, listen to me, I told you ,Alexander and I never had an affair, now he's trying to use the media..."

"Jenna, everyone is telling Alexander's version of this story, except you and Adam. My heart wants to believe it's not true, but

I'm not a compete moron. The whole world is convinced that my girlfriend loved this man. In fact, now they are convinced that she is still in love with him and that they are getting back together! I call you, hoping that I'm just overreacting and who answers the phone in your room but Adam, who for all I know, is possibly an ex-lover as well.

Jenna bit her lower lip in anguish. Her entire life was falling apart, she seemed to have no control over it whatsoever. The entire world was convinced that she was this slut that the media had invented, at this point in her life, she couldn't even imagine having sex with anyone...ever!

"Matt I swear to you there is nothing between Alexander and I, and you know that Adam and I are just friends. I should have never come here, I had no idea that the media would react the way that they did, no one was supposed to know, there was a privacy clause..." Jenna could hear her own voice fading away, she could only imagine that everything she said, just sounded so lame, to a man who thought she was sleeping around on him.

"I already saw the pictures Jenna, you can't deny what the two of you feel for each other. It was completely obvious in the photos, I could see the passion between the two of you," said Matt, his voice was breaking with emotion.

Jenna drew in a stunned breath. She her heart was breaking over the fact that Matt had seen the photos, she could only imagine, what he had thought when he saw them. She imagined that to the outside world, they would seem amazingly convincing. Jenna cringed as she suddenly realized, everyone in the states was going to see those photos. That had been Alexander's plan from the very beginning, the cold, calculating bastard had planned it that way. She was struggling to breathe, this was a nightmare!

"Matt, no..." Jenna couldn't think of anything to say to Matt, that could possibly explain how she had ended up wrapped in Alexander's arms like that. There was no way she could explain to him, the mental and physical hold Alexander still had over her. He was controlling her even as they spoke, he had worked his way into her brain, turning it into a useless pile of mush.

"It was all a lie, you told me that he pursued you, you told me that you felt nothing for him. I wanted to give you time, I thought your trepidation with me was related to the rape, but now I realize, you didn't want me to touch you because you were still in love with him," snapped Matt, Jenna could hear the barely disguised disgust in his voice.

"It wasn't a lie Matt. There is nothing between Alexander and I. That photo was set up, he overpowered me and kissed me, it was a media stunt. I didn't kiss him back," she breathed, her voice was fading away to nothing. Her head already knew what her heart could hear in Matt's voice. He'd already made his decision, what they had was over.

"Well it sure as hell looks like you're kissing him back from here. It looks much more passionate than any kiss I got when the two of us were in St. Kitts together!" he cried angrily.

Jenna felt her heart aching, apparently her struggling and distress with the situation had come out as passion on the photo, of course,

Alexander was a brilliant actor, he'd played his part to perfection. Jenna had cringed when she'd seen the photos, she would have never expected that anyone would believe that they were lovers, but the photos were very deceiving. She could only imagine the pain Matt was feeling at this very moment, the kisses they had shared in St. Kitts weren't passionate at all, and Jenna knew she was the one to blame.

"Matt please, Alexander set me up. He's getting back at me for the charges I filed against him in Paris. He told me that I ruined his life but..." Jenna couldn't continue, her voice was breaking with emotion, her heart was breaking.

"I feel like a moron. I've been so stupid I couldn't see what was happening. Personally, I think a picture is worth a thousand words. I think the newspapers are right and you've been screwing this guy all along. How am I supposed to know what you've been doing all summer?" cried Matt, angrily.

Jenna was fighting tears, it hurt that even Matt didn't believe her side of the story.

"Matt, please listen to me," she pleaded. It was too late, he had already slammed down the phone in her ear. The line was dead.

Jenna drew in a ragged breath and fought back tears. She was stunned that Matt was so angry, he wouldn't even hear her side of the story. Adam sighed and gave her a wry smile. He had heard Jenna's side of the conversation, so he knew exactly what was going on. Jenna was uselessly fighting to regain her composure.

"Why does everyone think I had an affair with that arrogant, hairy bastard? He almost killed me!" cried Jenna. She felt as if she was near her wits end. She fought to breathe as the room swirled around her. She was fighting panic and she silently wondered if this was what it felt like to have a nervous breakdown.

"Unfortunately for us, Alexander is a very skilled actor. Don't worry about Matt. I'll talk to him tomorrow, after he's had a chance to cool down a bit. You need to relax and calm down before our program tonight," said Adam, putting his arm around her shoulders and leading her over to sit down on the sofa.

"I can't do the long program," whined Jenna.

"If you don't perform tonight, then Alexander has accomplished exactly what he set out to accomplish. If you think he kissed you just for the heck of it, you are wrong. I believe it was all part of an elaborate plan to completely destroy you," said Adam.

"He's already completely destroyed me. My reputation, my relationship with Matt. Just seeing him here has brought back every nightmare I've struggled so hard to forget" Jenna told him with a sigh.

"It's a mind game, don't let him control you. You are the master of your own destiny," said Adam.

Jenna shook her head numbly. She no longer felt like the master of her own destiny.

Jenna wasn't sure how she could possibly perform tonight. It was true. Alexander had infiltrated her brain and completely messed her up. The very thought of Alexander anywhere near her was enough to send panic rushing through her entire body. Jenna wasn't sure if she could even make herself go to the ice arena, she was so scared by the possibility of encountering Alexander again.

Adam walked over to the radio on the dresser, he turned the dial until he found a radio station playing soft classical music.

"Alright, come over here," said Adam, he was standing there next to the bed. Jenna was giving him a quizzical look.

"What?"

"I'm going to help you to relax, you are not going to quit on me, do you understand? We have come all the way to Denmark, we are in second place, I will not let Alexander take that away from us," said Adam, his voice was gentle but firm.

"Adam, I'm sorry. I thought I was strong enough to deal with this, but I'm not. I thought that now that Alexander was married...maybe he would just leave me alone..."

"I know Jenna..."

"No Adam, you don't know! I can barely stand to be in the same country with that man, and not only did he have the audacity to speak to me after what he did to me, but he kissed me...he made it look like we are still lovers Adam, that I want him..." Jenna sighed miserably, she felt like crying again. When would this nightmare end?

"Jenna, I know...I'm sorry. I wish there was something else I could do. Please, just let me try and help you to relax.

Jenna nodded to him in resignation and walked over and stood in front of him. Adam was her best friend, sometimes it felt like he was her only friend. He was only trying to help her. They'd come all this way to compete, there was no way she could disappoint him.

Adam sat her down on the side of the bed and then he ambled over to the mini bar and began rifling through it. "Bourbon or vodka?" he called out to her.

"Not vodka," she told him, distastefully.

"Here, drink this," he said, handing her the tiny bottle of alcohol.

"I don't think this is a good idea," she told him with a frown.

"Just drink it, you need to relax, a little bit's not going to hurt you," he told her.

Jenna took the bottle from him and obediently took a sip. The liquid burned a trail straight down her esophagus. Jenna cringed and tried to hand it back to him. She shuddered distastefully, she didn't know how anyone could drink that crap!

"Drink some more, I know, it's not pleasant at first..."

Jenna rolled her eyes and obediently took another sip, she was beginning to feel a warmth spread throughout her body and she was amazed how quickly she began to feel the effects.

"Are you feeling relaxed yet?" asked Adam.

"Maybe a little," she told him shrugging slightly. If he meant had she totally forgotten about Alexander, the answer was no.

"Lay down on the bed on your stomach, I'll massage your shoulders," said Adam, running around and turning off most of the lights in the room.

"Adam, I don't know...maybe this is not such a good idea," said Jenna, frowning at him uncomfortably. With the reputation she had right now, she wasn't sure what would happen if she were caught in another compromising situation.

"Don't worry, I won't let you seduce me, you little vixen," said Adam, flashing her a sly smile.

Jenna narrowed her eyes at him and gave him a look, she wasn't sure how she felt about that last comment, but she laid down on the bed anyway. She closed her eyes and tried to relax as Adam worked the muscles in her neck and her shoulders, she had to admit, it felt pretty good. Jenna had almost fallen asleep when she was jolted to attention by a knock at the door.

"I got it," called Adam, trotting over to the door. He opened it, to find Hans standing there.

"What the hell is going on in here?" cried Hans, angrily.

Jenna jumped up from where she was laying on the bed, her face was panicked. She was acutely aware of how this must look to poor Hans. The lights were low, she was laying on the bed, and they had an open container of alcohol in the room.

"I was just trying to help Jenna to relax, she's been quite upset and..."

"Get out right now!" snapped Hans, angrily.

Jenna was standing there staring at him with a dazed look on her face. She was dizzy, either from the bourbon, or her jump up from the bed. Hans turned around and glared at her, he was obviously struggling with anger. His mind was overwhelmed with all the rumors and lies that had been flying since their arrival in Copenhagen, at this point, he wasn't sure what to believe.

"What have you done?" he breathed, he appeared utterly shocked.

Jenna couldn't speak, she knew she looked totally guilty, regardless of what had actually happened.

"It's not what you think," said Adam.

"I said get out!" snapped Hans, angrily. Adam headed to the door hastily and let himself out. Hans turned around slowly and glared at Jenna.

"I want the truth from you now. What is your relationship with Alexander Peterov?" his voice was seething, and it burned Jenna to her very core. Now Hans, the man who had been essentially the only father she had ever known, was doubting her. She could feel the tears coming to her eyes once again.

"Hans I know how bad the pictures look. I saw them myself, but there is not, nor has there ever been anything between Alexander and I," she told him, her voice breaking with emotion.

"The whole world is convinced otherwise," said Hans, his voice was filled with disgust.

"Hans, I'm sorry, I know how it looks, Alexander is very convincing. He had Simone completely convinced that I was some accomplished seductress that had taken him away from his fiancee and went on to seduce nearly everyone else in the cast. When she found out otherwise, the guilt nearly ate her alive. It was what led to her emotional unraveling."

"And Adam...what have you done to my Adam?" asked Hans, his voice was thick with emotion.

"What have I done to *your* Adam?" Jenna mouthed numbly, those very words hurt her more than Hans could ever imagine. "Adam and I are partners and friends, there is nothing more,"

"I do not know if I believe you, I can see that things have been changing between the two of you. What would have happened here this afternoon, if I did not interrupt?" asked Hans, giving her a dubious look.

"Hans, nothing was going to happen. Adam and I spent the entire summer together, it's not like that for us," Jenna told him, shaking her head miserably.

"Then tell me, what did I interrupt? I am not such an idiot I do not understand the soft music, the lights low," said Hans.

"Adam was trying to relax me. This run in with Alexander has me so worked up, I'm not sure I can skate tonight," she told him.

"You will skate tonight, I will not allow otherwise."

"Hans I'm afraid. Alexander will be there and..."

"You will face many challenges over your life. This world we live in, is not always pleasant. You must choose to remove

Alexander from your thoughts and skate like I know you can skate.

Jenna tried to speak, but only a tiny whimper escaped from her lips, she wanted to skate...but the thought of encountering Alexander again seemed like a nightmare. What if he spoke to her? Tried to kiss her again?

Jenna, I can only imagine how awful it was for you, having to face Alexander, after all he's done. He is a monster. But if anyone can take on Peterov, it's you. I know you can do it. You are the strongest person I have ever met, man or woman. If you weren't, you would have never made it this far," said Hans, taking her hand and looking into her eyes, earnestly.

Jenna could feel the tears coming to her eyes. Hans never got gooey, it had thrown her off balance that he was showing so much emotion now.

"Hans I..."

"Please my love, I know that you are scared, but we are so close to this victory.

Don't let Alexander take one more thing away from you, he's a monster," said Hans.

Jenna could hold back her tears no more, she threw herself into Hans' arms and bawled like a baby. He stood there and held her while she cried. When she had finally straightened up a bit, he looked her over carefully and gave her an odd look.

"Have you been drinking?" he asked, peering at her suspiciously.

Jenna went over and picked up the bottle of bourbon and held it out to him guiltily.

"Bourbon?"

"Adam thought it would help me to relax," she told him with a little shrug.

"Yes, well it will also help you to have cirrhosis of the liver," he said, tossing the bottle into the trash can.

Jenna pouted at him and he gave her a smile.

"I have something much better to help you to relax," said Hans, hardly able to repress a devilish smile.

"What?"

"There is someone in the lobby waiting to take you for an early dinner, I do believe he'll cheer you up," said Hans. Jenna was giving him a blank stare. Who could possibly be here to take her out to dinner, she wondered?

"Who?"

"I shall give you a hint, he told me that he missed you terribly and that the two of you were going to have a splendid time together," said Hans, in a poor imitation of a British accent.

"Colin!" she cried excitedly.

"Yes, and you've kept him waiting long enough. You know the British, they are frightfully punctual," said Hans, still trying to pull off a British accent.

Jenna threw her arms around him excitedly and headed for the door. Colin was the one person she was certain could probably cheer her up

CHAPTER THIRTY SIX

When Jenna saw Colin standing there, she ran to him and threw herself into his arms. It was all she could do to keep from breaking down in tears. Colin was the one person, besides Adam, that she trusted implicitly. He had always been there for her, no matter what. He squeezed her tightly and she clung to him, unable to let go, she had missed him so much.

"My sweet Jenna, I have missed you so much," he said finally, holding her away from him and looking her over.

Jenna was almost too emotional to speak, she had missed him so much. "I missed you too." she managed to mumble somehow.

She was subconsciously aware that at least half a dozen photographers were nearby, recording their emotional little reunion on film for everyone else in the world to gawk at and speculate about. Jenna imagined most of the world would think Colin was just another conquest for her. She almost giggled at the thought, the media would think that poor Colin was just another hopeless victim of the ruthless, sixteen year old seductress. It almost seemed comical.

"Let's get out of here," said Colin, taking her by the hand and leading her out of the lobby. He rolled his eyes at the photographers as they strode out the front doors to a waiting taxi.

The restaurant was only a few blocks away, so Colin had originally planned for them to walk there, but the throngs of reporters and photographers in the hotel lobby had changed his mind. He had worried that the photographers and reporters would follow them and he didn't want their dinner interrupted by the media.

They arrived at the restaurant and the host was kind enough to seat them out of the main dining room, in a secluded corner. Jenna was happy to be somewhat shielded from the eyes of the curious public. She had sat there for several moments, staring blankly at the menu, which was not in English, when Colin took her hand gently.

"How are you doing Jenna?" he asked, the concern in his voice nearly brought tears to her eyes once again.

"Terrible," she told him, ruefully.

"I realize how hard this is for you, but you cannot let Alexander destroy you like this," said Colin.

"I don't know what to do Colin. It was bad enough for me, just knowing that he was here in Copenhagen. Now that he got to me, and started this ridiculous media frenzy, I'm not sure that I can even perform tonight," she told Colin, miserably.

"If you withdraw, then Alexander has won. You cannot let him control you like that," said Colin, pleading with her.

"Colin, I wish it were that easy. I am still far from being over what Alexander did to me. Of course I've put it behind me and moved on, but unfortunately, I'm not over it at all. The thought of him anywhere near me, completely creeps me out. The very idea that the entire world thinks that we had an affair, and that I am still madly in love with him, is killing me!" I exclaimed.

"You have to put all of this out of your mind and win tonight. I know you and Adam can go home with the gold medal, your short program was perfect, and your long program is even better," said Colin.

Jenna sighed, Colin knew that she was capable of performing well under pressure, but this was different somehow. She couldn't seem to let go of the fear that enveloping her entire body. Alexander had completely invaded her brain, and her mental destruction was eminent, she was sure of it.

The waiter arrived at the table to take their orders, he came to Jenna first and smiled politely at her. She gave him a wry smile and a little shrug, she had no idea what to order. Colin immediately sensed her discomfort.

"What are you in the mood for? How about salmon and the house salad?" asked Colin, giving her a little smile.

"That's perfect, thank you," she told him. He proceeded to order both their dinners for them with perfect ease. Jenna had to smile as she watched him conversing easily with the waiter, in Danish. She shook her head in astonishment, Colin was completely amazing.

"Thank you for ordering for me, I was more than a little lost. I had no idea you spoke Danish also," she told him with a shy smile. Colin also spoke French and Italian fluently. It seemed as if she was always learning something new about him.

Colin also knew Jenna like a book, she didn't even need to know what else was on the menu, he knew exactly what she preferred and he never forgot, even when they'd been apart.

Jenna usually ordered a salad and some sort of fish or chicken, though salmon was always her favorite. Most pork or beef dishes were way too heavy for her if she was going to have to skate. She tried to avoid anything too fancy that might upset her stomach.

"Anything to get to spend some time with my favorite girl," he told her. Jenna blushed, she knew that Colin was gay and not really interested in her as more than a friend, but he was always very lavish with the compliments, he could always brighten up her darkest days.

"Colin..."

"Well you are my favorite girl, I'm not just toying with you, you know that," he told her, giving her a sly smile.

"Thank you for bringing me here and trying to cheer me up. You are the greatest friend ever," Jenna told him.

"Bloody ell!" he exclaimed, suddenly standing up.

Jenna whirled around in her chair to see a photographer right there behind them. He was excitedly snapping photos of Colin and Jenna having what appeared to be, a very intimate dinner together. Jenna gave the man a stunned look, he took one final photo, turned, and quickly headed for the main dining room.

Colin started to go after the man, but he thought better of the gesture. Jenna just sat there, shaking her head disgustedly. No one in the media cared about the truth, they were all looking for the most sensational story. The man obviously thought he was quite clever "catching her" having diner with Colin. Jenna almost hoped that tomorrow all the newspapers would be speculating that she had dumped Alexander and was now pursuing Colin.

"Well..." said Colin, picking his napkin up and placing it back on his lap as he sat back down. "I rather cannot wait to see what the tabloids will be spewing out of their horrid pages in the morning. I imagine it looks as if I have stolen you away from Alexander after all," said Colin, giving her a pleased smile.

"Well, you *are* much better looking, and it's no secret that I've always adored you," she told him, smiling back.

"Not half as much as I have adored you," he said, smiling broadly.

"I will not allow you out compliment me tonight Mr. Anders, you crafty devil. You think that by stroking my ego you can make me forget all about Alexander and win the gold medal tonight," she told him, giving him a sly smile.

"I have to admit, that was my intent," he told her.

"Colin, I wish that I could just put Alexander out of my mind. Believe me, I've tried," she told him.

"I know darling. I promise, if you go to the ice arena tonight, you will be safe. Alexander will not be able to touch you," said Colin.

"I'll never feel safe from Alexander, what he wants, he gets. It's not fair Colin, I thought that I believed in Karma, I thought that as long as Alexander and I weren't alone together, everything would be alright. I was wrong Colin. It was worse!"

"Someday Alexander will get his due. He will rot in misery in his own lies. His ill deeds will be repaid," said Colin.

"I seriously doubt it," said Jenna, frowning.

The waiter arrived at their table with their food and Colin and Jenna used the diversion to busily feed their faces. Colin thought that Jenna was safe to go to the ice arena, but she knew the truth...she would never be safe from Alexander.

CHAPTER THIRTY SEVEN

Jenna was in the locker room in her skating dress, distractedly putting on her makeup. She was light headed and her stomach was upset and she knew this was much more than the standard case of stage fright.

Tonight was the long program, their best program by far, but Jenna still wasn't sure she could do it, she felt as if she were an emotional mess. Being an emotional mess, is not really conducive to winning a major competition.

Once again, Jenna and Adam were in the last group of four pairs to perform, they would be performing second, right after Alexander and Marika. Jenna could barely breathe at the thought of having to share warm up ice with them.

Everyone had tried to divert her attention, Adam, Hans, Colin. What they didn't realize was, this was deeper than any fear she had ever experienced before. The very sight of Alexander could send her heart racing...but, not in a good way.

An official stuck her head in the door and told Jenna her warm up would be in two minutes. She put on her jacket and headed toward the door. She still wasn't sure if she could do this, the thought was completely overwhelming.

Adam met her in the hallway and gave her an encouraging smile. He took both her hands in his and squeezed them.

"You can do this, I know you can. You're the strongest person I know," said Adam, he smiled in encouragement.

Jenna gave him a weak smile. She didn't feel very strong right now. As they neared the ice entrance, Hans appeared in front of her and gathered her up in his arms, in a huge bear hug.

Jenna clung to him half heartedly. She wanted to win the gold medal for Hans more than anything, but she wasn't sure she had it in her. Jenna's messed up mental status was consuming every bit of energy she had in her body. Four minutes on the ice seemed like an eternity!

Jenna and Adam skated out onto the ice for their warm up. There were a total of four couples on the ice, all warming up, including Alexander and Marika. Adam and Jenna worked on their throw jumps and their side by side spin. When the warm up was nearly over, Alexander skated right up to Adam and whispered in his ear.

"Does it bother you, knowing I had her first? It was so beautiful, I'd do it all over again. Did she ever tell you that I brought her to a beautiful climax?" whispered Alexander.

"Get lost asshole," cried Adam, who immediately assumed a stance of someone who was about to become involved in a fight. Jenna had stopped short and was staring at them both blankly. Alexander laughed heartily and turned toward her.

"Ha, your husband is a bit angry with me. I told him how perfect we are together. He doesn't want to believe that I actually made you writhe in ecstasy, he still believes you were just an unwilling victim. Go ahead darling, you might as well tell him the truth," said Alexander, as he skated past her.

Marika skated up to him, her face a mask of barely concealed rage. "We are married now, you will not speak to de slut!" she cried angrily.

Jenna was frozen in place, Adam had skated up beside her and took her hand as Marika stared her down angrily. He was obviously concerned that a cat fight was about to ensue.

"She cannot help it Marika. I told you, we were in love, she still loves me. She is upset that we are now married and I will never again make love to her," said Alexander, pulling Marika away by her arm.

Jenna was staring at them both with a stunned look on her face, Alexander was completely insane! She turned and abruptly and began skating quickly toward the gate. She was sure that she couldn't do this. There was no possible way she could skate tonight, not with Alexander here in this arena. Adam was right behind her as she approached the gate.

"Jenna wait," cried Adam, trying to catch up to her.

"No Adam, I can't do this," she told him. She could feel the hysteria ready to overtake her body. Jenna wanted to go back to her hotel room and hide under the covers, she did not want to be in this ice arena with Alexander!

Jenna skated over to Hans, who had seen Alexander's little stunt, he was furious. He took her hand as she stepped off the ice and slid her jacket over her shoulders, pulling her into his arms protectively.

"Don't let him shake you up, it was a cheap shot. He's messing with your head," said Hans.

Jenna turned to glare into Hans' eyes. "I cannot stand to be in the same country as Alexander, let alone the same ice arena. I cannot deal with him Hans, I want to forget the man lives and breathes," she told him, the emotion was seeping into her voice, she just wanted to scream. Why couldn't anyone listen to her?

Jenna stalked angrily out into the tunnel that wove beneath the rows of seats. She couldn't perform tonight, Alexander had seen to that personally, if there had been any chance, he had eliminated it by taunting her during their warmup. She could barely even walk straight at this point!

Jenna looked up to see Colin standing right in front of her. He gave her a gentle smile and soon he was leading her down the echoing corridor with his arm around her shoulders as they announced Alexander and Marika for their long program.

"What did Alexander say?" demanded Colin.

"I'm not exactly sure what he said to Adam, but he was taunting me with lies," Jenna told him ruefully.

"Please darling, you must put Alexander out of your mind," said Colin, looking into her eyes very earnestly.

"Colin, how can I put Alexander out of my mind? He not only got off with barely a slap on the wrist for what he did to me, but now he's got the entire world convinced that I wanted it!" cried Jenna, tears filling her eyes.

"I know Jenna, it's not fair, but..."

"Now he's here, flinging it in my face, when all I want, is to forget it ever happened. Did you know that the media is convinced that we're getting back together again? Convinced that we were in love! I fought him Colin, I fought him as hard as I could, and still, he won..."

"I know Jenna, I'm so sorry," said Colin, folding her into his arms and holding her tight.

"Now he's here...taunting me. As if I needed any reminder of what he did to me."

"He is trying to use your fears against you, make you into an emotional mess. He will mentally destroy you, in an attempt to make you fail, but if you take the gold tonight, like I know you can, there will be no victory party for Alexander," said Colin, looking into her eyes earnestly.

"Colin, I don't think I can..." tears were already coursing down her cheeks.

"Where's that brave girl, I know she's in there? The fighter that has never backed down from a challenge in her life. The one who ended up on her own in Paris, at just fifteen years old."

Jenna sniffled, Colin was right, she'd never backed down from a challenge in her life. The very reason she was alive now was because she had fought Alexander. She wasn't going to give in to him now.

Jenna turned around to see Hans and Adam staring down the cold concrete corridor toward her. They both looked completely crushed. Jenna knew that Adam was certain that she was completely freaked out and it was all over for them. She took a deep breath, she couldn't quit. She couldn't let Adam and Hans down, they had all worked so hard to get here.

Jenna took one tentative step toward them. She thought she saw a flicker of emotion cross Adam's face, but they both remained completely still, afraid to hope...

"Adam!" called Jenna, her voice rang out down the corridor.

"Jenn?" his voice was hesitant.

"I can't quit! I'm going to do this!" she called to him.

"That's my girl!" he cried, running toward her.

Jenna ran to him and they were both so exuberant they literally crashed into each other. He threw his arms around her and spun her around excitedly. Jenna looked up to see Hans mouthing the words "Thank you" to Colin.

Adam and Jenna arrived at the edge of the ice, just as Alexander and Marika were skating around, picking up a few of the flowers that were being showered onto the ice.

As they came through the gate Jenna shrunk behind Adam and tried not to make eye contact with Alexander. Alexander was so cocky, he was literally strutting as he passed her.

"Best of luck my darling," he said, as he brushed past her, his body making more contact with her, than necessary. Marika glared at her, like a woman plotting her eminent death. Jenna shuddered at the hatred in her eyes.

"Asshole..." breathed Adam, uselessly trying to place his body between Jenna, and Alexander and Marika's.

Adam and Jenna had a short warm up while Alexander and Marika's scores were computed. Jenna was almost dizzy when the announcer read them off. They were nearly perfect, putting them solidly in first place, with just three more couples to skate.

In moments, they announced Jenna and Adam, and they skated to their places on the ice to wait for their music to begin. The crowd was loud and rowdy and Jenna suddenly felt very scared and lonely, standing there at the center of the ice waiting for their music to begin. She closed her eyes and tried to focus. She was convinced that their program was the best, and the most technically difficult. If they could make it through, Jenna was sure they could win the gold medal.

The music began and Jenna immersed herself in it. She was on autopilot. She knew this program would lack the personality it usually had, but what could she do?

They'd chosen music that was, for the most part, very fast. It was their style...though now Jenna regretted it. Their sequences were fast and intricate, it left no room for error. Jenna only hoped that she could pull it off.

Things were going well till their split twist. Jenna had rushed it a bit and ended up completely over rotated. Adam was able to right her, but she'd ended up too close to the wall, and on the wrong edge of her blade, she had to do a desperate little hop to get back on track.

Then came their side by side spins, a flying camel into a three position sit spin. Jenna was too close to the wall and ended up skimming it with her blade, then she pulled her leg in prematurely, thus putting their sit spins out of sequence.

Jenna was now panicking, wondering how far she had set them back. She struggled to focus and make the rest of the program perfect. The rest of the program seemed to go nicely, till their last lift. Jenna had only made it about halfway up in the air when Adam set her gently back on the ice. Jenna glanced at him quickly and realized he was tiring, knowing Adam, he was probably as anxious about everything as she was. The anxiety was draining, she was almost surprised that they both had made it as long as they had.

They managed to finish their program and skated to the center of the ice to take their bows. Jenna tried to smile as she faced the audience and sank into a deep curtsy. The applause was thundering through the arena and flowers were raining down on the ice, but Jenna was well aware that her and Adam would not be standing on the podium tonight.

She was sad knowing that her and Adam would not be going home with a medal tonight, but she was still happy that they had made it all the way to Worlds, even though she would have preferred it, if Alexander were several thousand miles away.

Jenna was proud that she had made it all the way through their long program, despite her fears, she never quit. Even if Alexander walked away with the gold medal, which she was sure that he would, at least she didn't hand it to him. She had given it her best, given the circumstances.

As they skated toward the gate Jenna could see Hans standing there with a broad smile on his face. She skated off the ice and right into his arms, immediately bursting into tears. She guessed that they were tears of relief more than anything else. She was happy that they were done in this competition and soon they would be flying back to St. Louis.

"Jenna, you were fabulous, I knew you could do it," Hans whispered in her ear. Jenna could only cling to him and bawl like a baby. Finally, they headed to their seats in the "kiss and cry" area to wait for their scores.

They watched as the scores came up on the monitors, actually, they weren't too bad, considering. They were currently in third place, though there were two more couples to skate, the West Germans were seeded second, Jenna assumed that they would knock her and Adam off the board with their performance.

They waved to the crowd as Hans led them from the arena to an area where Jenna and Adam could watch the rest of the performances and be out of the reach of the media, for now.

Of course, the West Germans gave a perfect performance, the other couple, who was Canadian, also gave a stellar performance putting those teams in second and third place respectively. So unfortunately, Jenna and Adam would be going home in fourth place.

As disappointed as she was in their fourth place finish, she was happy that Colin had persuaded her to skate tonight. She had been completely overcome with her fear of Alexander, but Colin had gently reminded her that she was not a quitter.

As the closing ceremonies wrapped up, Jenna assumed that everyone from the media would be swarming around Alexander and Marika, who for the second time in two years, had won the gold medals, making them once again the reigning World Champions. Jenna found there were an equal number of reporters soon swarming around her and Adam!

Jenna was clinging to Adam and Hans in a desperate attempt to avoid being separated from them again. The crowd that only moments ago, had been a sea of screaming, adoring fans, was now a crazed mob of pushy reporters and photographers.

Hans was in front, pushing aggressively through the crowd, using his body to shield Jenna from the crowd the best he could. Hans was only 5 foot six inches tall and Jenna was five foot nine without her skates, so it was kind of an act in futility. He was pulling her along behind him, as she dragged Adam through the surging crowd.

The reporters were also pushing through the crowd, yelling out questions to them, sticking their microphones as close to them as they could manage. Jenna was doing her best to ignore them as the three of them were jostled toward the exit. They emerged in the tunnel, an area that was off limits to reporters finally. Jenna got her things to head back to the hotel.

When they arrived back at the hotel, Colin was waiting in the lobby for them, he was holding a huge bouquet of flowers. Jenna ran into his arms and squeezed him tightly.

"I meant to give these to you at the arena, but the crowd was crazy, I couldn't make it anywhere near you," he said, kissing her on the cheek affectionately.

Jenna was vaguely aware that there were photographers there in the lobby, excitedly taking pictures of her and Colin, but she didn't care. Jenna had decided she would much rather have her name linked to Colin, than Alexander.

The next day, Jenna was glad they would be boarding a plane and leaving Copenhagen and the World Championships far behind them. She trailed numbly though the lobby behind Hans. Adam was behind her, keeping his eye out for Alexander. They were all determined to get out of the country without encountering him again. Jenna spotted Colin standing in the lobby with his coach, surrounded by their bags. She ran to him and threw herself into his arms.

Colin hugged her and held her, as happy tears coursed their way down her cheeks, Colin was once again a World Champion and she was so proud of him.

"Oh Colin, I don't know what I'm going to do, I'm going to miss you so much," she cried, vaguely aware that cameras were flashing all around them.

"We'll be together soon love. I'll see you back in Paris in April," said Colin. They would be resuming their roles with The Theater company in just two months.

Hans and Adam stood there patiently, as Jenna buried her face in Colin's neck, unwilling to let him go. He was murmuring in her ear, trying to reassure her.

"Did you by any chance see the papers this morning," asked Colin, flashing her a sly smile.

"Oh no, why," cried Jenna, pulling away and looking into his eyes very seriously.

"You've made the headlines again," said Colin, smiling at her.

"Oh no," breathed Jenna, fearing the worst.

"Not only did I win the World Championships, the whole world is convinced that I won you as well," said Colin, handing her the front page of the paper.

Jenna looked down at the headlines in shock. <u>New Men's World Champion Colin Anders, Wins The Heart Of Fellow Skater Jenna Bruce.</u>

"Well this is probably the truest headline I've ever seen, but this is not really breaking news. You won my heart a long time ago Mr. Anders," said Jenna, smiling at him.

"It is a lovely picture of the two of us, is it not? Much better than that photo of you and Alexander," said Colin.

Jenna looked at the photo, snapped of her and Colin at dinner. He was smiling at her and she was laughing. It truly looked like they were a happy couple.

"I get the feeling my boyfriend is not going to like *this* photo either," said Jenna, sighing miserably. Though she wasn't sure she could still call Matthew her boyfriend, she was getting the distinct feeling that they were breaking up. Adam had promised to talk to him, but she wasn't sure he'd had time. The point was probably mute anyway, she was sure it was already over for Matt.

"As a matter of fact, I *do* like this photo better," said a voice from behind her.

Jenna spun around quickly to see Matt standing there behind her. "Matt?" she breathed, hardly able to believe he was here.

"I'm sorry," he said, giving her a wry smile.

"What?'

"I wanted to tell you in person...I love you. I'm sorry for everything I said," said Matt, looking into her eyes.

"But..." Jenna didn't know what to say. How did he end up here in Copenhagen, and what had made him change his mind? She was stunned, he'd been so angry.

"It was stupid of me to cause you more pain when you were already hurting so bad. I know you Jenna, I know you would never lie to me. I was worried because Hans had discouraged me from coming along. He had told me that he didn't want me to ruin your concentration, but I guess I thought he wanted me to stay away because you and Alexander were an item.

When I got off the phone with you, I felt like an ass. I knew I had hurt you and I started to call you back, but instead I called the airport and got on the next flight here. I just wanted to come to you and apologize," said Matt, looking into her eyes earnestly.

Jenna couldn't speak, she just threw herself into his arms and he held her as she cried.

In a few minutes Hans put his arm around her and told her they needed to leave for the airport. The media was still anxiously snapping photos of Jenna with this new man, who had appeared out of nowhere.

Jenna flew all the way back to the states snuggled in Matt's strong arms. She was happier than she had been in months and it seemed as if Matt couldn't stop kissing her.

They returned to Chicago, weary from their long flight from Copenhagen. Matt got to spend just two days with Jenna before he had to return to Boston. She had tears sliding down her cheeks when he had to board his plane. She worried how they would continue their long distance relationship.

Now that Matt was away at Boston University, she rarely ever saw him, and Jenna and Adam would be returning to Paris the first weekend in April, so it didn't seem like Matt and Jenna would be spending any time together, any time soon.

Jenna was looking forward to a new season with the European Theater company and a new cast. She felt as if she had grown up completely in the last year. She was no longer that naive little girl, that had been so frightened and alone. She felt more confident then she had ever felt in her life. She smiled to herself, she no longer feared what the future would bring...

Jean Marie Stanberry

ABOUT THE AUTHOR

Jean Stanberry was born and raised in St. Louis, Missouri. She spent a great deal of her adult life there as well. Nine years ago Jean and her family left the hustle and bustle of a busy metropolitan area behind, to live a slower paced life in the Rocky Mountains of Northwest Montana. Jean and her husband Gary wanted their kids to be able to finish their high school years in a place where they could enjoy all the outdoor recreational opportunities that abound in Northwest Montana.

As a busy wife and mother who worked full time as a nurse in surgery, Jean didn't have a lot of time to pursue her love of writing, but several years ago when her daughter graduated from high school she decided she would give it another try.

Jean got her start writing articles for various sports magazines and working as a guest blogger for a figure skating blogspot. On

February 14th, 2013 her first book was published, "Laying Low In Hollywood", and that novel's phenomenal success led her to release "One World United" just two months later.

"Blood, Sweat, and Fears" is the first book in her series of books, "The Heart of a Phoenix Series", a series of books based loosely on her experiences growing up in a dysfunctional family, her career as a competitive figure skater and traveling throughout Europe with "Holiday On Ice".